D1421038   023

GRACE

Robert Drewe

Grace

HAMISH HAMILTON
an imprint of
PENGUIN BOOKS

HAMISH HAMILTON

Published by the Penguin Group

Penguin Books Ltd, 80 Strand, London WC2R ORL, England

Penguin Group (USA) Inc., 375 Hudson Street, New York, New York 10014, USA

Penguin Group (Canada), 90 Eglinton Avenue East, Suite 700, Toronto, Ontario, Canada M4P 2Y3
(a division of Pearson Penguin Canada Inc.)

Penguin Ireland, 25 St Stephen's Green, Dublin 2, Ireland (a division of Penguin Books Ltd)

Penguin Group (Australia), 250 Camberwell Road,

Camberwell, Victoria 3124, Australia (a division of Pearson Australia Group Pty Ltd)

Penguin Books India Pvt Ltd, 11 Community Centre,

Panchsheel Park, New Delhi – 110 017, India

Penguin Group (NZ), cnr Airborne and Rosedale Roads, Albany, Auckland 1310, New Zealand
(a division of Pearson New Zealand Ltd)

Penguin Books (South Africa) (Pty) Ltd, 24 Sturdee Avenue,

Rosebank, Johannesburg 2196, South Africa

Penguin Books Ltd, Registered Offices: 80 Strand, London WC2R ORL, England

www.penguin.com

First published in Australia by Penguin Group (Australia),
a division of Pearson Australia Group Pty Ltd 2005
First published in Great Britain by Hamish Hamilton 2005

1

Copyright © Robert Drewe, 2005

The moral right of the author has been asserted

Set in Perpetua
Printed in Great Britain by Clays Ltd, St Ives plc

A CIP catalogue record for this book is available from the British Library

ISBN-13: 978–0–241–14172–4
ISBN-10: 0–241–14172–9

For Sam and Anna

In late September the dunes

Stop moving, as if a seasonal migration had ground to a contoured,

abrasive end.

ANTHONY LAWRENCE

ONE

ESPLANADE

Grace didn't feel insane any more and the realisation was exhilarating. Merely ordering the meal – the fish, the salad, the wine – made her feel like she was emerging from a long convalescence in some grey institution. Suddenly the restaurant itself and the passing parade on the esplanade seemed extraordinarily bright and fascinating.

As she savoured the scene, two small boys as skinny as burnt sticks, their open faces, dusty ragged clothes and bare feet indicating their recent arrival from the desert, ran up to the Trocadero's fishpond and stood there gaping and pointing. They couldn't believe the carp. The fishes' blatant accessibility and size astonished them. For a moment, toes hanging over the pond's edge, they stood silhouetted against the sunset. Then a look passed between them; they were about to pounce on these ridiculous fish when a waitress shooed them away.

In any other mood Grace would have found the carp bloated and repulsive; this evening, sitting at her outdoor table on the esplanade's verge, she noticed only how their fins and flanks glistened in the day's last rays. She faced the sun setting in the sea – a red submerging whale – and watched the gamy breeze parting the mangroves in the bay as precisely as a comb on a wet scalp. The same warm gusts caressed her bare legs and made her skin tingle. For once she felt invigorated instead of weighed down and overwhelmed by her situation.

On the esplanade, young tattooed fathers with big bellies and hairstyles as old as themselves strutted like lords beside their women and hectic children, smoking cigarettes and swigging beer. (Good family men, she decided.) Buskers of varying nationalities and talents, too, had come out to perform in the sunset. Many of them were backpackers trying to raise money, probably no more skilful than the evening strollers watching them, but with her newfound serenity she gave them full marks for trying.

Showing all the ability of someone who'd been practising for perhaps a week, a beautiful Asian girl in flared pants and a bikini top was trying to juggle three fire sticks. She started confidently, then soon dropped one stick, and in attempting to flick it up into her hand with a bare foot, accidentally kicked the burning end.

She gave a squeal and the wind blew the flame onto a billowing pants cuff, which puffed into flame. She shrieked again and was batting ineffectually at her burning pants when a grinning surfer stepped up and stifled the flames with his beach towel. Brushing her hair from her eyes, the girl, rather surprisingly, bowed deeply to her audience, as if her audacity and beauty were accomplishment enough. The evening crowd was prepared to indulge her, rewarding her with a scattering of coins and cheers not entirely ironic.

Grace relished it all: the human byplay, the shoreline's fertile muddy aroma, the warm evening wind on her body, and especially the meal – the fresh barramundi, the Greek salad, the chardonnay. It was the first food she'd enjoyed in ages, and the knowledge that she no longer felt anxious and depressed was making her scalp prickle and little nerves twitch at the corners of her mouth. She found it impossible not to smile.

It seemed that everyone this evening was good-natured and entertaining, particularly the young Aboriginal woman with crimson hair who had suddenly entered the restaurant, slowly circled the tables with a queenly air, then sauntered purposefully up to a table of white businessmen.

The men's conversation stopped and they looked up warily, as if expecting to be denounced or mocked. Having reached her target, however, the girl seemed to forget why she was there. She stood by the table, swaying to some inner melody. She was thin, about six months pregnant, and her exposed bare belly pushed out a silver navel ring. Perhaps a minute passed. Gradually conversations ceased and silence spread through the restaurant.

The street noise seemed louder. The suspense was killing.

Eventually the girl blinked several times, as if to clear her head. Affecting a posh voice, she said loudly, 'Good evening, gentlemen. I hope you're having an enjoyable meal. May I trouble you for a light?'

The men looked relieved and quickly produced cigarette lighters. The oldest one, perhaps the other men's boss, nudged a young freckled beanpole and said, 'Yours, Ken?' and they all chuckled.

The girl drew on her cigarette in the manner of a forties film star and blew a neat smoke ring across the men's table. The smoke drifted and dissipated in the night. 'You wish,' she said. Then she flicked her narrow hips at them, once, twice, and sashayed out of the restaurant.

Grace raised her glass to the girl's departing back. She felt like running after her and wishing her luck. How appropriate that she should share her own sudden confidence in life. Each sip of wine, like the gin and tonics earlier, seemed to be stripping away a layer of old anxiety. Tensions sloughed off her. When a bush mouse scuttled across the esplanade from the mangroves to nibble the crumbs under the table her reaction was childish delight rather than repulsion. As the mouse tickled her sandalled toes she felt – *what an old, familiar feeling!* – tenderness towards it.

'Hello,' she murmured. She'd had a pet mouse as a child. 'Do you like olives?'

Eating and drinking with unaccustomed appetite, surreptitiously dropping olives and fetta for her mouse, watching the pink sky fade over Indonesia and the moon's reflection rise triumphantly out of the bay, she found it impossible not to share her euphoria with the human diners as well. She beamed sociably around her, flagrantly eavesdropped and guessed at neighbouring lives. Those two blond women gossiping at the next table, what was their story? They were in real estate and hotel reception, she gleaned from their conversation. Hunched conspiratorially over their wineglasses, they were busily exhuming relationships, defaming their exes and crowing over their replacements.

'Glenn's very sensual.'

'Oh, tell me about it. So is Matt.'

'Glenn's mad for lingerie. I suppose I'd better buy some new lingerie.'

Grace drank all the wine. The icy dessert, too, was the most delicious she could remember, and when she finished she sighed with satisfaction, left a generous tip and methodically brushed her dinner crumbs onto the floor. 'There you go, mousey!' The two blond women had been observing her with interest but they, and the restaurant at large, seemed surprised when she sang out to them, 'Good night! Good luck with your new lingerie!'

Snorts of laughter followed her progress into the street. For a few minutes she had to concentrate on getting her bearings. It was hard to remember directions. There was the dark bay; there was the town. When she looked back at the candlelit white table-cloths of the Trocadero, the restaurant seemed to be on the wrong side of the road.

With the changing light and tide the scenery had somehow shifted, just as the proportion of black to white people on the street had altered. Blacks now predominated. Also, the wrecks of two ancient pearl luggers had mysteriously surfaced in the bay below and the boats' mud-bound ribs were exposed. They clutched at the air like claws.

The breeze smelled of frangipani, warm mud and garlic. Along the esplanade someone strummed a guitar and a woman's husky voice sang a snatch of country song that ended in giggles. Two drunken men squatting on their heels, or trying to, eyed Grace from a lane across the street. One crooned something in singsong tones, then toppled over on his side. Four kids shot past her on the one bicycle, like a circus act.

But she was blithe, only half aware of all this. What held her attention was the amazing sky: the moon performing simultaneously above her and on the tidal mudflats below. Around it the sky sizzled with nursery-rhyme stars; they seemed to be alive and intent on leapfrogging each other.

Walking back to Clara's was like being in an early-morning TV cartoon; she had to shut one eye in order to keep up with those mischievous stars.

GRACE OF
THE CROCODILES

Some relevant facts about Grace Molloy. Apart from being named after a 100 000-year-old skeleton whose age, owing to advances in radiocarbon dating technology, had twice increased in increments of twenty thousand years, she was twenty-nine and for much of the past three years she'd been hiding from a stalker.

Fleeing him and the city for the country's northwest frontier, the remote Kimberley, she'd ended up living and working on the outskirts of Port Mangrove, in a wildlife park which specialised in the reptiles of the region, particularly the country's biggest and fiercest predator, the saltwater crocodile (*Crocodylus porosus*).

She felt she'd come a long way in more ways than one. For her first three months in the Kimberley, still constantly looking over her shoulder, exhausted, depressed and battered by the heat, she'd been apt to break down without warning at a particular combination of cumulus clouds and the setting sun, for example. And, of course, at the moonlight reflecting on the tidal mudflats – that famous Port Mangrove phenomenon requiring an absence of clouds and a receptive imagination – like a silver staircase to the moon.

She wept copiously at television's nightly terrorist-atrocity roundup, at the mere mention of Bali. Bombings sent her to bed with her dinner untouched. In dry-eyed moments she was her grumpy self, annoyed that her emotions seemed unable to differentiate between tragedy and beauty, between dead children and the mirages of moonlight on mud. She felt she'd escaped the loony bin by the skin of her teeth.

Lying low, but too restless and anxious to stay for more than two or three days straight in the one place, she tottered back and forth between three coastal bed-and-breakfast bungalows run by pearling and cattle widows of her father's acquaintance. Reduced to eking out their dwindling inheritances with paying guests, the widows were gravel-throated, kind old ladies with romantic tropical histories and a need for evening drinking company.

The widows provided animated conversation, set outlooks and a gritty sympathy. Over their nightly gin and tonics behind the bougainvillea they also evoked lives so vividly lived that after a couple of months in their company Grace was surprised to feel her equilibrium slowly returning.

Under the mosquito net in Clara's or Louise's or Marion's sleepout, while moths and beetles battered against the louvres, she'd replay the widows' sagas in her head. They were like old Technicolor movies with grand themes and Vistavision landscapes. Revisiting their palmy and tragic storylines helped her put her life in perspective. They probably accomplished more in two months than Dr Garber had managed in two years. Psychotherapy lagged way behind those verandah tales of drowned, gored, broken-backed or bankrupted husbands, sons and brothers. All the pearling and cattle fortunes won and lost, the grisly accidents, the aircraft and marine disasters, the wartime bombings, the interracial battles, the exotic lovers, were surprisingly effective therapy. Alongside their lives, hers appeared trivial and egotistical.

Every Port Mangrove narrative was punctuated by vivid memories of a different tropical cyclone – Mavis, Faye, Norma, Edna, Kevin – as ferociously individual as its name was now unfashionable. How could her troubles compare with the tempests these old women had lived through? In this place of wild hurri-canes and emphatic colours – where any combination of sky, sea and landscape, indeed any view framed by any window, suggested the flag of some passionate equatorial republic – stalking seemed simply too grey and urban to exist.

Stalking. The widows passed the word gingerly between them like a magazine printed in a foreign language. In their mouths it was just another term for 'trespassing' or 'annoying', something undesired and inconvenient. But mindful of her feelings, they coughed politely on their Dunhills and kept their viewpoints to themselves. One evening, however, she overheard old Louise Foy mutter, 'I don't get it. Is there some reason why she didn't just shoot the bastard?'

Then one July evening in Clara Aherne's garden she caught herself about to weep by habit at a prettified sunset – a scarlet travelogue sun, a seductive dusk rouged and powdered by the smoke of Indonesian forest fires across the water. Abruptly she saw herself as a pathetic bystander in this exotic panorama and she stopped the tears in their tracks. *Jesus, it was over.* There was no need to keep looking over her shoulder. She'd escaped him.

She took another swig of gin and tonic. Despite the humidity she felt surprisingly cool and clear-headed, also hungry and unusually aware of the tropical air wafting about her thighs and armpits. The landscape loomed sensually around her. You could almost see and hear things growing. The palm fronds, the bougainvillea spikes, the mould on the deckchair canvas. Suddenly even the words for her surroundings had a taste and smell – guava, tamarind, papaya, pomelo.

She sniffed the breeze like a dog; it brought scents of night-blooming flowers and every so often a whiff of smoke from the latest captured Indonesian *prahus* burning on the beach north of town. As the boats of the trochus poachers smouldered on the shore they gave off pungent foreign smells. Sweat, oily canvas, burnt fish, gluey plywoods.

Hawks and fruit bats twirled above the garden as usual, smaller birds chattered and flapped in the palms, anonymous nocturnal creatures rustled in the shrubbery. And suddenly none of this exotic smoke, twitter and croak was the least strange or disconcerting.

Clara and Louise and Marion Dwyer had grounded her. She'd never mixed with women in their eighties before. Perhaps the extra generation made all the difference. These women were grand-mother vintage. They were a welcome relief after her mother and her cronies.

The Dabblers, she called those inner-city baby-boomers – the Judes and Janes and Maggies and Carols – with their dated poli-tics, semi-religions, scatty professions and middling artistic skills, their dodgy diplomas in self-improvement and shamanic healing and regression therapy, their sexual and spiritual oscillation and fad diets and herbal teas and echinacea. Yogalates topped it off. Their latest craze. That cross between yoga and Pilates that sounded like some new low-fat dessert summed up for her their foot-in-each-camp worlds.

In recent years her mother had become an even more annoy-ing mystery to her. In the early stages of the stalking, when it was a problem, a worry, rather than a threat, her mother had constantly urged her to take back control of her life. Whenever they met she was subjectively impatient with her daughter's low state of mind. Sooner or later she always shook her head, threw up her arms. 'But I was never like that.'

Perhaps because a man was involved – an obsessively enthusiastic and romantic man — she'd appeared to hold her anxieties against her. Get over it; get over *him*, she seemed to be saying.

In the meantime why not try these wonderful exercise routines with her and Jude and Maggie? Forget her troubles by stretching and clenching and firming? If Jude, who was physically disabled, could tackle Yogalates, what on earth was stopping a young healthy woman like her? Yogalates was the answer to whatever ailed a woman. Panic attacks and depression? Of course.

Lately her mother had developed new lemony hair and a confusing and nostalgic relationship with her body. She seemed to confuse her body with her daughter's. One minute she'd be talking loudly and embarrassingly in coffee shops about her pelvic floor, the next she'd turned into one of those women who self-consciously pull their tops over their hips or shyly flap a hand behind their buttocks when they rise from a table or leave the room. As if that nervous little hand flutter could reduce her beam.

'Listen, more and more ballet dancers are doing Yogalates these days,' her mother said. 'Have you ever seen anyone more serene than a ballerina?'

'Even a ballerina with a lunatic after her?'

The Yogalates session with her mother had indeed made an unforgettable impression, the reason being that people farted throughout. Her mother hadn't mentioned that the stretching, clenching and firming exercises favoured by her Yogalates group seemed specially designed to shake up and loosen the intestines.

But it wasn't just the intermittent blasts, peeps and whiffs from the leotards of septuagenarians and thirtysomethings alike that shook up her daughter. It was the particular Yogalates etiquette. The class decorum was that when someone was about to break wind they should, near the point of no return (but more often simultaneously, or indeed, rather abjectly, just afterward), make the polite warning announcement, 'Release!'

Release! In her fragile emotional state she found this pure slapstick. When the warning came, what were you supposed to do? Run for cover? No, the unspoken protocol insisted that no one should avert their face, certainly not hold their nose or show repugnance. *What fart?* They were stoics, these Yogalates people.

Of course she couldn't concentrate on the exercises. Every time someone gave that prim little alarm, what muscle tone she did possess turned abruptly to jelly. The effort to stifle her laughter was so great her own intestines were in danger of exploding. And between announcements the suspense got to her. Waiting for the next *Release!*-and-fart combo, she began to snort.

Her mother and her friends were mortified but she couldn't help herself. She found the class's prim disapproval and stockinged feet desperately comical. As one, they huffily turned their backs on her. But just looking at the rows of taut leotarded bottoms was enough to set her off again. *Release!*

She was on the brink of hysteria when the Yogalates instructor, a bossy South African blonde with suspiciously high breasts, a dolphin-shaped nose stud and a self-approving manner, clapped her hands for attention. 'I really think the girl with the giggles is spoiling this experience for everybody. And it's really a shame because her body looks as if it would really benefit from these exercises.'

So I'm unfit as well as insane, she thought, and padded quickly out of there.

The widows weren't dabblers or amateurs or stuck in some intermediate zone between hippie and yuppie. They were unashamedly of yesteryear, and their nightly Beefeater-and-Dunhill monologues about the past, their generous hearts and settlers' pragmatism, had finally driven her to find a new present.

Her confidence still intact despite her hangover, she began looking for a job next day. The local paper advertised the customary Situations Vacant – seasonal waitresses and bar workers – but it was the position of general assistant at Crocodile Gardens that caught her eye. Forget the usual jobs – a proper tropical occupation seemed the appropriate next step.

As part of this exotic new backdrop – the colours, the heat, the wildlife – crocodiles were in the back of her mind in any case. Perhaps they'd been lurking there since her desperate Forbes Street days. She had a vision of herself behind barred doors, hunched before the TV news: an item on a novel scheme to discourage

asylum seekers. The federal government had made a film on the
perils refugees should expect to encounter during and after their
risky voyages to democracy. The film was to be distributed on video
throughout the Middle East and Asia.

Awaiting all refugees, the film warned, were crocodiles, sharks
and venomous snakes. It went further – it implied that if Australia's
notorious wildlife didn't kill the misguided asylum seekers, the
grim detention centres in store for them in the desert would make
them wish it had.

Hunkered down with the television, she'd taken it as a spoof
at first, a comic anti-tourist promotion. (Cut to stock footage of
slavering crocs, writhing death adders, a great white's gaping jaws.)
But the newsreader didn't smirk; his eyes didn't even twinkle afterwards; he didn't seem to think it was a zany idea. Nor did the press
columnists satirise the scheme in the days that followed. It was
accepted as the government intended: a unique but sensible plan
to deter unwanted boatloads of dubious foreigners.

Her mind was disturbed and quirky back then. Maybe only she
confused this political campaign with black comedy. But it was the
croc-as-refugee-deterrent episode that now determined her job
choice. In this restive mood, stressing the zoology unit in a long-
discarded science degree, she applied for the Crocodile Gardens
position.

The widows vouched for her. Their word still counted in the
Kimberley. The old women went a step further and invited Garth

Stroller, the proprietor of Crocodile Gardens, for cocktails at Clara's bungalow.

It was hardly necessary for Clara to remind Garth of her late husband Padraic's generous loan back in the sixties that had enabled him to buy the fifty acres of coastal sand, swamp, paper-bark trees and red pindan dirt which had become the park.

'Remember that, Garth?' said Clara. 'Back before you were an Outback Identity?'

'The poor girl's had a rough time,' Marion chipped in.

'You must know her father,' Louise said. 'The anthropologist John Molloy. Been coming to the Kimberley for years. He found a fossilised fish on our old property once. From when it was all under water hundreds of millions of years ago. Lovely thing, older than the dinosaurs – I've still got it on the mantelpiece. Not his area, he said. He asked us to keep an eye on Grace.'

Garth Stroller sipped his drink. He found the old ducks unnerving en masse. Clara had brought out a dusty bottle of single malt and the widows sat facing him in a semicircle of Dunhill smoke. 'What's the catch? She's not a junkie, is she? A lezzo or something?'

'Excuse me?' said Clara.

Louise took another tack. She patted his hand. 'Garth, you can help Grace bounce back.'

Clara's sigh was impressively drawn out. 'I know Paddy would've given her a break. He believed in giving people a helping hand in life. When it was warranted.'

What choice did he have? He agreed to give her a six-month trial while she convinced him she fitted in. But a novice from Down South needed watching, he insisted. 'I'm not running a convalescent home.'

'Of course you're not.' Clara topped up his whisky and blew smoke out the side of her mouth into the bougainvillea. 'You're running a crocodile home, aren't you?'

It didn't take long for the euphoria to wear off. In the beginning Grace wondered whether Garth Stroller's belittling banter was part of his seasoning process. From her first day he insisted on calling her Sydney. The nickname and his cracks about pampered city slickers and left-wing southerners and their bohemian and deviant ways were delivered in the same blunt, ego-battering manner he used to show friendliness. Not that this was his habit alone. Up here, she discovered, even affection – especially affection – was demonstrated like this.

While she felt strong enough to take his teasing in her stride, his conversations with her, even if no one else was present, always seemed to be playing to a wider, more appreciative audience. But she was determined not to rise to the bait or to sink back into depression. She would be a good sport, a different, more agreeable person. She'd keep her head down. After all, she was lying low.

He'd started her as a sales assistant in the Crocodile Gardens gift shop. Croc-schlock seemed to be a thriving industry. Working the cash register, replacing stock, endlessly folding and refolding T-shirts, she felt like a little girl playing grown-ups. She hoped her enthusiasm in flogging reptile souvenirs to tourists would do as much to prove she fitted in as her efforts to overcome her natural fear of the living animals.

All day she was on her feet selling the crocodile-tooth necklets and crocodile-skin boots, the belts, bags and wallets, the croco-dile-claw backscratchers, the taxidermised baby crocs, the plastic and rubber crocodile toys, the crocodile T-shirts and tea towels, as well as rubber snakes and fluffy marsupials and the growing range of Garth Stroller books and memorabilia. Her feet hurt from the cement floor, her jaw ached from constantly smiling, her fin-gers stank of musty crocodile skin and damp money. But at least she wasn't frying up croc burgers next door in the park's Hard Croc Café.

On her second morning she was folding a pile of children's T-shirts, each featuring a bloody bite-shaped gash across the chest and the words 'I Fed the Crocs at Crocodile Gardens', when Garth Stroller sauntered up to her.

'Grab a length, Sydney,' he said, grinning tightly, and looped a diamond python around her neck.

Time stood still. This snake wasn't made in China. The weight was part of the shock, but outwardly at least she took the sudden heaviness and tension, the fear of strangulation, calmly enough. She was concentrating on breathing properly and avoiding a choking.

As the python's coils undulated in a mildly curious but pressure-less fashion over her body she forced herself to stroke them. Funny, it was nothing like the evil anthropomorphic serpent that had stalked Jennifer Lopez and Jon Voight in *Anaconda*. Her fingers traced the undulating kaleidoscope of scales and eventually she muttered, although she hardly recognised the raspy voice, 'It's beautiful.'

'Kills by constriction,' Stroller said helpfully, nonchalantly turning away to rifle through some paperwork. 'Wallabies, rats, the occasional dog.'

She waited for what she thought was a decent interval, batting the word 'constriction' back and forth in her mind, before remarking as casually as she could manage, 'A really interesting sensation. Back to Daddy now.'

Stroller said nothing, but as he unwound the snake from her torso and hefted its weight back into his arms, he winked at her. As soon as he left she took ten deep breaths and one of her emergency Xanax tablets.

The same afternoon he returned to the gift shop and dumped a fluorescent-green tree snake, more garish than its nearby plastic replicas, in her hands. He was annoying her now, but again she steeled herself to pass the test, not to flinch or utter the mildest protest, much less scream or even hint at the helpless city girl.

She'd had enough of flinching and helplessness. Anyway, the Xanax was still working.

There was little weight this time. With the snake coiled neatly and not uncomfortably around her forearm, she faced the sinister myth and peered into its eyes. And she found the stereotype inaccurate. They weren't evil-looking, merely indifferent, like the eyes of some self-absorbed men she'd known. She recalled some film stars skilled at playing shrewdness. They were Jack Nicholson eyes, Christian Slater eyes, Michael Douglas eyes, Lee Van Cleef eyes. Gunslinger and cardsharp eyes. Hollywood eyes.

But it was ridiculous to load sneaky human characteristics onto them. As the snakes tentatively investigated her – and she, more cautiously, them – their feel and passive, trusting manner were a pleasant surprise. Of course these specimens were used to being handled, but they weren't cold or slimy or repugnant. They were surprisingly dry and warm and rather sensually muscular.

She thought of sex then, and in a way not entirely threatening and nasty. However, she couldn't be sure she was thinking of sex just because you were supposed to associate snakes with sex – the obvious symbolism and all that – or because sex had actually sprung unbidden to mind.

Whatever – she was very tired of analysing things – snakes weren't so bad.

On her third day at Crocodile Gardens she was on her lunch break in the café, shooing flies off her sandwich and writing to her father, when Garth sprang more surprises.

'Follow me, Sydney.' Across the gardens, behind the sign saying DANGER — STAFF ONLY — NO PUBLIC ADMITTANCE, he led her into the back reaches of the park. 'You need to see the whole picture.'

Away from the trim lawns and public gaze, here was the crocodile farm — the breeding unit, abattoir, refrigeration plant, incubation sheds, variously sized concrete pens and galvanised-iron sheds. Surrounding them were kidney-shaped cement ponds, turned mossy and fungoid but still resembling swimming pools left over from 1950s Hollywood mansions. The sort of pools that Lana Turner and Tyrone Power might have lounged around, where Cary Grant and Randolph Scott worked on their tans, where film producers seduced starlets. Hollywood crocodiles.

A light musty stink caught in her throat.

'*Crocodylus porosus* HQ,' Garth announced proudly. 'We're a fully integrated facility, from egg to shoe.' He waved a hand towards an open-sided shed where racks of pink flayed skins were stretched out to dry. They looked like cartoon crocs flattened by steamrollers.

'Luxury leather,' he went on, 'high-fashion products, ladies' shoes, boots for rich cowboys, handbags, luggage, belts, wallets, other fashion items. The whole skins, naturally. Trophy items. Meat, of course.'

Meat. The sun beat down on her scalp. Odours grew richer

in the stale air. From somewhere nearby came the wild hot smell of blood. In the parallel ponds of live crocs, reckless water birds – ibises and egrets and coots and an occasional gull – strolled and pecked a wing-flap away from lounging snouts. In the humidity nothing else moved. Several floating reptiles had egrets standing nonchalantly on their backs like surfers.

The blood smell seemed trapped in her sinuses. She shuddered with distaste. 'I hope you're not going to show me where the Hard Croc's burgers come from.'

He looked sharply at her. 'I'll tell you something. What we do isn't gruesome or cruel. This is a farm – the only difference between crocs and cows is that these are dangerous animals with very rudimentary personalities. They want to eat us and we've always wanted to kill them.'

'Not everyone,' she said. How soon she'd reverted to the green and sanctimonious city girl. Had she ever given crocodile welfare a second's thought in her life?

'Listen, I'm here to keep the species alive and thriving. Believe me, people won't tolerate having crocs around unless we extract some benefit from them.'

Benefit? she wondered. Necklets and wallets and backscratchers and bar-room accessories.

'This is an ancient battle. Human–croc relations have been shithouse since Day One. You know why? Because deep in our DNA we know they see us as food.'

She felt dizzy. What was the correct position on this: senti-mental or pragmatic? She had no idea. She followed him to a soupy pool enclosed by a cyclone-wire fence. A stew of algae and leaf mould, the pool's surface looked thick enough to walk on. The whole enclosure appeared lushly vacant. It reminded her of the empty compound at Taronga Zoo when the lone panda died, and how desolate it had made her feel at the age of six. With the panda dead, the bamboo it had kept tamed and gnawed down to the roots instantly flourished; within weeks it had taken over the cage.

No egrets or ibises strolled this compound's boundaries. Still the sun beat down on her. Across every surface, heat mirages pooled and flickered; the false pools appeared far more fluid than the real ones. From somewhere Stroller picked up a heavy mooring buoy the size of a big medicine ball and heaved it over the fence.

The movement was faster than her brain could react to it. In the same split second as the skin of the buoy tipped the surface of the pool there was a blur of fierce intent and huge jaws surged upwards and engulfed the buoy. It burst like a party balloon and water roiled and billowed over the rim of the pool.

In a churning dash the beast continued out of the water towards them, the crushed buoy hanging from a front tooth. Grace leaped back, her heart hammering in her throat. As if a switch had been thrown, the crocodile stopped just short of the fence and was instantly composed and motionless.

Its jaws remained half open. Up close it was mossy, brown-toothed and prehistoric, straight from the swamps of myth. The surroundings were suddenly misty and all bird noise had stopped. The crocodile dominated the landscape and the whole steamy world.

Now its eyes met hers with such deadpan engagement she could hardly stand it. Even the buoy dangling from its tooth like a busted red balloon didn't diminish its predatory authority and alertness for action. At the same time it was imperturbable. It didn't bat an eyelid; the eyes could have been marbles. The stare was primal and infinitely patient.

Hey, meat. It's just a matter of time.

Still the crocodile didn't blink or shift its gaze. It was she, the eternal prey, who was forced to break eye contact and turn away. She felt faint, and the heat mirages flickered at the edges of her vision like the beginnings of a migraine. She smelled its humid, rank breath.

'He's the new boy.' Stroller's voice came from somewhere. 'Haven't named him yet but he'll probably be Gunter.'

'Gunter?'

'After a Swiss backpacker.'

'Oh.'

He squeezed her shoulder then, a fleeting touch she found surprisingly welcome. 'It's okay to be scared when a predator threatens you. We're all born watching out for the Big Bad Six – lions, tigers, leopards, bears, sharks and crocs. If our ancestors hadn't been shit-scared of them we wouldn't be standing here today.'

She wanted to sit down. Her legs were tottery but she made herself keep up with him as he strode along spouting breeding information. With great effort she set her face in a professional expression. 'Of course.' She slapped at an insect. 'The collective unconscious and all that.'

He'd already moved on. Captured wild crocs like Gunter, he was saying – 'the big troublesome salties' – provided the best breeding stock, the boldest beasts with the finest skin quality. But she was still thinking of those jaws – the huge brown teeth snapping the buoy. This wasn't a normal animal. It was megafauna from another time, when reptiles roamed and ruled.

'Crocs are protected now,' he went on, 'but me and the government have a deal.' He captured the problem crocs that had attacked humans and brought them here. He paid the government a hundred dollars for each male he took, two hundred for females. 'The citizens are made safer, the money goes towards conservation, I've got my breeding stock and everything's hunky-dory.'

'Sounds like a good deal.' She sounded stupid to herself. By now she'd fallen into a sort of daze of repulsion, fear and fascination. Oddly, her shoulder still retained the pressure of his hand. She felt so malleable and weak she wouldn't have been surprised if her flesh was indented for ever.

For want of anything better to say, she muttered, 'It's interesting that the females are more valuable.'

She was even more annoyed at herself. The phoney note in

her voice irritated her, and the way she always felt giddy when an expert imparted expertise – particularly unusual expertise, from a male expert. This susceptibility was a lifelong habit; she couldn't fight it. For that reason, despite Dr Garber suggesting it would be helpful, she'd been determined never to submit to hypnosis. She knew she'd go under right away – fall under the spell, lose herself.

She had an image of a suave bearded man resembling Mandrake the Magician. Black slick hair, evening clothes, patent-leather shoes, maybe an opera cloak. He snapped his fingers and she was cackling like a chicken in ten seconds flat. Another click and she was barking and crawling on her knees. She presumed sex came into it somewhere and she resented this, too. At the same time, the thought of Stroller's soothing touch made her cheeks hot with embarrassment.

'Females,' he was saying. 'They like it cool.' His eyes were shrewd as an old lizard's. 'Can you answer me something, Sydney?'

She shot him a glance but he was merely asking whether she knew a croc's sex was determined by temperature.

'No, not really.'

'Males like it hotter. The higher the incubation temperature, the faster the embryos grow and the more chance they have of being male. But not too hot – over thirty-five centigrade kills them. Thirty-two's ideal for getting both sexes. Between thirty-two and thirty-three gives you mostly males. Thirty degrees and less, only females.'

He gave her a teasing glance. 'Colder and slower development means a female. Make of that what you will.'

On cue, continuing the irritating sex-war banter they
seemed to have adopted, she said, 'I guess females are more
carefully made then.'

'Depends who's making them.' He looked smug. 'You can
guarantee a far greater success rate than nature when you control
the temperature.'

Her brain was still in a fog. Now he was ushering her into
one of the stale-smelling sheds and (how was this happening?) she
was stepping over the side of a big bathtub and standing knee-
deep in a morass of squirming baby saltwater crocodiles. That
cleared her head.

Hundreds of identical foot-long hatchlings were scrambling
over each other in their panic to escape to the farthest corner of the
trough. For a few seconds she panicked, too. As the crocs bustled
over her feet and squirmed between her calves she was reduced to
girlish helplessness. Every nerve in her legs was desperate to react,
to avoid and kick out — especially to run. This was not possible.

She wanted to cry out. Back in Sydney there had been a
mentally disturbed man who roamed the inner-city streets shouting, 'No!' at the world. In the night his noes from the lane below
sometimes invaded her dreams. She'd wake with her heart racing,
protesting sudden nightmares and repeating the No Man's cries.

She needed to yell it now — *No!* Or had she done so already?

Get a grip! She wondered which of them had muttered this sentence, too, and realised it was her own involuntary sound. Holding her breath, she willed herself to stand still and not topple into the nightmare scrimmage of tiny jaws. It was like a familiar bad dream.

But as the seconds slowly passed it dawned on her that the little crocs, cheeping and scattering like anxious chicks, were more terrified than she was. The experience began to seem even more familiar. Up to her knees in crocodiles, yes, she felt like the female co-star in an Indiana Jones movie. While she was trembling and mockable, the taciturn hero was in his element. Now he confidently plunged a tanned forearm into the writhing mass of bodies, extracted a single snapping infant and held it up for the co-star's delectation.

The hapless feminine sidekick supposed she was expected to accept the reptile and, furthermore, to appreciate it. Its mouth, she noticed, could open to about eighty degrees and contained needle teeth. A delicate pulse throbbed in the throat.

She took the creature and held it. And, carefully watching her fingers, she discovered that crocodiles, the babies at least, were also a tactile surprise – unexpectedly warm to the touch, their bellies like satin, those lumpy dorsal scales smooth as river pebbles. Perhaps she could even convince herself, as had the other female rangers, Tenille, Skye, Ingrid and Monique, that the chirpy little reptiles were as cute as any pup or cub.

There was more. Stroller's tour wasn't finished. 'Notice the difference,' he announced, flinging open the door of an adjoining shed to display another trough of crocs. 'These are six months old. Better stay where you are.'

An unnecessary instruction as this snapping melee charged the invaders, clattering against the sides of the trough. They were twice as big – about half a metre long – and definitely aggressive.

So crocodile personalities changed with age, size and confidence. It wasn't necessary for him to climb into their trough and invade their territory, especially not to wade knee-deep into the chaos of their bodies, to illustrate the point. As waves of reptiles swelled and dashed against his bare legs, he slipped over – in slow motion, it appeared to her horrified eyes – and skidded on his back into the scrum.

Her brain was still trying to react before he was torn to pieces when he abruptly sat up and clapped his hands like a schoolteacher. As the claps reverberated, the crocs dropped as one from his body. With a wild drumming sound, like hail on a tin roof, they scampered to the rear corners of the trough.

He was grinning as he stepped out of the trough and dusted himself down. 'Reckon that routine would work with the public?'

She couldn't speak. In any case he was stamping off again.

Along the way he picked up two reeking feed buckets. 'Are you getting the gist of this?' he sang out over his shoulder. 'Getting the full picture?'

'Yes.' Surely there couldn't be more?

In the wild, he went on, because of heat, flooding, genetic malfunctions, predatory animals and Aboriginal hunters, most of their eggs died. Only a quarter survived to hatchling stage, and only half these survivors lived twelve months. 'In the wild only one per cent of crocs reach five years old. Not great odds, eh?'

'No.'

'In the wild, everything wants to eat the hatchlings – fish, goannas, snakes, dingoes, Aborigines. But if they grow up they get even. They eat everything – they don't draw the line.'

Warily she followed him and the feed buckets into yet another shed, this one larger and more ominously dark than the others.

His voice came out of the gloom. 'It's different here than in the wild.'

Again the shed enclosed a long, chest-high trough which seemed at first to be dark and empty. Then he banged a bucket twice against the side and instantly there was a disordered scrabbling noise, like excited dogs running on lino. The scrabbling grew louder and five (or was it six?) beasts from science fiction or a nightmare squirmed into the daylight. It registered on her that these were all mature crocodiles. They were also genuine monsters.

These things could have come from another planet. The first creature to appear had an underslung lower jaw like a scoop, and no top jaw. The next one had the opposite: a long snout but no bottom jaw, giving it a comical, chinless, bucktoothed look.

Corkscrewing along the ground towards them meanwhile was a third twisted creature with a kinked spine and curled tail. It was followed by a crocodile which would have been a huge specimen, easily five metres long, if only it had possessed a tail. However, its two-metre-long body ended at its back legs in a pair of oddly chubby, human-like buttocks.

'Good God!' She was transfixed by the tail-less croc. Out of shock and embarrassment, like a five-year-old spotting red-arsed zoo animals doing rude things, she gasped, 'It's got a bum!'

Bent over the feed buckets, Stroller said nothing. He seemed to be avoiding her eyes.

The buckets contained chicken carcasses, strangely reptile-looking themselves: bedraggled, attenuated things, all neck and claws. One by one, Stroller solemnly doled out the scraggy bodies. As the buttocky croc gulped its meal and waddled off to the side, the fifth and sixth creature suddenly spun like a catherine wheel in their general direction. Its aim was erratic, marred by its actually being two crocodiles fused together. It, or they, possessed one body with four legs, and a head at each end. Because each head was competing for the same target, the food bucket, the creature was in a constant whirl of frustration.

Stroller's arm hovered patiently, then aimed a chicken into each roaming mouth. 'I regard Buster as the one fellow. The one old chap,' he said softly. He cleared his throat. 'He just happens to have two heads and two sets of sexual apparatus, a doodle and a tweedle.' He fed the heads another chicken each. 'Tough luck for Buster they're not positioned so he can take advantage of them.'

She was tempted to ask if Buster, too, was named after some-one. It was difficult to take all this in. The oppressive humidity and the musty aquarium smell were making her head burst. She felt she was participating in a fantasy. What was this like? A TV cartoon? A nuclear-test aftermath? No, it was a *Star Wars* bar scene brought to life.

She gaped at the yawning intergalactic denizens and then back at him. What was Stroller doing nurturing these things? Back and forth he flung the chickens. Now the scene also reminded her of *The Island of Dr Moreau*. The Burt Lancaster version. There was a slightly embarrassed restraint about Stroller's movements, as if he were withholding his usual tenderness towards them.

'Of course in the wild these animals wouldn't have sur-vived.' What was it he'd said about determining the outcomes by controlling incubation temperatures? Again he self-consciously cleared his throat. 'Or even hatched successfully.'

He fed the mutants until the buckets were empty. Then he locked the door on them. For a few moments she could still hear the noise of Buster's whirling claws. The scrabbling sound faded away as she moved out of the shadow of the shed into the beating sun.

Surprisingly enough, she seemed to have passed the Stroller test. As she worked at turning her fear of reptiles into a cautious respect, he eased up on the city-slicker cracks. Assisting the rangers, mucking in, gradually put her at ease with the non-venomous snakes and the smaller, more timid freshwater crocs – and of course the marsupials, dingoes and birds. Anyway, apart from Stroller and his son Brett, with their legendary wildlife-wrangler genes, only the senior rangers were permitted to handle the venomous snakes – milking their venom for the antivenene used to counteract snakebite – and tend the big saltwater crocs. With all the other creatures she became a dab hand.

During staff drinks one Friday night, emboldened by alcohol, she hinted at a wider knowledge. They were drinking at a backpacker haunt, the Mangrove Moon, and the bar's air of youthful adventure and sexual optimism was contagious. She was feeling particularly upbeat, cheered by all the international flirting and gender display, and especially by the T-shirt slogan on a solemn Japanese girl delicately sipping something tropical and fizzy at the next table:

Ride the Wind Beautiful
Standing Obeytion
For Winner

Garth Stroller was expanding into ecotourism. He'd seen the writing on the wall. He was acknowledging the changing face of the wildlife business, the commercial imperative of ecotourism. You could guarantee that most European, American and Japanese tourists who ventured this far off the beaten track were ecologically aware. And even as the Koreans and Malaysians dropped their Coke cans and plastic bags overboard and flicked their cigarette butts into the shrubbery, they too probably appreciated knowing that sensitive attempts were being made to conserve the dugong and bilby in all their shy splendour.

Grace thought it was time to bring up the additional plant-ecology and anthropology units in that uncompleted science degree.

Time to ride the wind beautiful.

'I studied ecology at university,' she said.

'No kidding. I thought you were pretty green.'

But his reaction was not discouraging. He knew little about university degrees but he appreciated a hard worker. This girl was wasted selling backscratchers and T-shirts. He had to admit she was bright and keen. She could change a tyre, operate an outboard motor and had yet to bog a jeep. While she turned away when an animal had to be put down, she didn't make an embarrassing fuss. In any case, the looking-away was acceptable, even preferable, in a female ranger. He didn't want hard bitches working for him.

'Ecology, eh?' She also looked good in khaki shorts. Having tanned legs and looking plausible was an important part of wildlife tourism.

The next Friday night at the Mangrove Moon he bought a bottle of champagne and announced her promotion to Eco-Adventure Tour Guide. A European soccer match was on television above the bar and he had to shout above the competing cheers of drunken backpackers. 'Put your hands together for Sydney!'

She hugged him. 'Grace,' she said.

'Okay. Grace.'

However, Garth Stroller firmly believed there was one tourist attraction that would never change. Tourists craved thrills. Everyone wanted to see at close quarters – just out of striking range – creatures that could kill them. The more teeth or venom, the better.

More than anything, they wanted crocodiles. So he provided them, on the premises and, for the more adventurous, in the wild. He displayed them, bred them and farmed them. He sold products made from their bodies. *Fully integrated, from egg to shoe.* As his tourist brochures and television advertisements proclaimed, he was Mr Crocodile.

The 'adventure' in Grace's new title recognised and promoted the desirable hint of danger. In truth the risk was not great. Of course accidents could happen (this was the wilderness, after all), but her tours, educational recreation for the most part, steered away from the riskiest locales and creatures. Hazardous or not, however, her job was as remote from her previous occupation as she was physically removed – three and a half thousand kilometres – from home.

In Sydney she'd been the film reviewer for *Now,* a weekly celebrity and gossip magazine, seventy-five percent of whose content was American (eighty percent of that emanating from Los Angeles), and seventy-two per cent of whose readers were females aged from fifteen to thirty-five. In a generally declining magazine market it was extraordinarily successful.

As a matter of production design, *Now* ran suitably glamorous photographs of its movie, TV, video, DVD and music reviewers above their columns. Her stalker's first letter indicated that it was the black-and-white head shot above her reviews – young, dark-eyed, dark-haired, black-clad and, at least when reduced to two square centimetres, resembling a moodily elfin film star – that had caught his attention.

My dear Grace

I hope I don't insult your obvious education and intelligence to say that I first made your acquaintance at the checkout counter at Bi-Lo. I flipped open the mag alongside the chewing gum and pink lady razors and there you were. The same serious and studious beauty (glossy hair, expressive eyes, sensual mouth, delicate neck and so forth) of my favourite actress, Winona Ryder. You two could be twins! But looks aren't everything and I am educated enough not to put an attractive woman on a pedestal. Your brains are another matter! Since following your career I've learned what a clever mind and delightful turn of phrase you possess.

I'm known as a tough nut to crack romantically but credit where it's due you've accomplished it! You've won me over Grace Molloy! I'm even no longer offended that you are often sarcastic about films I like(d). Now I take your criticisms 'on the chin'. After six consecutive viewings of 'Moulin Rouge' I must admit I'm coming round to your way of thinking. I included a copy of your review (ouch!) in my last letter to Nicole where I pointed out some things about her performance, sexuality, hair, voice, height, standoffishness, attitude to Scientology and so forth that she neglects at her peril.

Is that a jealous frown I detect? No need to worry. I'm afraid I can be pretty blunt when dealing with insincerity and treachery. Anyway Nicole's and my relationship is over, finito, kaput. Frigidaire Kidman can go back to the arms of the Vatican and Microsoft and the Pentagon for all I care. Enter 'the Gates of Hell', Roman Catholic Nicole, for flirting away in that photo with Bill Gates and George 'Monkey Boy' Bush. Hugging them! What's the matter with a dignified handshake for someone in your position? Once a Mick always a Mick, I say! Who cares if you have dinner at the White House with the Masters of Evil? No one respects a flirt, as my mother used to say.

Getting back to us, darling Grace, why you are frowning in

your photo is a mystery to me when you have the entire film-going and magazine-reading nation at your feet. Or is that just you being intellectual and 'interesting'? (Relax, I didn't take it personally!)

Don't get me wrong, I'm sure it's our mutual appreciation of each other's intelligence, charm, wit and so forth rather than shallow 'sex appeal' that will bind us together. Bottom line, our natural charisma will win the day. (One in the eye, hey, for that charisma-free zone Bill Gates!)

If I may be so bold how about this idea in the meantime? Ask the editor to run a full-length (enlarged) photo of yourself in the next issue. Why should you end at the neck just because you're an intellectual? No reason on earth why a brainy woman can't also be a 'fun chick'.

I recently read this important gender-studies academic stating that feminine garb (push-up bras, short dresses, stiletto heels and so forth) were 'empowering' for bright young women! The headline was Babes Fight Back. Right on! I like to keep up to date with contemporary ideas. Far from being a mindless macho moron (I hate beer, drugs, rap 'music' and 'foolball'), I am definitely a 'male feminist' in my attitudes. I am incredibly sensitive to a woman's needs. It will soon be obvious that I have 'been around'. You are dealing with 'Mr Experience' here.

Since 'Now' introduced us to each other I must say it has become my 'Bible'. Who would have guessed how much vital intelligence it provides? Like that recent candid photo of Winona leaving the AIDS benefit with Gwyneth Paltrow, which reminded me that although Winona is tiny she is also 'full-figured'. (Gwyneth? Forget it! Another member of the breastless Vatican-Pentagon axis.) Correct me if I'm wrong but ever since starring in 'Girl, Interrupted' with Angelina Jolie, Winona seems self-conscious about her feminine shape. Like all us mere mortals she has had her 'problems' with authority but why on earth kill your inner 'chicky babe'? (She should take a few tips from Angelina!) Next thing she'll be binding her chest like in days of old so no one realises how 'stacked' she really is!

Can your editor have a word to her agent and tell her to throw back those milk-white shoulders? The loyal readers have spoken! And their words are, 'If you've got it, flaunt it, Winona!'

Here's another idea that came to me in bed last night. Why not proudly show your readers the similarities between yourself and Winona? (But not the bust-denying Winona!) You could wear various strapless gowns, swimwear and so forth resembling hers. Here are some suggestions — 'Now' magazine clippings, Winona-website printouts and my own artwork attached. I'm no da Vinci but notice how successfully I have superimposed your head on Winona's body . . .

Then had come his first cleverly engineered contact, over the free coffee, spring water and potato chips in the foyer before a magazine reviewers' six p.m. screening of a re-released *Nashville* at a struggling arthouse cinema with no security and a hunger for publicity. It should have shown him she was neither particularly moody nor elfin, indeed considerably taller and less delicately featured than Winona Ryder. But he was not deterred.

'You're Grace Molloy,' he said as he materialised at her side. 'I'm your greatest admirer.'

He was tall, thin and youngish, with piercing eyes and a white face waxy with sweat, perhaps from the bustle of the evening's peak traffic or from being too warmly dressed for Sydney's late-spring humidity. He wore a hand-knitted turtleneck sweater. It was clear he'd been hurrying – whiffs of body odour, damp wool and pungent chemicals came off him and he was still panting slightly. Even his hair, standing up in pale ginger spikes, appeared urgent. It was hard to guess his age, maybe late twenties. A studenty-looking cloth shoulder bag held a couple of manila folders bulging with press clippings.

This guy is anxious and keen, she thought. Her first impression was that he was a reviewer for a foreign-language magazine. His light, lilting accent with its upward inflection made this plausible. There was also something foreign about the way his raw, chewed-looking fingertips peeped out of the sweater's frayed and too-long sleeves. An expression of her father's occurred to her. *Just off the boat.*

'You're so knowledgeable about films, even the humdrum ones,' the pale boy said.

She gave a self-conscious laugh. 'Thank you.' Of course she was civil. She didn't put two and two together. In the bustle of work, the city, life in general, she'd forgotten the nutty fan letter. Most of the readers' letters the magazine received were pretty sappy and lowbrow and needed strict editing to be publishable. Babbling flattery was not particularly unusual. Half the readers didn't know that their favourite TV soap characters were actors. When they got married or had babies on screen they sent them presents.

And it wasn't as if the boy stood out in these surroundings. Scruffy urban pallor was hardly a rare style for assertive cinephiles. Many of her fellow reviewers kept the film-student look going well into middle age. But in the cryptic and clubby atmosphere of a critics' screening session – especially a thinly attended one like this – flattery from an intense stranger was as unsettling as his intimate smile (a redhead's small lemony teeth) and the fact that he was standing too close. But he was foreign, she reasoned, and a new reviewing colleague, so she gave him the benefit of the doubt.

To cover her slight embarrassment she passed him one of the gratis bottles of spring water. He took it with such loudly repeated thanks (clasping it to his chest but not opening it and drinking from it) that her friends Saskia Banks of *Vibe* and Griff Aarons of *Alley* caught her eye. Saskia raised an eyebrow. Griff winked.

'That's okay.' She laughed self-consciously again. 'It's on the house.'

The interloper's light voice murmured something else over-grateful and complimentary. In his excitement, with his attention shifted to the water bottle, his manila folders were in danger of dropping their load of cuttings.

'Careful,' she said.

'Oh, *thank you*.' He leaned closer. 'You don't know . . .'

She nodded politely enough but took a step back as her friends half turned their backs on him in a simultaneous amused demi-shuffle of black leather, for the moment casting her off as well, and resumed their film-buff banter. He was still standing close enough for her to smell his breath and skin – an acrid clash of mouthwash and aftershave.

'I can't begin to tell you —' he was saying.

'Are you an Altman fan?' she interrupted.

Marooned between this intensely smiling stranger and her earnestly chattering colleagues, thinking it rude to ignore him but keen to jettison him as soon as possible, she only had time to add, 'He's always interesting, isn't he – even his disasters, like *Popeye*.' Mercifully the lights went down then. 'Movie time,' she said brightly, hurrying inside to join Griff and Saskia. She made sure she sat between them.

Denied her company, and after some indecision and heavy sighing, the stranger moved heavily into the row behind – not directly behind her, but obliquely, two seats along. The best available seat, it occurred to her, from where to check her out. But

44

buffered by Griff and Saskia she was amused rather than unnerved by all this attention.

'Who's Old Spice?' asked Griff, rather too loudly, and they began to giggle.

She wondered what nationality he was. For some reason – his damp pallor? – she thought perhaps Icelandic. Not that she knew any Icelanders.

And then he wouldn't sit still. He lacked a reviewer's concentration. He wasn't interested in the Robert Altman classic, even this director's cut. It was also odd he hadn't bothered to pick up a copy of the film's production notes from the stack by the door. They were useful for the storyline, cast biographies and technical information, and especially for the credit list. A real buff with prior knowledge might get by without them, but why would you? Production notes could make even the dumbest teen-magazine movie reviewer sound like a cineaste.

He kept sighing and shuffling through his folders, at the same time adjusting and readjusting his legs as if he had a cramp. Like a six-year-old forced to sit through *Sleepless in Seattle*, he kept squirming and pressing his knees against the seat in front, making the old leather seats in both rows squeak and strain. Although she kept her eyes on the screen, she could feel his Arctic stare and sensed he was aching to move closer and speak to her.

Then he did so. His head hovered over the back of her neck. The chemical smell grew stronger and she felt his breath on her skin. He cleared his throat. 'Thank you again for the water,' he declared. 'I appreciate your kindness.'

'Jesus!' an exasperated voice hissed behind them. 'Cut the noise!' At that, he jerked back in his seat as if mortally offended, gathered up his rustling paperwork and left the cinema.

The Icelander. After eighteen months she'd almost stopped anticipating his gingery head in the landscape. She still had anxious flashbacks, especially in the sweatbursts of night, but in the sharp Kimberley daylight she felt the security of vast distance.

For the past six months she'd even stopped scrutinising the faces of her new tour groups as they stepped off the bus. She told herself this was healthy of her. At the same time she was still often sharply reminded of home, which was also natural. This wasn't homesickness so much as the sensation of living in a parallel yet detached world, existing side by side with her former city self, the movie nerd of daytime darkness, enclosed spaces and professional fantasy. This was the self who'd emerge from a critics' daytime screening like a nocturnal animal, blinking into the headachy sunlight. A pink-nosed urban possum who viewed and reviewed life and art as a three-act drama.

Ever since she was a child she'd absorbed Hollywood films and their foreseeable outcomes. She accepted the certainty of their structure – the security of the beginning, middle and end – above all, the satisfaction of the upbeat finale.

You could depend on it. The judgemental arrangement of every ancient myth and campfire tale, the Joseph Campbell template in Hollywood and beyond – the hero's or heroine's compulsory journey. All those movie storylines shaped like the letter W: the hero's situation plummeting, then rising, then sinking, then finally ascending. Ordinary decency eventually rewarded, the bad guys getting it in the neck, the conflict resolved – after epic tribulations – in the third act. Romantically entwined at the end, the main characters always achieving redemption. The audience getting its emotional payoff.

Her own situation defied the screenwriters' manuals. Motive remained unclear; conflict was irregular but traumatic, and maybe never-ending. Something blurred those easy Hollywood boundaries, she thought, or was it just the times, the twenty-first century, that had done that? As she lay in bed in the rangers' cottage at the rear of Crocodile Gardens, she felt more than ever that her own storyline had been left dangling. If she considered her personal narrative, the life of Grace Molloy, it seemed to be shaped more like a Q than a W.

Listening to the bats squabbling in the mango tree beyond the louvres, she could easily imagine herself back in her old bedroom in Sydney. The time and distance that had elapsed between Forbes Street and the wildlife park seemed negligible.

Of course Sydney had bats as well. On hot nights the More-ton Bay fig tree in Forbes Street shook with bats as they flapped and screeched and scattered chewed figs on the road. An elec-trocuted fruit bat had dangled from the power lines outside her kitchen window all her last summer there. She saw why they were called flying foxes: the dead bat was surprisingly big, tan, furry and canine-looking, so *foxlike*.

Despite the summer humidity, the bat's relentless dead grip had forced her to keep the window shut against the stink. But even-tually the smell had faded, and the fierce foxy muzzle had shrivelled up, and two months later the claw tendons had finally given way and the desiccated leather umbrella of the body had blown away in an autumn gale.

Slow to fall asleep nowadays, she lay on her back considering other similarities. This bedroom window faced east, too. Even lying here, her body repositioned diagonally across the continent, the first rays still struck her face each morning at the familiar southern city angle. And both bedrooms looked down on similar scufflings, grunts and shrieks of indeterminate nocturnal menace.

What's more, she thought, in both places reptiles roamed below. Under her inner-city window they'd been the men sidling through the door of the Golden Peach brothel next door, or trawl-ing in their cars for girls or boys or in-betweens. Or they were the muggers and gangs and drunks and junkies, the pimps and dealers and crazies, the bouncers and bouncees – all the assorted lurkers, ferals and drifters of the night. Not forgetting her special lurking crazy – her own personal erotomaniac. Up here, of course, the reptiles were merely scaly animals.

She thought the rangers' cottage was inaccurately named. It looked more like a small two-storey factory or warehouse than a cottage; maybe a surfboard-shaping factory or an auto-electrician's business.

My home is now this cement-block shed northwest of nowhere, at the arse-end of a sort of reptile zoo. This thought could get her down if she didn't consider it in a certain optimistic way. Not her permanent residence, by any means. More a temporary tropical getaway.

Just for the moment, she told herself. For the near future. Merely for the experience. It helped considerably if she imagined herself as a character in a film, an intrepid contemporary person doing reckless things in an exotic and cinematic environment. A Woman Escaping the Past.

I could even be a WOTO, she thought wryly, WOTO being the publishing acronym for Woman Overcoming the Odds, an important story genre in *Now* magazine. Readership and circulation surveys showed WOTO stories attracted great sympathy and were proven big sellers. This remained the case even though the classic WOTO subjects had subtly changed since the genre's inception.

In the beginning WOTOs were Aboriginal girls who became university deans, or farmers' widows battling drought and the banks to save the family acres, or pop singers fighting breast cancer. But now a WOTO was any beautiful female celebrity who'd been dumped by a man – to great career advantage in most cases.

Or, she thought, let's apply the heroic-narrative template instead: Grace is the heroine. She is being hunted. She's driven forth from the common-day world into a region of supernatural wonder. Fabulous creatures and evil forces are encountered there. Along the way, perhaps under a lone tree in the desert, she meets the god of love and death who assails her and shatters her self-absorption. A decisive victory is won and Grace the heroine returns from this mysterious adventure with the power to bestow boons on her fellow man and woman.

Great. Boons all round. But in her unpainted cement-block bedroom in the rangers' cottage it was a struggle to sustain heroic fantasies. The only faintly cottagey feature was the tangled wisteria vine covering the northern wall. Out of public view at the back of the park, the building did, however, have the privacy of a cottage in some leafy Cotswold lane – upstairs at least. The top floor, reached by an outside staircase, had three bedrooms for live-in staff, the other two bedrooms vacant since Troy Parfitt, the crocodile-farm manager, and Tenille Stokes, the marsupial and bird keeper, had moved in together in a farmlet down the highway. Still pinned to Tenille's old door was her cardboard sign with the copulating cartoon kangaroo and cockatoo cheerily announcing FUR AND FEATHERS DEPARTMENT — IF YOU HEAR THE BED ROCKIN' DON'T COME KNOCKIN'.

Upstairs there was also a bathroom, and a tearoom-cum-kitchen containing a sink, fridge, portable TV, vintage microwave and electric kettle, a dartboard, an assortment of unmatched chairs and a Formica table speckled with cigarette burns from Troy's Wednesday-night poker games in the days before he and Tenille linked up.

Downstairs was an emergency generator (Tropical Cyclone Shane had once knocked out the electricity and shut off the croc-egg incubators) and a big storeroom for park-maintenance equipment and animal-food supplies: the marsupials' and waterbirds' pellets, the echidnas' and platypuses' earthworms, the parrots' and cocka-toos' seed, the cages of mice for the snakes, and, in a big Norge freezer, the crocodiles' and dingoes' meat. At night the wet news-paper and ammonia odour of the mice cages blended with the rich algal aromas of the crocodile pens and drifted up through the louvres into the rooms above.

Despite the crocodile-pen and mouse-cage aromas, she assured herself that it was still a more suitable place to live than the city for a woman escaping her past, overcoming the odds, lying low. It was actually a better-smelling backdrop, too. After rain, the drains in the Golden Peach next door had regularly overflowed and drib-bled their repulsive refuse into her yard. After one summer deluge the backyard view from her bedroom – scores of condoms – was of a scummy shoreline matted with jellyfish.

Her bedroom here overlooked the cloudy lime-green surface of Clifford's pool. Clifford was a five-metre saltwater crocodile trapped five years before by Garth Stroller in a tributary of the East Alligator River after he (she found it impossible to think of Clifford as *it*) had killed and partly consumed a Saturday-night reveller named Clifford Emu Greentree. Either momentarily disregarding his twenty-year knowledge of the crocodile's existence, or over-estimating the speed of his own freestyle sprint, Greentree had resolved to take a short cut home from the pub by swimming across the river.

This was how almost all the victims died: foolhardily. And surprisingly often (this, she'd discovered, was the fate of Gunter the Swiss backpacker) right in front of a large illustrated sign in several languages warning of the presence of saltwater crocodiles.

Naming the crocs after their victims was a droll and necessary touch, Stroller believed. Something had to wake people up. But judging by the regular complaints of tastelessness in the 'Your Comments Please' column in the visitors' book, it made the tourists edgy.

'I'm not surprised,' was his response. 'Seeing most croc victims are dumb tourists or drunks. Or often both.'

As it happened, Clifford had a quandary presently making itself known to Grace. It was the start of the breeding season and he had lately developed his seasonal love song, a series of grunts deepening to a louder, low-pitched rumbling growl, to advertise his presence to the female crocodiles in the neighbouring pens. But every crescendo of growls reminded the bats nesting in the tree above him of his presence, sending them shrieking and panicking into the air. Their numbers were dropping off daily as they sought safer accommodation. She'd wondered idly why Clifford didn't wake up to this. Clearly his sexual urge overcame his taste for fruit bats.

Thanks to Clifford, Grace found it even harder to sleep than usual. By now she was accustomed to the standard cacophony of bat squeals, gecko chirps, owl hoots and frog croaks, but tonight Clifford's additional grunts and rumbles tipped the balance. As she climbed out of bed and padded down the corridor to the bathroom, wondering idly how many toilet frogs she'd find tonight, Clifford accompanied her steps with a bass stomach drum-roll that shook the louvres.

The personal assault of his noise reminded her of any inner-city Friday or Saturday night, the menacing *doof-doof* of the marauding car stereos from the outer suburbs. For several seconds the crocodile's low-frequency call was so deep-toned its reverberations filled her chest cavity and seemed about to crush her heart.

She'd more or less overcome her nervous distaste at the frogs living under the porcelain toilet rim, their mouths and little spatula fingers only a few centimetres from her flesh. Every toilet had its resident frogs. You just had to get used to sitting on top of them. As shiny apple-green as their gift-shop replicas, they clung to life, literally, just a froggy fingertip or two, and occasionally a tiny protuberant eye, showing above the rim.

Their secret lives and risky existence remained a mystery to her. She had never seen any of them arriving there, or any venturing outside the toilet bowl. If they did breed in there, she wondered, why didn't you ever see their tadpole stage? And wouldn't tadpoles simply be washed away? She didn't like to think what the frogs lived on. She very much hoped it was the clouds of insects attracted to the night-light.

Only when she stood and flushed – as they struggled in the maelstrom to avoid being sucked down the sewer pipe into oblivion – were their actual numbers revealed. Or was it oblivion? Maybe it was frog heaven. She recalled a cartoon character on early-morning television when she was four or five. She saw herself sitting at her little TV table eating peanut-butter toast while a cheeky frog defied his bigger, dumber nemesis. (A fox? A cat? A human?) It was a variation on the Uncle Remus story of Brer Rabbit and the tar baby. The frog pleaded pitifully for his enemy not to wash him down the bath plughole. Any punishment but that! For a moment she'd held her breath on the frog's behalf. But of course he was really delighted to be sluiced away down the pipe to the safety of his home in the swamp.

Tonight she counted six frogs swimming steadfastly against

the cascade. Her record was nine. Brett said nine was nothing; one dawn during the dry season he'd found twenty-two goggling up at him.

As she walked back to her room, Clifford's sudden silence struck her. It was the first breather he'd taken from his love calls in several hours. She stared down at his algal haunts, but despite the moonlight he was impossible to spot. Not a nostril or dorsal scale tipped the oily sheen of the pool. Meanwhile the bats kept up their flapping and shrieking, two of them squabbling recklessly in the tree fronds dipping over the water. But only for a moment.

He didn't waste any undue effort. It was one of Clifford's smaller vertical explosions, but still so fast it didn't register on her until he was sinking back with a mouthful of wings and fur and the bat colony, a frenzied cloud, was rising into the night.

Crocodiles, bats, frogs. Their presence, their unholy racket, should have forced the Icelander out of her mind. By day this was so. But at night she had these recurrent flashbacks.

Dr Garber had said this was to be expected. 'Try not to think of it as *your* problem,' her psychiatrist stressed. 'It's unfortunate that this particular erotomaniac crossed your path, but he's the one with the problem, the delusion. You're handling this in a perfectly normal way.'

Handling it? Normal? This was back when she'd have a panic attack just driving past a movie hoarding for the latest *Star Wars* film or glancing at the entertainment ads in the *Herald*.

It had been dark when *Nashville* ended and she and Griff and Saskia had come out of the cinema singing 'I'm Easy' and affecting country-music accents. They'd kept up the twangy voices through their wine and omelette supper at La Luna nearby and then a couple of drinks afterwards. When she said goodnight to them in the street and walked to her car it was about ten-thirty. It was that lull between crowds; the carpark was full but quiet, the regular movie and restaurant crowds hadn't yet emerged.

She regarded underground carparks as a terrible film cliché. Give thriller directors a carpark scene and they went overboard with the sound and lighting. None of them could get over the Deep Throat scenes in *All the President's Men*. Carparks had been maligned ever since. As she approached her car now, for instance, she could barely hear her own footsteps. They didn't tap nervously, or *ring out*. (No one ever wore rubber soles in a movie carpark scene!) And they certainly didn't echo.

Underground carparks in the movies were always barely and menacingly lit, all blue-black shadows and evil portent. (How did people ever find their cars?) Whereas this carpark blazed with a yellowy fluorescence, a 24-hour public-toilet or operating-theatre hyper-brightness, which easily enabled her to see the familiar magazine page lying on the cement floor by the driver's door of her car, to recognise the typeface and heading, and of course her own face.

In a typical thriller, she thought, the clipping would have been placed under the windscreen wiper and not merely dropped on the ground by her door. And some key word or phrase, and especially her photograph, would be circled or underlined. Maybe some cryptic or threatening message would have been added. And now she'd be hearing either the ominous amplified squeak of some villain's shoes or the frenetic squeal of fleeing tyres.

There were none of these carpark clichés. The page might have blown there, or been accidentally dropped. It was just haphazardly *there*. It might just have been coincidence. What were the odds of that?

In any case it made her do something that for some unfathomable reason thriller heroines in scary carpark circumstances always forgot to do. Her car was a two-door hatchback, a big squeeze for any villain, but she carefully checked the back seat before she got in. Of course there was no one there.

ADORATION

My darling

What hell it has been to wait but I had to postpone writing until your 'Nashville' review came out. What suspense! Since our meeting I have been unable to sleep (not that I need more than an hour or two a night) out of embarrassment at my behaviour and fear that our intensity would make you call 'Time Out' in our relationship. What a relief that the reverse was the case!

I got the message loud and clear in your review and I accept The Critic's 'rap over the knuckles'. I deserve it. It's not my place to suggest what garments you should drape over your gorgeous body if any. And I detected a hint of jealousy at my mentioning a certain Ms Ryder (and the unmentionable redhead N.K.).

Let me say that after repeated private viewings of 'Nashville' (I think I've worn out Video Ezy's copy!) I understand how you could

have trouble deciding whether I am the famous 'director' throwing
his weight around or the coolly sexy but shiftless Keith Carradine
character singing 'I'm Easy' as he calmly seduces all and sundry in
the country music world.

Rest assured that I am not a Keith. That was not the real 'me'
but just a Keithlike 'mask' I present to the world. We all wear a mask,
don't we? Even that homo fag with you in the leather jacket with the
arty farty air posing as your 'boyfriend'. What's his problem? Don't
bother, I know the type. Film school perhaps? Or media and cultural
studies I bet. The arrogant possessive way he let his elbow lie up
against yours on the armrest it was all I could do to keep my cool and
not rip his arm off!

But the 'director'? I get it! (Altman = Alternative Man = Yours
Truly.) You're definitely on to something there. What insight! I am
very flattered.

My thanks again for the gift. I will always treasure it. Already
it has pride of place in my residence. (I'm gazing at it as I write!)
The best presents are the simple ones, aren't they? And water is the
mainstay of life after all. 'If I were called in to construct a religion
I should make use of water.' So says the noted poet Philip Larkin in
my Oxford Book of Quotations. Phil obviously knows his stuff! How
sensitive of you to instinctively know that too! If I turn the bottle to
the light in a certain way I can still see your fingerprints on it. Such
delicate spirals, and so complex, like the amazing vortex of your mind.

That's how I see our relationship. As close as a fingerprint on a

Cool Ridge spring water bottle. (You are the fingerprint and I am the
bottle!) Pardon me getting all poetic but I believe our love will also
boldly stand out if only we can expose it to the sunlight.

Never fear, unlike Keith I am not 'easy'. I am 'hard'. A hard
nut to crack but true. No one but you (no, not even Winona!) has ever
cracked open my heart and stolen the kernel of my love. That you
regard my 'direction' as a triumph (to quote you — 'He brilliantly
controls his mosaic of human relationships') is a blessing I shall
remember all our days together . . .

Erotomaniacs believe their victims love them, despite all evidence to the contrary. The Icelander certainly believed Grace loved
him, and he publicly declared this delusional belief many times,
during his court appearances and also in front of the *Now* editor,
Rainer Jensen, and a wide range of intrigued or amused staffers in
the magazine's offices.

With the same indignant pride, he loudly announced their love
for each other at the Valhalla, Chauvel, Academy and Verona cin-
emas, in three film distributors' city screening rooms, and in various
pubs, clubs, restaurants, coffee shops and bookshops in Leichhardt,
Enmore, Darlinghurst, Newtown and Paddington. He made similar
romantic proclamations to her in a sandwich shop in South Dowling
Street, at the Coles supermarket at Bondi Junction, the Paddington
markets, the Centennial Park Café, and during the Tropfest short-
film competition and the Festival of German Cinema.

Once – she'd believed dawn sunlight and seawater might provide a healthy break from her anxiety – he suddenly grasped her bare shoulders from behind while she drew breath after swimming laps in the Bronte ocean pool. Her heart almost stopped. He'd stripped down to saggy grey Y-fronts. His milky-blue goose-flesh embraced her, then pressed against her. Despite his shivering, his burbling cry indicated he was in heaven.

'My darling lover! At last we're together!'

Even as she screamed he was trying to draw her closer. Near naked, he seemed taller and bonier than ever. Genitals, ribs and collarbones poked out. Orange hairs ringed his nipples and drifted like kelp from his armpits. A snot string dangled. Clinging desperately to the wall of the pool, she thought, I mustn't faint or I'll drown. She dug her feet so hard into the wall's shelly encrustations she could feel her toes slicing and bleeding.

A dozen bemused swimmers looked on. The 'darling lover' declaration had made them cautious. At her further screams, three men finally intervened and dragged him from the water protesting and splashing like an angry toddler.

As the men saw him off, she stumbled to the shallow end, taking deep breaths and willing her panic to subside. Her temperature had plummeted; she was freezing. Then something stroked along her thigh and she screamed again. It was seaweed: fronds as softly insinuating as his body hair.

Shivering, she watched her rescuers release him on the promenade.

His hangdog form slouched north towards Tamarama – every few steps mournfully turning back in her direction – and eventually climbed the steps up to the street. Then she ran for her car.

In the early days and weeks – it was almost too easy for him back then – he'd also followed her home to the Enmore house where she was living with Joel. To her – and Joel's – annoyance, he'd turned up for an imagined date one Saturday night, standing beaming on the doorstep, slicked down and spruce and holding a bunch of freesias. From his shoulder bag he produced a box of Cadbury's Fiesta. 'The film starts in thirty minutes,' he remarked amiably, 'but I've got the tickets already.'

Of course she shut the door in his face. But, looking back, this was the evening when everything had begun to unravel; that spelled doom for Joel and her. He began looking at her oddly, every now and then snorting his disbelieving, unamused laugh. His cynical actor's laugh.

Then he left. The underwear clinched it. They had barely stopped bickering over her 'hot movie date', as Joel referred to it, exhaustingly, when the first of a stream of presents arrived, at home and at the office: a Winona Ryder biography and a bottle of Baileys Irish Cream. Then followed a necklace of little silver hearts, flowers three or four times a week, fruit baskets, bottles of Tia Maria and crème de menthe and Drambuie. More ominously somehow, a pair of swimming goggles. Then, as frightening as they were disgusting, frilly, frothy panties and bras, in her correct size.

Even more unnerving than the home stalkings, however, were those in the darkened theatres and screening rooms. While she was absorbed in the movie of the moment her guard was down; her imagination and emotions were necessarily open and exposed. Usually his personal scent, the chemical adoration of his breath and body, announced his arrival. His smell struck her a split-second before the touch on the shoulder, the soft obsessive voice in the gloom.

Darling Grace. Beautiful Grace. Brilliant Grace.

And finally, so odious she could barely think it, the most nightmarish greeting of all.

Hello, my wife.

It made her job impossible. She worked long hours in the dark. The dark was her professional milieu. And if in daylight the fear was less distinct, it was still ever present. Even at the magazine it never went away. Every time the lift doors opened she anticipated him. In each door squeak and footfall, in every sudden whiff of the editor's or copy boy's aftershave, there were sinister hints of the Icelander. At night only pills enabled her to sleep.

As a consequence her brain was foggy and her moods erratic. Bouts of anxiety and confusion struck her throughout the day. Before this she'd rarely been aware of her heartbeat. Now her heart seemed to be guttering like a candle flame. Or booming so loudly against her ribs she was surprised that people weren't commenting on it.

Not that her colleagues understood her dilemma or the stalker's condition. Far from it – they thought she was either exaggerating or merely suffering from a particularly annoying ex-boyfriend. One bitchy conversation overheard in the Ladies insisted she was just big-noting about her devastating power over men.

Attempting to explain the continuous harassment, she struggled to think of a film that illustrated what she was going through. Nothing came close. None of the standard stalker movies, the 'bunny-boilers' featuring the usual fatal attractions, the knife-wielding evildoers waiting behind the apartment door, accurately showed what he was subjecting her to. Not homicidal hatred in her case, but relentless adoration – from a mental case.

'Think of a female-victim version of *Play Misty for Me*,' she told them. 'Without the sex,' she hastened to add. This still wasn't close but at least the males should be able to identify with it. 'Or think *Cape Fear* – both the Robert Mitchum and Robert De Niro versions. But forget the ex-convict revenge angle and make the stalker worship the victim instead.'

She knew she was rambling now but it was the nearest she could get. Unlike most psycho-thriller victims, she was innocent of any cause or come-on. It was imperative everyone understand that.

She persevered. 'Imagine a deluded stalker believes they're secretly married or intimately connected to you, and that while you're cruelly avoiding him in public, in private you're passionately leading him on. Make him pale and bony and sweaty and gingery.'

It nauseated her to describe him. She couldn't forget that milky blue-white chest, the orange nipple hair like kelp fronds, the grey prodding Y-fronts. The fact he bought her underwear.

'Oh, and make his breath and skin stink of sickly chemicals.'

Her colleagues regarded her uneasily. Sweaty and gingery? Chemical smells? She was pitching some very odd images here. They'd seen all the presents arriving for her – the flowers, the fruit baskets, the syrupy liqueurs. Snorts and embarrassed laughter were the order of the day.

'But she's my lover,' the Icelander had asserted to the Central Court magistrate while protesting yet another restraining order. 'As you can clearly see from the evidence,' he added, producing one of the ubiquitous manila folders from his shoulder bag. Magazine cuttings fluttered to the floor: her movie columns, with sentences high-lighted in fluorescent pink. Proceedings halted as frowning court orderlies, sighing heavily, bent to pick them up.

'Grace is both my wife and mistress, you know,' he solemnly informed the Waverley Local Court a week later as he faced a fur-ther trespass charge: this time for being unlawfully on the premises of the Verona Cinema during a critics' screening of *Run Lola Run*. His face showed no sign he saw any relevance or coincidence in the film's title. The backdrop wasn't important; it was the foreground that concerned him: the precise location of his beloved. 'How can I recognise this court's decision when it's my responsibility on this earth to watch over her?'

In mitigation of his offences this time he brought out the heavy guns: Franz Kafka, Kofi Annan, Osama bin Laden and both George Bushes, as well as Microsoft, Afghanistan, Iraq, Iran, North Korea, Kosovo, IBM, NASA, and the brutal unfairness of both the Academy Award voting system (the blatant conspiracy against Winona Ryder) and tertiary student grants. His sixth court appearance, this, and yet another conviction thrown out because of his mental state. More press clippings fluttering to the floor. Another apology by the defence solicitor, another promise to seek psychiatric treatment.

But out of the court appearances came a name for the record – Carl Gerard Brand; also a date of birth, which made his age then twenty-six; and an address, a boarding house in Glebe. Carl Brand gave his occupation as student, although he was not currently enrolled at any tertiary institution. Apparently he had attended three universities. It was not stated that he had ever graduated or held down a job.

In court it sickened her to look at him. As the applicant for the restraining orders, however, she'd been instructed to attend. In the dock he appeared pathetic and rumpled. By comparison, his appearance back at the *Nashville* screening had been calm and reasonable.

Carl Gerard Brand ran his fingers through his hair spikes like a decent, shocked fellow at the end of his emotional tether. He presented as a disturbed young husband whose devious wife was driving him crazy. As the usual legal barriers were officially put in place, he bared his teeth in an anguished smile and forlornly reached out for her. That faded cloth shoulder bag made him look like some messenger bringing news from sadder, poorer, less knowledgeable regions. A court attendant blocked his way.

'What about our marriage vows before God!' he cried. 'Surely the court must recognise our holy union of body and spirit! That we are one flesh!'

It worried her that his mental condition looked like genuine bereavement. She turned away. Was he really this mad, or just laying it on for the court? The magistrate didn't seem unsympathetic. Perhaps it was her imagination, but Carl Brand's beseeching chemical breath seemed to fill the courtroom. It reached down into her very lungs.

If Carl the Icelander thought he was a martyr to love, what did that make her? A pathetic runaway. She moved house to escape him – to Forbes Street in the inner city. Waking with a thumping heart before dawn every morning, frightened then indignant, she thought, Why me, you bloody lunatic?

Under the shower, behind the recently installed double lock

on the bathroom door (*Psycho*'s effect, of course), she'd feel her adrenaline surge so strongly she could at that moment have kick-boxed him to death, or run a marathon. By seven a.m., however, just before her first Xanax of the day, the depression struck and she'd collapse in tears.

She couldn't get over his unshakeable, psychotic belief that they had a passionate romance. Erotomaniacs believed this even when they'd never met their so-called lovers. If, like the Icelander, they'd not only met the 'lover' but exchanged pleasantries and been given a present (a free bottle of Cool Ridge spring water!), the delusion became even worse. It became a fantasy romance of *Casablanca* proportions. Bogart and Bergman. Carl and Grace.

It didn't matter that their 'communication' was entirely one-way. Erotomaniacs had all the answers. Carl insisted she was communicating with him via a secret code in her film reviews, writing passionate entreaties only he could decipher.

Not that the 'code' was too difficult to crack. Any praise for direction, cinematography or performance was meant for him; any criticism was directed at the unkind, sour world of bit players and minor technicians that schemed to keep Carl and Grace apart.

But she couldn't let herself think of him as Carl. Naming him only played into his hands and made him familiar and intimate. He remained the Icelander.

Her heart could no longer stand the shock of him materialising beside her in a darkened theatre. Or, for that matter, in daylight. The anticipation of his abrupt appearance was almost as nerve-racking as the reality. Panic attacks struck her from nowhere and made her want to scream out in protest like the No Man. She had no choice but to stop work for a while, take a break from reviewing. Anyway, she could no longer write.

How could she express herself with any fluency or insight when she knew he was poring over each review, devouring every word in his relentless search for evidence of their blessed and passionate love? And because all her opinions and utterances were grist to his mill, each word she wrote felt like a little suicidal knife-stab in her chest.

My own words are helping to destroy me.

It didn't take long for her to lose her witty, acidic touch. As she found herself resisting any strong viewpoint that could further inflame him, her critical faculty was next to fall away. So her reviews read as either weak and weepy or depressingly subjective. Increasingly self-conscious, she was soon too emotionally battered to write a coherent paragraph.

It was Rainer Jensen – *Now*'s smooth-faced young American editor, dutifully serving time on this overseas-posting rung of the corporate ladder – who suggested the break just before she did. 'Take some sick leave, kiddo.' Her gratitude and the concentrated effort not to cry initiated a shameful cloudburst of tears. Rainer Jensen couldn't have been more sympathetic.

'The mag is totally supportive,' he insisted, sending her on inde-terminate leave with a handsome boxed arrangement of gerberas, irises and tulips, a taxi voucher home, and the firm impression that the Icelander's disruptive appearances had finally stretched office bonhomie to breaking point.

'The human condition, my God,' he empathised. 'We gnarled old New York hacks aren't fazed by this stuff, Gracie, you know that.'

He walked her to the lifts and chivalrously pressed the Down button for her. His cheeks gave off the sweet tang of magazine perfume-ad inserts. It occurred to her that from this moment his consoling arm around her shoulders, the kneading fingers, probably no longer risked employer-gender protocols.

'God knows, we're streetwise enough to put up with most fruit-loopy things, but Human Resources and the security guys have had it up to here with your crazy boyfriend.'

She could barely whisper. 'Not my boyfriend. A complete stranger. An erotomaniac.'

'I know. That word again. *Erotomaniac*. Sounds sexier than it is, obviously. Very ominous in reality. And distressing. Well, keep in contact. Sort yourself out. Get the old touch back. No hurry. If we can do anything. Don't hesitate.'

When her lift arrived he gave her a hug and transferred some of his cologne to her cheek. As the doors closed he stood to attention. From his jaunty salute you'd think she was heading off to war.

In the following two months of hiding and sheltering, a virtual prisoner inside the Forbes Street terrace, she learned all about erotomania. Erotomania was almost all she thought about.

There were many anti-stalking websites on the net. Although she found them grimly unsatisfying, she couldn't stay away from them. Determined to get to the bottom of the condition, she was online most of the day. She was compelled to know her enemy.

The sites all stressed that stalking victims could stay safe only by remaining constantly vigilant. *Vigilant!* They all carried a warning in bold type: a victim should never assume that a stalker would respond to a restraining order. Delusional stalkers – by definition – couldn't be reasoned with. This assumption had proved fatally naïve. Plenty of prominent people had died. John Lennon sprang to mind.

A magistrate declaring 'Stay away!' made no difference. A stalker didn't understand and never would. Someone who'd created in his head an entire relationship, one with the power to transform his pathetic life, wouldn't be put off by a magisterial rap on the knuckles and an official piece of paper.

Her feelings exactly. All those restraining orders she'd obtained had proved a waste of time, energy and emotion. The Icelander simply ignored them.

There was another important point the websites agreed on. The media's increased obsession with celebrity had caused a dramatic rise in the number of stalking cases. The irony of her working for *Now*, the epitome of celebrity worship, wasn't lost on her. That she prided herself on the rigour of her reviews, regarded them as quite distinct from the glossy twaddle in the front of the magazine, only made the irony more bitter.

She swore by popular culture. But as she'd been heard to complain at too many movie-première after-parties, having just grimly observed from the sidelines the red-carpet parade of local 'celebrities' – the bratty chefs and soapie actors, the hairdressers and dressmakers, the bouncy TV weather girls and skeletal blond newsreaders – 'I don't see why it has to be mindless crap.'

She didn't suffer fools. In the tabloid and glossy-mag world she had a reputation as a grump. A bit too clever. A bit up herself.

But her line was, 'Why should popularity and quality be at cross-purposes? Look at *Casablanca*, *High Noon*, *Singin' in the Rain*,' she'd argue over the third champagne. 'How about *West Side Story*, *Bonnie and Clyde*?' She could rant all night about quality work that was also commercially successful. But *Casablanca* usually shut everyone up. *Casablanca* had won quite a few late-night arguments.

Was it only at last year's staff Christmas party that a flushed Rainer Jensen had raised his glass to her? 'Cheers, Gracie. Most of us are just star-fuckers but you're a critical bitch.'

She'd taken it as a professional compliment. When she'd mentioned it later to Griff, however, he'd shaken his head in wonder at her obtuseness.

'Isn't star-fucking the whole point of the magazine?'

Too bad. If she thought a $200 million high-tech spectacular was formulaic rubbish she said so in print, and watched the hate mail surge in. A new generation of *Star Wars* worshippers protested when she unfavourably compared George Lucas's later efforts to his early films. Her provocative belief that Steven Spielberg's work had gone sentimentally downhill ever since *Duel,* his first film, brought a similarly heated response.

At the same time, brickbats flew from the university media and cultural-studies crowd, for whom *Now* was an important text. She responded to their caustic emails. 'I couldn't be less interested in your *Lara Croft: Tomb Raider* paradigm,' she wrote back. And: 'What nonsense. *Exit Wounds* is not as significant as *Rebecca* or *Rear Window.*'

Her critics either took her to task for letting down the side (i.e., youth-targeted Hollywood trash) or presumed she'd fudged her movie-page photograph and was really much older.

Perhaps she'd too often drawn unfavourable comparisons between the movies of 21st-century Hollywood and those of the 1970s. But she believed the seventies' put today's in the shade. *Chinatown*, *The Godfather* (parts I and II), *Raging Bull*, *Five Easy Pieces*, *The Last Picture Show*, *The Chant of Jimmie Blacksmith*, *Taxi Driver*, *Wake in Fright*, *Deliverance*, *One Flew Over the Cuckoo's Nest*, *Don't Look Now*, *Amacord*, *The Tin Drum*, *The French Connection* . . . She could go on all night, and frequently did.

But it was a good decade, the decade of her childhood. Of course she hadn't seen these films herself until a decade later, well into her adolescence. They'd been her father's Saturday-night video choices and had since become her favourite films of all.

Not that she was a film snob. She'd never regarded her reviews as cinema criticism. That would be too pretentious a description of her weekly appraisal of current movie releases. (She'd promised herself never to write the word *oeuvre*. It set her teeth on edge when her friend Saskia airily referred to cinema, or even film, singular, for films collectively. 'Aren't you the little cineaste then?') No, in her heart of hearts she saw her reviews as intelligent pop culture.

Of course she beat herself up over this. Her proud professional standards hadn't prevented her from taking *Now*'s salary, exploiting its cab vouchers, stretching its expenses, accepting its Christmas-gift champagne and food hampers, scoffing and guzzling at its expensively catered parties.

And if she were honest she scanned the front-of-the-mag fluff and gossip as avidly as any other 15–35-year-old female in *Now*'s circulation catchment area. Yes, she kept up with the Hollywood scandals, the messy divorces and affairs and rehab admissions. While she scorned those who took this trash seriously, not many breakdowns, drug arrests, boob and lip jobs or bulimia 'tragedies' slipped past her.

How strange now for this opinionated crosspatch to share the stars' worst fears! Who could scoff any longer at their elaborate security arrangements or retinues of ex-Secret Service minders and Samoan musclemen? The stalking problems of Madonna and Spielberg and Jodie Foster had once been mere Hollywood gossip, not worth more than a second's idle perusal at the hairdresser's. Now their agonies were also hers.

Online, absorbed in one stalker's case history after another, she hunkered down all day behind drawn curtains, rarely bothering to change out of her pyjamas. And from this parade of sorry misfits she learned that the typical delusional stalker was a socially immature loner from an emotionally barren or abusive background, unable to establish close relationships and with more than a touch of psychosis. Probably a virgin.

Desperate to merge with someone more socially desirable, he or she picked an unattainable victim, someone in the public eye, someone rich or famous – a film star, a pop singer, a TV personality. Or they chose someone who initially reminded them of someone famous. *Winona.* This was a portrait of the Icelander. It gave her no consolation to see he was a classic case.

There was no solace for her on the net. She shuddered to learn that erotomaniacs were the most tenacious stalkers of all. At the same time she squirmed at the black humour stalking brought out. One droll website had even come up with the erotomaniac's anthem: Dean Martin crooning 'You're Nobody Till Somebody Loves You'. The net had no answers beyond mordant fatalism.

Another site listed stalking jokes. 'Did you hear about the

recently arrested stalker who used his one phone call to harass his victim from prison?' Except this wasn't a joke, it was a common occurrence. Gaoled stalkers had even been known to call their victims collect.

Another 'joke' made her laugh until she began sobbing and couldn't stop: 'I've learned that you can't make someone love you. All you can do is keep stalking them and hope that they panic and give in.'

The letter of termination of employment came via email, the firing method of choice of the new *Now* editor, Martin Hart.

At short notice, Rainer Jensen had been promoted and posted to London. Hart was the first Australian to be entrusted with the editorship and he was keen to impress on the New York head office that he could run a leaner, hungrier operation than his predecessors.

Under the terms of her employment as a film reviewer, she was dumbfounded to read, she'd been regarded as a 'permanent casual' employee and therefore not entitled to severance pay.

'You will surely appreciate,' Hart's email message of termination continued, 'that *Now* has been extraordinarily generous in paying your wages for the past eight weeks, notwithstanding that you provided no writing services for us while enjoying the company's time to sort out your personal problems.'

Enjoying? Suddenly she desperately needed to get drunk. For the first time in two months, with a commiserating Saskia and Griff in tow, she ventured outdoors after dark. They bar-hopped all evening, never staying longer than one drink in each place (compulsory stalker-avoidance tactics), and by the pre-dawn hours all three had at some stage wept tears of rage and frustration on her behalf.

At their last port of call they were slumped over an anodised metal benchtop in Short Cuts, a chic, monochromatic bar favoured by film buffs. By shunning any clichéd Hollywood portraits (decidedly no Bogarts, Bettes or Brandos; indeed, apart from a lone clapperboard for *Wings of Desire* above the bar itself, there was no movie paraphernalia whatsoever), it signalled deep cinematic credibility. It seemed the right scene for a final frank appraisal of her situation.

Griff gave her an intense look. The amphetamines were making him grind his teeth. 'You know that big sign outside the Chinese doctor's in Parramatta Road? DON'T TELL ME WHAT'S WRONG WITH YOU. I'LL TELL YOU WHAT'S WRONG WITH YOU!' He prodded himself in the chest and then tapped his forehead. 'Very true words. None truer.'

'What are you getting at, Dr Wang?'

'I know you've taken a lot of hits lately. A lot of evil shit.' He patted her cheeks like a speedy uncle, *ratatatat.* 'But I can help. I've got just the job for you. Mudcrawling.'

'What?'

Since last month he'd been mudcrawling on the side himself, he confided. '*Great* work.' He toyed with his Death in Venice and winked elaborately. 'Pays better than reviewing. Just sit at the computer, work whatever shift you like 24/7 and earn big bucks. This company needs cool young media-type people who know the ropes.'

'The ropes? I don't know the ropes.' She'd even forgotten the name of the drink she was sipping; after the Belle de Jour and the Blue Angel she'd lost track. Anyway, it was vodka-based, had a pale mauve sheen and resembled Palmolive dish detergent.

'I'm sacked and I'm stalked and I've got no ambition to crawl in the mud as well.' The tears streamed effortlessly down her face again. At the same time she had the impression she was smiling inanely and that her cheeks were on fire.

'Mudcrawling's just what the tech-heads call it. An inside joke. Officially we're content verifiers. CVs. Internet super-surfers. A vital profession in this day and age.'

'Just what we need, more bloody initials. More IT globalisation gobbledegook.'

'Porn trackers,' Saskia murmured, staring into her Kiss Me Deadly. Its fluorescence seemed to have drained all the colour from her face, except for her eyes, which reflected the drink's pinkness. 'You were boasting to me that you were a porn tracker. Being paid to look at porn all day. "Porn is actually cool," you said. Your very words, Mr Porn Tracker.'

'Only if you have a sense of humour and the right attitude, I think I said. Like if you don't *need* to watch it. It's like Jelly-wrestling Night, or Wet T-Shirt Competition Night, or Golden G-string Night at the pub. It's a giggle if you're not sweating on it like some poor lonely pervert.'

'Then why are you blushing?'

'A prawn cracker? Why would he boast about that?'

'Because he's such a tasty little prawn cracker, that's why.'

'Bite me, then.'

By the time she and Saskia had laughed themselves to the verge of hysteria, suffered loud coughing fits, barely avoided throwing up, reeled into the Ladies and finally returned, the night was drawing to a close and the conversation was too fractured and silly to continue.

Grace had forgotten about the job suggestion when Griff arrived all fidgety on her doorstep next afternoon, booklet in hand.

'I won't be put off by a violent hangover or your sexless jim-jams,' he called through the security bars. 'Depression is merely anger without enthusiasm, you know. I'm on your case.'

Once inside, he thrust the booklet at her. He had the tremors. It was a prospectus for a company called Bastion Technologies. 'Look at this bit,' he insisted. ' "The company employs only qualified staff with an *urban sensibility*." Urban sensibility – movers and groovers – is that you in a nutshell or what?'

Mover and groover? She felt like a depressed lump of soft

matter, some jellied organism washed up on the beach. Right now she lacked backbone, muscle, sinew and intellect. However, she supposed he was trying to be helpful. She squinted at the prospectus. Bastion Technologies declared its pride in successfully developing software for organisations and schools wanting to keep employees or children from looking at 'inappropriate websites'. She was dubious. 'It's just another web filter or censorware or firewall or net nanny or whatever they're called.'

'No, no. Read this. "These sites could be any of fifty categories, from hard-core pornography, anarchy, drugs and crime to such apparently innocent but time-wasting, anti-productive activities as chat rooms, gambling, shopping, investing, news reports, sports results, horoscopes and humour." See, it's not just sex and terrorism they're on about, stopping thirteen-year-olds from seeing threesomes or learning how to make bombs. It's a community service. Do you know how many hours of bosses' time were wasted online on 9/11?'

'Millions?'

'Beyond count. Immeasurable.'

'So? What would you expect?'

'Maybe that's not the best example. Anyway, mudcrawling's not just about the economic thing and the community thing and the moral thing. It's a privacy issue. Stops the invasion of the school or workplace. Remember, no one's ordered this stuff, invited it aboard, asked would you please provide Gosford High and the Star of the Sea Convent with a full range of perversions.'

'You're saying it's a good thing?'

'It's a very good thing. Mudcrawling actually helps freedom of speech. It stops medical and scientific and artistic and sexual-advice sites being blocked as if they were porn.'

'Blocked because technology stuffed it up in the first place.'

'Yeah, okay, it screws up sometimes. It's only machinery. Like a car or a toaster.'

'So what do you little mudmen do?'

'Bastion uses this automated tool called a spider to search the web for sites using certain keywords – say, 'sex' or 'bust' or 'grass' or whatever. Every site the spider finds is then examined by a human being. That's us.'

'How revolutionary is that!'

'Yeah, well you can't rely on technology to classify things properly. Sex and bust and grass might be completely innocent. Net nannies have been known to stuff it up and block the wrong things. Medical sites and safe-sex information. Classic artworks. Garden suppliers. They're not great at innuendo, a bit too literal and enthusiastic. The Swallows get listed as porn and they're really a Japanese baseball team. The Jewish Teens Club is blocked as paedophilia or race hatred. That sort of thing makes the internet-filtering business look really dumb.'

'And that's where the real live humans come in?'

'Yep. Actual humans check it out. People who know the scene. All the various scenes. Young humans preferably, cool people who know the euphemisms. Who can spot the subculture slang and word combinations the American porn capitalists use to try and sneak things through. But young humans with an education and strong stomachs, who don't faint dead away at scary *wooh-wooh* words like suck and dope and anthrax and the images and info that gush out. Young humans with no job. It's just the thing for you.'

'Thanks very much.' Her head was splitting. 'The thing is, I'm against censorship.'

'Who isn't?' His teeth were gnashing again. He looked as if he hadn't been to bed for a week. 'Look who you're speaking to – Mr Freedom of Speech. But Bastion doesn't block anything itself. This isn't some fundamentalist firewall. It just detects and identifies the nasty web invaders, then gives the customer the tools to blacklist them himself.'

'Leave it with me,' she said. These past months she'd forgotten about hangovers. The constant anxiety and the adrenaline flow must have flushed them away. Or had she lost the taste for alcohol? She could hardly remember how she used to be. 'I'll think about it.'

'You'd be doing something noble.' She'd never seen Griff looking so prim. He winked and ground his teeth in a grin. 'Protecting young boys from Pamela Anderson's honeymoon video.'

The Content Verifier Supervisor, a short-stepping, fast-walking, goatee-bearded boy with no visible lips, met her in Bastion's lobby. He was wearing a leather jacket, silver drop earrings – from one of which dangled a Christian cross and from the other a Star of David – and an English-style cloth cap turned back to front. His tweed-capped head barely reached her chin.

'Justin Beesley,' he said, frowning up at her, then setting off at a quick clip. 'Good to have another chick on board.'

To minimise offence, the content verifiers worked in an office positioned farthest from the lobby. 'The company doesn't want to freak people out,' Justin confided over his shoulder. 'Some old blue-rinse wanders in accidentally and next thing we've got the embarrassment of the vice squad.' A sign on the door said NO ADMITTANCE – AUTHORISED PERSONNEL ONLY. 'We call it the Mud Room,' he said proudly, ushering her inside with a heel-turn so militarily brisk it set his religious insignia swinging.

A dozen mudcrawlers, mostly dark-clad student types, some sipping milkshakes or munching takeaway food, sat at computer screens. Only two of them were female, both overdressed for the stuffy temperature in shaggy coats and scarves. Their faces bare of makeup, the young women had a raw, ruffled, cold-sore-prone look about them, their standoffishness enhanced by the shopping bags, magazines, water bottles and parcels set around the perimeters of their workstations.

No one glanced up as Grace entered. Several of the mudcrawlers were humming to themselves or murmuring cryptic asides to nobody in particular. She saw Griff typing away in a corner but he was too absorbed to notice her.

'Welcome to the domain of the Sinful Six,' Justin declared. 'Pornography, Anarchy, Criminal Skills, Racial/Religious Hatred, Drugs and Gambling.'

'Gambling?'

'You'd be surprised how evil its effect is on the soul of the nation.'

'A major sin?'

He sighed patiently. 'At the end of the day more insidious than terrorism. Drains the workers' wages and lifeblood. Hits the poorest people heaviest. Destroys families. Statistically connected to the overuse of tobacco and alcohol.' He raised an eyebrow. 'Wouldn't you call that a major sin?'

'I suppose so.' For all Justin's sanctimonious attitude, however, or Griff's spiel about the importance of cracking down on office cyberslackers, none of the mudcrawlers seemed to be categorising gambling, or online news, sport, horoscopes, or shopping sites for that matter.

From the images that jumped out at her as she followed Justin down a row of screens to her computer – to her left a screenful of multi-hued naked male automatons gripped, bobbed and thrusted, while on her right a solemn mélange of ballooning blondes squirmed, grimaced and bounced – and the intermittent expletive or amused snort from the verifier concerned, Grace gathered that most of them were looking at porn sites.

'What we're doing here,' Justin explained airily, 'is searching and categorising new websites within the Sinful Six, using special scanning software to search for specific keywords.'

'The dreaded spider?'

'You've heard of the spider?' He frowned again, blinked a couple of times, puffed out his cheeks and slowly exhaled so his lipless mouth made little popping sounds. He seemed miffed. 'Are you a Christian?'

'Ah, sort of, more or less.'

'We get a lot of Christians here. They seem keener. Ironic really, them being at the epicentre of the internet porn industry.'

'Really?'

'Yep. The more deeply religious a society, the more porn sites. America wins hands down, of course, but the Pacific islands of Niue and Tonga host as much porn as all Asia and Latin America combined. Niue alone hosts three million porn pages compared to the Netherlands' two million – and yet it's the poor old Dutch who've got the naughty rep! Then there's Tuvalu, Vanuatu. Forget coconuts, all these little desert islands live off porn revenue.'

She'd never even heard of Niue. 'Is that so?'

'So much for the missionaries, eh? But we don't discriminate against people of different faiths,' he added primly. 'It's all part of the great smorgasbord.' He handed her a list. 'These are your words for today. Sexual connotations only.'

She quickly scanned the list. None of the four-letter perennials seemed to be there. The words were arranged alphabetically:

Asian, bear, blonde, buff, chocolate, ebony, farm, flesh, fresh, golden, hot, hung, hungry, hunk, ivory, juicy, Latin, mature, meat, peach, pink, shower, silky, slit, teen, tight, tiny, twink, wet, young.

At a stretch she could read something toilet-wallish into about half of them. Thirty humdrum adjectives or nouns to be investigated to prevent the images they represented from invading cyberspace. Perusing them, she felt at the farthest remove from an 'urban sensibility'. Suburban, more like it. Even rural.

'Use them in any combination you can. Plurals, too, obviously,' Justin instructed. He was already marching away. 'Enjoy!'

Sarcasm, she decided.

It took only minutes to realise that in her present emotional state she was too vulnerable for this. *Young? Tiny?* She'd never felt less hip in her life. Even before she typed in the Google search for the first word, 'Asian', she felt squeamish. Asian what? 'Tight hot Asian teens', it turned out, was the bonanza here.

By the time she reached the last word on the list, the briefest and most horrifying of her investigations, she'd guessed why the female mudcrawlers chose to dress so bulkily and unattractively. It was to neutralise themselves. It wasn't just their sexuality they were hiding, but their youth and gender. Their presence. Those piles of bags and magazines were barriers to make their territory unassailable.

They made her reappraise her own limits. She was some-one who earned a living observing the human image on film. She'd twice sat through Pasolini's *Salo*, for God's sake! Visually unshockable was how she'd always regarded herself. And now she found herself drained and aghast. Had she changed so much? Would this stuff have worried her a year, two years, ago?

Some of what she'd just seen was simply kinky and ludicrous. People stimulated by belly-button lint, earwax, babywear, pith helmets or gumboots were just harmless Martians – not of her planet. Men who got off on imagining women mating with donkeys or dalmatians, or men themselves enamoured of toothy rodents or Muscovy ducks – even these pathetic creatures were of no concern to her.

What wrung her out was the 'normal' heterosexual porn with its crass images and brutal narratives. It was the dully compli-ant eyes of the women performers that affected her. She hadn't expected those bruised, stoned and numb souls. Or that this stuff would burst, tumble and pop onto the screen with such manic urgency. As if by typing a simple, everyday word into a search engine – merely a hint, nudge or wink to Google and Yahoo and

AltaVista – she'd triggered some brooding, dormant force lurking there.

How strange, all those body parts, those swollen organs and protuberances, lying in wait for technology to release them. Just as the puritanical churchy extremists had always insisted (indeed, their very words!), it felt as if she had *opened the floodgates*.

She strived to be the objective critic once more, to take the sophisticated view, the intellectual view, the cool and urban view. *Get a grip!* But the porn was too dumbly bludgeoning and lacking in both sensuality and artistic merit. Really, so unlike even the worst Hollywood trash. At least Hollywood strived to be sensual and sexy. This wasn't cool. It was crap: the after-lights-out fantasies of reform-school adolescents.

Her brain spun with questions. If it were true that cyberporn made even more money than Hollywood these days, did it make porn now the king of popular culture? So why was the standard so swamp-bottom low? Or was that the reason for its success? How curious was this? A multibillion-dollar business built on mud.

She noticed her hands were shaking on the keyboard. Nausea welled up in her throat and she was close to tears. Surely that old seventies feminist argument of her mother and her cronies couldn't be true: that the men who enjoyed this stuff – and millions obviously did – hated women and wished to degrade them.

Her generation had never believed this. Even if she'd considered it for more than a second, she'd thought she could handle it.

Live and let live. Each to their own. Whatever turns you on. Don't knock it till you've tried it. But now she felt as personally threatened as she had by the Icelander. And somehow betrayed.

Her despair wasn't just that the violent international studs on the Mud Room terminal would shadow her, follow her home and invade her head, as of course they would. The horror was that now she felt stalked by all the average Joes logging on around the world. All those clerks and mechanics and orthodontists and bricklayers and lawyers and farmers hunkered down over their computers in quiet rooms in cities and suburbs and sunny rural acreages with views of the mountains, cows grazing in the scenery and fresh winds riffling the paddock grass.

If she thought all men were after her was she finally mad? She certainly couldn't return to the Mud Room. The thought was more than she could bear. If she had a vestige of sanity left, another day with the shameless organs and orifices, the demeaned eyes, would tip her over the edge. She couldn't stomach Justin of the speedy footsteps and religious earrings, and she couldn't face those raw-skinned girls hiding behind their shopping-bag barriers. What would become of them? She couldn't think of them without weeping.

The Mud Room experience had worsened her condition. How could it have come to this? She'd never imagined being an anxious and depressed loser. She contemplated an existence dependent on unemployment benefits and handouts from her father. Right out of a Victorian novel, a sentence kept ringing in her head: *What will become of me?*

She was sinking fast. 'Embrace the positives,' said Garber the shrink. 'List them, count them, dwell on them.' Easier said than done. Her only consolation was that the Icelander seemed not to have discovered the Forbes Street address. There had been no contact now in the two months since she'd left Enmore. Maybe – if only she could believe this – he'd given up on her.

'Well, isn't that the best, most positive news you could have?' said Dr Garber. 'Why don't you take it on board?'

Then one afternoon towards the end of May, after she'd stayed indoors for almost three months, her computer brought some news that jolted her out of her chair: 'Erotomanic delusions on average last ten years. But often they last the stalker's – or the victim's – lifetime.'

A lifetime.

Minutes, or hours, later she found herself sitting behind the grate in the boarded-up fireplace, her knees under her chin and the cold of the old stone hearth numbing her buttocks through her pyjama pants. She was shaking and sobbing and finding it difficult to breathe.

The sensation of being trapped in a narrow, airless, unlit space, a coalmine or somewhere underground, enveloped her.

She couldn't straighten her shoulders or hold up her head. When her breathing and heartbeat eventually became regular again she thought, Ten years of this – or a lifetime! A gaol sentence would be preferable.

'*No!*' and then again, '*No!*' shouted the No Man in the back lane. Or had she imagined it? '*Yes! Yes!*' yelled some stoned neighbourhood rent boys, taunting him.

She rose in a daze, wondering why the front of her pyjama top was soaked, and realised that tears were still streaming down her cheeks. The hands angrily wiping them away were bony and unrecognisable and her right wrist ached from its obsessive onslaught across the mousepad.

'Delusional stalkers can become vengeful and violent for many reasons,' the computer screen continued. 'When their victims obtain restraining orders against them, for instance, or if they marry. And especially if they should attempt to flee.'

The logical next step in her disintegration was to flee from the computer to bed and stay there. For company she kept the television on all day and night, waking abruptly before dawn to the jarring fashions and fuzzy sideburns of detectives from an earlier decade, or to the curvaceous, round-eyed heroines of esoteric Japanese cartoons. Three days later the Icelander finally tracked her down to Forbes Street.

Considering its content, his letter was quite succinct:

To Grace the Murderer

Although I have become used to your cold-hearted cruelty
nothing could prepare me for the shock of your latest brutality.
It tears me up to even write the word 'abortion'. Even in my
wildest dreams I never thought you would destroy our unborn
child.

Devastated

Carl

Next day her neighbour Olga, the madam at the Golden
Peach, spotted a man on the brothel's security cameras. He was
trying to scale the back fence and she presumed he was a drunk,
stoned or deranged would-be client.

There was Olga with her elaborately pierced midriff standing on the front doorstep apologising in her East European
accent. 'Sorry, darling. Is a weirdo climbing in your yard.'

Grace ran to the kitchen window. Even before she saw the
ginger hair spikes, the desperate face, she knew it was the Icelander. It came as no real surprise. She could only think, There's
an inevitability about this. My condition willed it. She was an
emotional vacuum abhorred by nature. It had to happen, and she
was too numb to be shocked.

'Not to worry, babe,' Olga called out. 'My security's onto
it. Those Tongan bastards enjoying catching screwballs. They getting bored and fat without their fighting. Dickhead must've got

our address screwed up but he needn't think he's getting inside my place either.'

The man's shoulder bag was caught on the Golden Peach's razor-wired fence and he was hanging there kicking and struggling, providing an amusing on-camera show for the girls and their clients. Rapidly shredding clothing and skin, he was moaning what sounded like, 'My wife! My wife!'

In the circumstances, Olga implied, that was unusual enough in itself.

Two giant Tongans with shaved heads were launching themselves at the fence like rugby forwards, trying to dislodge the pale figure from the top of the palings. After several minutes he finally kicked himself free of the fence and the Tongans' outstretched tree-trunk arms and fell headlong into her yard.

Even as he stumbled towards her back door, strips of bloody cloth drifting around his white legs like a hula skirt, she was running for the front door. She had little strength, only desperation. It took an age to unlock the security grille, then open the heavy wrought-iron gate. Eventually it swung free. Out in the street cockroaches popped and burst under her bare feet. From somewhere nearby came pungent competing aromas of lemongrass and rotting seafood. A florid, well-dressed man sidled out of the Golden Peach looking self-conscious; his eyes widened momentarily at the sight of her in her pyjamas but he quickly turned away. Behind her she heard the door-banging begin and the plaintive calling of her name.

In tears, she fled Forbes Street and drove straight to her father's house in Randwick. She didn't hear the protesting roar of the car's engine; she'd driven three blocks and through four sets of lights before she remembered to change gears. In her fearful trance it was surprising she didn't have an accident.

What choice did she have but to leave? Her father went back for her things. She never returned.

TWO

THE FIRST
MODERN WOMAN

Although this wasn't immediately apparent, the woman turned out to have a small, pretty skull. It had been cremated and smashed into hundreds of fragments, so that each piece resembled the tannin-stained shard of a broken teacup. When they finally solved the jigsaw of the head – reconstructed the two hundred and twenty-one salvageable pieces – they concluded that she had been hardly more than a girl.

Of course the actual finding was accidental. As usual the first bushflies had woken John Molloy at dawn. His brain could block out parrot screeches and magpie calls, but the insistent gagging crows and the relentless buzz and tickle of flies on his skin made him dream he was desert carrion.

Outside the tent the air still smelled of night-dampened dust and the sand displayed the tracks and scufflings of nocturnal animals.

As he trudged away from the camp to urinate, his eyes wearily followed a trail of minute footprints – even the tiny claw points sharply defined in the sand's overnight crust – to where they ended in a dusty skirmish and a droplet of blood. A puff of fur still trembled in the air.

Near the little death scene, early sunrays glinted on a piece of that teacup. The woman had risen to the surface.

By the time his shouts woke Fischer, he'd uncovered another six pieces of skull, loosely cemented into a carbonate block. Crumbs of red ochre fell from them. The skull pieces separated easily and settled in the palm of his hand. He was still kneeling in the sand in his underpants, ignoring the sun on his neck and the ants on his legs, too excited to stand up in case he mislaid this vital spot, this pinprick in the desert.

'Henric!' he yelled again, and held out his handful of cranium bits.

Fischer had taught him that a finding was usually an informed accident. You spotted a piece of skull or mandible or femur exposed on the surface, like this one, bared by wind or water or the scratchings of animals or humans. Most of the Leakeys' African findings had happened near the surface. In China many of the famous ancient remains had been found by peasants quarrying or tilling the ground. The peasants called these mysterious discoveries dragon bones and regarded them as good-luck talismans.

Lacking metal and improvising shovels out of tree bark, the

early humans in this country had buried their dead where the ground was soft. Wherever there were ancient sand dunes near the site of an ancient water supply there was an outside chance of finding ancient skeletons. Where there had once been a water-course, you might find bits of tools and the remains of long-ago meals; with luck, human remains. But there were an awful lot of sand dunes in the Great Sandy Desert.

'Not quite a needle-in-a-haystack situation,' Fischer said, 'but almost.'

What Molloy respected about Henric Fischer was his grand aim, the grandest possible intention for a palaeoanthropologist. Fischer wanted to reconstruct the history of the continent itself. He hoped to solve the mystery of the world's oldest land mass: where had its first humans come from? When? How? Who were they?

To an idealistic young doctoral student like himself this was a fine ambition. Australia was a country of deserts; Fischer's starting point was to reconstruct the history of the desert. As far as Molloy was concerned, that was reasonable, too. Fischer's curiosity had been aroused by reports from geologists scouting iron-ore deposits. Their aerial photographs of the western edge of the Great Sandy Desert had indicated what ground-level surveyors had missed or thought insignificant: a chain of lengthy shallow depressions that Fischer believed might be long-dry lakes.

Luck was with them at the start. Two successive tropi-cal cyclones had begun their excavations for them. When they reached the site, five hundred and twenty kilometres inland from the northwest coast, they found that Cyclone Betsy had blasted away the dune shoreline around the biggest depression. A month later Cyclone Craig spread open the dune like a child's pop-up picture book.

Fischer named the big waterless depression Lake Salt End. Far from the sea and from any inland rivers, here were middens of mussel shells piled high above the original shoreline. Around these bleached and weathered pyramids they found stone tools: a handful of rudimentary knives, some axe-heads and many burned and scattered animal bones. But that was all. Their initial excitement gradually ebbed away. For five weeks they searched the beaches of the invisible lake for human remains and found nothing.

As Molloy would recount it afterwards, laconically downplaying the moment, 'Then one morning I woke up, went for a leak and found the girl.'

While Fischer was strangely calm as the girl's other bones revealed themselves – some large femur pieces first, then another sliver of mandible – his own fingers had trembled to touch any delicate fragment of her.

Only as her head gradually reclaimed its shape over the following weeks did his hands become merely careful rather than reverential. Then he was vividly reminded of the wigless and frayed bride doll in the constant embrace of Scottish Margaret back at the farm.

Fischer indicated the skull's thinness and the unfused cranial plates. In turn, Molloy eagerly pointed out that while the base of her spine had unified, the inner ends of her collarbone still hadn't fused. This put her age at late teens or early twenties. Her elegant femur and tibia indicated someone slender and athletic, about five-foot four or five. She was built like a ballerina.

The girl was about his age when she died. This gave him a shock. For some reason it seemed important. He was still unnerved by the skeletons of young people – not that he was much easier with the remains of the old, but at least they'd lived their natural span. At night in the cool dunes the past and its cast of characters loomed much nearer and more intimately than they did in the city. The generations closed in. Ghost winds blew over the phantom lake. At night the excavation sites turned back into graves.

When assessing a skeleton's age at death he tended to flesh out the person, to make comparisons. Of course he put himself in the picture. Is this fellow bigger than I am? Would I have found this woman attractive? If the woman was young he always presumed so, and immediately pictured their mating – quick, dusty and wordless. She wasn't one for foreplay. What would their children look like, these hominid kids who spanned the ages and races? Probably thin, he imagined, with light brown skin, a few freckles, straight hair, a slight Asian look – like many cheeky mixed-race kids from the western Kimberley nowadays.

But this fantasy gradually petered out with the difficult vision of domesticity: his and his early-hominid mate's life together in the Great Sandy Desert. Of course it wasn't a desert then – the lake was full, the land was lush and green, protein abounded. They ate fish and shellfish and jumbo-sized marsupials and reptiles and birds, all tossed on the fire. Between meals they chewed nuts and fruits and gritty tubers gathered by his diligent spouse. He could see himself lounging around the embers, gnawing the more man-ageable bones of a wombat as big as a Volkswagen.

Imagining their relationship was harder. Without movies, politics, books, music, sport, television, all that stuff that clogged the modern brain, it was a struggle to conjure up their early-hominid evenings around the campfire. What would they talk about without Vietnam, without America? Some hunting-and-gathering smalltalk, he supposed: local terrain-tracking difficulties, tribal politics, perhaps some com-munity gossip and animist storytelling. Then, before the light faded, some necessary weapon and tool maintenance and shelter construct-ion for the cool night ahead. And more love in the dusty moonlight.

Or would they already be making plans for their steady trek south and east across the continent? Were they being pressured by more recent invaders? Or were they themselves plotting to conquer the previous arrivals, to drive them from these rich and fruitful lands?

For someone like himself, oddly unmarked by the Anglicism of the farm years, it was especially difficult imagining his and his early-hominid wife's spirituality. The only vivid scene was their nightly roll in the sand.

Then he'd remember the condition of the girl's skeleton. He'd conjure up the death ritual and the deep beliefs involved and feel guilty, not for the first time, for being young and crass and too fixed in the hedonistic present for a career in prehistory.

In order to feel more objective about the remains of the young it helped to retreat into science, to recall textbook terms: synostosis and epiphyses. *The sacrum unified between the ages of sixteen and twenty-three; the clavicle fused at about twenty-six.* It made them seem less like real dead people.

On that subject, it was frighteningly easy to picture himself as a skeleton. Just cleaning his teeth, he'd yawn widely at the mirror and be shocked by the grinning horror-film skull within the flesh. To throw back his head and inspect the gruesome gaping arcs of his jaws was a preview of his own mortality.

Waking from uncomfortable dreams and aching from another desert night on hard ground, he'd find himself rubbing his own still-unfused collarbone – the ground's pressure roused other stiffness, too – and be immensely grateful to be a young hominid alive and well in the here and now.

He'd been taught not to generalise from an individual body, but the exciting anomaly was that this young woman was anatomically 'modern'. Anthropology had taught him to expect the ancient skeletons on this continent to be robust rather than gracile; of stocky, not delicate, physique. They looked like the skeletons of rugby players. The big surprise was her petite ballerina's frame.

The cremation was also dramatic and unprecedented: the fact that her body had been burned and her skull smashed into hundreds of pieces. Just as awe-inspiring was the result of the initial radiocarbon dating, which estimated her age at about 60 000 years. This made her funeral ritual the oldest human cremation ceremony encountered anywhere in the world.

As the continent's earliest hominid remains, their skeleton would become known to science as Salt End Woman. Having heralded her as the First Modern Woman, however, the newspapers stuck with that. They loved her being so old (the older the better) just as they loved her being so poignantly young at the time of death.

Newspaper artists gave their impressions of how she'd look today, fleshing out her bones with a beachgirl's curves. They dressed her for the weekend feature pages in a bikini, a leotard, a miniskirt. Naturally they put her in cavewoman animal skins as well. Numerous articles enthused that she'd put the continent on the evolutionary map. The stories had a self-congratulatory, nationalistic tone (the first!), as if she'd won the nation an Olympic gold medal or an Oscar.

All this was acceptable hyperbole to her discoverer, 21-year-old John Molloy – barely a BSc (Hons). Why wouldn't he love all the fuss? It was interesting how his previously reticent and scholarly mentor, Dr Henric Fischer, head of the school of anthropology at the University of New South Wales, leader of the Salt End Expedition, appeared to lap it up as well.

Salt End Woman. The First Modern Woman. Right from the beginning, the unexpectedly gracile nature of her physique determined what he and Henric called her among themselves: Grace.

The excavation of Grace took eight weeks: two months spent collecting her fragments, gently brushing away the ochre dust that many millennia ago had absorbed any vestiges of flesh and liquid. Then another six months back in Sydney reconstructing her shards and splinters into a recognisable human.

But still they were no closer to solving the mystery of her death. There was nothing like that extraordinary ceremony in traditional Aboriginal rites: the ritual cremation and the skull so painstakingly smashed afterwards.

It played on his mind both awake and asleep. Movie images whirled. He pictured a circle of chanting, painted elders wielding heavy clubs to an ominous *bonga-bonga* drumbeat, like a scene in a Tarzan film. Had she been sacrificed? Murdered? Had she broken some tribal taboo? Was she a sacrificial virgin? A witch?

Whatever her status, it certainly appeared as if her tribe had gone to great trouble to prevent her spirit returning.

EUREKA!

Just as he relished the thought of Grace defying her undertakers after tens of thousands of years and rising to the surface again, he was delighted to be her discoverer. If the dune-levelling winds and torrential rain of Tropical Cyclones Betsy and Craig had been chiefly responsible, it was he, John Molloy, who'd played the final, decisive role in her resurrection.

There was more than professional pride in his discovery. He knew it had changed his life. It was a scientist's *Eureka!* moment. He'd never felt more keenly the lack of people to show off to. It was like when he learned to ride a bike, and a horse; it was like his graduation ceremony. A parent or two would have come in handy.

He badly wanted to bask in the approval of someone special. But who? Kate?

On his return to town he'd intended to sit Kate down, perhaps over a boozy meal at the New Hellas, and detail his rich mixture of feelings. It shouldn't be too hard to place her for a moment in this rare role of congratulatory head-stroker. But when he got home he found them both hungry for more than stewed lamb and stuffed capsicums. The expedition's success had increased the usual homecoming lusts. Success made you randy, no doubt about it. After eight weeks in the desert the excitement his 60 000-year-old woman aroused was overwhelmed by his desire for a particular twenty-year-old woman, for the equally demanding, olive-skinned body of his girlfriend, Kate Prowse.

Barely considering neighbours or nourishment, they made hectic love in Kate's tiny Glebe room all weekend. When they surfaced for drinks and the occasional snack or Buddha stick, or to change her Rolling Stones records, he started to tell her the basic facts of Salt End Woman.

Sitting up earnestly, the sheet tucked under her armpits in Hollywood après-sex mode, she showed a polite enough interest. 'Dramatic stuff,' she said, passing the joint.

'It was.'

'But will it change anything? A discovery should change the status quo, shouldn't it?'

'It should fill in some gaps. Make people rethink accepted theory – if the evidence is there.'

'Not overnight then?'

'Not quite.'

He lay back watching the breeze rustling her wall posters. No Che, Mao or Ho portraits for once. Instead, stern and muscular Chinese workers built a dam. Stern, muscular Latino workers hoisted baskets of grapes, melons and citrus fruits on their shoulders. A miniature mirror ball on the ceiling cast a frivolous rainbow of dust motes across their resolute endeavours. By way of contrast to socialist realism, Aubrey Beardsley's stern Salome had John the Baptist's head on a platter. The posters fluttered. Mick Jagger sang 'Brown Sugar'. The breeze brought a whiff of tomcat spray and frangipani from outside the flat.

'Seriously, you're a clever boy.'

Nevertheless he felt his desert drama was lost on her. The dunes couldn't compete with the streets. Fitful dusty luck seemed pretty lame compared to direct action. In her campus fashions and attitudes she was 'politically involved' and 'committed to changing the status quo'. She was idealistic Political Science, not bland, unfashionable Science. He'd wondered aloud once whether she thought science should be overthrown as well.

'Parts of it,' she'd shrugged and added, 'like anything else. Breaking up the old hegemonies.'

Normally she'd be playing Country Joe and the Fish, Grace Slick, Dylan, Baez. Outside this bed, this room, this weekend, she had Students for a Democratic Society and the next anti-war moratorium on her mind. Marches, demonstrations, office occupations, sit-ins, fund-raising concerts, student newspapers: she was *involved*. Yes, she could indulge in the raunchy, ingratiating and politically neutral atmosphere of the Stones. And she could reward a boyfriend's quirky passion for old remains by trickling baby oil over his sensitive living flesh. At the same time he got the impression he should be grateful.

And he was. So he made no real effort to convince her of his discovery's unique importance. Anyway, the mood was hardly suitable. In the salty damp tangle of her sheets it seemed inappropriately scholarly as well as immodest and elitist – a wank – to recall how *noble* he'd felt walking the sandy shorelines of the ancient lake.

He'd trodden in the footsteps of the first occupants of the land – the first *Homo sapiens*. How to explain the magnitude of that to a sexy young woman between bouts of lovemaking? How could he get across the wonder of the piece of broken teacup in his hand? In any case he had other *Eureka!* moments on his mind. Right then he was Contemporary Man, feeling his correct and healthy physical age, supremely 1970s.

After that weekend, of course, life moved in its new arc and the moment was lost for ever. Back at the university he was soon engrossed in the complexities of Salt End Woman and her scientific and career consequences. Indeed, the whole riddle of ancient-yet-modern Grace didn't leave his thoughts for long. Even throughout the turmoil of Kate's own discovery three months later, their impulsive registry-office marriage – against all expectations – and their daughter's birth the following April, Salt End Woman held her ground.

Perhaps it was inevitable that later, during one of those long argumentative evening walks he thought of as a Five Jetty Night, Kate would throw it back at him that he'd named their daughter after a pile of old burnt bones.

This argument, at least, was a half-hearted one. He reminded her that she'd gone along with the name. Of all people, the Kate Prowse of the early seventies, the Kate still in brusque political transition from Catherine, via Cathy (activist Kit was still to come), was not immune to the political kudos of the First Modern Woman. The favourable connotations had appealed to her from the start.

Anyway, by the time they broke up and left their cottage on Lion Island, their own Grace was a chatty and chubby two-year-old of confidently individual character and appearance. And, as always happens, by then no name but that one suited her.

THREE

———

ADVENTURE TOURS

The eroded sandy delta and leaf litter of the tidal creek, the freshly torn and stripped branches upstream and the newly uprooted trees indicated the path of the cyclone. But in a place of such thick mangrove forests and wildly variable tides, the storm damage was hardly discernible. Where you noticed a cyclone's passage was in a town. Roofs and power lines down, smashed windows, crushed cars, trees in bedrooms, dazed and broken-winged birds, dead pets in the swimming pool. It was now early autumn; surely it had been the last cyclone of the season.

Inevitably, as the turbid water of the creek rose above the waists of the English couples, and the mud, roots and snags of the creek bed increasingly hampered their progress, they were beginning to mutter about crocodiles.

It had taken them almost two hours to voice their fears. Grace considered this some sort of record. That elaborately bush-kitted German party last month, so pocketed and epauletted and orna-mented with retractable technology that they resembled human Swiss army knives, had started seeing imaginary crocodiles within ten minutes.

Two hours earlier, the Mainsbridges and the Horsleys, intrepid middle-aged schoolteachers from Salisbury and Devizes, had been relishing their latest outback pursuit, the Mangrove Crab Adventure. Laughing self-consciously in their new Crocodile Gardens and Eco-Adventures T-shirts (no pretentious safari-wear on this lot), they'd climbed out of the Eco-Adventures jeep, removed their shoes, taken up their hessian sacks and crabbing hooks and followed Grace in a sliding scramble down the shore dunes and into the creek mouth.

But two hours ago the outgoing tidal creek meandering gently into the sea had been nowhere more than knee-deep; they still had firm white sand under their toes. The sun was still several hours from full strength and the water reflected the startling azure clarity of the northern sky.

Furthermore the sandflies hadn't yet discovered the delicious moisture of their eyes; even the ubiquitous bushflies were still deterred by the party's brisk, splashing progress upstream. And the Mainsbridges' new duty-free Sony camcorder, primed to cap-ture quirky antipodean creatures for display on this year's family Christmas cards, had not yet fallen, during a stumble by Hugh Mainsbridge, into the creek.

On the other hand, that unique wildlife they'd travelled thousands of miles to see had paid off handsomely. Already this morning they'd spotted a goanna running on its back legs just like a *Jurassic Park* velociraptor, a frill-necked lizard, several dusty dozing wallabies, and a single pied oyster-catcher, whose lifelong monogamous habits, Grace told them ('They always come in twos'), meant that this little bird, frail as a child's drawing, would forever pace the shoreline alone, pining for its mate.

As usual, that made them thoughtful – at least until the crabs appeared. Thousands of crabs.

Limited as it was by the four hours of lowest tide (the twelve-metre tides on this coast were among the biggest in the world), the Mangrove Crab Adventure had seemed a novel way of spending the morning, with the bonus that any suitable catch would be cooked and delivered to them for supper. Bare-legged and sensibly hatted, coated from scalp to toe with tropical-strength sunscreen and insect repellent, the teachers had set off upstream, scattering hermit crabs before them.

As the disorientated hermit crabs fled across the sandbanks, Grace paused in midstream as usual so her clients could take in this little comedy. She quite liked this lot. 'We're not *tourists* as such – we're seasoned *travellers*!' they'd corrected her with great earnestness, as if travelling were a vital endeavour. It certainly could be, she thought, if you were travelling in order to escape.

No one wanted to be called a tourist these days. Tourists visited hackneyed places like Paris and Venice and Rome, and disliked hardships. Her clients were here because at this stage of their lives they enjoyed being intrepid.

Her *travellers,* these adventurous temporary friends, amused her. The older ones – the Grey Wanderers, as the rangers called them – were so bloody jolly. Their bland conversations, inevitably about meals, pets, grandchildren or travel mishaps, were as intense as they were inconsequential. Without exception their grandchildren were all geniuses or Olympic prospects – and their cats, dogs and budgerigars weren't far behind them.

It intrigued her how the female Grey Wanderers regarded their husbands like pets or babies, and how the husbands, those big, stolid children, put up with it. Their viewpoints barely registered. In company the wives behaved as if the men were invisible.

'He'll eat anything you put before him. Absolutely anything.'

'Oh, yes, so will mine.'

'No, I won't. I won't eat tropical fruits. I won't touch them.'

'But he doesn't like tropical fruits.'

'I can't stand pawpaw, mango, passionfruit, kiwi fruit, breadfruit. Too sickly and sweet. Even pineapple. What's that one we had yesterday? Jackfruit? Disgusting. Something about the tropical taste, it's unnatural. And persimmons. Don't talk to me about persimmons!'

'Absolutely refuses to eat them. Says they're too sweet for

him. It makes it a bit difficult in the tropics. He hates persimmons most of all.'

'*Wait a minute, I tell a lie. I like guavas.*'

Today's clients exposed paper-white thighs, calves, ankles, feet and arms. Rather than travellers, they were human road maps. Their bodies' highways and byways were written on their skin: blue freeways, purple turnpikes and delicate red and purple overpasses – even mysterious greenish winding lanes.

She was glad they liked her hermit crabs. They were totally dependable, her hermits. No matter how many times the crabs encountered her tour intrusions, they never became accustomed to them; their hysterical reaction was always the same. She pointed out those more anxious crabs which discarded their old residences too early (there were always some desperate panickers) and then, unhoused, suddenly vulnerable and facing fierce opposition from the existing tenants, frantically tried to take over already occupied premises.

'I love the way they hold their helmets on their heads and then stampede in all directions,' she said. 'They remind me of the Keystone Kops.'

The teachers laughed and agreed. Of course they got it. When she'd pointed out this similarity to Brett, he looked bemused. 'The *what* cops?'

The first of the Brett Stroller disappointments. While he'd brought her here a year before ostensibly to teach her mudcrabbing, they both knew it was really to present himself, to air his comprehensive Kimberley knowledge – the tropics, the desert, the coast, the tidal streams, the mangroves. The mud.

As she squelched and slid upstream behind him that day, recalling mudcrawling in its recent city context, this coincidence had given her a moment's pause. But her attention wavered only for a second. How far away all those intense city anxieties seemed on an optimistic tropical morning with its vivid azures and creamy aquamarines. Suddenly it was enormously impressive that Brett knew every piece in the environmental jigsaw.

Yes, Brett was even an expert on mud. *Mud*, which, as he pointed out, the little crabs were presently eating and filtering of nutrients and then spitting out in tiny ornate patterns. They were so delicately arranged, these patterns, that she recalled *National Geographic* photographs of her childhood: the cicatrices on the cheeks of traditional African brides. For a brief moment this was a male who made mud beautiful to her.

And mangroves. Who could possibly know more than Brett about mangroves?

'See this little mangrove leaf?' He held it in his fingertips and rubbed them together, and even this small tension made some tendon and muscle twitch in his forearm. She found herself fascinated by the fine blond wrist hairs of a boy talking of mud and mangroves. 'Mangroves filter mud, too, you see,' he said, 'and they sweat out salt through their leaves, just here.'

Mangroves, all thirty-seven local varieties of them, he went on, were the nursery and supermarket of the ecosystem. They nurtured the world's most delicious fish, the barramundi, and the best-tasting crab, the mangrove or mudcrab – the famous muddie.

It didn't matter that he was reciting a ranger's well-worn spiel. He spoke so tenderly that the daze was on her again. The old secret swoony feeling that struck her when faced by someone calmly and methodically conveying expert knowledge. A subtle but thrilling sensation stroked the back of her neck and crept across her shoulders and scalp.

She was having difficulty standing. She felt that if his skin were to brush hers at this point, if he should casually touch her bare forearm with his hand, say, while indicating a crab hole in a mud bank, she would embarrassingly crumple into the creek and float away. Either that or sink into his arms in the mud.

Only the elements and her surroundings brought her back to reality. The beauty of it all, she thought, taking a deep breath. The way he fitted into the scheme of things as neatly as any crab or goanna or waterbird. He must have read her thoughts. To prove how harmoniously he blended into the tropics he nonchalantly removed his shirt.

So she trudged behind him upstream, stunned now by the gleaming orchestration of his muscles. She couldn't remember ever noticing anyone's shoulderblades before, but his coppery back, too, made her dizzy. It was hard to concentrate on keeping her footing while his blond ponytail swung like a metronome and his body moved so languidly yet athletically in front of her. Harder still to keep her emotional balance.

It proved she was well again. More than well. Back on track. She was astonished at how thoroughly she'd acclimatised. Usually she was no fan of the outdoor male, the surfer or sportsman. Back home her preference had been for indoor and interesting. Creative types. Johnny Depp rather than Brad Pitt. Graphic designers, musicians, struggling writers and painters, fine. The occasional lounge lizard, why not? Some quite scrawny theatre and nightclub denizens had been granted favour on their sense of humour alone.

But Brett was sinewy and lean and his muscles looked more casually capable than the gym-manufactured stacks of no-necked Sydney footballers and vain beachboys. Not only did his body appear to work well, like an indigenous animal's it looked as if it served a very useful purpose.

Back in her grumpy days she might have muttered tartly to such a showoff, 'Shouldn't you cover up in this sun?' Taken the wind out of his sails. At least said something sensible about skin cancer and 30+ sunscreen. After all, the Adventure Tours jeeps carried buckets of the stuff. But not this time. After half an hour plodding behind Brett as he bounded over mud banks, lunged into nests of mangrove roots and deftly produced huge crab after crab for her perusal (sensitively returning them to their holes afterwards), she was plotting her moves on this bronze-skinned nature boy.

Then, halfway up the creek and surrounded by anxious hermit crabs, she abruptly changed her mind. And that was the beginning of the end of their potential affair.

As far as she was concerned, his failings had multiplied that morning when, on their return to the creek mouth, he'd suggested freshening up in the ocean.

'A swim? Sure, absolutely.' She was muddy and hot and suddenly thoroughly depressed with herself and her stupid mood swings. She badly needed to dive under, to calm down, in the sea. They were only ankle-deep, however, when he abruptly pointed to a dark shape only metres away.

'Shark!' he yelled.

Was there any warning on earth more electrifying? Bravely interposing his own body, Brett dashed forward, grabbed the shark by the tail, leaned back and swung it around his head in the manner of a hammer-thrower – his ponytail also swinging dramatically – and tossed it towards the deep.

As the surprised shark, a five- or six-footer, scooted off, he turned to her with a modest grin. 'That bugger won't bother you now.'

'My God! Thank you!' She was impressed and grateful all over again. She found herself gripping his forearm.

'Not a problem.'

'What sort of shark was it?'

Why was he grinning? When she thought about it, the shark did have a flat, guitar-shaped body and smaller dorsal fins than you'd expect. It took a moment to wake up to his ploy. The shark was a shovel-nose, a harmless shoreline browser, a muncher of crabs and shellfish. In the shark world, a shovel-nose was to a great white or tiger shark what a tabby kitten was to a lion.

'I love to pick sharks up,' he said. 'It spins the chicks out.'

Whistling through his teeth, he undid his ponytail then, rather too languidly, and shook out his hair so it fanned across his back. Then he sank slowly below the surface. For what seemed a dangerously long time – and a difficult feat, what with defying buoyancy and the tide as well as holding his breath – he sat cross-legged on the sea floor like an underwater yogi. His merman hair billowed around his face in the currents.

Eventually he sprang up again, leaning forward so his hair fell heavily over his face and chest. With another upward leap, he tossed it back in a sweeping arc of spray and winked at her. 'I *love* this job.'

'I can see that.' Suddenly she felt old and sour and strangely out of sorts. The shark-throw was just another performance, like the torso exhibition: his sexy tour-guide routine. She supposed the hair billowing and tossing display was intended as a macho grand finale. Instead it reminded her of *The Little Mermaid*, and Brooke Shields in *Blue Lagoon*.

He was still grinning, slyer now, and continuing to spring from foot to foot in the shallows. 'If a tour party's European — French, German, what-have-you — and cool about it, I usually shed the shorts about now,' he offered hopefully. He was as keen as a kelpie. 'Skinny-dip, have a bit of a frolic.'

'I bet you do.'

'What do you reckon? Are you up for it?'

'Not this trip, captain.' What had happened to the tender mud lover and his thirty-seven varieties of mangrove?

He turned briskly away, dived underwater, surfaced and refastened his ponytail. On the way back to the jeep he looked hurt and sulky. She noticed five or six other shovel-noses cruising the shoreline, nosing the sand for crabs. They looked more like rays than sharks. Brett ignored them.

'Thanks for the orientation tour,' she said.

'No problem.'

They drove back to the park in silence. For several weeks she was in turmoil again and resented it. This was ridiculous. She'd been too harsh on a mere flirt, a boy trying to impress a girl. So what if displaying his body was his habit during any activity involving both sunshine and female tourists? Ninety per cent of the time, in other words. The vain bastard.

Then she was disappointed and angry with herself all over again. She'd thought this was the turning point: conclusive proof she was well again, that she could imagine touching and being touched by a man.

Then again maybe it did show she was her old no-nonsense, brittle self. This confusion made her obsessively return to the initial moment of her disenchantment. It wasn't as if she was a fan of corny old silent comedies. The wet Saturday afternoons of her childhood came to mind. The days before grown-up films. Sitting with her disappointed father, in movie-educational mode, in front of flickering black and white comedy classics, with only Buster Keaton – certainly not the hammy, simpering and over-praised Charlie Chaplin – measuring up three generations later.

Wasn't it understandable for an outdoor boy – a physical boy, a crocodile ranger, a mudcrabber – never to have heard of them? Yes, he was a show-pony. *And yet* . . . A try-hard seducer of tourists. *But still* . . .

He was gormless. There was no getting away from it. How could she ever wake up alongside someone, no matter how pretty, who'd never heard of the Keystone Kops?

He'd been merely a confusing flicker on her radar. The Icelander had killed her libido. She'd gone off sex for good. Anyway, she could live without men. She would become one of those calm, enigmatic women you saw meditating on empty beaches at sunset.

To visualise this bitter-sweet scene was easy and even vaguely comforting. She could taste the salt on her lips just thinking about it.

Now as her mudcrabbers splashed upstream past the panicky hermit crabs, the firm sand of the creek bed merged into silty gravel, which quickly turned into swampy slush.

'Take it slower here,' she advised.

The faces of the English party were already registering surprise at the ooze sucking at their ankles – and at the changed surroundings. Mud-mounds loomed like hippos along the banks and in midstream, quivering in the seepage of the tide. Occasionally they shifted position and belched out streams of gas bubbles.

Faces became more serious. Who knew what was lurking under their tentative toes in the trembling mud and murky pools? The men looked increasingly dubious, but the women exchanged glances and suddenly threw out their arms to embrace the creek, the mud and the silent mangrove jungle pressing around them. They were proud of themselves. They embraced their own adventurous spirit and the unique nature of their situation.

'Look at us!' laughed the muddy, drenched women, and suddenly helpless with amusement, they clung to each other so they wouldn't topple. 'Will you look at us!'

It was while attempting to capture on film this distinct moment of swampy jubilation that Hugh Mainsbridge stumbled sideways, swore, and sat down heavily in midstream, the hand holding the camcorder forced by the weight of his left buttock into the water and then the ooze of the creek bed.

'Oh, no!' Grace said. 'Poor you.'

Her commiserations were brief. She'd warned them of the risk to expensive equipment on the Mangrove Crab Adventure, even mentioning the fuss of the Germans' dropped Leica. Everyone had had to sign an exemption form before they set out. As the tickets and brochures for all Eco-Adventure Tours stressed, 'This is the Wilderness. The company takes all care but no responsibility for life, limb and equipment.'

'Let's keep moving right along,' she said, mentioning how the crab species changed with the terrain. Sure enough, at some invisible line in the silt the territory of the hermit crabs suddenly became the habitat of larger and better-organised fiddler crabs, which swept across the mud banks like waves of windblown red blossoms. Their scuttling legs and clicking claws were a bayonet-rattle in the still air, then a chesty, asthmatic wheeze. As one platoon of crabs after another plopped out of sight, the wheeze faded to a sigh and then silence.

For the next hour, as they trudged upstream, the party struggled to keep up with the guide. She was leaping in and out of the creek to inspect those holes in the banks, protected by portcullises of mangrove roots, where the big mudcrabs hid. However, no muddies seemed to be at home. While Hugh Mainsbridge kept grumbling about needing to find a Sony dealer in a hurry, the women tried resolutely to keep up their earlier enthusiasm. But as they trudged further from the fresh air of the coast, and the softer mud tugged at their legs, their mood turned to resignation and their smiles became strained. The rancid air seemed to press them deeper into the bog.

'I'd better find you a crab or I'll have a mutiny on my hands,' Grace said.

She beckoned everyone closer. As they stumbled nearer, each step a battle of balance versus suction, she extricated herself from the ooze and clambered up a mud bank. Selecting a hole barely revealed by the tide, she parted the roots meshing its entrance, squatted on her haunches and peered inside.

Surely she must slide down the bank into the creek. But she hooked her left arm around a mangrove root and dug her toes into the slope. The party watched her take her crab hook, the most basic of hunting implements – a length of thick fencing wire bent into an elongated L – and poke it into the hole. Her arm, then her shoulder and head, darted in and out of the mud cave as she prodded and twisted the hook.

'Come on,' she urged the hidden crab. 'I'm an evil intruder. Grab me.'

Eventually she withdrew slightly from the hole, paused, then a little further. They could see the tension in her shoulder, the individual mud droplets glistening in the hairs of her forearm. Then she withdrew it entirely. A crab the size of a dinner plate gripped the hook with one claw. The other huge claw snapped at the air.

Although the creek-bottom slush was now up to their knees

and the water here reached their chests, the party watched her even more keenly. Unsure whether to wade or swim, and not sure they could accomplish either, they were near to floundering.

The same thought process showed on every face: the crab's grip on the hook looked tentative, as if it were deciding its next move. At the same time it seemed angry and threatened. If it chose to let go, it would drop into the creek in their midst. At midriff level. *Right in front of me!* the anxious faces said.

In its anxiety to escape, the crab would probably be aggressive – and invisible in the turbid water. How could their vulnerable bodies – their protuberances! – avoid those enormous snapping claws?

Grace slowly drew the crab towards her, turned it over and examined its underside. 'It's a girl. I have to let it go.' It was sound ecological practice to release the females and youngsters. 'We only take the big boys, the mature males. Females are too important in the scheme of things. Right, ladies?'

Someone always cracked a joke at this point. The women were too busy trying to keep their footing. Ian Horsley obliged. 'Same old story.' His grin looked forced. 'Mind you, I've known a few crabs in my time.'

Grace steered the crab back to the cave entrance, deftly twisted the hook, and the creature was instantly disengaged. Waving an uncertain claw, it sidled back inside.

'Who's next?' she asked. 'Find a hole and just poke your

hook in until you hear a sound like metal on metal. That's a claw. That means you've got lunch. Or lunch has got you.'

No one looked enthusiastic. The sandflies had discovered their eyes, that small proportion of their bodies not covered by insect repellent, mud or water, and the part the sandflies preferred in any case. Unsuccessfully attempting Garth Stroller's broad accent, Ian Horsley loudly repeated a vivid piece of Stroller bush lore from the day before. '"The reason your eyes itch and go red is because the sandflies like to suck their liquid and then piss in them."'

No one laughed or gasped this time. Self-consciously, Horsley stomped forward and began jabbing perfunctorily at a small mud hole just above the waterline. His scrabbling was the only sound in the silent mangrove thicket. All bird noise and insect hum had abruptly ceased.

In the stark silence the tangle of trunks and roots seemed to be growing before their eyes. The mesh of mangroves thrust up shoot-spikes like stalagmites from the bog. The creek mouth, ocean and white sandy beach seemed months and miles away. They were aware of rank vapours and the disappearing sky. The jungle ceiling pressed down. It was now that the muttering and anxious sidelong glances began.

Horsley voiced everyone's question. He pretended to be interestedly prodding the mud bank with his crab hook. His attempt to sound as laconic as a TV wildlife expert didn't come off. 'Incidentally, what's the croc situation around here?'

Grace had been anticipating this. 'Crocodiles end at seventeen degrees latitude,' she said firmly. 'They don't come this far south.' This was an unshakeable local belief and certainly Garth Stroller's firm conviction. Crocodiles ended at seventeen degrees, full stop.

However, as usual her tourists had crocs on the brain. After spending a day at Crocodile Gardens, where the Strollers scared the cash out of them with the omnipresence of crocodiles, she could hardly blame them. It was asking a lot for them to forget crocodiles.

'I guess the crocs carry maps then,' Horsley said. 'Compasses, perhaps.' The women giggled nervously. *This far south?*

'Yes, they do actually,' she said. 'In their brains – little computerised maps of territories and boundaries.'

'What's our latitude now?'

'Oh, at least eighteen,' she said. 'Probably more.'

Not for the first time, she thought, One pathetic little degree. The same climate, food supply and habitat. The same creeks, crabs, turtles, wallabies, mangroves and mud. What indeed was to prevent saltwater crocodiles – the man-eaters they'd seen yesterday exploding out of the water for bedraggled chicken carcasses – from setting up habitation here?

'All I know is they've never been seen this far south. Not here, not once.' So she'd been told, by someone who'd been told. Brett. On that first mudcrab trek.

'Aren't mudcrabs the staple food of saltwater crocs?' Horsley continued helpfully. 'I saw it on the Discovery Channel. When they can't get a buffalo or a turtle or a kangaroo, that is.'

'Or a person,' added his wife, and having frightened herself gave a little squeal. Then another shriek. 'I've got one!' she yelled, thrusting her crab hook as far from her as possible. 'It was just sunning itself on the bank and I gave it a little poke.' The way her arm was shaking, the crab gripping the end of the hook seemed to be the one controlling the situation.

'Hold it still,' Grace ordered.

She was moving towards the woman, her sack ready, everyone's eyes on the small drama of the capture, when a mud-caked creature, panting shrilly, burst from the mangrove thicket and slid down the bank into their midst. At the hubbub of screams and gasps his swollen, bloodshot eyes roamed wildly about, skated over the astonished men, and fastened on the grey, grandmotherly head of Anne Mainsbridge. With a deep sigh, he slithered across the ooze to her.

Grace struggled for breath. For a moment she'd thought . . . She stared at him, her heart drumming. He was smallish and bony and his face was too dirty and scabbed with infected insect bites for his age and race to be apparent. His eyes were dull as slate. Either out of exhaustion or deference, he remained on his knees by the English woman, although in that position the mud and water rose quickly to his bony haunches.

He was still ardently clasping the calves of Mrs Mainsbridge, about to unbalance her, while she wailed and frantically flapped her hands in the air just above his head. She appeared distressed for both him and herself but seemed unwilling to touch his matted hair.

Then Grace moved quickly through the slush. 'I'll take him,' she said.

Exhaustion had made the boy passive and apathetic and there was little gratitude evident in his dull eyes. He didn't speak. As he trudged behind her, allowing her to steer and haul him through the mud and water back to the creek mouth, she felt in the listless grip of his hand that he'd passed over to her all responsibility for his existence.

It wasn't that he necessarily trusted her, rather that he'd come this far by himself and now it was up to someone else.

Soon he gave up trudging altogether and let himself be half dragged in her wake, his limbs trailing, like a child in a seaside game. But a younger boy would be pretending to be a speedboat or a surfboard and would probably be grinning and threshing about, whereas his upraised chin parted the water in a grim bow wave.

Back by the ocean shore, as he slumped on the sand, she produced the tour party's lunch hamper from the jeep. He gulped down a litre of water and scoffed four sandwiches and a banana.

Then she said, 'Let's see who you are, mister,' and handed him a wet towel to clean himself.

He belched, looked blankly at the towel and made no move to take it. When she attempted to clean him he leaned so defiantly away from her dabbing hand that she gave up.

'What's your name? How old are you?'

He didn't reply. He snatched a second banana and stared out to sea while he peeled it and ate it in three mouthfuls. She couldn't tell whether he understood English.

'Never mind.'

Her brain was racing, recalling jerky images on the TV news. The trailing edge of Tropical Cyclone Sean striking the detention camp in the desert. Turmoil in grainy black and white. Panicky guards running bent against the wind. Dust swirling in angry willy-willys. Rubbish blowing flat against the perimeter fence. And outside the wire, the demonstrators choosing a distracting moment of nature's destruction to ram a weakened section of the fence with their vehicles.

In this silent film recorded by the camp's security cameras, three noiseless trucks charged and reversed over the fence. Like ants from a disturbed nest, men and boys instantly streamed over the flattened barrier. Some of them first threw mattresses and coats over the razor wire, but most clambered over regardless.

Mouths agape in mute yells of triumph, they poured out into the flat, unknowable desert.

The footage of the mass escape had been supplied to the television networks to help identify the escapees. She couldn't recall any clear faces, however, just raucous jubilation and blurry images in the spinning dust. A mob of excitable Middle Eastern males – it could have been any evening on TV. Despite the absence of sound, she seemed to remember wild shouts and the howling victory of the wind.

All the way back to Port Mangrove he remained silent, slumped beside her in the jeep's front seat, indifferent to the leached-out sea-level surroundings, staring incuriously at the termite mounds and lone grey trees and patches of khaki vegetation.

For a while the travellers in the seats behind continued to speculate about him, but Grace didn't join the conversation and eventually they took the hint of her silence and succumbed to the afternoon heat, the fatigue of the morning's Mangrove Crab Adventure and the motion of the jeep. The only sound was the soporific drumming of the tyres on the road.

The highway was so flat and straight that any vehicle on the horizon could be spotted instantly, looming out of the heat mirages like a liner on a glassy sea. In an hour they passed only two, a dusty road-train and a four-wheel drive with Victorian plates. There were no roadblocks or signs of pursuit or agitated authority, just more ant hills the shape of wigwams, an occasional crow on a furry smear of roadkill and, every five or ten kilometres, a solitary, palely loitering and improbable-looking Brahman bull propped up against the landscape like a nineteenth-century naïve painting.

She recalled the government spokesperson, followed by a local police sergeant, coming on screen to insist that the 'illegal immigrants' would soon be rounded up. With the appearance of the authorities, the TV picture had returned to colour and clarity. The spokesperson, a cross, overweight woman with severely plucked eyebrows, referred to the escaped refugees as 'fugitives' who had 'now compounded their initial illegal entry into the country'.

As the last squalls of the cyclonic wind hissed into the fluffy TV mikes, the cop posed a reasonable question to the cameras. He was self-consciously struggling to hold onto his hat in the wind. It was a new-looking, outback-issue, wide-brimmed, khaki police hat, hard to control in the gale. Eventually he gave up the struggle and reluctantly removed it, only to strike new on-camera strife with his flyaway hair, parted low and grown disproportionately long on one side. His scalp secrets revealed to the nation, his cowboy image shot, he shouted plaintively into the pitiless wind, his voice breaking in an effort to make himself heard.

'How long can the fugitives survive in this weather and wilderness?'

Farewelling the English couples at their motel, Grace apologised again for curtailing the Mangrove Crab Adventure. 'But we seem to have a human drama here.'

The teachers had already worked it out. Hugh Mainsbridge muttered knowingly, 'A breakout, eh?' He patted his drowned camcorder, rueing missed photo opportunities. 'Flown the coop.'

'I think we all grasp the situation,' Grace said.

They nodded their understanding; they were schoolteachers, after all, by definition educated, civilised and well inclined towards the young. They'd been in the Kimberley long enough to see the television images, to hear and read the charged words: 'boat people' and 'asylum-seekers' and 'illegal migrants' and 'detention camps'.

The men still looked edgy, however, self-consciously circling the jeep and peering into the distance, as if anticipating a sheriff's posse. Smiling sympathetically, the women shuffled around the boy's side of the jeep, aching to reach in and pat the muddy head lolling against the window. The way Anne Mainsbridge was sighing and tutting, she obviously regretted missing the earlier opportunity to touch him.

Grace could see they were reluctant to extract themselves from this news story and resume their travelling. She climbed back into the jeep. 'We'd better go. Police station next stop.'

'Good luck!' the teachers chorused wistfully as the jeep moved off. As if it were a departing pony, the vehicle was sent on its way with many farewell pats.

She'd made up her mind on the drive back from the creek. She had no specific plan, no idea what she would do, but she couldn't hand him over to the authorities. How could she, of all people, do that? He was being hunted. People were chasing him.

She motioned the boy to slump down further in his seat, then she drove around the back roads of town, killing time until Crocodile Gardens closed for the day. Although his eyes were shut, his frown indicated an aloof disengagement from events. Eventually she pulled up at the rear gate, used mainly for the dawn refuse collection – the exit for the park's more unsightly, smelly and non-recyclable garbage.

'You can sit up now.'

He didn't bother moving, merely lifted his gaze a fraction. The steel gate and cyclone-resistant security fencing were his first shock. Then he saw the warning sign, TRESPASSERS WILL BE EATEN, and sat up in a hurry. An understanding of English was hardly necessary. The crocodile on the sign was crunching a human torso in its jaws.

As she got out to unlock the gate, he began gasping and wildly shaking his head. At the same time he cringed under the dashboard. At first she mistook the sound – the low husky panting of a trapped animal – for one of the park's creatures under duress. Back in the jeep, she saw it was the boy.

'It's okay. We're home,' she said, and drove inside. He kept up his panting. 'Relax, mister.' She patted his shoulder. 'Are you going to speak eventually?'

It was after she'd locked the gate behind them and he spotted the first actual crocodile that he spoke at last. Rather, screamed. Suddenly the listless body in the jeep was all squirming bones and angles. Tears shot from his eyes. Past experiences showed in his savage fists and feet and whirling knuckles. His bared teeth made him look as if he were fighting for his life.

A blow to her nose made her eyes water. His hands were calloused and hard and his nails were long and dirty. A scratch stung her cheek.

'Stop it!' This was more than fear she was seeing; he seemed to be reacting to her apparent treachery. Betrayed yet again. 'No, no,' she cried. 'Stop fighting! Jesus! You don't understand. You're safe here.'

How could she reason with this furious little shit? He was too strong for her. Again she tried to coax him out but she hadn't the strength to withstand his fury, much less drag him from the jeep and upstairs into the rangers' cottage. Eventually she stood back to curse and catch her breath and he quickly slammed the jeep door, closed the windows and locked himself in.

Her cheek was bleeding and her eyes streamed from the blow on the nose. She was really rattled and panting herself now. 'Keep this up and you're going straight to the cops!'

She still had the keys. He's going nowhere at the moment, she thought. Hurrying up the cottage stairs, she snatched up some tourist brochures and ran back. He was still in the jeep, of course, cringing away from the window. His head had left muddy smears on the glass.

'Look!' she insisted, flapping the brochures at the jeep. She flicked hastily through photographs of children picnicking on the park's lawns, frolicking in the pool and speeding down the water-slide. She pressed more pictures to the window: delighted blond toddlers with parrots perched on their shoulders, boys posing with carpet pythons looped around their necks, mothers and babies feeding kangaroos.

She rapped on the glass and indicated a photo of children positioned safely behind the cyclone wire; they were watching a ranger hand-feed a crocodile. Though of imprecise origin, the food the ranger dangled over the gaping jaws looked feathery and bedraggled, and not at all like a portion of human being.

'Chicken,' she said. 'We feed them mostly chickens.' And minced kangaroo meat, she thought but didn't say.

His expression didn't change. He just stared dully at her as she displayed more pictures of happy children and waved a frantic arm about her. 'Same place! A fun place! Wildlife park! Gardens! Animals! Reptiles! A sort of zoo!' Her own fake vivacity was driving her crazy. 'Come on, sonny. Give me a break. All this fun is happening right here!'

Maybe he understood English, because he responded then by slowly swinging his head to take in their actual surroundings: the asphalt truck-parking area around them, the compost heaps and garbage bins and the lichened concrete rear walls and slimy ponds of the crocodile pens. They didn't look the least entertaining. He raised one eyebrow and seemed to sneer, then slumped down on the seat once more.

Suddenly exhausted, on the verge of exasperated tears, she unlocked the jeep and tossed the brochures on the seat beside him.

All she could do was wait him out. From the cottage fridge she brought out all the food it contained, her meagre bachelor-girl rations: bread, butter, half a takeaway chicken, a jar of marmalade, a tub of Neapolitan icecream, two tomatoes, a bottle of orange juice, a Diet Coke, a Mars Bar and a tray of ice cubes. Into his view she dragged a picnic table and set out the food and drink. She poured two glasses of Coke and dropped ice into the glasses. She raised a tinkling glass in a toast and took a thirst-quenching swig. Then, just as theatrically, she began to eat.

She wasn't the least hungry, sitting there in the ugly back reaches of the park amidst the humid reek of reptiles both dead and alive. But she pretended. Despite her throbbing nose and cheek, she hammed it up. No TV-commercial model could have nibbled a drumstick so seductively, or so relished a spoonful of melting ice-cream. She hardly glanced in his direction, but after every mouthful she ostentatiously drew attention (*Oh, no!*) to the dwindling amount of food and drink. However, she left the Mars Bar untouched.

Half an hour passed. Dusk was falling and she was becoming anxious about being discovered. While it might just be possible to explain away the boy's presence in the daytime (a young backpacker, an overseas tourist who'd mislaid his parents?), it would definitely seem strange at night.

She was thankful that Garth and Brett were away leading five-day tours, and for the fact that nowadays Tenille hurried Troy home to their lovenest at closing time. She weighed up other chances of discovery: the cleaners had already cleaned up the day's litter and departed. So, too, had Verge Action, the big, silent Maori gardener nicknamed after the customer-safety sign Garth Stroller made him display while mowing the lawn edges: WARNING: VERGE ACTION AHEAD. (Garth was ever watchful for insurance claims.) The croc-farm, gift-shop and office staff should also have left for the night.

It was the nightwatchmen who worried her. Their shifts started soon. Darren Ahmat and Lou D'Angrusa, better known to the young staff as Armed and Dangerous, carried .308 semi-automatics to defend themselves against trespassers or any escaped or illegally released crocs. Armed and Dangerous held typical security-man views on territory.

As Garth often remarked, shaking his head in wonderment, 'You'd be surprised how many morons are desperate to break into a crocodile park.' The culprits divided into three categories – drunks, gun lovers and religious nuts. Their intentions, however, could not be more different. Whereas drunken stag-night and football-club revellers merely relished the escapade of releasing man-eating reptiles into the streets, and the gun heroes badly wanted to kill crocodiles, the religious cranks wished just as fervently to be killed *by* them.

Break-ins had not been a problem until crocodiles became a protected species in the 1970s. Suddenly there was no more croc-shooting for fun and profit. It was greatly resented in some gung-ho quarters that Garth Stroller was permitted not only to capture and display crocodiles but also to commercially farm them.

The park's attraction to potential suicides and religious martyrs, on the other hand, had only seriously begun with the fatal impulse of one Conrad Bax, a member of an esoteric religious cult, the Oracles, in 1986. The seven copycat attempts since, four of them successful, were sometimes blamed on the *Northern Register*'s detailed reporting of the Bax suicide.

From Conrad Bax's scaling of the perimeter fence and his deliberate choice of Leslie, their biggest specimen at that time, to the jarringly jaunty farewell note ('See you later, Alligator!') and the Bible with bookmarked references to leviathans (Job 3:8, 41:1; Psalms 74:14, 104:26; Isaiah 27:1) 'miraculously left unscathed' in Leslie's pen, to a description of the remains found next morning (the head, right leg and Adidas sneaker), the report left nothing to the imagination.

The police attention, paperwork and inquest appearances were a nuisance for the Strollers. However, as Garth noted drily, once any insurance worries had been cleared up, there was no doubt that after each suicide the park attendances increased dramatically.

It was 7.30 p.m. and she was running out of bait. As careful as she'd been, the chicken was almost gone and what was left of the icecream was murky liquid. Now she was definitely worried about the time. Around the park the automatic lights had come on. Either Armed or Dangerous would start his night rounds in half an hour.

All she could see of the boy was his matted mop of hair the colour of mud and the dark eyes staring blankly through the wind-screen. In desperation she went through her food-relishing act one more time. She began to slowly unwrap the Mars Bar.

It might have been the temptation of the chocolate, perhaps the terrors of the encroaching dark in such a place. One moment he was in the jeep affecting total lack of interest, the next he was beside her, wiping his nose on his wrist and hovering over the remaining food. He looked around him nervously, then snatched up the Mars Bar in one hand and the chicken carcass in the other.

'Yes, eat, for Christ's sake.' All the emotional energy she'd regained over the past eighteen months seemed to have drained away. She was whacked. Unlike Mrs Mainsbridge, she wasn't tempted to touch his filthy hair. Her scratched cheek still stung. She hoped it wasn't infected from his filthy nails. They sat in silence while he chewed the Mars Bar. The mosquitoes were out; the park's nocturnal creatures, the marsupials, were beginning to stir and rustle. 'What am I doing?' she said aloud.

His wary, dull expression didn't change. He finished picking at the chicken bones and sat staring at the darkening crocodile pens, licking the grease and chocolate from his fingers. Perhaps he noticed her expression of distaste, because he suddenly picked up the tray of melted ice cubes and made a great show of pouring the water over his filthy hands, revealing shiny round scars, still pink and angry, on his palms.

Cigarette burns. They did it to themselves, she'd heard.

Mosquitoes buzzed around their ears and necks. Time had run out. She stood up, sighing, and pointed towards the rangers' cottage. 'Take it or leave it, buster. The cottage or the crocodiles.'

The bats were awake and beginning to squabble in the mango tree. The rotten-fruit smell of their droppings wafted on the air. A bush rat ran past them and scooted up a palm. From Clifford's pool a couple of questioning grunts sounded and reverberated against the walls of his moat. The boy stood up quickly.

The cottage door stood beside a tangle of bougainvillea. It was like walking into a tunnel. There was a light at the top. She'd turned on the lights upstairs, and the TV, to try to ease his fears. Flippant, sit-com voices came down the staircase. As they climbed up she told him her name.

BATHROOMS

Each morning when the rain began like tentative footsteps on the tin roof the boy woke with a start. There was always faint thunder in the distance. Each morning, too, a bird cried mournfully somewhere nearby and was answered by another further away. The boy lay there breathing hard as the raindrops stuttered and stopped, remembering his current situation. He recalled the wild animals below and all around.

He avoided looking down at them. Much of his waking time the past three days had been spent at the bathroom mirror, combing his hair and savouring the novelty of his reflection. The stained and broken mirrors at the camp had distorted it, and his mind itself had come to match the disarranged image in the cracked glass. This face was new but vaguely familiar, like that of an older relative met after a long absence.

Although he relished the disappearance of childhood's soft-ness from his features, the person he saw still lacked alignment and coherence. He was no longer K167, but neither was he his old name and self. He was barely tied to that other life. The person of three years before was part of another story, one submerged under fathoms of loss and stifled memory.

He dismissed the scabbed insect bites and took in the deeper frown lines and the newly visible down of a moustache. The moustache hair was fine but just long enough at the ends to roll between his fingertips. He turned his head to observe the moustache from several angles. Then he touched the scabs on his lips. All in all, the boy in the mirror looked older and tougher than he was used to. In a small way this was not an unsatisfac-tory feeling.

He could tell the woman wondered at his incessant hair grooming. He didn't care. It was she who wanted him clean and neat after all, he thought sulkily, his eyes sliding along the row of bottles, jars, tubes and boxes of female mysteries lining the win-dowsill. It was she who'd bustled him into the bathroom with the soap and shampoo, then – when he finally emerged – pointed out the mud still behind his ears and in his nails and sent him back. It was she who'd thrust the brush, comb and hair gel on him, as well as the nail scissors and the clean clothes the same as hers.

Women's clothes. Even though the khaki shirt and shorts could have been male clothing, the fact that they belonged to a female was upsetting. Worse, they were too big for him. Glowering defiantly at the mirror, he combed and recombed his hair.

'Eat and rest,' she'd said when he was finally satisfactorily clean. 'You're safe here.' Her mood was more agreeable now. 'Do you understand? Don't try to run away or they'll catch you.'

When she left the cottage she locked the door behind her. If he'd chosen to speak he could have said there was no need. Crocodiles outside. Girl clothes on him. How could he leave?

At night, watching the news with her, he barely recognised the camp. It was after the cyclone. Workers were mopping up. The fence had been put back. Close-ups showed the wilted flowers that protestors had threaded into the fence wire. The TV no longer ran the same wild blur of escaping faces. The authority figures were still solemn but looked more confident. There were scenes of brisk behaviour with vehicles and radios, and calm images of police roadblocks on long straight roads that ran into the sky. Then dusty, hollow-eyed men limped forward, gave themselves up and snatched thirstily at water bottles. They barely remembered to flash peace signs for the cameras as they were bundled into the police wagons.

He strained forward in order to see people he knew. Each recaptured prisoner made his heart thud. In their bedraggled twos and threes, they were rounded up on screen every night like stray goats. Finally there were no more. Last night, sitting before the TV, eating his KFC nuggets and drinking his Coke, it had struck him that he was probably the only one still at large.

Now his hair-grooming concentration was broken by a gecko's sudden chirp. In mid-comb he nervously glanced around. Three years of the camp's ablution block had sharpened his senses to a bathroom's denizens and undercurrents. The toilet frogs and the lizards scuttling in its seeping shadows were the least of it. But they stood for all the loitering men with busy eyes and undone flies, the blatant and aggressive stools and pools, the dramatic smears of FREEDOM painted in wrist blood across the walls and broken mirrors.

An orange gecko clinging to the interstice of wall and ceiling brought them flooding back. Madly beaming Mr Aziz fountaining blood as he endeavoured to cut off his own head with his safety razor. The three Nasser children cramming into a toilet cubicle to drink disinfectant. Above all, in the week before the breakout, Ibrahim and his acid scream.

Another anxious glance around the bathroom reassured him that Ibrahim's ghost wasn't rocking on his heels in this particular shower stall. There was no ghostly pacing Ibrahim here, his sandals slap-slapping in the wet while he gathered courage to swallow drain cleaner. The presence of ghost-Ibrahim had forced him thereafter to urinate outside in the yard, incurring anger and punishments from the guards. Of course his bowels had knotted up as well, but it was impossible for him to enter the ablution block again. So after a week his concreted intestines forced him to join the breakout. His stomach felt like stone. From the waist down he was a statue. There was no choice. Flee or shatter.

But ghost-Ibrahim would not come here. In the woman's bathroom there was no assaulting stink, no scoured and frothing Ibrahim screaming and coughing simultaneously. He'd never forget the way Ibrahim had so quickly bloomed purple, changing colour as fast as a chameleon. Lips, gums, tongue, throat bubbling into the one purple balloon of tissue and blood that choked him.

No Ibrahim, no Mr Aziz, no Nasser kids vomiting up their Pine-O-Cleen. Just the gecko and the toilet frogs. Everything else was as it should be in the crocodile woman's bathroom.

Something else. The smooth-haired male in the mirror reminded him he was no longer locked up in the detention camp. Instead he was locked behind another razor-wire fence, still caged, this time in a strange daydream where crocodiles and chattering children roamed below. A fantasy where an indecently bare-legged young woman hid him from the authorities and provided two-litre bottles of Coca-Cola and fried chicken or fish and chips every evening. And still kept him prisoner.

But he could view this new, older version of himself in another light. He could pause in his grooming before an unbroken mirror and admire his satisfying hairstyle. And again this calmed him.

It seemed to annoy her, but he wasn't concerned at the time and care he took with his hair. What caused him discomfort was her uncovered legs, so smooth and long and tanned in their male-looking shorts. Yes, the legs and also the picture on his bedroom door of the bird mating with the kangaroo. Even in this strange country with its peculiar animals that couldn't be possible. He would have to remove the picture to save further embarrassment. But there was nothing he could do about her shameless legs except look away.

At last the hair was falling on his forehead just like the hair in the film. If he were back home now, he imagined, people would definitely be commenting on the striking resemblance to Leonardo DiCaprio. After all his trial and error, assisted by the woman's hair gel he had finally got his hair the way he wanted it. He had managed *Titanic* hair.

Despite the risks involved, all the boys had coveted *Titanic* hair. It was remarkable how the craze had swept the study groups, the province, the whole country. When he visualised his old friends now, stood them back in that shambling row in front of the village barber shop, all their heads defiantly featured that long-in-the-front, floppy look. They would shortly be punished for their *Titanic* hairstyles. Just as people were gaoled for possessing videos of the film itself, they would be marched inside at Kalyshnikov gunpoint to have their heads forcibly shaved by the barber. But there were numerous copies of *Titanic* in the village. Everyone had seen it many times – it was the most popular film in memory. And hair grew back.

Just thinking about *Titanic* lifted him for a moment. Then

a great wave of sadness welled up and swept over him as he thought of the ending, and other shipwreck endings.

If he wasn't strong he could sink right now. His knees felt weak and his head spun. Standing at the bathroom mirror, gripping the sink with both hands to steady himself, he endeavoured to hawk up a gob of saliva, but since his escape he seemed to have sweated all the moisture out of his body. Concentrating hard, he eventually managed it. He rolled the phlegm around in his mouth and took a deep breath. He was rebellious but heroic Leonardo DiCaprio standing there at the ship's rail with his fashionable hair, impressing beautiful rich girls by spitting into the Atlantic Ocean.

He moved to the window, slid open the mosquito screen, aimed carefully through the louvres and let fly into the careless country of crocodiles and blond children down below.

She was awake now, too, and knocking on the bathroom door. 'Are you in there? Are you okay?'

She still didn't know his name or his age, where he was from, whether he had family. Sometimes he appeared older than his height and physique, like a jockey, as if detention had stunted him. Other times – that interminable business with the hair – he looked and acted quite juvenile, barely adolescent. She questioned him several times a day, even wrote down the questions, but he ignored them. He wouldn't speak to her in any language.

After three days she'd come to believe he understood her. But he wouldn't give in, wouldn't cross the line he'd drawn. The only time he'd shown any animation was during a commercial for the following week's Sunday-night movie – *Titanic*. Leonardo DiCaprio stood heroically on the bow once more, his floppy hair blowing in the gusts off the Atlantic ice floes, and suddenly she understood the boy's hair fetish. He was just an ordinary teenager, susceptible to fads like any kid. When the film was not immediately forth-coming he was crestfallen, then angry, and disappeared into the bathroom.

He was always moody. Most of the time he either ignored her or, at best, orchestrated some ambiguous physical action to communicate a response. This time he ran the tap, then flushed the toilet. *Yes, I'm okay.*

'Will you please come out? I need to use the bathroom.'

Eventually he emerged in a wave of clashing sweet aromas, his hair stiff with gel. A forced sort of forelock dangled in his eyes.

'Very smart, Leonardo,' she said. She held up a new backpack in camouflage tropical-green. 'This is for you.'

He looked at it distrustfully. *What's the catch?* On the front the backpack said, *Eco-Adventure Tours*. She zipped it open to show him the T-shirts, pants, underwear, baseball-style cap and rubber sandals she'd bought at the gift shop. 'I hope I guessed the right sizes.'

He noticed the T-shirts had the same crocodile motifs she wore on her shirts. But it was the underpants – boxer shorts of a thin, shiny material – that commanded his attention. He'd never seen anything like them before: snorting buffaloes and rams and angry red bull-ants. Boy-type cartoons, but . . . He ran suspicious fingers over the shimmery fabric and frowned at its silky feel. *More girl clothes!*

'They're supposed to be good in the heat,' she explained. 'Very fashionable. All the boys here wear them.' She'd also packed a Crocodile Gardens towel and water bottle, sunglasses, sunblock, insect repellent, a Swiss army knife, and a comb and brush set in a crocodile-leather pouch. Even with the staff discount, she'd spent more than a week's wages on him. He gave the items only a fleeting glance as she itemised everything aloud and then zipped up the backpack.

'You're all set,' she said. 'You're moving on.'

It was almost six-thirty, the park would soon be busy. Already there were workday sounds coming from the farm: machinery hummed, shed doors clanged open. Somewhere on the lawns, Verge Action's mower roared into life. She had to start work herself at eight. She'd backed the jeep up to the cottage door the night before. He just stood there holding the backpack like it was an unpleasant burden.

'We have to go. More adventures for our young hero.'

This was just like a hundred familiar films, she told herself. Everyone from Joseph Cotten to Harrison Ford had done this sort of thing. Breaking the law in a good way. Defying the enemy in a French Resistance sort of way. It was perfectly in keeping for a Woman of Mystery.

But who was the enemy again? It was hard to accept the television's suggestion that it was a bewildered country cop with a new hat and flyaway hair. The TV hadn't spelled out who the refugee hunters were. There was no footage of them. She'd read something about inspectors from the Immigration Department's compliance section. They were 'working hand in hand' with federal and state police. It was all a bit shadowy and mysterious. Suddenly she felt shaky and nauseous.

She managed to get him into the jeep without him being seen. From the nervous way he kept dabbing at his hair she saw he was anxious enough already. How to explain that they were keenly hunting for him? But of course he knew that.

'You have to keep moving. Not stay too long in one place. I'm not deserting you. I'm trying to keep you safe.'

She repeated this in the jeep on the way to Clara Aherne's. She couldn't tell how much of it sank in. As usual his expression was both dulled and wary. He seemed diverted by his reflection in the rear-vision mirror and by the way his hair fell on his forehead. His fingers twiddled and patted. To get the full-head reflection he had to lean halfway out the window.

'The hair is fine,' she said. 'The hair is bloody gorgeous. Do me a favour and leave it alone for five minutes.'

He took no notice at first. A few minutes later he turned away from the mirror with a pained sigh and slumped down in his seat.

'Okay,' she said. 'Sorry.' She was feeling anxious too – more than she'd expected to be.

Out of desperation she'd turned to Clara. Casting her mind back to her own first numb Kimberley days, she'd recalled one highly charged evening with the widows. The old ladies were arguing over the asylum seekers. Discussing the *situation*, the *problem*, they were even more stroppy than usual. Beliefs and anxieties had clashed. The dusk backdrop was the same as always – the frenetic bird chatter in the palms, the western sky roseate from Indonesian forest fires – but their banter had an edge she hadn't heard before.

Clara was reminiscing teary-eyed beside the bougainvillea, linking the subjective to the wider picture. She bemoaned the state of the nation and the deterioration of hospitality. 'We used to be good-natured people, generous people.'

She was bewildered at how her husband's final coronary had changed the world order. 'Paddy used to bring foreigners home from the pub for dinner – complete strangers, black, white and brindle. He didn't care if they were Muslims or Seventh Day Adventists, he'd give them a bed and cook them breakfast himself next morning. Grill them a barramundi, and a compulsory Bloody Mary to go with it. A breakfast cocktail on the verandah, if you please. The full treatment. He wouldn't let me lift a finger.'

Old Marion said, 'Not many left like him, darl. One in a million, Paddy and his Bloody Marys and that apron he always wore.'

'Apron? Only when he was entertaining, mixing drinks. Just to keep his tropical whites natty. Prided himself on smartness as well as hospitality, my old boy.'

'He certainly cut a dash in it,' Louise murmured.

'Six splashes of Worcestershire, he'd count them out. Five drops of Tabasco. Lemon juice. Salt around the rim of the glass. The celery stalk cut into a frill. Fatherly advice if they needed it. Long talks into the night. A few dollars if necessary. Wouldn't take no for an answer. No one ever wanted to leave.'

'Mind you, he had a bit to make up for.' Marion again.

Clara, instantly icy: 'Really? Do tell.' Her veiny, freckled hand gripped her drink with real tension.

'No, no, not him in himself. Paddy was a saint. It's no secret we all tossed our hats in the ring there. And he chose you, pet, the beauty of the bunch. And very wisely, too. Turned out for the best. No, heavens, I meant the way his father used to treat our indigenous brethren. I don't need to tell *you*, darl. Not many of Frankie Aherne's pearl divers saw the old corroboree grounds again.'

Louise adding drily: 'Not too many saw terra firma again.'

No response from Clara beyond the faint shaking of her head. The fine grey hair hovering over her scalp. Dead straight hair, wispy as a baby's, ebbing from her forehead. In old age her

Asian genes more prominent. The eyes, the scalp, the smooth cheeks. Hardly a line on her.

Louise backtracking now. 'My God, the Kimberley wouldn't have got off the ground if we'd worried about a touch of the tar-brush.' She patted her crêpey freckled bosom. 'Even our mob's supposed to have a bit of Portuguese in there somewhere. On my mother's side.'

'I thought your old man had a touch of something darkish, too?' said Marion.

Louise ignored this. 'Where would pearling be, cattle, without our distinctive multiracial culture that they're all suddenly crazy about down south? It's not as if we all jumped out of Debrett's in our tiaras.'

Marion chiming in again: 'Speak for yourself, pet. My father was a Montagu.'

'Pardon me, duchess.'

'It's such a long way from the Middle East it beats me why those sheiks and what-have-you want to fetch up in our desert.'

'Grow up, dear. It's our democratic way of life they envy, not our bloody camels.'

'I thought they detested our way of life. I thought that was the whole problem.'

'Well, they've got me worried. I feel faint every time that Coastwatch plane flies over.'

'I find it a great comfort myself.'

'No, it brings back the morning the Japs strafed the flying boats in the bay. All those women and kids. I can't get it out of my mind lately. Those poor beggars strapped into their seats waiting to fly south to safety. The wounded ones trying to swim for it. Mothers holding their kids above water.'

'Don't forget the sharks.'

'I hadn't.'

'Or our aircrews with their grandstand view of proceedings from the pub. Our boys having one for the road in the Continental while their planes were shot up in the bay. My word, those pilots used to put it away.'

'Whenever I broached flying south my Gordon said, "Nothing to worry about, dear. Zeroes can't fly the five hundred miles from West Timor with those piddling fuel tanks." So the Japs put on bigger fuel tanks, didn't they.'

'I suppose the men'll be in the pub again when we're caught napping this time. Those fanatics won't be in old wooden *prahus* and rust-bucket fishing boats either. It won't be people smugglers and trochus poachers.'

'It'll be missiles. The North Koreans will beat the fanatics to it without even leaving home.'

'Listen, what's the nearest city to where we're sitting now? Denpasar, Bali, am I right? Where they've bombed us already. What's the nearest bit of foreign land? Still West Timor as far as I know, where the Indo militia now run the show. And who's always saying how much they hate our boozy Christian guts? The Indos, correct me if I'm wrong.'

'I've got a lot of time for the Timorese. That pretty little Maria in the hairdressers, her family wiped out by the militia and she still sings "Que Sera Sera" around the salon all day like Connie Francis.'

'Which hairdressers?'

'The Cut Above. I'm never going back to that other place. Stuck-up little bitches.'

'I think you'll find "Que Sera Sera" was Doris Day.'

'Doris Day, Connie Francis, who cares?'

'Doris Day was definitely "Que Sera Sera" and "Buttons and Bows". Her signature tunes. I'd bet the farm on it.'

Clara shaking her head through this crotchety hubbub, then fumbling for a fresh cigarette, struggling with her lighter, scratching unsuccessfully for a flame, interrupting their squabble with sudden hopeless tears.

'Sixty years ago. You two are so . . . Those families are in the camps right now. I don't know. The poor kids with their dead eyes.'

Clara's chastened cronies falling silent, suddenly respectful of the one most recently widowed, remembering with a jolt she'd already lost a yachtsman son to a storm at sea. Giving her emotional leeway, Marion and Louise now bustling around her, lighting her cigarette, refilling her glass, patting her knotted wrist.

Clara sympathised with the refugees – that was how Grace recalled the evening. She wondered now if she'd accurately read Clara's feelings. It was eighteen months since that evening. If the old settler establishment still existed up here, Clara defined it. Original British family, conservative – and, back in the early pearling days, a glamorous Eurasian grandmother. Things could go either way. It was a risk.

In the end she'd had no choice. She was a stranger here. Who else in Port Mangrove could she turn to?

On the phone Clara had listened to her in silence.

'Leave it with me,' she said.

The time of day, her haste to start work, indeed her sudden wish to be rid of the overwhelming difficulty of him, made the handover easier. He stood uncomfortably on Clara's verandah, clutching the new backpack. His new clothes still had their creases. He looked like a schoolboy on his first day at a new school, frowning as Grace brushed a loose thread from his shirt. Some bird screeching nearby made him blink.

'Here he is,' she presented him to Clara. 'Mr X, man of mystery and adventure.'

The heat was already beating down. The day seemed cruelly bright. She still saw the sky anew every day. The colours up here were so intense that tourists were told to get their holiday snaps developed locally rather than when they returned home. The photo shops in the south toned down the photographs because the colours seemed artificially vivid.

'Don't forget to wear your cap,' she told him. She sounded like a mother, she thought. Of course he wouldn't wear it. He wouldn't want to mess up his hair. Well, he wasn't her problem any more.

'Good luck. Take care,' she said, and unthinkingly went to kiss his cheek. But he flinched from her, jerked away so vigorously that her mouth knocked the side of his head and she bit her tongue.

In her pain and embarrassment she laughed. 'That's what we're dealing with.' She put on a brittle smile and kissed Clara thanks instead. 'Not surprising, what with all they've been through.'

'Well, then,' Clara murmured uncertainly, and stared off into the bougainvillea. She'd already taken in his scabbed lips, his elaborately oiled hairstyle. Obviously she'd been expecting someone sweeter-faced and younger. A sad-eyed foreign waif. Someone less sullenly adolescent and decidedly more grateful for the risks they were taking.

Grace drove off then, leaving the old woman and the boy standing as rigidly as stick figures on the verandah. To cheerily wave goodbye seemed somehow inappropriate, but she did so anyway.

She was halfway back to Crocodile Gardens when she began to crumple. She'd never felt quite so dashed. On the main road she pulled the jeep over on the verge, turned off the ignition and,

as passing road-trains hurled red dust against her, allowed herself to sob bitterly.

All morning he impassively watched television and occasionally combed his hair while the old woman hovered uncertainly
nearby, smoking and plying him with snacks and iced drinks.

Around noon he signalled that he'd like a cigarette, too. She
hesitated. She recalled from somewhere that fugitives were known
to smoke. Prisoners, men on the run, people with terrible, messy
lives, were forever smoking. In prisons, she seemed to remember, cigarettes were used as currency. Maybe in detention camps
as well. Anyway, his body was young but his face was old. She'd
hardly be introducing him to the habit.

She handed him the Dunhills and lighter. In the rising heat
she turned on the air-conditioning and they sat silently together
on the sofa like longtime companions, smoking and watching
American soaps.

Lying back smoking, he was intrigued as always to see middle-
aged men with no beards nevertheless managing to impress and
arouse beautiful, passionate women. However, he noticed that the
beardless old men seemed to infuriate these stormy, big-breasted
women as often as they enthralled them. There were many fiery
arguments and angry departures. Doors were slammed and

telephone calls cut short. The *Titanic* commercial did not reappear, nor did anyone with the Leonardo DiCaprio hairstyle.

Eventually, in the bird-racket of sunset, two nuns from the Little Company of the Holy Charity drove up to the bungalow in the convent's Landcruiser. They opened the rear door, indicated the mattress on the floor, and told him to lie down and make himself comfortable.

Through the back window he could see leaf fringes, telephone wires and an expanse of pink sky. Across his vision wafted traces of smoke from the trochus poachers' burning *prahus*. This late in the day some bats were entering the air, while sporadic hawks still circled over the mangroves.

He thought briefly of the crocodile woman. For a moment he regretted not speaking to her. He thought of her by name for the first time, as a person rather than a pair of bare legs. *Grace.*

Surely he could have spoken to Grace to say goodbye. Once he would have been polite. Back then. Before the boat. But it was painful to think of then, of the boy he'd been then. He dismissed the past, forced it away, and his mind went blank again and the nuns drove him off.

FOUR

THE CAPRICORN MUG

When the day's mail arrived Molloy was in his office in the
Anthropology Department at the University of New South Wales
drinking his morning coffee, as he had for more than twenty
years, from the mug his daughter had given him the Christmas
she was nine.

'Capricorn the Goat', the coffee mug announced, displaying
an ornately horned animal perched on a craggy hill. Strictly speaking, the mug's illustrator had erred in drawing a North American
bighorn sheep instead of a goat, but beneath the ornately horned
wild sheep the mug offered the usual critical appraisal of his star
sign's character:

Those born under the sign of Capricorn (December 22–
January 21) prefer to be in positions of authority, but their

grand ambitions, if unrealised, can make them lonely and melancholy. Despite being good and faithful friends they do not suffer fools gladly and should avoid the tendency to criticise.

Twenty years on and the mug's disapproval, like the painted 'goat', had hardly faded.

Back then he'd asked Grace, 'Is this what I'm like?'

'Only a little bit.' To prove the mug wrong, he'd had to smile at that.

Still sharply defined in black script around the mug's sides was a list of typical Capricorn characteristics and connections. Most of them were gloomy. Did a sort of over-striving wretchedness really loom over his one-twelfth of the world's population? All those millions of cynical, ambitious Chinese farmers, he thought; those legions of pragmatic but melancholic Indian labourers.

Their planet was Saturn, of course; their element was earth, their stone garnet, their metal lead, their colours grey and black, their flowers hemlock and ivy, their herbs hemp and comfrey. So poison and pot were his lot. Not satisfied with that mixed bag, the mug offered gratuitous employment advice. 'Most suitable careers for a Capricorn: politics, engineering, science.' At least science. 'Famous Capricorns: Mao Tse-tung, Joseph Stalin, Richard Nixon, J. Edgar Hoover.'

The mug ('Regal Heritage Tableware – Made in China') had a

most selective view of ambitious, morose Capricorns. He happened to know that Joan of Arc, Albert Schweitzer and Humphrey Bogart were Capricorns – also Elvis Presley, Muhammad Ali and Marlene Dietrich. Or were they sore losers too? Well, there was always the Capricorn trump card, Jesus Christ.

Despite its implicit disapproval, he'd always felt warmly towards the mug. As he took his first sip of coffee each morning he recalled the chirpy nine-year-old who'd shopped for it, gift-wrapped it and proudly presented it to him that Christmas. The memory brought a sentimental pang and a stab of anxiety for the unhappy woman recent events had made her.

What also struck him this morning was the realisation that his relationship with his daughter was the only one that mattered to him. He had the usual amicable professional relationships but no intimate associations. His love affairs had all seemed to vanish into the ether when he wasn't paying attention. Trailing particular scenes or conversations, the occasional husband or pungent memory behind them, the affairs had all just faded away. No restaurant walkouts, or belongings tossed on the street. Definitely no screaming dramas or scissored clothes or hiding the knives before bedtime.

It was as if Carol Rothman and Jenny Spiers and Diana Wakefield and Susy Vidor had all excused themselves to go to the Ladies, and after a while – maybe a week or so – he'd looked at his watch and realised they weren't coming back. All gone to more congenial jobs, climates, cities, men. Not forgotten – he could still conjure them up with little effort; indeed, he thought he could have kept most of them with a little effort. (That was another story – the story that began and ended with Kate's departure.) But definitely gone just the same. Kaput.

And then Tina Fischer. Strange, the tumult Tina had aroused in him. He'd never even kissed her more than socially, or been alone with her, much less slept with her. But shrewd Henric, with a mentor's precise intuition, and the survival instincts of the older husband – he had twenty-five years on this second wife – had sniffed out the potentialities before they'd even dawned on his protégé.

The possibilities had apparently been clear to Henric, even though Molloy had regarded the boss's wife as strictly off limits. Weren't they the same age? Didn't she light up like a teenager when he appeared on their doorstep? He realised, much later, that he probably lit up, too. They found each other amusing. They were both film buffs. At a certain stage of any evening they gravitated together. Then, independently realising this, they deliberately kept apart, which must have struck Fischer as more brazen still. But he'd never called him on it. For indeed, what was happening between them? Nothing.

Then one evening he'd openly flirted with her. It was the end of the week and she'd driven to the staff club to pick up Henric after work, a wifely Friday-night habit to enable him to unwind without worrying about the breathalyser squad. Henric and he were on their second bottle of red. As soon as she entered the bar he'd flattered her outrageously, blithely disregarded the raised eyebrows, paid her in public the compliments he'd always kept buried deep. Oh, they welled up in him. How pleased and somehow relieved he was to suddenly sing her praises over the wine and little dishes of chips and cashew nuts. Her looks. Her unsung talents. Especially her looks. He thought he was being amusingly frank and spontaneous. He half recalled using the word 'adorable'. Maybe 'mouthwatering' as well. He was certainly thinking it. Just inoffensive words in any case.

In vino veritas? He must have been insane. His and Henric's twenty-year camaraderie – the mateyness of the desert, the laboratory, the staff club, the Salt End discovery – ended that night as Henric stood up from the table and the angry pyramid of shredded drink coasters he'd been constructing for the past hour, grimly took her arm and led her away.

Yes, the only lasting relationship had been his and Grace's. His love for his only child had always been sentimental, dutiful and boundless. From the astonishing moment when she entered the world, pointy-headed and so creamed with vernix that she resembled a tiny New Guinean mudman, he'd felt she was an old soul. Their lives seemed connected in ways that predated her birth. Naturally genetics came into it – genetics, the most emotion-laden and newsworthy branch of science. The one that caused him all the trouble.

As well as his sole genetic link to the future, she was his only connection to the past. In her physique, the shape of her nose and ears, her hair colour, her moods, her love of films (why not a gene for that?), she matched him. The same went for the angle of her walk, her distinctive running style (head thrust forward, arms pumping across the body), even in the way she chewed an apple. In her appearance and habits he hungrily sought clues to his own background. He thought of her as preceding him as well as following him.

He could hardly look at her without thinking of her genes. Her familiar characteristics were one thing (that seventy-degree running style); others were a total mystery.

Her affinity for the water, where had that come from? As a swimmer he was still a tentative London orphan boy, an easily sunburned and surf-dumped paddler. Her mother had been no sportswoman either. And here was this earnestly splashing, spitting toddler from Jellyfish swimming class turning into a solemn Crab, a buoyant Turtle, a sleek Platypus, then a Redfin, a Snapper, and finally – her body mysteriously lengthening and streamlining along the way – a lean and hungry member of the Barracuda Squad. Overnight she'd metamorphosed into a competition swimmer. Where had those genes come from?

She'd been a natural from the start. Even at five and nominally a jellyfish, she'd skittered across pool surfaces like a water beetle. Year after year, in a multitude of fuggy indoor swimming centres and breezy outdoor pools, condensation dripping on his head, his eyes smarting from the chlorine fumes, he'd watched with awe those endless laps. The little arms slicing the water, the relentless pat-a-kick legs. Inherently she understood the rhythm, the alternate breathing, the tumble turns, and when she skipped from the pool into the towel he proudly held out for her only her pinker cheeks hinted at the slightest effort.

Of course she was proud of herself and wanted his eyes on her the whole time. The universal child's cry: *Look at me!* Woe betide him if she glanced up between laps and caught him reading. She needed his ardent attention: the proud nod, the congratulatory thumbs-up. He gave them with gusto and she basked in his approval. *Look at me!* And he did. Many times he wondered, with a sort of loving envy, what that experience must feel like.

Not once during those countless dawns and afternoons as she churned up and down the pool had he imagined his daughter's future as less than limitlessly successful. With that focus and effort she could do anything she wanted. How confident and doting his love had been. How smug. Sitting in the stands, he'd feel for those hopeful endomorph parents watching their broad-hipped, chunky kids and dreaming of Olympic medals. You poor bastards, he'd think. They're not going to make it. Next time come back tall and slim.

He clung to the idea that in her genes his daughter preceded as well as followed him. He supposed it was because they had the other connection as well: the link to his discovery. Here, too, father and daughter went right back to the beginning of the age.

There were three letters in his mail. One was addressed to Grace, care of him. Of the other two, one carried a scarlet Ugandan stamp and was addressed 'Molloy John MSc, PhD, Anthropologist'. He opened the Ugandan letter first. It was from someone called Miriam Mirembe, return address a post-office box in Nsambya Road, Kampala.

> *Dear Friend,* her letter began – in longhand, but in different handwriting, he noticed, to that on the envelope. *Am glad to have this moment to greet you in God's name. Let me hope you are doing well healthwise and thanks to God for His great care!*
>
> *Allow me to introduce myself to you. Am 54 years old widow living with six children in a small house to rent. My husband died of AIDS and I regret to inform you that my youngest son and daughter and I myself are all HIV positive yet I have no income to look after this big family.*
>
> *I have now written begging you to help me with any funds to enable me to look after the family and if possible to let them attend school for the bright future and where they can have proper meals, accommodation and medical care even to easy the*

burden upon my shoulders.

Fortunately thanks to God my eldest daughter has been admitted to a 3 years nursing course but I can not raise $250 US for each year of her study and this is the only way she can support the family in future.

Let me hope to urgently hear from you and may the Almighty keep His blessing hand on your family and your efforts.

Your sister in the name of Jesus,

Miriam M.

PS: You can email me at <u>*miriamblessedfamily@hotmail.com*</u>

So speedily did his emotions range back and forth that only seconds bridged them: sympathy, followed immediately by cynicism, then doubt at his cynicism, then scorn for that doubt, then an all-encompassing sympathy for less fortunate mankind – especially the decidedly less fortunate mankind of Africa.

Especially East Africa, the – alleged – cradle of mankind. There his thoughts settled for perhaps a minute in grim contemplation before they swung back to cynicism, then sympathy, then cynicism again.

Obviously a form letter ('Dear Friend'). A rudimentary African scam. 'Miriam' had dredged his name – as printed, surname first, followed by his degrees – out of some international academic directory. Not of the magnitude of those legendary Nigerian scams, which promised for the mere loan of one's bank-account details vast cash deposits from the plunder of an ex-government minister, it depended for its success on far more raw and sensitive emotions than greed. Pity. Mercy. Fellow-feeling. It was therefore somehow more insidious.

He read the Ugandan letter again. Then he tossed it in a desk drawer.

It was in a contemplative and slightly rattled mood that he opened the envelope addressed to Grace. This letter had apparently originated as a fax to her at *Now* magazine, and the magazine had sent it to her last known address. As she'd arranged for all her mail, it had then been redirected to him at his work address.

What struck him at first was how the letter seemed relatively sane. He was no psychological profiler but the writer appeared to be trying to give the impression of normalcy. However, he hadn't pulled it off.

URGENT FAX TO:
Grace Molloy
NOW Magazine
Sydney
From: Carl Brand
Please pass on immediately to Ms Molloy!

My dear Grace

    *I'm sending this open letter to you at NOW on the off chance
you are merely on extended leave or working in an important 'behind
the scenes' capacity. <u>If not I presume your whereabouts are known to
the magazine staff and they will be kind enough to pass this fax on
with urgency and the utmost seriousness.</u>*

    *'Long time no see.' I hope you are as healthy and happy as I am.
Occasionally I wonder where on God's earth you are. As a loyal reader
and cinema lover I'm naturally curious why you suddenly vanished
from the public eye. I hope you aren't sick or in any way incapacitated.*

    *It has come to my attention that the film reviews are now written
by someone called 'Grant Walker'. At first I thought it might be
you playing journalistic tricks so I waited outside the Sydney Film
Festival and kept asking 'film buffs' (what poseurs!) in the theatre
foyer to point out 'Grant Walker' to me. Finally a nondescript chinless
guy came over to me looking confused and wearing the same glasses
and leather jacket as in the photo over the film reviews but with less
hair. What a loser! My heart sank at his existence but I am prepared
to acknowledge that he does seem to exist. I must say he was totally
disinterested as to your whereabouts and rudely walked away while
I was still questioning him.*

    *But enough of Grant Walker. He's wasted enough of my time
already. Not money, fortunately! These days I check out the magazine
in the supermarket rather than buy it. The checkout chicks don't
care. (Sorry, NOW editor. It's a fabulous magazine and worth every*

cent! Ha ha!) First thing every Monday publication day I'm at the supermarket checkout 'checking it out', praying today I'll strike it lucky and Grant Walker's goggle-eyed loser face will be gone and yours will be staring out from the film page again.

Stop rambling Carl! Bring her up to date on your life! Well, so much has happened since our paths last crossed. I have the best possible news! My Kafkaesque disagreements with the legal and mental health systems are now water under the bridge. I AM A CHANGED MAN!

After the embarrassing incident in your back yard (chemical imbalance, wrong medication, blah blah, plus undue harassment from the authorities, deepest apologies, enough said!) you might find this hard to believe but the confused 'perpetual adolescent' is no more.

Truly, I have a newfound calm maturity befitting my years and extensive education. Can I ever forgive those government shrinks and quacks and bloodsucking bureaucrats their damaging pseudo-science, their evil onslaughts into my bloodstream and nervous system and various artificially induced states of (un)consciousness? Yes I can! Because – after much trial and error – they worked! Thanks to a Simple Little Pill I am stabilized as the old Carl again!

Now you would go a long way to find a less obsessive personality than mine. The only nut I am these days is a health nut. Any more spring water and I swear I'll burst! (Only Cool Ridge of course!) I have given up meat, sugar, dairy, alcohol, tea and coffee and am much better for it. Tobacco is a little more difficult but I'm working on it

with nicotine patches. So far so good. Terrible taste though!! (See –
I have the serenity and insight to joke about myself these days!)

My current interests? Obviously the cinema because of our
deep shared involvement. I have also resumed my childhood hobby
of breeding bantams which I find very restful after the hassles the
'real world' has thrown up these past few years. Are you familiar with
bantams? I must say I favour the featherfoot breeds, Buff Brahmas,
Black Silkies and Porcelains, rather than the clean-leggeds. Beauty
versus drabness – it's no contest. I don't know the extent of your
bantam experience (some areas of your life are still a wonderful
mystery to me!) but in my humble opinion featherfoots are truly the
flower garden of the poultry world!

Just as successful as bantams in resolving tension are the many
new friendships I have made on the chat room circuit. Incidentally, let
me know your email particulars. My details follow.

I gather you've moved house. To a less sleazy and aggressive area
I hope! No offence, but I don't know how you could live amongst
those sorts of people. Or were you just 'soaking up atmosphere'? The
two 'confirmed bachelors' living there now were no help and quite
offensive to my civil request as to your whereabouts.

Do let me know where you're living and/or working now. We
could have a quiet drink or a meal and catch up. Don't be a stranger.

Yours with the utmost affection and the happiest shared memories,
Carl
coolcarl@ezymail.com

ONWARD MARCH

The coffee mug wasn't Molloy's only brush with astrology. He was a constant if slightly furtive reader of astrology columns. Waiting for barbers, dentists, doctors, or marking time while new tyres were fitted or pizzas cooked, he'd seek out his stars in the magazine at hand, no matter how tattered and out of date. Had he enjoyed a reckless but gratifying encounter with a stranger the previous September? (He very much doubted it.) Had he needed to be watchful for opponents' ambitions last April? (No doubt of that one.)

Of course he didn't take the stars seriously. He presumed all zodiac columns were written by fey Aquarians in caftans and dangly earrings. (He supposed this prejudice was typically Capricornian.) But despite astrology's spotty track record he was hooked.

He knew why. The only reason a Capricorn, or an anthropologist for that matter, would heed such a faintly shameful pastime was the need to know more about himself. Science could only go so far. All those front-page gene breakthroughs notwithstanding, he'd never know whose genetic blueprint he'd inherited. This was more than a vague yearning to know what made him tick. It was a black hole. In this vacuum his name and date of birth were all the personal background he possessed.

One thing he'd learned from years of fruitless inquiries: a blank personal slate wasn't unusual for an orphaned or abandoned boy caught up in the post-war child-migration schemes of the British Empire. As familiar as he was nowadays with the London of professional visits, nothing in the English cityscape or countryside rang an emotional bell. He got no hints from double-decker buses and black cabs, the ubiquitous heroic statues. Shouldn't the weather, at least, have nipped a little boy's knees and ears and nose and fingers enough to become a frosty physical memory? His boyhood England had no climate, landscape, buildings or inhabitants, beyond those of the two orphanages. And over time even the orphanages had melded into one in his mind. The England of his memory had become one redbrick Home – St So-and-so's. And four overriding smells.

The Home divided into four distinct odours which he knew now as carbolic acid, floor polish, gravy and urine. The smells dominated his early life, one or other of them characterising a dormitory, a dining room, a bathroom, an asphalt quadrangle, a fight (with a now faceless bully), several punishments (cane strokes on the palm) and an illness (chicken pox).

Sometimes the aromas flowed like waves over and through one another, or piled up like strata. Gravy overlaying floor polish represented the dining room. Floor polish mingling with piss stood for the dormitory. Carbolic acid and piss was the bathroom. Only one odourless place sparked any recollection: the 'picnic meadow'. This was the patch of sparse, wilted grass used for approved family visits. He'd received only one such visit and no smell attached itself to this shard of memory.

Generally, the word 'orphanage' didn't weigh as heavily on him as 'farm'. As for that emotionally freighted word 'mother', it seemed to skim lightly over him these days, only settling momentarily if he concentrated on the shadowy glimpse of the tall quiet woman looming over him and proffering a Milky Bar during that one visit in the picnic meadow.

Did he recall dark hair like his beneath a scarf, pale skin, dark lipstick, eyes earnestly on him as he stood there on the rare grass nibbling the Milky Bar? This woman stood vertical and rigid inside her coat. As she'd hardly spoken he couldn't be sure of her role, her voice. Not even her smell. Had her eyes seemed to drink him in?

With adult hindsight, the dimly remembered, tense woman might have been an aunt or some other relation. Perhaps a charity visitor. With the word 'mother' he'd always associated the barley-sugar smell, tender bitten fingertips and chirpy Cockney accent of

Betty, the young nursing assistant at St So-and-so's. The way Betty stuck out her lower lip to blow the hair from her eyes when her hands were busy or when she bent over his bath: he missed that sweetly futile feminine gesture to this day.

No, there was no mother's name, or official record of a father, or place of birth. Beyond the name John Molloy and his birth date, there were no records at all. He'd been a ward of the state, abandoned, an orphan, just like thousands of other children sent off on ships clutching paper Union Jacks to new lives in Australia, Canada, New Zealand, South Africa and Rhodesia. Then wiped off Britain's records.

The way he saw it, Britain had been masterfully keeping records ever since the Magna Carta. Britain kept tabs on its children; his details had to have been deliberately destroyed. For years this realisation angered him. Then he discovered he wasn't the only one. Thousands of children were denied their backgrounds. Any number of churches, municipal councils, charities and governments – a whole host of busybody, self-righteous organisations and individuals – had destroyed their orphans' birth records. Everyone from mayors to mothers superior did it. It was the accepted thing. Better for all concerned to clear the decks, burn the bridges, start life afresh.

These days he told himself his parentage no longer concerned him. Too many years had passed, and anyway the British Government had since apologised for such nineteenth-century colonial behaviour prevailing into the mid-twentieth century. Perhaps one day he'd even see a shred of truth retrospectively in what Brigadier Wansborough had impressed upon them each dawn assembly at Fernhope Farm, his reedy voice rising and fading over the parade ground like a faulty tannoy.

'You children are the lucky ones – free to soak up God's sunshine, eat his good food, breathe his clean country air, exercise your limbs in his decent manual work.'

There was no God's sunshine at five-thirty in mid-winter. He could still hear the quavering voices, thinned by the frost of the Southern Highlands, feel his bare feet freezing on the gravel, as Physical Training Sergeant Tallack patrolled their ranks, his enthusiastic cane flicking the calves of reluctant songbird and bedwetter alike.

> God bless our lovely morning land,
> God keep us in enfolding hands,
> Austra-lia.
> On Earth there is no other land,
> Like our enchanted Southern Land,
> Our own dear home, our Motherland,
> Austra-lia.

Although they took place every morning of the year, the dawn assemblies of his memory, without exception, occur in winter, the chilled chorus echoing in his head always underscored by the muffled sobs of the shivering bedwetters paraded naked in the front row.

The mortified mumble of the bedwetters. Forced to wear their incriminating sheets like cowls over their heads, they can never raise their voices above a monotone. Despite the cane's threat, they're either struck dumb with embarrassment or they blubber and stumble headlong towards that final *Austra-lia*. Boys and girls alike are desperate to end the humiliation, but know it will never be over. The next miserable night, the next smelly, yellowed, naked morning, lie ahead. And the suspense and taunts until the next, and the next. Pissing and suffering unto eternity.

As the winds of his memory fizz across the parade ground, the Brigadier rubs his hands together and repairs inside for his bacon and eggs. This leaves Sergeant Tallack to stand them to attention in military style, stand them at ease, then dismiss the bedwetters to the cold showers, the others to their breakfast of porridge and bread and Golden Syrup, his daily pep talk ringing in their ears.

'Work hard. Obey orders. Be grateful. You were once puny orphans. Sickly English flotsam and jetsam. Now you've got good weather every day and meat and three veg every night. Did you get lamb chops back in Pommyland, Mary Butterworth? *I don't think so.* Fresh milk, David Pratt? *I don't think so.* More spinach than Popeye? No, siree. Eat up, knuckle down and one day you'll be gainfully employed citizens of Australia.'

The pep talk is modified on weekends. Then, depending on the sergeant's mood and the state of his hangover, he passes along their ranks like a visiting general. Murmuring approvingly, 'You're building real muscle, young Brinsden' – or Mattson or Cowan or Brooker or Sullivan – he nominates his current blushing favourite with a matey ruffle of the hair, a teasing buttock-flick of the cane.

Gainfully employed farm labourers and domestic help are what Fernhope Farm actually anticipates for the children's futures. In the meantime the sergeant's golden-haired boy is encouraged to grow his fingernails so he can be gainfully employed all Saturday afternoon. Under the canopy of a favourite willow overlooking the dam, rainbow lorikeets treacherously chattering above them, it's his job to scratch dandruff from the sergeant's scalp.

It's the habit of Sergeant Tallack, proud of his thick silt-and-nicotine-coloured locks, to demand this scurf removal each weekend. To break in a new dandruff scratcher takes time. He has to instruct him on the correct friction and rhythm, and then some of them still don't get it, even with the threat of the belt. So he prefers to stick with one of his long-nailed favourites. By Saturday night the boy of the moment is slumped on the leather sofa in the sergeant's bedroom, his eyes fixed on the framed photographs of the 1953 Melbourne Cup and the 1952 Rugby League grand final.

He has spent the afternoon scalp-scratching, then the evening parting the hair into little sections and trickling Macassar oil onto that tripe-coloured scalp. He has combed the oil into the yellow-grey waves, creaming and layering them into furrows, while the sergeant leans back sipping his Yalumba sweet sherry. Now the exhausted boy is most likely praying for the swooning, slippery sergeant to fall asleep in his arms.

It's not enough that you're covered in his dandruff. That his scummy skinflakes are stuck to you with sickly grease. *In your arms! Tallack's actual slimy head is lying in your arms!* You want to vomit right there, protest, leap to your feet. Or maybe try to kill him. But of course no one does anything. A sleepy sergeant is preferable to a sherry-roused Saturday-night sergeant.

As soon as he, young John Molloy, cottoned on he became a nail-biter, right down to the quick, forever nervously nibbling his nails and tearing at his cuticles. Raw, blunt, spongy-tipped and often bleeding – most unsatisfactory fingers for dandruff scratching. If by misfortune he somehow draws attention to himself and is ordered to attend to the sergeant's scalp, he now trusts his ineffectual nails to gain him a whack on the head and a welcome curt dismissal.

Saturdays are farm work and dandruff duty and Sundays are church, prayers and preaching and the same five or six hymns – the familiar choruses welcomed with gusto – that, for some, help blur the memory of the previous day.

Praise my soul the King of Hea-ven / to his feet thy tri-bute bring / Ransomed, healed, re-stored, for-giv-en / Who like me his praise should sing?

Who indeed? Before nail-biting occurred to him, he would

carry a small rectangle of solace for his own sour and frightening Saturdays: a creased, faded and much-thumbed black and white photo of himself aged five. Betty had given it to him before the boat sailed. On the back was written his birthdate and the words, 'Thank you Miss Phillips for looking after John.'

He presumed Miss Phillips was Betty. He would concentrate his thoughts on the photo and it got him through the day. He took it as evidence his mother cared. And he knew Betty did.

Al-le-lu-ia! Al-le-lu-ia! Praise the ev-er-last-ing King.

So it's ordained he will be a farm labourer, or eventually, given unimaginable luck, a self-employed farmer. This is his destiny until the frosty morning he rams the tree stump with the farm's tractor and dislodges the beehive inside. When he regains consciousness he's lying in the male ward of the Southern Highlands District Hospital between a poultry farmer with kidney stones and a fireman with a hiatus hernia bulging from his pyjamas.

He's fourteen and the last thing he remembers is eating a Jonathan apple as he climbed onto the cold metal seat of the old Fordson Major early that Saturday morning. He'd gripped the apple in his teeth because he needed both hands to shift the gears. He doesn't remember bumping down the gravel road with orders to clear the lantana infestation in the bottom paddock.

Considering it's Saturday work, this is regarded as an enjoy-able chore. You not only avoided the daily milking and the weekly sheep slaughter, you weren't a candidate for dandruff scratching. It's a job with some status – you have to be fourteen before you're allowed to drive the tractor. He doesn't recall the cool gravel dust billowing around the tractor, the crimson rosellas exploding out of the wild oats beside the track, or the magpies warbling what always sounds like 'Pop Goes the Weasel', or deciding that it would be a good idea to knock over the hollow tree stump. Or indeed ram-ming it twice with the front-end loader, inciting the angry bees to swarm over him.

His tumble to the ground inches in front of a back wheel doesn't ring a bell. Nor does the fact of the tractor still being in gear, or the dogged resistance of the old spotted gum's roots which, refusing to budge any further, saved his poisoned and ballooning head from being flattened under the wheel.

Lying in hospital between the poultry farmer and the fireman, neither up to chatting, he has a week to consider his lucky escapes. The doctor, a rural codger named Sutherland with a remarkable, porous-looking nose like a pumice stone, informs him that he and the two nurses have removed one thousand, two hundred and thirty-three bee stings from his body.

'This is a record for me, son,' the doctor confides. 'The most stings I've seen before on the one body was five hundred and five – and she'd been wearing some exotic perfume and lying in a field of clover. I had to count them for the autopsy. Funny, the chap with her was naked as well but he was stung only half a dozen times and walked out of here.'

He's pleased to be part of a record. He feels contentedly unique lying here 'under observation', waiting for the swellings to subside and listening to the doctor saying how fortunate he'd been to be stung so massively. The huge exposure to bee venom had stimulated antibodies which protected him. A mere hundred stings might have killed him. 'Just forty or fifty and you could have kicked the bucket, sonny. I'd buy a lottery ticket if I were you.'

He's staring at Dr Sutherland's lava-rock nose, imagining he can feel the heat coming off it, when the doctor sounds a warning. 'I don't know how you're going to take this, being a country boy, but you're going to have to avoid bees for the rest of your life. The native Australian bee is harmless – no sting. But those bees you see in every field and garden are European honeybees. Beware the European honeybee. Any more stings could produce a devastating reaction. You'd be better off in the city. Or maybe the desert.'

This is a confusing thought. It's hard to hold anything against bees when you have no memory of them stinging you. He has to accept the doctor's word that he'd been seriously poisoned. And that the urgent search for the tiny bee stings and their attached venom sacs is the reason for his shaved head, armpits and genitals, the discovery of which on awakening mortified him for three days.

At this moment it's difficult to imagine life beyond the placid hospital netherworld of brisk, soft footsteps, the morning's milk-arrowroot biscuits and the evening's steamed fish. As he lies back scratching his itchy groin stubble and reading *Pix* magazine, even the farm seems a distant memory. As the days pass, however, a small concern takes hold and grows in his mind. It's all very well passing the time munching biscuits and perusing candid snap-shots of Ava Gardner and Hedy Lamarr looking smoky-eyed and tousled in nightclubs, but he needs some direction and advice.

Unusually, his new direction comes about because one of Fernhope Farm's six-year-olds, Scottish Margaret, so named to distinguish her from the farm's Welsh and English Margarets, is brought to hospital by Matron Pagett after licking plum jam off her fingers.

The children had been warned to keep their fingers away from their mouths; the jam was laced with strychnine. A regular Sunday-afternoon relaxation for the younger ones was poisoning rabbits. The task involved spooning dollops of poisoned jam across the entrance to their burrows. When the rabbits got jam on their feet they painstakingly licked it off, then died painfully in their burrows. But Scottish Margaret got her fingers sticky, forgot the warning and did the natural thing.

Luckily, Margaret hasn't licked a fatal dose of jam. But as he listens to her howls – she hasn't lost her accent yet and screams in Scottish – and sees the hospital staff rushing about, he thinks about both of them lying there in their poisoned states. Life seemed suddenly more tenuous if you could be killed by honey-bees and plum jam. It firms his resolve. When Matron Pagett is about to return to the farm he has the temerity to ask her, 'Next time you come could you please bring me my book?'

His request surprises Audrey Pagett, also his rash presumption that she'd be making another visit. 'I beg your pardon, Your Majesty?' she says. However, as it's she who purchases each child's Christmas present every year – and so must have chosen his book herself from the Anglican Homes Gift Catalogue – she can hardly refuse.

So for direction as well as solace he turns to his favourite book, indeed his only book, his Christmas gift of three years before. It's called *Humanity's Onward March*, by Herbert Courtney Hon. D. Litt. Unlike Scottish Margaret's furiously protected bride doll, the book has stayed intact, attracting no envy or vandalism from his companions. No other child ever coveted *Humanity's Onward March*. (Consequently it was on his study shelves still, its cover and frontispiece forever brown-speckled from the accidental spray of some excited child's annual bottle of Coca-Cola at that year's Christmas party.)

Humanity's Onward March begins with a chapter called 'In the Beginning' and ends with one called 'The Fight for Democracy'. Ever since that Christmas morning three years before, he has been pretty sure it will change his life. Lying in hospital waiting for his four patches of hair to grow back and the bee venom to leave his body, he's certain. Anyway, what choice does he have?

'Were it possible to commandeer the stars,' begins Herbert Courtney Hon. D. Litt. with a flourish, 'and they were equally shared out, each one of us would become a landholder of some importance. There would be approximately sixty stars apiece for the two billion men, women and children who presently inhabit the earth.' He likes that idea, although even on the clearest starlit nights in the Southern Highlands he has found it impossible to count more than a dozen of his share before losing his place.

'This is not to suggest that the world is overpopulated,' continues Herbert Courtney Hon. D. Litt. (What a naïve orphanage boy he'd been! Until university he'd assumed the author possessed a strangely elongated and staccato name. He thought of him as Herbert Litt.) 'Human beings are merely inefficiently distributed. Accommodation for every person could be found on the little Danish island of Bornholm. It is quite pleasantly situated in the Baltic, and has an area of two hundred and twenty-five square miles . . .'

At this point he always imagines Herbert Litt, whom he sees as a ruddy, shoulder-to-the-wheel type resembling Mr Vern Walkhope, the peach and apricot farmer from the adjoining property, pursing his lips in a little smile.

'. . . but there would be standing room only.'

Humanity's Onward March celebrates the romance of mankind's relentless migrations. Among Herbert Litt's many uplifting anecdotes – of British wanderlust in particular – are several lauding the bravery and navigational acumen of eighteenth-century English explorers. There is one tale, however, about the Pacific voyages of Captain Samuel Wallis in 1767, that has him wondering. He isn't sure where it fits into humanity's onward march but he finds it extraordinarily exciting and he reads the passage almost every day.

> When Wallis and the *Dolphin* were in Tahiti, the Englishmen found the Tahitian women surprisingly affectionate. The women would readily exchange intimate favours for iron, and in their urgent search for this material the sailors began pulling nails out of the ship. They were removing nails at such a rapid rate that Wallis had to order them to stop because the ship was falling apart.

He pictures the *Dolphin* riding at anchor in the sparkling lagoon and the giggling Polynesian women paddling their canoes out to the ship. Some carry pineapples, coconuts and fish but the younger, more beautiful women bring nothing but the bright flowers threaded in their hair and looped around their necks. He sees the flowers bouncing against their bare breasts as they paddle.

After a long erotic interval the women paddle slowly back

to the beach with their cargoes of nails, their canoes riding much lower in the water. Now they are even more prone to giggling, and they comb and fidget with their hair. (Their decorative hibiscuses are rather crushed.) Drawing their outriggers up on the sand, they turn and face the ship and toss the bruised flowers into the receding tide, waving and singing fond goodbyes. Their sweet harmonies dip and rise in the balmy trade winds, the flowers drift and bob around the ship, and with an exhausted, creaking sigh the *Dolphin* pops its final timbers.

Surprisingly affectionate! Intimate favours! The way he visualises it, the swooning, sated sailors, all non-swimmers and sinking fast, wave contentedly back.

Herbert Litt was a romantic who wrote inspiringly of the grand sweep of migration over the ages. *Where did we come from?* Herbert Litt posed this question and then answered it himself with great verve, a handful of facts and an untramelled imagination. Man's evolution, he implied, keeping a respectful distance from the Creation question, was like a track-and-field relay race, with the *Homo erectus* runner passing the baton to the *Homo sapiens* athlete and then expiring politely on the side of the track. While the Neanderthal runner was lumbering along behind in an outside lane and *Homo habilis* and the Australopithecus team were way back in the field, *Homo sapiens* shot to the front and breasted the tape.

From Herbert Litt, moreover, he understands anthropology

to be quite a detective story – indeed, the world's first detective story. And one whose plot is still far from solved. Unable to make any headway with the mystery of his own past, he decides to absorb himself in this bigger mystery.

He leaves hospital with his mind made up. No more fields of clover, no tree stumps and no honeybees. Forget farming. The bees have decided him. Fortunately the bees carry weight with Brigadier Wansborough – the bees and the firm letter from Dr Sutherland pointing out the possible consequences.

Luckily he has been a good student, the brightest boy in his year at Southern Highlands High. Now he's allowed to sit for an entrance exam to a far-off selective high school, James Ruse Agricultural High. At James Ruse it is assumed that a profession or university career will follow, and not necessarily in agriculture. So he becomes the first Fernhope child to attend university, and there he transfers his longing and curiosity about his background to the bigger picture, the study of mankind.

As for his eternal questions about himself, he finds scholarship certainly helps. Science is a balm. Science tells him to be curious, to test the bee-sting peril. He does. It hurts. His arm swells a little where the bee has stung him. The pain and swelling soon stop. He is not allergic.

There was no denying that his discovery had made him envied in his field: the young man who'd discovered the First Modern Woman, who'd brought the Out of Africa theory into question. And at only twenty-one – not much more than a boy. His youth was part of the news angle, the whole long-haired, gangly, orphan-hippie look of him:

Modern Woman Found
by Ultra-modern Man

Whereas Henric was five-seven, even then middle-aged and portly. Anyway, Henric, let's not forget who found Grace, who first spotted her and held her skull pieces in his hand. You were still asleep and snoring in your tent, one eye eerily half open and rolled sideways as usual.

Herbert Litt had been on the ball. How percipient the warning in *Humanity's Onward March*: 'The search for answers to mankind's evolution is a highly competitive endeavour, fraught with blind leads and clashing theories and egos.'

Clashing theories and egos had not occurred to him back then. Territory as a force of nature applied to animals, football teams, native tribes and ancient forms of mankind under scientific investigation. He hadn't yet linked the notion of territory to science and to those theories he admired. He didn't see territory in the everyday. Naïvely, he could barely imagine scientists squabbling across the globe, much less fighting bitterly in the same building.

Political motives and intense competition were still unknown to him. Department versus department, university versus university, country against country, theory against theory, scientist versus scientist. One side of the tearoom against the other. And the first to publish wins.

Back then he was still a romantic about scholarship. It had already dramatically changed his life for the better. Universities were still all about intellectual curiosity, calm reason, a drink after work in the staff club, and agreeing to disagree. As for anthropologists, weren't they all laconic outdoor scientists with beards and shady hats who knew their red wines?

Herbert Litt had been right on the money. Just ask Professor Henric Fischer.

But he'd prevail, he assured himself. His view would come out trumps. Next month his new paper would be published in *Nature*. In print and on the internet he'd proclaim his new, incontrovertible findings on Salt End Woman. The latest dating technology proved she was one hundred thousand years old. Not sixty or even eighty thousand. It would take things forward – and backwards, of course – another huge step. In the meantime he could surely afford a self-congratulatory moment. And a philosophical one, too. The longer he studied the regular surges of humanity's passage across the earth, the less important became the transgressions of his enemies – and former friends.

Reflecting on the *Nature* article, how eagerly and anxiously he awaited publication, it occurred to him that if he were contemplating a memoir, a brisk sort of chronicle to set the record straight (not that he was vain enough to do so), he'd start by marking his life as a series of pinpoints.

The first would indicate a classic *Homo sapiens* of Anglo-Celtic origins. At twelve he'd proudly discovered the name Molloy was Irish, meaning 'proud chieftain'; at forty the gene for haemochromatosis, common among Celts, had come to light during a life-insurance medical – so his ancestors had evolved a way of retaining iron and fighting the Potato Famine! Add a typical Caucasian skull and skeleture and a body type tending to the ectomorphic and you had the typical man on the street; well, thirty percent of them.

This man, due examination would show, had trodden the earth with varying amounts of pressure, differing degrees of success and failure – evidenced by the ground-down molars, sun damage to the pale Celtic skin, occasional liver twinges and the beginnings of arthritic joint deterioration – for fifty years.

He could then pinpoint being five years old, and easily recall that age because all the children in the Home aged five were marched into the assembly hall in their pyjamas to have their heads clipped and inspected for lice. He remembered being shunted down the line of iron beds and the hair falling on the floor. Next, the smell and pressure of the chloroform pad on his face, the doctor ordering him, 'Count backwards from ten.' Nine. Eight. Reaching seven as he fell unconscious, waking with a puddle of blood on his pillow and his tonsils removed. And being sent to bed early a few days later because the next morning they were going to Australia.

Age five was also the ship. Of course he could pinpoint the journey: the ship that supported them in the boundless rocking sea and swept them away in that below-deck miasma of porridge and vomit. The thick porridge smell of the children's quarters almost but never quite succeeding to counter the whiffs of vomit. Vividly he recalled the daily drama of bath time, and the ship's huge baths, deep and wide enough to swim in. But none of the kids could swim; they were too tense and terrified even to float.

Contagious hysteria overtook them at four o'clock every afternoon – the line of panicking children stretching along the passageway and up the stairs to the open deck. Even the nine- and ten-year-olds clutching at the nurses and shying from the huge taps and fierce steaming pressure of the bathwater. Seawater, not fresh. Everyone believing that the ocean pouring so fiercely into those big deep baths could just as surely flush them down the plughole into its vastness.

The first week at sea it took two and sometimes three nurses to bathe each child; to physically restrain them, support them and wash them. The children screaming at the hot salt stinging their throats, so overwrought they coughed up gobbets of old tonsil blood into the bathwater.

He remembered his shipboard secret – the intense pleasure of surreptitiously picking paint off the ship's rail. If he couldn't get near the rail, any painted metal surface sufficed. It was an obsession. Whenever on deck he'd urgently run his fingers along and under the rail, searching for congealed paint drips. More and still more; his busy little fingers couldn't stop their restless search. There were never enough salty paint bubbles and lumps to burst, pick and tear, never enough strips of paint skin to peel off and flick into the ocean. His fingers wanted more.

Was he was trying in his small way to scuttle the ship? Perhaps to disable it enough so it had to give up its one-way voyage to the colonies and turn for home? What he did remember was that it was his pleasure, and his alone. Each night, as he lay in his bunk breathing the porridge-and-vomit smell, while the ship creaked and throbbed and the children moaned and tossed in their anxious dreams, he dug the day's scraped-off paint from under his nails with a feeling of sly satisfaction.

Five was a big year. He also remembered owning two toys at five: a little cream-painted wooden truck with a sign on its side advertising Wall's Ice Cream, and a sailor doll, handed out just before the voyage.

The charity woman giving out paper flags and sailor dolls at the gangplank had trilled, 'Congratulations, dear. You're a little child of the Empire.' The sailor's cap said SS *Adventure* but their ship was called the *Strathaird*. All the boys received identical sailor dolls and the girls were given teddy bears. He would have preferred a bear and to stay with Betty but no one asked him and he didn't say anything.

The third, drabber-looking envelope in the morning's mail had escaped his attention. He opened it now. It contained a single sheet of unsigned purple paper, headed ATTENTION ALL 'SCIENTISTS'.

Your pompous, so-called enlightened portion of mankind is a fool's paradise. You have attempted to explain the possible origin of all life as we know it! What ignorance, stupidity, even arrogance to question the miraculous perfection, symmetry, harmony, balance in all of the immensity of the universe that we are in and constitute a part of!!!

You misguided 'enlightened' people profess to understand our origins and thus the workings of the human mind. Through your supposed educational 'anointing' you claim to have gleaned the processes of man's soul.

No! No! No!

Let your puny little minds grasp this fact. The only reason you 'intellectuals' are standing in your white coats on this planet today is because you are meant to live out your time on a purpose-driven basis. The inexplicable life-force energy that keeps your hearts pumping exists purely for the fulfilment of His Manifest Destiny.

The Origin of Life came about only to worship Him, to serve His ministry, to become like His Son, above all to observe the clear command in the Bible:

'You Must Be Born Again.'

He tossed the letter in the bin and took another sip of coffee from the Capricorn mug. He thought for a moment, then he reached into his desk drawer for the Ugandan letter.

Didn't he have some traveller's cheques left over from the last trip? In the back of the drawer he found three US$50 cheques still in their little plastic wallet. Now he countersigned them, put them in an envelope and, sighing, gave Miriam Mirembe of Kampala the benefit of considerable doubt.

FIVE

THE NATURE WALK

The boy came into Grace's mind as she led the first tour party of the day around Crocodile Gardens' new Ecosystem Nature Walk. The track was made of woodchips laid on the red pindan sand, and an unseasonal overnight rain shower and the pressure of the visitors' feet had brought out the smell of freshly cut timber. Lifting a woodchip to her nose, she sniffed and announced authoritatively, 'Bloodwood.'

Her little joke. While she'd learned much about the local flora and fauna and how it was that so many diverse species managed to thrive in such abrupt and harsh conditions – tropical coast one minute, inland desert the next – she'd also noticed the termite-infested bloodwood tree being sawn down and chipped a fortnight before.

As it happened, her party, a travel-industry group of eight

from the southern capitals, didn't bother to even feign interest in
her ecological know-how. They were merely checking the recent
makeover of a well-known tourist drawcard to fill in time between
flights. Some of them had visited Port Mangrove before on junkets,
back in the days when the Ecosystem Nature Walk was just
an unnamed gravel path around the crocodile park's boundary –
before the advent of the free-range kangaroos, the bilby retreat,
the flying-fox arbour and the sand-goanna basking area. Anyway,
their pallor, sunglasses and subdued wisecracks indicated severe
hangovers this morning. They played hard, these people.

A light sheen still lay like lacquer on the surrounding vegetation, but within half an hour the Ecosystem Nature Walk would
look and smell dun and dusty again. From mid-morning the desert
began pressing in. The desert always reminded you of its closeness.
You could smell it in the easterly wind, taste it, catch its grit in
your eyes. She wondered whether the boy was being hidden
in the desert. Or in a coastal town, a southern city? She'd kept
a close watch on the news. There had been no reports of him
being caught.

Was it easier to lose oneself in the country or the city? She'd
chosen the farthest reach of the country herself – but then she'd
been desperate to escape the city. It would be easier for the boy
to disappear in a big city. Dressed in typical street gear, the baseball cap, the compulsory brand names, he'd go unnoticed in the
racial mixture of Sydney. He could be quietly working somewhere

out of the public eye, maybe as a gardener for an order of nuns, she thought, and improving his English and education at the same time.

The image didn't last. Somehow she couldn't visualise him with his Leonardo DiCaprio hair solemnly weeding a convent rose bed or trimming the grass around a Holy Mother and Child out in Burwood. It was easier to picture him slouching around a cineplex or amusement centre, on the edge of trouble. She saw slot machines, violent video games, junk food, bad company, drugs. What was next? Gangs? Weapons?

As the tour party moped along the woodchip path, she dutifully pointed out the various local grasses, plants and trees: the spinifexes and grevilleas and hakeas, the occasional eucalypt and the more tropical fringe of pandanus palms and mangroves around the park's swampy western side. A big domed nest of mud-dauber wasps bulged from a gum tree and she indicated its two or three sentries flashing warning orange in the sunlight.

'Wasps, really?' someone murmured sarcastically. Bugs didn't count. Eco-friendly or not, you didn't stress bugs. On the contrary. Nor vegetation, unless it was rare and beautiful or *very* old, old enough to have been munched by dinosaurs. Just like ordinary tourists, the travel specialists gave the flora a perfunctory glance and hankered after the fauna lurking within it. Even banal old crocs and pythons were preferable to wasps and spiky grasses and cardboard-coloured shrubs.

Behind her a male voice muttered to no one in particular, 'A tough sell or what?'

'Who can tell any longer?' a woman's voice answered. '*Exotic* works, *wilderness* works, the croc thing definitely works. Crocs get sexier with every new attack. They don't want New York or Bali any more, I know that much.'

'I'm Nine-Elevened out,' another woman complained. 'I'm so over it.'

A grevillea bush suddenly rustled at the edge of the path and the last speaker, a bulky, perfumed woman tropically clad in white cheesecloth arranged in descending layers like a rainforest-floor fungus, bustled from the group and addressed the vegetation with exaggerated vehemence.

'Come out and show yourself! I don't even care if you're poisonous. A bloody lizard will do.'

Like a comedian from the wings, a wallaby duly peeped out, sniffed the air, and vanished back into the shrubbery before the woman had time to remove the lens cap from her camera.

'God, even that kangaroo thingie won't stick around. And they're not exactly *rare.*'

'Oh, Maggie, do settle,' said a silver-haired man in a hibiscus-print shirt. He threw a tanned arm around the cheeseclothed woman's upper layers and shook her in mock annoyance. Although still frowning impatiently, the woman didn't discourage this contact, her shoulder continuing to veer towards his arm for some

seconds after he removed it. 'We've had the full crocodile introduc-
tion,' he continued, 'and the venomous snake number, thank you
very much, and now we're getting the ecosystem experience.'

'If I wanted animals I could have taken up Garuda's offer to
pat bloody orang-utans in Borneo while there are still a handful
left. But there was hiking and canoes involved. No thanks.'

'Speaking for myself,' said the flowery-shirted man, 'I *do*
like a good palm.'

Grace, meanwhile, was coaxing the wallaby from the bushes
with some feed pellets from her pocket and starting her ranger
spiel: 'This fellow is called an agile wallaby. He comes out in the
early morning and evening and feeds on grass, leaves, fruit and
roots. During the heat of the day he rests in shady depressions in
the sand.'

'Eats, roots and leaves,' a man sniggered. 'Same old story.'

'You should know,' a woman said.

Grace felt suddenly self-conscious, like a visiting celebrity
doing a photo-op and worrying that the koala she was hugging
would piss on her for the world's front pages. 'Did you know they've
found agile-wallaby bones that are twenty thousand years old, from
the time when Indonesia and New Guinea were connected to the
Australian land mass?'

'Looks pretty lethargic to me,' grumbled the cheeseclothed
woman.

'He can move fast if he needs to,' Grace muttered, mildly

enough for someone who heard the agile-wallaby crack several times a day. Indeed, having discovered food, the wallaby was showing a turn of speed, zigzagging along the path beside them, nosing their legs and sticking close by.

The travel party's attitude was bad form, she thought, especially since the park tour had been specially arranged (she'd started work an hour early) to suit their schedule. They had seaplanes to catch mid-morning, they kept stressing, to a remote resort called Impossible Bay, a tiny reef-ringed jewel ogled, over the centuries, by such notables as the buccaneer William Dampier and the crew of HMS *Beagle*.

'And the Rockefeller boy who went on to New Guinea and was eaten by cannibals,' enthused someone else. 'He fell in love with the place.'

Now that the ozone was easing their hangovers they were cheering up and becoming excited about this next destination. Apparently Impossible Bay had what the world's rich and celebrated demanded in a hideaway these days. Nicole Kidman had recently looked in, and Russell Crowe, and some younger Murdochs. It was imperative they check it out and report back to the travel market.

'The word is *complete* barefoot luxury,' said the man in the hibiscus shirt.

'Yes, but define barefoot luxury,' interposed a brisk, blonded woman. 'The way they keep moving the parameters, I'm never sure these days.'

'Oh, the standard definition,' he said. 'Ten guests max, total privacy, no kids, no party animals, holistic nurturing, top chef, wet-edge saltwater pool, safe lagoon, white sand, natural fibres, hardwood floors and near-impossible access.'

'Access to nearby indigenous cultures?'

He gave her a quizzical look. 'Oh, *sure*,' he said, and everyone laughed.

Well, she'd be happy to be rid of them, Grace thought. 'If you have planes to catch, shall we move on?'

Now that they were on the verge of leaving, however, they were dragging their heels, irritatingly stopping to snap ironic photos all over the place. Suddenly everyone was grinning and posing with the palm trees and the SNAKES AHEAD and CROCODILES THIS WAY signs, and of course with the now-gregarious agile wallaby, and breaking up into chatty groups.

'Everything was perforated,' the Maggie woman was announcing fiercely. 'Every organ. A complete system breakdown. That's the only reason I accepted this bloody trip. For the relaxation. *Ha!*'

'Poor old Mag,' mollified the man in the flowery shirt. 'Well, tonight it'll be a massage and a spa and Moët under the palms and the sun setting over the Timor Sea.'

'I could be in Machu Picchu or Guadeloupe right now,' she grumbled. 'Or Budapest. Incidentally, Budapest is the next Paris, in my opinion.'

'No, you made the right choice, darl. Considering your health. I wouldn't want to be in Guadeloupe with a dicky tummy. No thank you.'

'I was on life support, on the drips, couldn't take solids. Everything shut down. The doctors said I'd been asking for it. It was a lifestyle thing.'

'I know where you're coming from.'

'I know you do.' She touched his arm suddenly. 'I'm not telling *you* anything you don't know. You know what we have to put up with.'

'I'm with you. I've cut out eating lunch altogether.' He patted his flat stomach. 'I thought, This can't go on, mister. You have to draw the line somewhere. It's just not worth it.'

'You know something weird? I turned the corner the day Marlon Brando died. How do you explain that? Brando croaked and that day I felt much better. Spooky or what?'

'Life's funny,' agreed the man in the hibiscus shirt.

CHARITY

Far from hiding in a desert town or a southern city, the boy was presently kicking a soccer ball with five prisoners on the front lawn of the Little Company of the Holy Charity convent only five kilometres away in the centre of Port Mangrove.

The prisoners were convicted trochus poachers, boys of around his age serving their hundred-day to twelve-month sentences in semi-custody. In theory this meant they were supposed to be performing some form of community service. For these five prisoners, semi-custody was interpreted by easygoing courthouse officials as doing the nuns' gardening; by the prisoners on this unseasonably temperate coastal afternoon – as they passed the ball back and forth across the shadows cast by lichened Catholic statuary – as playing soccer.

They were from fishing villages in the south of Sulawesi and from the island of Roti, south of Timor. Since the sixteenth century, their ancestors – trepangers, Macassans – had sailed their *prahus* of timber planks caulked with paperbark to this same coast to collect trepang – bêche-de-mer or sea cucumbers. Nowadays national fishing zones were strictly enforced and the *prahus*, fitted with engines but hardly less flimsy than those of five hundred years before, were regularly captured by Navy patrol boats. Foreigners convicted of unlawfully fishing in Australian waters forfeited their boats, equipment and catch. The boats were then burned on the beach. A cupful of kerosene and a match was all it took to destroy a *prahu*.

And still they came, *prahu* after *prahu*, year after year. The same men and boys, and new boys, younger sons and brothers, generations of them from the same impoverished villages. The chances were they'd be arrested again. Then they would clog up the court system, and be too poor to pay the increasing fines for repeat offenders, and be sent to prison in lieu of the fines – and crowd out all the gaols in the north.

So semi-custody evolved as the pragmatic way of handling these offenders. After all, they were mostly too young for gaol and not the most heinous of criminals. They themselves were cheerfully fatalistic about semi-custody. The notion of semi-custody was soon well ingrained. It enabled them to sleep in more comfortable hostel or dormitory accommodation, eat McDonald's and KFC and pizzas, update their baseball caps and T-shirts, renew friendships and play for the local soccer teams.

Apart from the not unpleasant prospect of semi-custody, what was it that brought these Indonesian teenagers here in a constant tide of *prahus*? Not sea slugs these days so much as the trochus, a big sea snail with a cone-shaped shell coated with nacre. Treated and polished, the shell was turned into simple mother-of-pearl jewellery and ornaments — tourist-market and bazaar kitsch. Trochus fetched ten dollars a kilogram on the Asian market. If it managed to elude the Navy boats and the Coastwatch plane looking for people smugglers, a *prahu* could take home eight hundred kilos of trochus.

The boys were employed as divers to pluck the trochus shells from the coastal reefs. With no breathing apparatus they dived all the hours of daylight for a month at a time, plunging repeatedly to a depth of twelve metres or so. Holding their breath again and again. Back on board, they'd pack the shells under the deck. All fifteen or sixteen boys slept on deck above the appalling stink of sea snails rotting in the tropical heat. The trochus flesh was inedible. They ate weevily rice and whatever fish they could catch. Many became sick from burst eardrums, ear infections or bad drinking water. Some drowned. There were other dangers. Sharks. Stingers. Cyclones. It didn't take much of a cyclone to sink a *prahu* made of planks caulked with paperbark.

But for this they were paid fifty dollars per voyage: enough to support their families for three or four months. It was good money back in the village. And if they were caught, they shrugged and smiled. Semi-custody, free food and new soccer uniforms loomed.

All this the boy gleaned from his chatty new companions.

They were a different sort of prisoner. After the detention-camp inmates, these ones were lively and confusingly cheerful. Even though they, too, were separated from families and friends, they were full of mischief and, yes, gratitude. Gratitude to this land of the trochus and the Hawaiian pizza and the Happy Meal. A country so rich it gave children free toys with their food.

He liked them well enough. They had some things in common. Soccer. Their ages. Bits and pieces of religion, though none of them were particularly devout. They knew about Leonardo DiCaprio. Of course they had seen *Titanic*. However, he couldn't understand their occupation: diving deep into the sea. Underwater. That they could live and work all day on and, worse, *in* the ocean mystified and troubled him. It made him feel dizzy if he thought about it for long. It brought back bad memories.

In the beginning they were curious about him and where he came from. The nuns had told him to say nothing – not that he would have. When he wouldn't discuss it and played dumb they didn't keep on. The nuns told them not to bother him about it, saying there were language difficulties and a deep sadness involved. Anyway, the entire world of the happy-go-lucky trochus poachers revolved around their fishing village and this Australian place. He wouldn't let on that he and they shared the one thousand kilometres of sea in between.

This time the nuns had decided on a different approach to refugee concealment: hiding in plain sight. The whole town knew the convent officially detained a constant stream of youthful trochus poachers – even if the Little Company of the Holy Charity was more haven than detention. Dark-haired, brown-skinned, wiry boys were often to be seen kicking a ball around the convent, mowing the lawn and trimming the bougainvillea hedge on the streetfront, splashing in the municipal swimming pool, cramming noisily into McDonald's with their team after a soccer game.

The town liked the young prisoners. It appreciated their happy natures and their football agility and sympathised with their poverty. It wasn't as if they'd been caught dynamite fishing – like the older fishermen back in Indonesia, blasting the reefs away – or poaching local lobsters or prawns, or even sharks, cutting off their fins for the Asian market and throwing the bodies back into the sea. They weren't affecting the town's livelihood.

Who here was interested in trochus shells? They were environmentally protected in any case; no one was allowed to take them except the Aborigines from the north. As a nod to old traditions, a sentimental gesture, the northerners were allowed to collect trochus, but only by hand, and only from reefs exposed at low tide. Not surprisingly these people, whose own blood carried the genes of generations of visiting Macassan trepangers and trochus gatherers, held a different view of the poachers' competition.

Although this was just talk, they'd been threatening to kill them and burn their boats for decades.

No, Port Mangrove saw the young trochus poachers in a friendly light. It wasn't as if they were illegal refugees either. They hadn't tried to sneak into the country through the back door; they hadn't jumped immigration queues; they weren't seeking asylum. They just wanted to do their unspeakably tough job and take money back to their families in the village. You couldn't blame them for that. Moreover the town was accustomed to seeing them around, used to passing the self-conscious conga line of new arrivals at the courthouse, used to the ever-changing but somehow familiar faces on the soccer field.

The nuns guessed that one more young brown face would hardly be noticed. Thanks to the poachers' own genetic inheritance – over the centuries, Arab and Indian traders had regularly visited Macassar – the boy even looked like them.

Experience had taught Sister Joseph the best way to do things. East Timor and the slaughter of Catholic innocents had toughened her mind and honed a skill for subterfuge and secrecy she hadn't known she possessed.

The first refugees she'd hidden were a sailboat load of Timorese escaping the militia. A family of five with faith in the weather, the mood of the Timor Sea and a backup, twenty-year-old Evinrude outboard: Catholics running from Muslims, and then from Australian Immigration. She'd regarded what she was doing then, and thereafter, more as sanctuary than subterfuge – the historic proper role of the Church. Since then the refugees' religions had ceased to matter. She'd hidden or passed along the line Muslims, Buddhists, Hindus, Coptic Christians, even a couple of Chinese Presbyterians. She believed that children were worth going out on a limb for. So, she'd decided as time went on, were a great many adults. Her conscience could not have been clearer.

If you were trusted you might approach Sister Joseph, or one of her feisty counterparts in another country town, through certain of the local Catholics. She'd say, 'I'll deal with it,' and get in touch with her network in the country and the cities: 'I've got a small problem that needs attention for a week or so.'

Sister Joseph's commonsense and imagination had fashioned several rules and modes of operation for passing people around. It was easier to hide someone in the city, of course, and make the changeover there. In Sydney, for example – so you could test whether you were being followed – you might park the car in George Street and walk the subject through the bustle of Central Railway Station and meet the changeover person on the other side, in Elizabeth Street. Easy to lose anyone following; to catch a series of trains, buses, cabs, or have a car waiting. In the country, however, it was easier to move the subject from one convent or presbytery to another – provided the lay staff didn't inform on them.

You worked out a system of codes, places and exchanges. It was best not to use the telephone – and never a mobile phone – but if you had to, you used a code: 'I've got those vegetables for you. Can you pick them up at five o'clock on Monday?' And both of you knew to add, say, three in each case, so the handover would actually take place at eight p.m. on Thursday. Then you arranged the meeting place somewhere with a lot of activity or none at all.

It just amounted to lateral thinking and foresight. You learned to drive to a handover point via a circuitous route, to set off in the opposite direction, or in a roundabout way. You worked out where the surveillance officers expected you to be, then you moved in an unpredictable, seemingly random pattern. Not that they were too hard to spot: in a country town, surveillance officers stuck out like the proverbial outhouse in the desert, always trying to look like tourists so the locals wouldn't suspect them. They were generally spotted nevertheless and the old warning went out on the grapevine: 'Strangers in town.'

In the country you quickly sensed if you were being followed. What you did then was drive right on the speed limit. Stick to the traffic law. No ordinary country driver ever did that; the other car was going to have to pass you. Mind you, someone with a sophisticated camera in their car could still nail you when they drove past.

The local police might be sympathetic, you never knew. They were supposed to work with the federal police and the immigration inspectors and make the actual arrests, but they might be Catholic and sympathetic. Or their wives might be. Generally speaking, if a husband and wife were involved in hiding someone it was the wife who started off as more sympathetic, especially if the refugee was a lone child. But then the husband would usually come round; next thing, he'd be kicking a football with the boy (the lone children were always boys), taking him to the beach with his own kids. Husbands wouldn't inform on their wives, not in her experience. They might be on tenterhooks the whole time, and hasten the next handover, but they wouldn't turn them in.

The people who turned them in were often fruitpickers. She never let her adult or teenage refugees work as fruitpickers. Better to go without work. In the countryside the first stop for the surveillance officers was always the local fruitpickers because they were the cheapest unskilled labour. The police relied on fruitpickers' tipoffs. Fruitpickers were prickly and envious and itinerant, always annoyed at the refugees undercutting their wages. In the city the officers always checked the brothels first. Why the brothels? What did nuns know about brothels? Well, the men had been locked up for a couple of years, hadn't they?

Lately Sister Joseph worried that the level of surveillance was intensifying. Some of the refugee collectives had been infiltrated. Such an unwieldy amalgam of ethnic and church groups, political activists and students, disgruntled successful migrants avenging old battles and latter-day treacheries — you couldn't overestimate those ancient furies and more recent doublecrossings, the warlord rivalries and religious schisms and sect-splinterings — that she supposed it was inevitable.

Word had come down the line that increased pressure and manpower were being exerted to catch particular escaped detainees, especially witnesses to politically sensitive events. Apparently a special list had been drawn up. In these cases there was great hostility towards the individual refugee and the threat he might represent.

How long should they keep the boy? What was his background? She didn't know.

The man had visited him just before the cyclone. Before the breakout. Sweating in his city clothes, face pink in the heat, no moustache or beard, no hair on top either. An interpreter with him. The TV crews outside the fence filming the city man coming through the gates. The demonstrators there too, watching and holding their signs for the cameras. FREE THE CHILDREN! ASYLUM NOT PRISON! The air very still, the dark clouds building up from the coast. A strange green tinge in the sky. The guards bad-tempered and nervous. Everyone waiting for the cyclone.

He didn't let on he understood English. Not with any sort of authorities.

Tell him in his language that I'm very sorry for the loss of his family. Very, very sorry. It's hard for me to express how sorry I feel for him, especially at his age. That's why I'm here, why I have come so far to see him — to help. I am acting on his behalf.

Does he understand that I'm a lawyer, not the government, not immigration? I am a lawyer for the people, a civil-rights lawyer. Not the government! Please make that clear to him.

Tell him I need him to answer some questions about his voyage here. Not so much the first, overland part of the journey — the final stage of the journey in the boat from Indonesia. I need to hear what he knows and remembers seeing. This is very important. For him and the other survivors. And especially for the people who died. Three hundred and fifty-three, wasn't it? Including his family.

Tell him I mightn't get the chance to talk to him again. I've come a long way to see him. From the other side of the country, three thousand, five hundred kilometres away. It was difficult for me to get inside the detention centre. I've been allowed only half an hour and they've already wasted fifteen minutes shuffling me about. They might cut short this interview at any time.

My father paid for our passage with the money from selling his shop and my mother's gold jewellery. I think it was four thousand dollars, one thousand for each of us. He gave it to the man who organised the trip to Australia. It was supposed to be a luxury boat. The man said it had an entertainment area and a swimming pool.

When we saw the bad condition of the boat we didn't want to leave Indonesia. None of the passengers did. Everyone changed their minds. The boat looked rusty and unsafe. It was a wreck. You could hear water sloshing about below. But the Indonesian police wouldn't let us go back. They waved us aboard with guns and stood by in the background. The organising man followed us aboard with a gun and prevented us from leaving. My mother and sister were crying – my sister was only five years old. Everyone was all crowded up on deck and down below. Four hundred passengers – the boat was sitting very low in the water. Even in port, waves were washing on the deck. The organising man jumped off the boat before it left.

The boat stayed afloat for a day and a night. It was struggling in every wave. The engine was weak and water was always coming over the sides. Everyone was nervous and panicking. People were praying and moaning. No one could sleep. When we got nearer to Australia the pump broke down and we began to sink in the night and suddenly we were all in the ocean.

Ask him if before the boat sank he noticed any sort of tracking device on board. Maybe hidden somewhere.

(Shrugging.) There was a sort of radio, not hidden.

What did it look like?

A radio.

Other survivors have reported that two big vessels soon arrived and shone their lights on the people struggling in the water. Ask him is that so.

It is so.

How soon did they arrive?

Very soon.

How many people were in the water? Were you expecting they would rescue you?

Of course. About half of us, about two hundred people were still alive when the boats arrived and shone their lights on us. People were sobbing with joy because we thought now we would be saved.

Ask him what sort of boats they were. Big? Small? Boats made of wood or metal?

Quite big metal boats. Ships. Big, but not as big as the *Titanic*.

What? No, I guess not. Anything else?

A smaller boat was cruising around the two large boats. And I heard a plane circling overhead.

Did you see the names of the ships? What colour were the ships? Black? Grey? Were they Navy boats?

The ships were shining lights on us, in our eyes. I couldn't see that.

How close did the ships come to you and the other people in the water?

The ships came to about two hundred metres from us. Close enough that their engines disturbed the water and made waves over us. In one voice we all screamed so they would hear us: 'Please help! Please help!' We blew whistles, too, and yelled out and waved at them. Their lights were shining on us. They could see us. There were so many of us, it was impossible they didn't hear us, too. We couldn't believe they weren't rescuing us.

How long did the ships stay?

They shone their lights on us and watched us for about five minutes, then they turned the lights off and circled us for another half-hour, and then they left us.

Are you sure of what you have said about the ships?

Yes.

Have you told anyone in the detention centre that you saw the ships come and then go away?

(Another shrug.)

I don't want to upset him any more than necessary, him having lost his parents and sister during the night, but can you ask him how he was rescued?

Some Indonesian fishing boats picked us up next morning.

The forty-five who didn't drown?

Yes.

Tell him I'm sorry to upset him . . . Can you ask him how he's being treated in here?

(He shrugged.)

Have you been bashed?

(He shrugged.)

Have you been molested?

(He shrugged and looked away to the side.)

Have you been in solitary confinement?

(He shrugged again. Still not answering, but this time maybe wanting to answer – but how to talk about solitary confinement? About using a plastic bag as a toilet – when it quickly filled the first time, calling out to the guards that he needed the proper toilet. Four guards rushing down the corridor in riot gear and bursting into the cell with their blocking cushions. Pushing him back against the wall, one guard holding his legs, another forcing his hands behind his back, the third gripping his neck so he thought he would choke. The fourth guard just standing there swearing at him, then punching him unconscious.)

Yes.

You're very thin. Have you been on a hunger strike? Have you harmed yourself? (The man was staring at his lips, his hands.)

(He shrugged.)

Jesus, that wind is picking up. Ask him to sign this, please. Tell him thanks and all the best in the future. We're working on his case. Tell him to take care. What time is that cyclone supposed to hit?

Sister Joseph allowed the prisoners to each choose a video every week. His first week, the boy roamed the Video Ezy racks until he found *Titanic*. The trochus poachers didn't mind too much, although they'd already seen it. They grumbled when it was his choice again the following week, however, and vigorously protested the week after that. But he was so adamant that Sister Joseph eventually gave in.

'You had your own choices,' she told the others, 'and some of them not very appetising, I must say – explosions, car chases, shooting, Arnold Whatsisname. This means something to him.'

The third time he watched it alone, sitting at a grey formica table in the bare refectory, oblivious to the noise of the others outside: the clamour and plunk of table-tennis, the adolescent cheers and groans. When she passed the refectory door Sister Joseph noticed he was crying. She began to enter and comfort him but stopped when she realised the importance of the moment to him. He preferred watching *Titanic* alone.

She presumed the *Titanic* fixation was something to do with his being a 'boat person', as the papers called the refugees. He identified with the characters. She wondered which boat. One that sank on the way?

Lately Sister Joseph had decided to accept conspiracy theories. She would believe them initially and only discount them if and when they were revealed to be exaggerated or false. Nowadays she found this more sensible and safer than the other way round.

Being naïvely, Christianly trusting, always presuming officialdom's best motives, then having your faith destroyed, wasted so much time and emotion. Once you lost ground that way it was impossible to make it up. By then the bad things had happened and the lie was set in concrete. The officials had got their story straight. Or the person had been captured. The situation was irrevocable.

The latest conspiracy theory to come up the line was about the unnamed boat that sank on its way to Australia carrying four hundred refugees. Three hundred and fifty-three of them had drowned. The theory, as Sister Joseph heard it, involved the federal police and agents of the Indonesian police – bribes taking place all round. Acting with a well-known people smuggler, they'd encouraged the departure from Indonesia of a spectacularly unseaworthy and overloaded refugee vessel. This encouragement had extended to placing a tracking device aboard the decrepit (perhaps even sabotaged) boat so they would know where and when it was sinking. The aim – the theory went – had been to make an example of this leaky tub; to show potential asylum seekers how dangerous was the voyage to Australia. Best that it sank in Indonesian waters, though.

Murky waters, thought Sister Joseph. At best, the government hadn't detected for three days a human disaster in the middle of its intensive reconnaissance operations, and through simple ineptitude had let a boat full of refugees drown. (Sister Joseph couldn't believe this scenario of dullwittedness.) At worst, as the conspiracy theory suggested, it had arranged for the boat to sink. She thought the truth probably lay somewhere in between. The government had known it was sinking and had stood by and let it happen.

If it were possible to make prayers retrospective she would have prayed that such a callous thing had never happened. She could certainly pray for the souls of all those who'd drowned that night – that part was no theory – and also for those who'd survived and who were now presumably locked up in a detention centre. That wasn't theory either.

Her mind rambled over the prayers to come. Strangely, only that old heartfelt and sober Protestant hymn 'For Those at Sea' came to mind. That catchy, swelling chorus – *O hear us when we cry to thee / For those in peril on the sea.*

She had to know if the boy had been on the boat that sank.

Titanic finished and she waited while the credits rolled. A gecko clung to the wall above the television set; it disappeared behind a picture of Our Lady. From the change in the noise level outside, the trochus poachers had moved onto the lawn and were kicking a football around in the dark. The gecko reappeared with a spider in its mouth. The boy was still sitting there composing himself. She'd made him a cup of hot chocolate, an odd drink for this climate but one he usually enjoyed – an Anzac biscuit to go with it – but he hadn't touched them.

Wherever he came from – what with the conspiracy theory and the questions at McDonald's – she knew it was only a matter of time before things got difficult. A couple of the soccer team fathers had started asking questions after the games.

'That guy on the wing did okay again. Who *is* he – the one they call Leo that doesn't talk? Over there next to young Jayden and Dylan hoeing into the McChicken? Different accent to the trochus boys. If he's a Leo I'm Mohammed. Hey, Sister, we're not aiding and abetting an escapee, are we? Not that there's anything in the club rules against it as long as he keeps kicking goals. Just joking, Sister. You're doing a great job. No picnic, I bet. Teenage boys are hard enough. Different cultures, *whew*. Keep up the good work.'

Then she'd spotted the two strangers parked outside the convent; not an official car, of course – an Avis Toyota Prado. No dust on it. No bags. A fishing rod on the roof just for show – not very professional. She saw the Prado again parked behind the police station. Going through the court records, she guessed. Ticking her boys off their list. One of the Catholic constables, young Max Kennedy, said her guess was right but he couldn't say any more.

She sat beside the boy at the refectory table and took his thin brown hands in her stubby freckled ones. On his palms the scars shone like new five-cent pieces. There were smaller scars dotting his lips.

There was a limit to hiding in plain sight. 'You're a marked man, boyo,' she said. He didn't pull his hands away for a minute or so. His eyes were moist and huge.

She asked him. He nodded yes.

She sighed. Sometimes she felt like a mother. *Then they're really looking for you.*

SIX

PARK NOCTURNE

A Tip Top bread truck swung off Oxford Street through the gates of Centennial Park and stopped by a blue gum on the side of the hill below the reservoir. The truck driver climbed down and sat on the truck's front bumper in the tree's shade and began to play a clarinet. The notes streamed down the grassy slope, trickled through the ragged pines and flame trees and over the sandstone buttresses onto the sandy track where Molloy was strolling. 'How High the Moon'.

The music reached him as aptly as birdsong. Drawn by the clarinet, he climbed the hill towards it. The clarinet's lilting currents swept up other park walkers, a few jogging couples and several cyclists, and they all drifted towards the music. Soon about twenty people were loosely gathered around the truck. The clarinetist's deep concentration kept them a respectful distance from him.

He was young and dark-haired but his face was hard to make out with his head down and his eyes closed. The tree's shadows played across him as its leaves moved in the wind.

Seemingly oblivious to his growing audience, he segued into 'Caravan', then 'In the Mood' and 'Take the "A" Train'. People were squatting down among the pinecones and bracken, perching on rocks and leaning against trees to listen. Other curious passers-by joined them. Heads nodded, feet tapped. Their smiles were contagious. They were charmed by his music, by an exuberant 'Tuxedo Junction'. He was hitting his stride. An unexpected swerve into Mozart's *Clarinet Concerto* raised his audience's eyebrows before he swooped confidently down into 'Moonlight in Vermont' and 'Harlem Nocturne'.

Then, as abruptly as he'd started, he stopped playing. The moody notes faded into the upper branches, drifted into the background birdcalls and cicada buzz. Oxford Street hummed again. His lips still set in embouchure, he removed the reed and wiped off his spit with a cloth, wiped off the keys, removed the mouthpiece and wiped it, too, shook it and put it in his pocket.

Only now did he seem to notice his audience. He licked his lips, stretched his mouth and glanced around self-consciously. Perhaps there was a beat of three before the crowd clapped vigorously. The clarinetist gave a little bow, jumped back into the bread truck and accelerated away.

People were loath to break the spell. Heads dreamy with

melodies, strangers smiled and nodded wistfully at each other as they dispersed. Cyclists pushed off again, struggling for momentum; joggers limped and faltered back into their own thudding rhythm. Lives seemed suddenly clumsy and inept.

Molloy, too, felt unsettled by the Tip Top clarinetist. Unexpected music was an experience worth sharing, one of those minor jubilations that gave a sudden sting to living alone. He knew Grace would have enjoyed it. This was a favourite spot of hers: the southerly blowing in her face, the green, breezy view over the Centennial Pavilion and the ponds and the length of the park and Randwick Racecourse, downhill all the way south to Botany Bay.

They went to the movies together here. On this hill an open-air cinema operated each summer: the Moonlight Cinema. The evening after Joel left her they'd sat on the grass watching *Day for Night*. He'd thought it might get her mind off the breakup. Joel had finally had enough of the stalking. Joel had told her the situation was 'too full-on' for him; he found it difficult to believe she didn't know the stalker from somewhere, or that she hadn't had any contact with him.

Maybe she was leading the guy on. 'You often give the impression in a social context of being sort of available,' Joel had said.

That was too much. Joel being jealous of a man she didn't even know. Indeed, someone she detested; a lunatic who was making her life a misery. The trouble with Joel was that he wanted an uncomplicated life. He was an actor – not an especially good, or good-looking, actor, a would-be character actor – so he spent a lot of time at home. He depended on TV commercials requiring zany young types who suffered humorous indignities. Too much chilli in the burger. Girlfriends who ate the last Snickers Bar. The rest of the time he wanted to smoke his dope, drink a beer or two and partake of the current party drug. He didn't fancy any dramas ruffling his surface.

Her mood swung back and forth that night at *Day for Night*. Tears came and went as they waited for darkness. He made a joke about the appropriateness of having to wait for the night to be dark enough for the film to start. She didn't answer; she was checking her text messages again to see if Joel had been in touch in the last five minutes.

'I don't get it,' she said. 'You'd think he'd want to stay and protect me. Fight for his woman.'

'Leave it be,' he said mildly. 'You've broken up. You dislike him now, right?'

'I know he's immature and selfish but I don't completely blame him,' she said. 'How could he be expected to understand? He's an actor. He's got a vivid imagination. He was scared of being murdered in his bed by a mad prowler.'

Down towards Botany Bay, aircraft lights dipped and rose in quickening succession over the flat plateau of the airport. Around them the park was finally beginning to blend into the backdrop of the city. Surrounding palms and roofs loomed in sudden silhouette. Bats weaved melodramatically over cupolas and gables and widows' walks.

He recalled that the week he and Kate were breaking up he'd seen portents of chaos everywhere. The week of the drowned dog. The sky was sullen and electric, the sea frothed with dead sea creatures. Cormorants washed up around the island as if a plague had struck them. Daylight was mayhem, with spiked, jellied and tentacled corpses lying everywhere. Each eyeless leatherjacket and ballooning pufferfish seemed like a personal message. And in the gusty evenings the barrage of palm fruits on the tin roof could have been the stones of a mob.

Even the sun's rays and ocean tides had struck him as aggressive and personal. That last week on the island the biggest king tides in memory had eroded their front yard and tossed their scummy flotsam on the doorstep. One bleak morning he'd found a bull terrier, pink-white as a pork sausage, crouching on the remains of the lawn.

It took some minutes for him to face the dog. It was too much of an omen. Unmoving, observed by the dawn's first cautious crows, it still looked ready to pounce. Marine bloat had stretched it taut as a toadfish but didn't moderate the menacing slant to the albino eyes or the rictus snarl. He tossed a stone at its stomach; it bounced off. He gingerly prodded the dog with his foot. It was truly dead, no doubt about it. And even then he half expected it to leap for his throat.

He had a ferry to catch. He told himself he'd deal with it later. But when he returned that evening the drowned dog was gone. Someone had removed the carcass from his yard and buried it, he presumed, and in the maelstrom of his own domestic tempest he instantly forgot about it.

But to his astonishment there it was next morning, crouched in the yard again, in the same position, on the very same spot of bedraggled grass. This was eerie. Maybe there were degrees of death? Once more he had to leave it there. He gave it a wide berth as he left for the ferry. When he returned home that evening it was gone again.

Later that night, the anxieties and arguments spinning in his brain making sleep impossible, he was sitting on the verandah when the tide turned. Soon a pale shape loomed. Rolling and swaying on the incoming waves came the ghostly dog, surfing all the way up the beach to his frayed lawn. There the waves set it down in its customary position, its head facing the house.

For several hours he sat watching the tide lapping at the carcass, then gradually inching down its length and retreating in measured stages down the lawn to the beach. In a daze he sat considering the selective choice of tides, staring at a dead white dog crouching in the darkness. At the first wan rays of daylight, exhausted by omens, he buried it where it lay.

How different the sunrises had been during their early days on the island. That one unforgettable, enamel-painted morning when he'd risen to find the yard and beachfront mysteriously carpeted in green capsicums. Thousands more, shiny and buoyant, bobbed like plastic bath toys in the waves.

The whole ridiculous capsicum day stretched around their shack like a bright cartoon. Kate and he couldn't stop smiling, imagining some fanciful capsicum freighter jettisoning its cargo. In the green ocean light he handed Grace a capsicum. The baby gripped it solemnly in both hands while he sniffed the breeze in her scalp and briefly entertained the fantasy of manna from heaven.

And the capsicum sunset: a young couple making love at dusk in the warm green shallows.

That night at the Moonlight Cinema, the skyline began to hum and glow as Grace prattled on. Searchlights defined the clouds. A helicopter clattered north, and a slow and heavy Hercules troop carrier followed it, lumbering low overhead. Grace had to raise her voice to be heard above the racket. She was on a new tack.

'How can I put it? Yes, I'm sorry to see him go but I'm not devastated. The individual, quirky looks, the deep and meaningful actor thing, got me in for a while. But he was never going to be there for the long haul. He was surplus to requirements.'

'Requirements?'

'I have to keep my wits about me. I've got to narrow things down to the essentials.'

'Of course you do.'

She said something else that he couldn't quite hear. In the semi-darkness on the hillside nearby a man was kneeling on the grass and struggling with a corkscrew and a wine bottle. 'Now the bloody cork's broken,' the man complained. 'Jesus, I don't need this.'

'Push it in then,' said a more blurry and bulky male figure. 'Push the cork right in.'

'What do you think I'm trying to do?'

'Give it to me,' the second man said.

'No, I can do it.'

'Oh, just give it to Gary,' said a woman's disembodied voice.

Another woman laughed. A younger voice. A mobile phone rang with *The Lord of the Rings* theme. The laughing woman answered it and between shrieks told the caller in some detail where she was at present, where she'd been and where she was going next.

He still hadn't caught what Grace was saying.

'I'm fully stretched just dealing with the Icelander. I don't have the energy to focus on Joel's problems as well. I've realised I have to be selfish.'

Selfish. This was not her usual style. It was a new, brittle side to her. He murmured something else supportive but again he missed what she was saying next. He was trying to listen but he was increasingly distracted by the people around them and the angle of the seating. The ground was hard and sloping – his back ached easily these days – his wallet kept sliding out of his pocket onto the grass.

Finally the night became dark enough for the movie to start. 'Thank God,' he said.

Throughout Truffaut's film about films she lacked concentration. She fidgeted, and twice he was aware she was crying silently. Then in the car driving home to his house she suddenly quoted the movie's narrator about a film shoot being like a stagecoach trip.

'"At first you hope for a nice ride. Then you just hope to reach your destination." That sums up my life at the moment.'

'What do you mean?'

Her profile was pale and long-suffering; her eyes looked weary and lined, no longer a girl's. Right now this tall dark woman loomed beside him like a stranger.

'I wanted to go places once. Now I'm just hoping to reach my destination. In one piece.' Her laugh was more like a snort.

Surely she was being overly pessimistic. 'You'll be all right, I promise.' As he squeezed her arm he wondered suddenly whether she remembered the morning of the green capsicums. She'd been too young, of course.

'Oh, I'll be absolutely fine,' she said sharply. 'Now I'm on medication.'

When they reached his house she strode to the gate ahead of him. His house was always her refuge but even on the street verge there was a different, moody air space between them this time. Umbrage, misunderstanding, insufficient sympathy? He seemed to have failed her in some sort of uncomprehending male way.

He watched her heading grimly up the garden path. A dark and frowning study. His daughter had become one of those unknowable women you see walking briskly along with their heads down and their arms folded across their chests.

How easy it was to recall their first park visit. How recently it seemed that Grace was toddling in the autumn leaves and throwing bread to ducks. Back then, her age still measured in months, he imagined her featuring in freakish park tragedies. Choking on bottle tops, mauled by pit bulls, asphyxiating inside discarded lunch bags. Just to see those ominous swamp hens with their black wing-cloaks and Darth Vader headgear was to imagine her carried off in their beaks.

She was on her first legs; whenever he set her down she hit the ground running. Drawn to danger, new curls bobbing, she headed unerringly for some park deathtrap or other. Within seconds, watched by swamp hens, she was tottering towards a murky pond. Even as he blocked her wobbly path and safely scooped her up, he was picturing the alternative, launching himself into that stagnant water, scattering disgusting eels and carp, plucking her pale body from the swamp.

So he'd perched her out of harm's way on that actual picnic table beneath that very oak tree over there. Then he'd worried she would swallow acorns. Surprisingly, however, she'd sat in a con-tented trance, nibbling duck bread and painstakingly removing and replacing the acorns' little hats – until an oak leaf hanging in the air caught her eye.

How mysterious the leaf looked, twirling yet refusing to fall. As it floated beside their faces her quizzical frown was years beyond her tender age. *What's going on here?* Knowing some elemental law was being flouted. Bending closer, he saw the leaf was tethered to the tree by a strand of spider web. She couldn't talk yet but when he indicated the connecting thread her expression said, *'Aha!'*

For several minutes the twisting leaf entertained her. She nestled her head under his chin, snuggled backwards into his chest, wrapped herself loosely in his arms. She was a tactile little girl, and becoming sleepy. The leaf had a hypnotic effect on them both. Maybe he was humming Brahms' 'Lullaby' as he breathed her hair. Meanwhile waterbirds clamoured entertainingly nearby. Sunlight filtered through the oak tree and normal autumn leaves succumbed to gravity. Even as he experienced the moment he was nostalgic for it. Then from beside her little thighs atop the picnic table a black sentence leapt out and mugged him: 'Cindy M is a skanky slut that sucks Wogs and smells like dead rats – TRUE.'

At once he grabbed up his precious daughter and moved away. That she was years away from being able to read didn't matter. Her proximity to that mood-altering combination of letters was foul and intolerable to him.

He remembered his furious discomfort that day. Was it just the brutal change of atmosphere, the ferocious stripping away of innocence and sentiment, that had angered him? Or the sudden realisation that Grace would eventually grow into an adolescent, and a woman?

He also recalled the graffitist's own fury. A raw, ridiculed boy? A girl whose boyfriend had dropped her for a rival? What had become of flirty, hated Cindy M? he wondered. The usual transformation, he supposed. Metamorphosed into a stolid, anxious mother of teenagers. Whereas his daughter was still on the run.

DARK LADY
OF THE CINEMA

Her latest postcard had arrived that morning inside an envelope with a Hobart postmark. Hobart was the furthest town in the country from her actual location. Obviously she was still using the elaborate snail-mail communication system she'd devised when she first fled to the Kimberley.

With the pressure off nowadays, the postal ruses had turned into a sort of one-way game. She always placed each postcard – one of scores she'd collected over the years from umpteen movie press kits, art exhibitions, drive-through country towns and scenic holiday spots – inside a pre-stamped envelope, or sometimes two, and sent it crisscrossing the country via the far-flung addresses of different friends. Mail from Grace was likely to arrive from Tasmania, Victoria or South Australia, even from overseas – or from two blocks down the street.

She still wouldn't risk pilfered mail revealing her whereabouts. As it happened, he found her postcards so cryptic in their messages, so misleading in their illustrations and pictured locales, he was sure that sourcing the sender would bewilder any mail thief.

They certainly mystified him. Today's postcard commemorated a Frida Kahlo exhibition at the Art Gallery of South Australia. The painter stared out from a lush self-portrait. As usual Molloy's eyes were provoked by Kahlo's implacable monobrow and moustache, and everything else in the painting – the monkey perched on her shoulder, the hibiscus it was nibbling – simply fell away. The card said, 'Keeping busy. Think Leonardo rather than Frida. I'm well and happy. Wish you were here.'

Leonardo? Did she mean da Vinci? Was this some art joke? The postcards were becoming more and more obscure. He wondered if there was a new boyfriend. She'd always kept her boyfriends under wraps until they were a *fait accompli* – usually at the point they were moving in together.

He'd pinned the postcard to his bookshelves with the thirty-odd others, the more tasteful ones from colleagues on sabbaticals overseas, but most of them from her. Kahlo and her monkey abutted Coffs Harbour's Big Banana and Elvis Presley's grave; above them were cards plugging *Nosferatu,* Bangkok by Night, a Picasso exhibition, a Melbourne tram, a Blue Mountains view and a Cairo bar called Oasis; below, the Musée d'Orsay, Kakadu National Park and a *film noir* festival. As he closed his office door and left for the day he thought what an eclectic collage her personality made when all its strands were pinned down.

Once again he was grateful and relieved that distance and time had proved successful. She'd escaped the lunatic's clutches. She was prevailing over her nightmare. He was glad he hadn't told her of Carl Brand's two letters: the fax sent to her at *Now* and the second one recently posted to his address.

She'd instructed him to open all her mail and only send on anything vital. He'd taken her at her word and kept these letters from her. What purpose would it serve to even mention them? Why worry her unduly now the experience was over and she was beyond the mad bastard's reach? He'd no wish to reopen the old wounds and to see her depressed and sick again.

When he'd read the first letter, the fax intended for general office consumption, it had seemed to be masquerading as a normal communication between friends. The writer was minimising his problem and boasting, anyhow, of having overcome it. But he was still an obsessive case.

The mood swing of the second letter showed him in his true colours – a raving lunatic. This one worried him. It seemed to be a definite threat to her. He had to remind himself that she was safely out of Carl Brand's range, thousands of kilometres away.

Did the letter legally constitute an offence? Three law lecturers he'd shown it to in the staff club hadn't thought so. Certainly crazy and angry, they said, but too indirectly phrased. They said it would be hard to make any charge stick. They looked at him strangely, as if they were wondering whether there might be some truth in it.

My Dark Lady of the Cinema

Yes, this is what you have become to me. Where once you stood high on a pedestal, a goddess out of filmdom's Technicolor myths, your head constantly surrounded by a golden light of purity and joy, now I see only a cold, dark cloud around you. Your aura is grey and malign, your lips are the black of deceit, your flesh has turned to icy white marble.

You defy everything I believe in. God Almighty knows I have been patient but this latest wanton behaviour has cut me too deeply to bear. My eyes have finally been opened. Your exhibitionist sexual behaviour takes my breath away. It wasn't enough that you fled our relationship like a thief in the night! That you aborted our babies! Now you humiliate me with blatant adultery.

There are so many counts against you that my patience is exhausted. Immediately return to your senses and passionate romantic nature towards myself. The clock is ticking. Resume your loving wifely duties towards me under Jesus Christ Our Lord or I can no longer accept responsibility for the consequences.

Carl

Betrothed but Betrayed

SEVEN

THE SKELETON HANDBOOK

The workmen had just begun repairing the cyclone damage to the Salt End Inn when they spotted the skull protruding from the collapsed dune which had undermined the motel's four back cabins. Just in time they yelled to the bulldozer driver, downed tools and shuffled around nervously, backing into the dry wind to light cigarettes, unsure what to do next.

As they huddled around the burial site their feet inadvertently dislodged more sand; it trickled softly and swiftly from around the skull, revealing the curvature of the forehead, one eye socket and the nose cavity. The skull was lying on its right side in a position of repose. Maybe the protuberance adjoining it was a shoulder bone, someone said. Perhaps they'd found a complete skeleton.

The men fell quiet and thoughtful and agreed they shouldn't

touch anything. They solemnly debated the cause of death. A sudden awareness of solitude, the distance from home, the passage of time and the vagaries of the elements showed in their expressions. The gusty breeze seemed cooler and mustier and they saw hints of mortality in each other's faces: sagging flesh here, broken veins there. They were a hundred kilometres along a dirt road from the nearest township, even further from the authorities. Suddenly the harsh censure of crows on the cabin roofs, previously ignored, was almost too loud and insistent to bear. Someone went to fetch the motel proprietor.

He appeared a few minutes later, a dark, lugubrious man, Evan Strachan, walking heavily like a cop and carrying a book covered in protective plastic. His face was set in long-established lines of bitter resignation. The cyclone had wrecked four of his cabins and cut the electricity and road access for two weeks. It had taken a month to get the insurance company to play ball, even longer to get the workmen out here – and he had to feed and accommodate them for the duration of the job. Now, in the first hour of their first day, here was another unexpected consequence of the cyclone. He knew the drill on skeleton discoveries. They could be a major headache.

A small willy-willy accompanied him on his way to the smashed cabins, whirling back and forth across his path, twisting and threading through the gravel and the clump of blinking workmen, spinning dust and leaves in their faces before blowing itself out on the driveway. They were rubbing the grit from their eyes as he reached them. He slapped the book against his thigh in a businesslike fashion. 'What have we got here?' he inquired in his old detective-sergeant voice.

He'd had *The Skeleton Handbook* since his police days, indeed since his last day on the force. It was government issue: there was supposed to be a copy in every police station and National Park ranger's station in the State. It was designed to help them identify old Aboriginal skeletons – remains from the prehistoric past and the early historic period – also to stop them presuming a modern murder victim and overexcitedly disturbing a grave. No more hauling the bones off to the morgue and upsetting indigenous cultural sensibilities.

Actually, the police had come to appreciate the handbook. Anything was welcome that helped them decide whether human remains were ancient or not, Aboriginal or not. A really old skeleton let them off the investigation hook. On the other hand it required a different sensitivity, and paperwork.

When he'd got the heavy hint from the Police Integrity Commission and taken early retirement, he'd pinched the station copy of *The Skeleton Handbook*. He thought it might come in useful where they were going – to the back of beyond, the Great Sandy Desert. He couldn't get far enough away from Perth.

Burning bridges right and left, he'd run away with probationary constable Kelly Burnish and bought the Salt End Inn on the edge of the Salt End National Park, ten kilometres from the burial site of the First Modern Woman. To buy it, he'd only had to touch two of the interstate bank accounts: it was a bargain. The owner, a baby-pink German whose alopecia had erased even his eyebrows and eyelashes, said he had to sell because of family problems back in Europe: some in-law trouble since the two Germanys got back together.

The motel was only twenty-five years old, built not long after the discovery of the famous skeleton, with tourists coming and going all through the dry season, as well as plenty of university, museum and heritage types. Hot and dusty ones, too, after a few weeks excavating in the field, searching urgently for more examples of the world's oldest *Homo sapiens* specimens. It was obviously thirsty work. Archaeologists, geologists, anthropologists, palaeo-this and palaeo-that; in this climate they all drank like navvies. The German had shown him the books, of course, with every last can of Swan Lager and bottle of Margaret River wine neatly itemised.

The motel not only possessed the only liquor licence and accommodation for hundreds of kilometres, it had the only water. *Jesus*, it had the only shade! And even after all the talk about changing the burial-excavation laws it still looked like a sound purchase. He seemed to be on a winner. The more intrepid tourists had discovered the Kimberley; the science types were still snooping around. Given the choice, no question they'd all prefer a cabin and a shower to a tent, and someone else – Kelly – to cook their evening meal and open the shiraz.

The hairless German had departed in a cloud of red dust, his sentimental Rheinland and Donau posters still rustling on the office wall whenever you opened or shut the door. And he discovered he'd been conned. The books had been well and truly cooked. The political climate was ultra-sensitive. In deference to Aboriginal sensibilities, it would soon be an offence to disturb or excavate any land 'with the intention of finding a relic', or 'to remove a relic' from any land.

He'd taken 'disturb' and 'excavate' to mean vandalism or souveniring by amateur trophy hunters; 'relic' to mean an old carved nulla-nulla or boomerang or somesuch. He hadn't realised that every burial site would be filled in and covered over, that Aboriginal site curators had been appointed from the local tribes, and that National Park rangers were empowered to strictly police the law. Tourists were barely tolerated; the graves were kept secret from them. The desert was definitely not thronging with hot and thirsty scientists doing fieldwork; for their research they had to make do with the bones they already had, and once their current projects were completed even these were supposed to be returned to the Aborigines.

So his plans for a contented outback future with Kelly were scuttled. As for his Kraut predecessor with the head like a kid's drawing, of course he'd asked some former colleagues to check him out. An address would be welcome. A vaguely fruitful outcome might still be possible with a little pressure. But his old cronies just laughed in disbelief and advised him to keep his head down.

There was nothing he could do. He knew he'd been lucky to be permitted to fade away and he had no intention of drawing attention to himself. He swallowed his frustration and anger, stayed put, and blamed the Aborigines for his troubles.

Strachan rarely voiced any overt criticism of them, their ancestral culture or spiritual beliefs – he was a businessman and had to live among them. But the rare motel guest having a nightcap at the bar – once the proprietor had sounded out his sympathies – could be subjected to a late-night lamentation on how politics had defeated science on the matter of prehistoric remains. The guest would be told dolefully how the Dreamtime had hammered Evolution into bloody submission.

'I'm right behind science on this one,' he'd declare earnestly. All this scientific activity on his doorstep – rather, the cessation of scientific activity – had made him an avid reader of science journals. It seemed to him, he said, shouting a round of drinks if his views received any encouragement, that lately something had gone wrong with the brains of the nation.

The later the hour, the more despairing he became. 'Our ancient remains that we're now forbidden to study – you've read about them, of course – mightn't they teach us important things about human evolution?' *Our. We. Us.* He liked to repeat the point made by some talk-show pundit: wasn't the Dreamtime just creationism with a cuter name? 'Funny how the Dreamtime is supported by the same politically correct crowd who shout down the Christian fundamentalists for flogging the identical horse.'

For his masterstroke he'd adopt a confiding tone and lower his voice. 'Did you know Salt End Woman isn't even Aboriginal?' He let this sink in. 'She predates them by tens of thousands of years. The Aborigines came much later. She was what the boffins call gracile. Slim and elegant. Most of the blacks around here today are robusts. Have you seen them? Built like bloody footballers.' As proof, he'd produce his scrapbook of articles going right back to Salt End Woman's discovery by the young anthropology post-graduate student John Molloy. Then he'd shake his head in stern bemusement. 'Mind you, no one's allowed to say that.'

Was it any wonder he was bitter? It amazed him how one piece of bad luck could lead so inevitably and seamlessly to another. Having stopped all burial excavations and discouraged sacred-site tourists, the government then saw no reason to proceed with its planned upgrading of such a now-minor thoroughfare as Salt End Road. It allowed it to erode and return to dust or mud, depending on the season, and sealed the alternative Clayfire Road instead. So the motel was left more isolated than ever. Even the redneck pleasure shooters bound for the feral-animal killing grounds of the Northern Territory, those trigger-happy scourges of buffalo, donkey, camel, pig, sambar deer and banteng cattle, now passed them by. Only the rangers and die-hard nature buffs and heritage-conscious elderly tourists, the SADs – the See Australia and Die brigade – called in now.

Meanwhile he'd drained most of the bank accounts, even the riskier ones that operated under the other names. They'd gone through most of the money that was supposed to last for ever – his 'pension' – and he was stuck like a cockroach in molasses. With fewer customers and less work to do, Kelly was growing more restive by the day. Every evening after the news she lost herself on the internet. She was about to hit thirty and she'd taken to reminiscing about Perth's nightclubs and beaches and making sulky references to 'life stages' and the 22-year age difference. She seemed to enjoy contradicting him on news items. They disagreed on the asylum seekers.

'I don't see anything wrong with allowing them in,' she said. 'And providing them with a home.' Then she'd suddenly brought up the Jewish business, her 'heritage'. This was news to him. As far as he knew she hadn't been in a synagogue in her life. Her surname was Burnish, for Christ's sake – what could be more English than that? She was a genuine blonde! She had a turned-up nose! She'd joined the police force – how many Jewish cops were there? 'I'm motivated by my heritage,' she said. *Jesus!*

'Okay,' he said, craftily. 'So you're a Jew then. And these are mostly Muslims sneaking in. You hate each other. What do you say about that?'

'My grandparents were in a similar position in World War II,' she said, this new argumentative Jewess in his life. 'If it wasn't for people smugglers in France my grandparents wouldn't have survived and I wouldn't be here today arguing with a grumpy old ex-copper in the desert.'

As he reached the workmen he was already opening *The Skeleton Handbook* to the 'Skull Comparison' chapter. This was the first step in identifying a skeleton, Aboriginal and non-Aboriginal skulls being so markedly different. He could have told them that. He'd banged a few of each in his day. A few minutes later he was on the phone to the local site curator, Byron O'Malley, at the ranger station five kilometres down the road. He would do this by the book. Under sufferance, but by the book nevertheless.

'We've uncovered a skeleton at the motel.' He couldn't bring himself to say, Maybe one of yours. Byron was from the local tribe. Or his ancestors were, the side that wasn't Irish. 'You want to come over right away?'

'Be right there,' said Byron.

When he eventually arrived at the motel twenty-four hours later, he sported an arresting new tattoo on the back of his shaved skull – a life-sized tattoo of his own face. The crown of his head had been straddled for years by a tattoo of an angry tarantula, but the spider now lurked above a Byron likeness in similarly aggressive mood.

The rest of him was memorable as well. Of his site curator's uniform he was wearing only the khaki pants today. Over his otherwise naked chest and shoulders, exposing his cavernous navel – from which a tattooed taipan emerged – was a black fringed leather vest of the type favoured by country singers. His wide feet were bare as usual.

He was a unique and imposing figure on two fronts. His fierce, goatee-bearded face dominated proceedings both coming and going.

The newer frowning face glared up disconcertingly at Strachan as they bent together over the skeleton. Strachan purposely didn't remark on it. Mentioning the tattoo, indeed making any comment of a personal nature to Byron, was not in the realms of possibility.

More sand fell away from the skull as they stepped closer to inspect it. A complete side view was now exposed down to the lower jaw. Strachan pointed to the identifying skull-comparison diagrams, tapping each one with his finger, then indicating the corresponding feature on the skull lying before them. It vaguely occurred to him that this might make Byron uncomfortable, for whatever reason, but from the annoying, brash way he was whistling through his teeth he didn't seem to be.

According to the diagrams, the distinguishing features of an Aboriginal skull were that the face was especially large compared to the rest of the skull; the skull itself was relatively long and low; the face as a whole projected forward, the teeth projecting further forward than the brow. The brow ridges were large and thick. The cheekbone was large and rugged. The roots of the teeth were large . . .

There were another dozen or so points of suggested comparison between Aboriginal and non-Aboriginal skulls but Byron stood up at this stage, still whistling through his teeth, and cadged a cigarette from one of the workmen, who'd all downed tools again and were watching proceedings. Strachan went through all the points methodically, grimly, pointing and comparing, doing it by the book like a stolid police officer, and eventually he stood upright, stepped back and said, 'As I said, my opinion is it's an Aboriginal one.'

Byron's original face blew smoke through its nose. His new face glared off into the desert horizon. Neither face looked at Strachan. 'Sure is, chief.'

Strachan knew the 'chief' was ironic, to do with his having been in the force.

'It's one of our old people,' Byron said casually. 'An old man, by the way.'

'I'll have to give the skeleton man a call. That's the next step.' *A white man, a professional, to deal with the paperwork, to make sure.*

'The anthropologist? Molloy? I've phoned him already, chief.'

They were having an evening drink on the motel verandah. Sunset was not long off and Strachan was drinking his second beer and watching ants hurrying to deal with an old crumb from his lunch sandwich before darkness fell. Magpies yodelled back and forth in the low casuarinas beyond the red-dirt airstrip. A dry breeze suddenly blew up and half filled the torn air sock and cranked up the windmill for several seconds. Kelly Burnish's eyes followed the plume of red dust as it gusted across the airstrip and disappeared into the dun-coloured scrub and desert beyond.

Another quiet day – only one cabin taken, the stupid photographic enthusiasts. They'd annoyed Strachan as soon as he saw them in their bloody camouflage bush gear with their cameras and light meters and tripods, the fellow with four cameras around his neck. Four. The wife weighed down with the tripods. No sooner arriving than bustling about and getting all excited and artistic about photographing the bloody windmill and the windsock. From every possible angle.

'What's that official-looking tape doing around that pile of sand?' they wanted to know. 'Is it a crime scene? What's under there?'

'Renovations,' he'd told them firmly, in the old sergeant's voice. 'Nothing you'd be interested in. Please keep away.' Serve them right to get a glimpse of a grinning skull. That'd set them back on their expensive hiking boots. Of course they'd soon got themselves exhausted racing around in the heat, and had to rest, and now dinner would be delayed until they surfaced. Maybe he'd knock on their door and wake them up.

He looked at Kelly, sipping her chardonnay and mineral water, half and half. The wind had dropped again. The ants still persevered with the breadcrumb; they'd brought in reinforcements: they were trying to break it up into more manageable portions. One of them was waving its legs as if giving directions to the others. 'I'm going to rouse the photo freaks,' Strachan said.

'It's only six-thirty.'

'Bloody inconsiderate of them.'

'Give them a bit longer.' She nodded towards the packed dry landscape, the haze over the land, the dust beginning to settle with the cooler air. Birds were becoming raucous with the sunset. 'I was thinking how much it looks like Israel,' she said.

Not this again. 'You've never been to Israel, as far as I know.'

She ignored that. 'It could have *been* Israel.'

'What do you mean?'

'I've been reading about it on the net. The Kimberley was going to be the Jewish homeland. Something called the Freeland League made plans for Jewish refugees to settle here in 1939.'

'You're kidding. Bankers and businessmen and doctors all flooding in here? I love the idea of that.'

'No, mainly agricultural guys who wanted to make the desert lush and productive. Seventy-five thousand scientific pioneers and farmers and settlers, in the first wave. They'd researched it all, worked out a scheme that suited everybody.'

'So what happened? Where are all the Jews?'

'Oh, the state government said fine. And the population up here was on side. There was a local slogan: "Better the Jews than the Japs." The Christian churches said okay as well. The opposition didn't come from Australian gentiles. It was from Australian Jews.'

'Why would they have knocked it? I thought Jews stuck together – one in, all in.'

She looked past him out beyond the old airstrip and sipped her drink. Black kites circled, spiralled down to investigate something tempting, then rose again. She recalled documentaries and travel articles on Israel – birds in the air, dry heat, fit and smiling young women doing their bit. Where the airstrip met the casuarinas she imagined citrus and olive groves, dry-stone walls, stock grazing peacefully. 'They wanted the Holy Land or nothing.'

He grunted. 'Hard to see it working, anyway.'

'Who knows? But if seventy-five thousand Jews had come out to the Kimberley in '39 I guess it would've saved a few lives. This'd be a different place, that's for sure.'

Her Jewish thing was getting out of hand. He hardly knew her these days. Whatever happened to the cute probationary constable on night shift: the willing driver, the takeaway-food fetcher, the patient operator of radio, computer and telephone? He couldn't remember any moodiness back then. He was suddenly nostalgic for those quiet nights before their affair began, when it was only flirting, when he'd look in at the station in the early hours and she'd get him coffee and a biscuit, pull up a chair, impressed by his vastly experienced words, wide-eyed at his old adventures. He'd hung around the station when he could have been out and about, God knows, but he'd hung about. Gladly. Because of her, the new girl.

'Anyway, war broke out and the federal government pulled the plug on the scheme.'

'Really? Why was that?'

'All foreigners were suspect. Foreigners from anywhere at all. They pulled up the thingumabob – the drawbridge.'

He got up to go and wake the photo freaks; he wanted his dinner. 'Well, I'm glad the Middle East got them instead.' His boot scraped the sandwich crumb and its enveloping ants off the verandah. 'Thank Christ we avoided that fucking shambles.'

INTO AFRICA

Ripening palm and mango trees ringed the town's old open-air cinema, and restless flying foxes, unable to decide between them, flapped heavily across the screen from one tree to another. Every few minutes a bat was captured, silvered and gleaming, in the projector's light beam.

Neither the bat diversions nor the hackneyed film bothered Molloy. Skimming along the light beam, the bats looked electrocuted, even radioactive. As they pierced the air it exploded like foam. Metallic dust motes spun and sparked in their wake. Like spacecraft, one bat after another rode the beam all the way to the screen, only veering off when a crash seemed inevitable.

It was a treat to be in Port Mangrove with his daughter, watching a film under the stars – even a bad Hollywood teen romance. He felt more than his normal mix of emotions at seeing her, just as he was unusually eager this time to be heading out to Lake Salt End.

All those trips over the years into the desert to the ancient lake bed for so little return. Nothing of importance since finding Salt End Woman. One skeleton (he had to admit, if only to himself in his blackest moods) was not a sufficient sample to shake the cast-iron faith in Out of Africa. If you were urging a whole rethink of the evolution of modern humans, fighting the sheer international political weight of it, you needed more evidence. Another skeleton aged eighty thousand-plus would be very handy.

Britain, especially, had to be convinced. America, too, but at least it had kept its options open; and China was on his side. Britain was the only country where everyone was a rock-hard Out-of-Africanist. It was like fighting fundamentalists. In a funny sort of way his opponents were really not much different from creationists. That's what they were – scientific creationists.

Well, all that fundamentalism and reserve and, yes, ridicule, might be about to change. For the first time in a long while he was grateful to be called in to look at a skeleton. Especially at his old stamping ground, where it had all begun. And his eager anticipation was bolstered by spending an evening with Grace in their favourite way together – dinner and a movie.

It hardly mattered that the film was a dud. Although it had begun with a reckless flourish it had soon turned predictable enough. If anything, the bat activity overhead, the flapping and screeching, the regular plop of falling fruit, gave it a welcome anarchic touch.

The plot was not original: a poor boy and a rich girl, peasant and princess, brought up to date in Beverly Hills. Through an uncharacteristically selfless act, a rebellious Latino boy from the wrong side of the tracks redeems himself and wins the heart and body of the beautiful blond bourgeois girl who previously scorned him.

At the point of consummation, the Aboriginal teenagers in the audience, having identified strongly with the boy's outlaw attitude, whistled and stamped their feet. To their confusion, however, the cynical antihero immediately improved his manners and channelled his aggression into coaching a multiracial misfits' basketball team to (unsurprising) success. The girl, meanwhile, defeated her own demons (snobbish rich parents), shed her pearls and pompous Ivy League boyfriend, acquired a modest tattoo, pierced navel and tighter clothing, and became 'real'.

Although both young stars had their names above the title, they were unknown to Molloy, though he did recognise several famous older actors in character parts. As the credits rolled, to a hip-hop beat that had little Aboriginal children bobbing and whirling in the aisles, father and daughter rose yawning and stretching from their deckchairs.

'Who *were* those actors?' he wondered.

She shrugged and smiled. 'Who knows? My showbiz days are over. I'm a daylight person.'

It suited her, he thought. As they edged down their row to the aisle it struck him again how healthy she looked. She'd grown her hair; it hadn't been this long since she was a teenager. She was tanned and fit and seemed to have regained her old confidence. A wildlife park was not where he imagined his daughter would end up, but she looked surprisingly settled. In the circumstances he could hardly argue with that.

Maybe it wasn't so surprising after all. He reflected on all the hours they had put in at zoos, circuses, aquariums, even reptile parks. A particular menagerie they'd visited when she was ten or eleven came to mind. On holiday in the Tasmanian countryside they'd found an eccentric zoo run by a testy farmer type. Indigenous fauna crouched in the dust beside humdrum farm animals and exotic importations. Runny-eyed kangaroos and scabrous wombats lolled beside ostriches; camels and sheep foraged competitively with alpacas and geese.

And she'd loved it. Rather, she desperately wanted to love it. He'd realised she was willing it to be terrific and although those desiccated paddocks depressed him mightily he kept his opinion to himself. Every animal was sulky and territorial: miniature horses shied at llamas, deer butted emus out of the way, and stags and donkeys attempted to mount nanny-goats. Displaced seagulls bickered and a bad-tempered monkey viewed proceedings from atop a guano-encrusted dovecote. Addled sheepdogs circled everything, barking incessantly. Every shred of vegetation was gnawed and pecked down to the ground and each creature, like the proprietor and his monkey overseer, seemed ready to bare their teeth and snap.

Aggressive familiarity was the man's style. Once he had their admission money he shook his head at their obtuseness. 'You would've done much better to come next week, champ. We're getting zebras and an albino water buffalo.'

For an extra charge the farmer enticed his customers to 'help feed the animals'. Naturally Grace went for the idea. So they boarded an open-sided van already jammed with families and sped recklessly down the hillside into the paddocks. The man's feeding method was to ring a bell for the animals; when they charged the van he would scoop up a pail containing chaff, bran and some concentrated feed pellets and throw it over a particular customer sitting nearby. Naturally, in their busload Molloy was *it* – the human dinner platter.

Wedged in his seat for the next half-hour, he was pecked and buffeted by an assortment of famished ostriches, camels and llamas. What registered most vividly was how alive they all seemed up close, and how massive their heads were. From an inch away the brown and yellow eyes were greedy and avid, totally single-minded. But as the farmer sped into yet another field, frenziedly ringing his bell and tossing feed, it was his eyes that looked demented.

Even as the next wave of animals thundered out of the

landscape, and more shaggy and beaky heads slammed and slob-
bered against him, Molloy couldn't believe it was happening, that
he was the necessary scapegoat. Demeaning the customers and
frightening children was the man's commercial modus operandi.
'This'll make your hair grow, boss,' said the crazed zookeeper,
grinning humourlessly and chucking more chaff and bran over him.
'Lucky for you none of them are carnivores!'

'Unluckily for you I've got a good lawyer,' he managed to
gasp out.

'Keep your shirt on, champ!' the man shouted, unfazed, frowning at such lack of humour and flinging another pail of feed in his
face for good measure.

Speeding down into yet another paddock, he thought his
ordeal would never end. From nowhere a wildebeest and a pug-
nacious red kangaroo bounded up to dine off him. So, horns and
claws, too. A new troop of camels and llamas blew their faecal
breath into his face and swung their heavy moulting necks against
him. Rough tongues scraped his neck. Snot ran down his cheeks.
Grains and twigs filled his hair, ears and nose and trickled down
inside his clothes. His head throbbed; all his skin itched with
dust and prickles and the detritus of animals.

What could he do but take the indignity sitting down? There
was no room to stand up, much less physically react. Would he
have done so, anyway? Grace hated to be embarrassed even when
he shooshed noisy cinema patrons. And now they were confident

they wouldn't be sharing his plight, the other passengers were lapping up the performance. Their grateful laughter forced him to be a good sport. But what he ached to do was knock the zoo-keeper to the ground, punch his lights out, then sue him for everything he owned, every last ulcerated wombat.

'What a weirdo!' she offered later, as she brushed him down and combed the chaff and mucus from his hair. 'I felt very sorry for you.'

From where he'd sat, his recollection was quite different. As each snorting muzzle burst into the van, his daughter's face had expressed fascination, wonder and something else besides, something harsher and colder – curiosity to see what would happen next.

Why wouldn't her fascination with animals overcome sym-pathy for her father? She was still a child. But for a few minutes a childhood sensation of his own had floored and almost overwhelmed him: the ache of betrayal. It was the Home, the ship, Lion Island all over again. He felt deserted again, small and young – years younger than her, in fact. Alone.

The feeling hadn't lasted beyond that half-hour on that peculiar Tasmanian afternoon. Back in their rental car, the cranky menagerie behind them, squirming as errant grains and chaff still itched his back and slid down between his buttocks, he could begin to joke about it.

Maybe she'd seen a glimpse of her future? Anyway, it seemed

the ranger life suited her. How different was her present healthy
glow to her grim pallor at their last movie outing? *Day for Night* in
Centennial Park. Another evening under the stars. Except her life
had been in turmoil back then: Joel had just left her; the stalking
agony dominated everything. Whereas this evening they inhaled
serene, mango-scented air and ahead of him his daughter seemed
to shine as she walked.

He made a comment about the film. The lights coming on and
the sudden audience movement were scattering the bats back to
their trees. Screeching territorial fights began to break out. She
didn't answer him. Apparently she hadn't heard him above the hubbub. Abruptly she seemed to stumble. Her legs crumpled and she
fell back against him.

He managed to steer her into a deckchair. In seconds the
colour had drained from her.

'What's the matter?'

After a few moments she stood up shakily, gripped his wrist and
peered intently along the row behind them. Unsatisfied, she pulled
away from him and hurried ahead to the foyer. He looked around
bemusedly. A few stragglers were still coming up the aisle: three
Aboriginal women carrying sleeping babies, several glazed-eyed
children, an elderly Chinese couple, two dreadlocked teenagers
lighting up cigarettes.

He spotted her in the foyer, still searching urgently about
her, before she ran out into the street. He hurried after her. The

street was almost empty. Apart from the departing filmgoers there were few other pedestrians and no motor traffic. A drunken man lay on his back in an estate agent's doorway, muttering in a pool of liquid. From several blocks away came the roar of a waterfront pub. The bats squabbled on behind them.

He caught up with her on the kerb. She was still jerking her head from side to side, breathing deeply and staring into the darkness.

'Sitting behind us. I thought I saw him,' she said.

By next morning, as they breakfasted together in a café near the cinema, she had changed her mind. She'd been mistaken about the man in the row behind them. Returning to the scene and seeing it in daylight had put things in perspective.

Really, how could the Icelander know her whereabouts? By day, the idea of the man at the movies being her old stalker seemed ridiculous, even frivolous.

The heat clamped down on such fantasies. Even at nine a.m., with three ceiling fans whirring over the customers and venti-lated wooden shutters open to the street, the big old Fahrenheit thermometer over the counter already registered ninety-five degrees. A yellow sun-shaped sign over the counter said WHEN IT FIRST HITS 100 YOU GET ANOTHER DRINK FREE! The 100 had been crossed out and 105 written in. Nevertheless by noon each day the café was usually crowded with backpackers.

In the dry season, she reasoned, the coast thronged with tall, skinny, uncomfortable-looking young men who appeared out of kilter with their environment, even some with spiky ginger hair. At any moment angular backpacking redheads from foreign climes were flapping past in their sandals and oversized shorts. Even the thin young backpacker presently perusing the menu with his blond girlfriend at the next table somewhat resembled the Icelander.

The blond girl was digging into her belly-bag and checking their money. 'It's manageable if we forget the bacon and hash browns,' she declared. Her accent was crisply English middle-class.

'As long as I have eggs,' the boy insisted in similar sharp tones. 'I'm holding out for eggs.'

'Eggs plural,' the girl said tonelessly. Her face was also expressionless. She put her purse away and raised her face to the ceiling fan and closed her eyes. The air current rearranged a few strands of her fringe. The hairs stood upright and alert, waving like little antennas.

'God,' she said. 'Another scorcher.' More fine hairs began to slowly come loose in the redistributed air. Her eyes were still closed. She seemed to be addressing the ceiling. 'We could have had bacon and eggs galore if we'd left the club at midnight.'

The boy didn't reply immediately. He pushed his fingers

through his hair, then drummed them on the table. His eyes roamed about the café. 'Fuck bacon. It's bad for you anyway.'

The girl seemed to come to a decision. She studied the menu again. 'We could stick to water today,' she said. 'They provide free iced water. In this heat we've got to keep our water up.'

The boy's fingers drummed louder. 'I'm rather desperate for an espresso. If it's not too much to ask.'

Grace finished her coffee and turned to her father. 'It was just my imagination playing up.'

'Are you sure?' He hadn't told her about the threatening letter: 'To the Dark Lady of the Cinema'. If she had any doubts at all about the man in the cinema he was loath to leave her.

'Yes.'

Again he wondered whether he should mention the letter. He was still in a quandary about it. But once again he wondered what it would accomplish. It would only set back her recovery. Last night he'd watched her revert to the disturbed and panicky girl of the past. For a moment she'd been completely disabled by fear. The sight had shocked him. Why do that to her again?

The uncertainty must have showed on his face.

'Seriously! I'm absolutely positive. I was being stupid.'

So that was that. He allowed himself to return to the matter at hand, the reason he was in the Kimberley: to inspect and date – as much as he was able – the skeleton at the Salt End Inn. The Land Rover stood packed and ready at the kerb.

He gave her a hug. 'I'll see you on my way back,' he said. As he left he remembered something and called, 'By the way, who's Leonardo?'

There was no need to go into that now. She was trying not to think about it. She smiled and waved goodbye without answering.

How eager and energetic he looked, she thought. Much more capable than he did in the city: an outback professional. It was the ancient skeletons that did it. Any bones more than fifty thousand years old always cheered him up.

She'd been thirteen when she first saw her father's name in the paper. There was an advertisement in the *Sydney Morning Herald* for a talk he was giving. It came as a surprise how important it made him seem. She cut out the ad and asked him if she could attend the lecture.

The World Heritage Association is honoured to present an address
by Dr John Molloy of the University of New South Wales:

**Out of Africa? Salt End Woman and
the Evolution of Modernity**

Dr Molloy, the scientist who discovered the famous *Salt End Woman*, also popularly known as the *First Modern Woman* – the oldest evidence of modern humans, *Homo sapiens*, in the world –

will explain his revolutionary findings about Australia's past at
the Sydney Town Hall next Wednesday evening at 7.30 p.m.

Out of Africa? Or *Into Africa?* Dr Molloy's revolutionary
work is currently refocusing the whole global debate on human
history. Resolving this central issue of human development will
influence international genetic research and notions of variation
within and between species.

With special reference to his famous discovery, he will
discuss existing knowledge of modern man, fossils and archaeological records going back as far as 100 000 years.

She was the youngest person in the auditorium by about forty
years. Everyone else was middle-aged or old, many of the women
eschewing both makeup and hair colouring, and most of the men
both bearded and bald. The women favoured straight grey hair
loosely pinned or drawn back in a bun. The men could have been
a separate subspecies themselves, with their ruddy faces and huge
brainy craniums like Charles Darwin's. It was a winter's night,
undoubtedly their season of choice. The tweedy jackets and ano-
raks and thick ribbed woollens spoke of plain habits and outdoor
preferences – mountain rambles and extreme weather and robust
red wines.

There was a frisson of excitement as her father stepped up to
the lectern. These were his people. He looked like a taller, darker,
better-dressed, more dashing version of them. He looked like their
leader.

'Once upon a time,' he began, mock seriously, and his voice

seemed deeper and more resonant than usual, 'I found some human remains in an ancient dry lake in the Great Sandy Desert in northwest Western Australia. It was the skeleton of a young woman, lying on her left side in a bed of ash. She had obviously been cremated on a funeral pyre.'

He was *performing*. And to her surprise – how often had she heard this story? – the audience found this old skeleton talk fascinating and suspenseful. All around her those bulging foreheads were pressing forward, leaning towards his presence and his accomplishments. They were hanging on his every word. No doubt about it, they thought he was a star.

At the same time there was something else in the air – a hopeful expectation of controversy. The receptive rosy and whiskery faces all looked as if they were willing him to say something defiant and iconoclastic.

'In some sort of funeral ritual after her cremation,' he went on, 'the skull of this young woman – this girl – had been shattered into two hundred and twenty-one pieces. We don't know why she was burned and pulverised, perhaps so her ghost wouldn't get up and walk around. Maybe people believed she possessed frightening powers, that she was a witch.

'Anyway, starting with a little piece of skull that looked for all the world like a shard of broken china teacup, we began to reconstruct her. It took us a long time. We estimated that she was approximately twenty-one years of age when she died and quite delicate, a very graceful young woman indeed. She had the physique of a ballerina or an athlete.'

He explained how, to ensure accuracy, they had employed relatively new methods of testing the age of Salt End Woman's skeleton; three forms of dating technology – uranium-series, electron-spin resonance and quartz-crystal dating.

He paused for emphasis. 'To put it simply, we found that she was the world's oldest human cremation. We estimated that she was approximately sixty thousand years old. She was the oldest dated point in Australia's past and the most accurately dated prehistoric skeleton in the world. Hers was the oldest human DNA yet dis-covered. As you know, Salt End Woman is now regarded by science as the first modern woman. As you also know, improved dating technology now puts her age at eighty thousand years.'

He allowed this to sink into those ruddy craniums. 'Just as important,' he went on solemnly, 'was her gracile rather than robust physique, her lithe – as opposed to stocky – build. Here all our previous assumptions of early *Homo sapiens* flew out the window. Some Aboriginal people still living in the Great Sandy Desert are skeletally almost indistinguishable from her. They are her direct descendants.'

Of course she'd heard the story of her namesake countless times, but she'd never really taken it in. If anything, the whole gracile/Grace business was a bit embarrassing and off-putting.

Until this moment she hadn't even seriously considered

what her father did for a living. As far as she was concerned he just worked at the university: he was an academic, he taught anthropology to graduate students, he conducted research, he kept skulls and whole skeletons in a room in the backyard. And every now and then he vanished into the outback for four or five weeks on some dusty dig or other involving more old bones and fossils, during which time she went back to live with her mother in Balmain.

However, at the town-hall lecture she suddenly saw him as both adventurous and acclaimed. Moreover it wasn't a big step to imagine herself in his respected mould: as a distinguished archaeologist, anthropologist or palaeontologist. Some sort of *ologist* anyway; one with a scientific calling, a definite mission.

At thirteen, fame was an attractive proposition; even a studious Madame Curie-meets-Jane Goodall sort of fame would do. Why not? She loved the outdoors; she wouldn't even mind the clothes: khaki shorts were coming back and she'd just started to secretly shave her legs. She'd be quite happy to be the person who rewrote the history of life on earth.

So had begun her high-school flirtation with the sciences, then, five years later, the attempt at the science degree at university. It had taken her another year to realise her mistake. She found the subjects increasingly complex and boring. She'd expected to be concentrating on the natural sciences; it came as a shock to find that her studies also relied on mathematics: biometrics, the statistical analysis of biological observations and phenomena. It was clear she wasn't a scientist in the making. If it was slightly pathetic to want to follow in her father's footsteps it was incredibly, foolishly immature to imagine any possible celebrity could come from it.

Increasingly she skipped lectures to go to the movies. She had an excuse, at least to herself: she was a film reviewer. She'd begun reviewing films for student newspapers, then for various free street mags, and soon convinced herself that her pleasure was work. Even if there was no money yet, there was definitely physical effort, imagination and prior knowledge involved. Anyway, she told herself, she was more interested in new culture than old cultures – and what art form, indeed what human endeavour, dominated contemporary culture? It was no contest. In any case, her father was responsible for her love of films, too.

However, as he stood at the town-hall lectern that evening with his slide projector and his maps of imaginary land masses and his confident assertions about mankind's origins, he'd seemed to his adolescent daughter to straddle the earth – its distant past as well as its present – more heroically than any film star.

He showed a map of how he said Australia had looked until ten thousand years ago: New Guinea and Tasmania were lumpy protuberances joined to the mainland, there was no Torres Strait and the South China Sea was only a trickle in the northwest.

Then her father, suddenly this articulate and charismatic stranger, this *actor*, painted a vivid word-picture of the continent those first humans had ventured to eighty thousand years ago. For a start, he said, it was one-and-a-half degrees cooler than today's average temperature. The sea was one hundred and thirty metres lower. Lake Salt End itself was about thirty kilometres long.

He described life around the living, water-filled lake as if he'd pitched a tent there only the week before. He was talking mega-fauna. She loved that stuff! This was what excited her: *Diprotodons*, three-tonne wombats as big as rhinos; *Genyornis*, a giant flightless bird with a sharp beak and legs with a lethal kick; the sabre-tooth marsupial lion, *Thylacoleo*; the carnivorous goanna, *Megalania*, seven metres long; and *Procoptodon*, a three-metre tall kangaroo with testicles like footballs. Her father's arms created tall red gums, open forest, shoulder-high reeds. In this fecundity of lake and swamp and plain there swam and grazed and slithered huge cod and tusked possums, ten-metre pythons, saltwater and freshwater crocodiles – of course – and also frightening land crocodiles that didn't need water and ranged over all the country.

'The first Australians weren't short of a meal,' he said. 'There was plenty of meat on the hoof.'

He declared that these first people had probably island-hopped from China. 'A few pieces of bamboo strung together into a flimsy raft were the beginning of the occupation of Australia.' Then his voice deepened further. 'I am convinced that the anatomical roots of the earliest people were in Asia and nowhere else.'

Suddenly that little piece of teacup in his palm assumed

huge proportions. It had changed the accepted estimation – then forty thousand years ago – of the arrival of the first people on the continent. Not only did it appear that they were graciles, not robusts, that shard of skull had wider repercussions. It tied in neatly with the discovery of Java Man; Salt End Woman's skull had great similarities to his. It threw the whole Out of Africa theory into question.

There it was – Salt End Woman went against scientific gospel. Her existence supported a regional theory of human dispersement. His handful of cranium bits contested the accepted theory of human evolution.

Throughout the auditorium, people were murmuring and nodding agreement. This was what they had come to hear. Forget Out of Africa.

'Australia was always a recipient of many different people,' he asserted. 'My competitors bandy the number sixty thousand about. Believe me, people have been travelling from Asia to the island continent for much more than sixty thousand years.' His voice rose provocatively. 'Indeed, I see no evidence for Out of Africa. Instead I see plenty of evidence for *Into* Africa.'

The audience was rapt. Amid the excited murmuring, a man in the row ahead, bulky and bearded and wearing green braces patterned with lyrebirds, farted loudly and unselfconsciously. 'Hear, hear,' he said.

Her father gripped the lectern with both hands. He was

enunciating very crisply and his stare took in every row of the auditorium. 'Our species and our modernity are universal. You could just as easily say that Man is descended from Australians.'

Then he took a couple of steps back, breathed deeply and ran his fingers through his hair as if to say to his scientific opponents, There, cop that!

He understood the power of the dramatic pause. He took down his map of lumpy, conjoined Australia and rolled it up tightly. He held it like a club, a spear. He waved it about. Seconds passed but there was silence throughout the auditorium. When he returned to the lectern he spoke quietly.

'You must understand that we are the one global species. Our unity exists despite our extraordinary complexity. We underestimate our complexity. Evolution is not simple – it's an intricate and tangled process and the forces behind it are greater and more irresistible than we realise.'

This was the voice of reason. His lectern could have been a pulpit; his congregation was silent and totally absorbed.

'Ladies and gentlemen, I'm an anthropologist. My job is to observe gene flow. You could say I'm fascinated by the big picture.' And he spread his arms theatrically and then chopped the air into a large rectangle. This canvas embraced a world beyond nationalities – 'a world,' he stressed, 'where evolution is happening everywhere and all the time, where any man and woman can produce children with each other.'

It had always been so, he said. 'We fling genes back and forth in order to keep the species together. Put it this way, the Mongol and Viking invasions, the Norman Conquest, the Roman and British Empires are all good historical cases of gene flow.'

She'd never looked at history like that before.

'There are plenty of other effective but less palatable examples in our time. It might offend delicate sensibilities to say so, but invaders always exchange genes. It's a given. I don't mean to sound harsh or insensitive, but morality doesn't come into it. It's necessary in order to keep the human species alive.'

At this there was a frisson, a thrill in the air, a rustling and throat-clearing from the front of the audience.

'Speaking of the Mongol invasion,' her father went on chattily, 'you know the most successful alpha male in human history was undoubtedly Genghis Khan. A much more likely candidate than poor old fairy-story Adam.' He was leaning on the lectern now as if it were a mantelpiece. He could have been relaxing after a dinner party.

'Seriously, Genghis Khan personally inseminated so many women in forty years of raping and pillaging across Asia that today at least seventeen million male descendants around the world carry his Y chromosome. Thanks to migration, Oxford geneticists are finding Genghis's Y chromosome in English greengrocers and dentists and car mechanics. Even Britain's royals are supposed to carry it. I would expect several people in this room to be descendants of the rapacious Genghis Khan.'

Laughter. A few hands went up. This was news to her – history was sex?

'All this is very interesting to anthropologists of course. You could say we're in the business of observing bonking.' A small smile telegraphed the final joke to come. 'Bonking, of course, is the technical term for gene flow.'

More laughter. The bearded and scrubbed faces glowed with understanding. The audience's good-humoured appreciation of the big picture – *bonking!* – seemed to be as great as her embarrassment.

It only remained for audience questions to round off his talk. He batted back friendly queries on Into Africa and Peking Man and Pleistocene cave art and the limitations of fossil carbon-dating. Then a woman stood up in the front row. 'Penny Kidson,' she said. 'I'm interested in your flippant comments on Genghis Khan and invaders and gene flow and so forth.'

'Yes?' he said. His facial muscles tightened.

'You say you're in the business of observing *bonking*, as you call it. Are you just as jocular about that contentious new study out of New York University that says women are more than twice as likely to fall pregnant after being raped than after having consensual intercourse?'

The woman looked familiar to Grace. Wasn't she a friend of her mother's? She recalled her holding forth at some Sunday lunch in Balmain, her eyes darting shrewdly around the table, airing inside knowledge and putting people in the picture. The other women had hung on her words, laughed in disbelief and kept her glass filled. They were loath to leave the room in case they missed a scandalous nugget.

Her father obviously recognised her too. A journalist. A columnist, what's more. His expression seemed bewildered and, for him, oddly naïve: *What's she doing here?* The audience's mood stiffened as well.

'Not my area,' he said firmly. 'And I'd need to be more convinced of those findings. I think the sample in that study was rather small – only two or three hundred women, I believe.'

Penny Kidson pushed on. 'Really? Don't anthropologists make definite pronouncements on the basis of the smallest possible sample – like one skeleton in the case of Salt End Woman, a few pieces of burnt bone?'

His laugh was more a snort. Grace recognised it as bewildered anger. *What's going on here?* He was gripping the lectern with both hands. 'Alas, folks from the Pleistocene period are rather thin on the ground these days. Believe me, I wish there were more early *Homo sapiens* around to add to the sample.'

Supportive laughter from the audience. They were still onside but some of them were frowning and others looked bemused.

'The New York study argued that men rape women for an evolutionary purpose. Isn't that what you're saying? That you're with them and Genghis Khan on this? Didn't you just say that rape was a great and irresistible force, a jolly good thing for the human race, merely part of the grand scheme?'

The light on the dais was suddenly harsh; it was draining the colour from his face. At the same time he looked as if he were coming up for air from several fathoms.

'I think everyone knows that my territory is the past,' he insisted. He gave the unhappy, snorting laugh again. 'The sweep of human history. God knows, it's much safer.'

This sounded pretty lame, even to his daughter. 'I'm a scientist, not a sociologist,' he went on. There was some murmuring at this. Then he drew himself up straight and endeavoured to claw back his thesis, the town hall, the whole evening.

'Listen,' he said, 'it's nature that eschews morality, not me. I would never absolve rapists or the crimes they commit – in the thirteenth century or nowadays. Or place any blame on the unfortunate victims, for that matter. I don't conduct random telephone interviews on contemporary behaviour. I and my colleagues painstakingly examine the physical evidence that human beings have left behind over the ages – without making simplistic conclusions based on contemporary laws and fashions in morality. We're the ultimate realists – we deal with what actually happened.'

'But you *do* reach firm conclusions, don't you? Like you did with the so-called First Modern Woman that you named and claimed?'

'What does Salt End Woman have to do with it?' He was shaking his head, either in disbelief or to cast around for support.

'Dr Molloy, do you say that rape has an evolutionary advantage – yes or no?'

'I say that I might wish it were otherwise but that the complex history of the human race says yes.'

'Thank you.' She exhaled deeply as she sat down. Grace had never seen anyone look so content.

He didn't leave it there, however; he couldn't stop himself. His eyes were glinting as he now addressed a question to Penny Kidson. 'Incidentally, have you had the DNA test yourself? You might easily be a Genghis Khan descendant, too.'

The article was not favourable.

EIGHT

BONE DRY

It looked as though someone had sprinkled red ochre across the body as part of the burial rites. The first thing he did was take a sample of the clay and sand at the edge of the grave. That was all he dared remove – a pinch of earth in a jar.

So now there was a Salt End Man as well. He was careful not to disturb the skeleton. Byron was watching him closely. Molloy realised he had been too optimistic. The era of Salt End Woman's discovery, when he would have patiently, even tenderly, excavated these bones, packed them up in a padded crate and transported them back to the university for examination and analysis, had gone. Aboriginal people now owned their past.

He would have to merely observe, take rough measurements and make estimates. Well, it wasn't a recent death, or a white man, or a modern murder victim. It was definitely old. He could state with some confidence the skeleton's race, gender and approximate age at death. It wasn't possible to say how long it had lain there.

The skeleton was Aboriginal, male and it appeared ancient. But how old? There were no clay deposits just here, so the mourners might have brought the ochre-coloured clay to the gravesite for the funeral ceremony. The clay was possibly from one of the lake's two arid phases – either twenty thousand or more than sixty thousand years ago. Of course he wished it to be from the earlier phase.

He noticed more clay embedded in the area between the skeleton's lower ribs and pelvis. He remembered that the Aborigines used to eat ant-bed clay for stomach ache. Some of the older people nowadays still ate handfuls of termite beds for 'sick guts'.

The skeleton reclined on its right side, knees half bent in a sleeping position, in a layer of calcium carbonate: this was what had preserved it. The man had been aged about fifty. Height approximately five-eight. Arthritis in the left, uppermost elbow – he couldn't see the other side without disturbing it. The skeleton was intact – no smashed skull this time. No cause of death apparent. No obvious fracture wounds. He presumed natural causes, maybe a stomach problem. Fifty. The coincidence of his own age again. Fifty would have been old back then. Things had changed, he thought wryly. Now fifty was the new forty. Fifty was barely middle-aged. At least this dry heat meant his own arthritis wasn't bothering him at the moment.

Without question it was a male. The height, the head diameter, the jaw were all indicators. Also the fact that his hands, like a golfer's, gripped something between his upper thighs. It was like discovering the final resting place of a weekend hacker, clasping his phantom sand wedge and buried right there in the same bunker that did him in.

The burial site was on the back slope of the lake's southern-most dune, on the opposite side of the lake to where he'd found Salt End Woman. There was another difference in the grave sites – she'd been lying in sand and ash; there had been no celebratory red ochre sprinkled over her.

Was Salt End Man the same age? Older? Only dating technology could tell. Without the bones he'd have to see what the sand and clay revealed. Like Salt End Woman, the man was of gracile physique, a relatively fine-boned individual, built for distance running rather than weightlifting. This was another early-modern human. It was just that it would be more difficult for him to prove it.

He knew Byron was of two minds about these relics, torn between pride at the discovery of his old people, the first *Homo sapiens* ('We're famous, bro!') and the belief that science shouldn't pry, that respect should be accorded the dead. His extra face made him seem even more ambivalent than usual. But of course Byron was curious, too. And superstitious.

He'd told Byron before, 'I can't initiate any excavations unless you authorise them. But this place has strong winds – after every big cyclone you'll have to rebury the old people. You know I'd conduct the excavation with dignity. I can ensure privacy, even organise a marquee around it, and chairs for the elders to watch the whole process. You'd see it all happen. You'd learn more about the people, more about yourselves. Byron, we're talking about Day One of our species.'

Byron scratched his new face. 'We've got the Dreamtime for that.'

'*Ngarrangkarni*, creation time. We're talking about the same thing, really.'

'Maybe.'

An ant crawled down the exposed femur to the knee. The bone was stained with ferric oxide. That pink thighbone, that skull, this prehistoric man risen to the surface, could help solve a lot of things. Molloy brought the matter up again, trying unsuccessfully to keep the frustration out of his voice.

Still Byron smiled and shrugged. 'You shouldn't be too curious about that stuff.'

'Look at it this way, this man is lying for eternity under a white man's crummy motel. This place doesn't even rate one star. No swimming pool, no TV reception; you're lucky to get a hot meal. You know Evan Strachan – he's not happy even serving you a beer. He was a cop. The old man can't stay buried here. Bad vibes, Byron.'

The sun blazed down on the skeleton. Molloy considered the expression 'bone dry'. Byron wouldn't look at it. His real face gazed off into the heat mirages across the airstrip; the new face scowled off into the dusty scrub. Crows made their blasé gagging noise.

Byron shrugged again. 'I'll give it some thought.'

They don't like touching the bones, Molloy said to himself. Even the site curators, the elders, those responsible for their upkeep. They glance briefly out of the corners of their eyes and they walk quickly past.

Molloy replaced the tarpaulin over the skeleton and climbed carefully out of the collapsed dune. His excitement had gone flat. Nothing would change. He and Salt End Woman were on their own. The workmen's building debris and Pepsi cans and Marlboro packets still littered the ground around the burial site. He brushed himself down, took off his boots and shook out the sand, dispersing atoms of ancient man into the detritus of the twenty-first century.

Bushflies crawled sluggishly for his eyes. The temperature was rising, the dust pushing skywards. This place was subject to the heat of the furnace one day, cyclonic rain and wind the next. He put on his boots again, the sun hitting the back of his neck. At least he could go and find some shade. As he set off towards the bar he felt a burst of fellow feeling for the poor bastard in the dune – lying there in the sand for millennia anxiously clutching his cock.

By day, he's still more than confident in his assertions: one hundred thousand is the figure he's sticking with. He tells himself he doesn't need the backup of Salt End Man.

The *Nature* article had received a decidedly territorial reaction. His claim that Salt End Woman was not sixty, not eighty, but one hundred thousand years old had met with enthusiastic support in Asia and anxious disdain in Britain and France. Germany was undecided and America was divided: the west coast went his way, the east stayed with sixty thousand years maximum and Out of Africa. Never in his experience had the boundaries seemed so definite, or a scientific wrangle been so overwhelmed by the furious grinding of axes.

But his European opponents stuck to old ground. None of them convincingly destroyed his case – that his new electron-spin-resonance and uranium-series-dating results suggested that the remains of Salt End Woman were between ninety thousand and 110 000 years old, and the sediment in which she was buried was between one hundred thousand and 120 000 years.

As he said in the *Nature* article, 'This revised dating effectively doubles the long-supposed date of the first occupation of Australia and indicates that, like the populating of the American continent, Australia was populated in multiple waves.'

At home in Australia his revised estimate of first human occupation had been respectfully if unexcitedly received. Perhaps he'd been foolish to expect the same applause that the original discovery had brought him. But at least he'd made a crucial judgement. He'd rewritten the history of human occupation yet again. How many of his contemporaries had managed that?

At night, however, he knows he's not infallible. After midnight his whole life is guesswork and full of gaps. He has a recurring nightmare that he's wrong about Salt End Woman. In the dream he's the laughing stock of science. Sometimes her skeleton turns out to be only a few weeks dead. Soft tissue still clings to it; it reeks – how come he missed that? *Nature* reveals it's a fake made of plastic. *The Journal of Human Evolution* goes further. It says it's the bones from a barbecue – lamb cutlets and pork spareribs and T-bone steaks.

In the dreams he's found out at last. He's really an uneducated orphan. A naïve farm boy. He's another Scheuchzer. This was the Swiss palaeontologist Johann Jakob Scheuchzer, so appreciated by generations of students, including him; the scientist who assured his textbook immortality by producing a skeleton of *Homo diluvii testis* – the remains, he announced triumphantly, of a member of the accursed 'original human race'. Scheuchzer claimed the skeleton was tangible proof of Noah's Flood – 'an ill-fated man, a witness to the Flood who had seen God'. Scheuchzer was right about the watery angle at least. The skeleton was a big aquatic salamander.

The dream has many variations but ridicule is the constant. In the worst, Salt End Woman is really a young woman dressed in a Halloween skeleton suit. She sits up defiantly in the sand and ashes and says, *Boo!* When she removes the skull mask he sees it's Kate.

The Kate of the dream is always in her early twenties. Sexy as the young Natalie Wood. Her capacity to surprise him is undiminished.

FIVE-JETTY NIGHT

The process of change is subtle at first. It takes him a few weeks to notice she's switched her everyday hello and goodbye kisses from the lips to the cheek – in every case. And speeded them up as well. At the same time his own kisses are gently evaded by her infinitesimally averted head.

Before long her new hasty kisses move north from his cheek to his forehead, then to the top of his head. It's only a small step to their being replaced by a pat on the head or shoulder – an amiable enough pat at first (*Good boy!*) but gradually more cursory and impatient. The vaguely affirmative gesture you might make if greeted by a friendly dog when you're in a rush.

And she's suddenly always in a hurry, so busy that eventually most daytime body contact stops altogether. Bolder now, she walks into a room complaining that it smells 'too male' and opens the windows. (What does 'too male' smell like? he wonders. Wet dog? Old boots? Jockstraps?) It's disconcerting enough that his hormonal unpleasantness can spoil a room, but one day he uses a favourite teacup of hers by mistake and he's really thrown. He sees her tip his tea into another cup and rinse out her cup with hot water.

He hadn't dreamed that the imperatives of territory extended – or, rather, narrowed down – to a particular teacup. Or that 'personal space', that buzz phrase of the time, covered so much ardour and vehemence. Where was the blithe, toothbrush-sharing girl of the old weekend sex marathons? When did she become so mad for femininity?

He'd thought territorial arguments were just another idiosyncrasy of the island. Islands were different; their deliberate boundaries were part of their charm. Moving to Lion Island had seemed a great idea for a young couple with a sudden baby and no income beyond his research scholarship. The ocean beach to the east, a spine of sandstone in the north, the river flats to the south and west – all patchworked by gum trees, palms and mangroves – what could be a healthier settling place for a young hasty marriage? And if he was yet to discover the special offshore viewing angle and light in which the island resembled a lion more than, say, a truck or a chicken, he imagined, romantically, that the moods of the tides and the elements would bring both stimulation and tranquillity to their lives. Passion plus serenity – it certainly looked like fun.

Kate's father Reece Prowse owned the real-estate business on the mainland at Rocky Point. He rented cottages on the island to holidaymakers and to permanent residents seeking solitude and cheap housing. What a godsend it was when he offered them the tin-roofed, fibro-cement cottage – a shack, really – facing the wide river mouth and the open Pacific beyond. Mariposa, it was called, named after one of the American tourist ships that plied the South Pacific route. Six times a year, if you stood at the cottage's front door with binoculars, you might spot the liner *Mariposa* or its sister ship *Monterey* approaching or departing Sydney Harbour with wealthy tourists. The cottage named Mariposa was a long way from the city and the university but it was more habitable than a cramped student flat, and it was free.

Reece Prowse was apt to drop into Mariposa at any time with a cooler of fish or prawns, perhaps a few dozen of the local rock oysters. Spotting him crossing the estuary in one of his amphibious cars, the distinctive maroon or emerald bonnet rounding the oyster beds, the sun glinting off the headlights and windscreen, his new son-in-law struggled just as hard with the notion of family as he did with the sight of a sedan making a bow wave. Dependent himself on the *Island Lady*, the Rocky Point–Lion Island ferry, and then the one-hour train trip into Sydney, he found Reece as ubiquitous as he was generous. Free accommodation had strings attached; Reece was often around.

Kate and he weren't the only recipients of Reece's seafood largesse. Divorced or separated women, single mothers, were drawn to Lion Island by the cheaper rents and the physical and emotional break with the past that an island provided. During school hours the amiable landlord found it necessary to regularly visit a selection of these tenants. His son-in-law suspected it wasn't just to collect the rent.

If it was a fine afternoon when Reece's old Trippel *Alligator* or his new Skoda *Amphibie* was spotted jauntily parked (or, at high tide, moored) outside Gina Cleaver's or Ariel Glaskin's or Sharon Burgess's cottage, any fisherman, oyster farmer or bait gatherer in the vicinity immediately spread the word. 'Reece is here!'

Weather-beaten men – descendants of grog smugglers, wreck pillagers and sandalwood loggers – would gather under the big Moreton Bay fig tree by the main jetty, rolling cigarettes and growling cryptic jibes at each other. Fishing rods, bait buckets, beachworm pliers and nipper pumps would be put aside and a procession of customers would start shuffling to and from the bottle shop. When Reece eventually chugged up in his aquacar – his appearance coinciding precisely with the arrival of the ferry carrying the island children home from school at Rocky Point – laughter would ring out under the fig tree and within minutes a beachside beer party was under way. It could last well into the night. *The old Reece,* they laughed. *Prowsie!*

There seemed an unspoken general agreement that this was Reece Prowse's territory. That surprised his son-in-law, given the insularity of the place and the fact that Reece lived and worked at

Rocky Point, which the islanders referred to as 'Australia' or 'the mainland', as if their island in the river mouth were an independent atoll a thousand miles offshore.

On this protrusion of sand, mud and Hawkesbury sandstone Reece had leeway and status. His family had owned property on the island for five generations, and had avoided excisemen for the first three of them. Reece had grown up here and had known these fellows since before primary school. He was one of them.

Even the Prowses' amphibious cars had been a tradition since the 1920s. All the Prowse Real Estate rental cottages had two or three framed photographs on their walls of Reece's father Mervyn at the wheel of his air-propelled 1927 Arnol *Hydroglisseur*, or his 1933 paddle-wheeled *Comet*. Merv had maintained an aquacar fleet of varying performance and floatability for forty years, including (the framed prints insisted) the actual 1934 Baulig *Land-Wasser-Auto*, 'the pride of pre-war Germany', which had successfully crossed the English Channel in 1935. Compared to the Channel, a mile of Hawkesbury River estuary, even during a fast winter tide, was a cinch for Merv Prowse's Baulig.

It was ridiculous how the bonhomie that swelled around his father-in-law made Molloy curious and envious. It soon became clear from the reluctant, tight-lipped service from Dawn and Frank Thirsk at the general store and the sneering response, if any, from fellow *Island Lady* passengers to his cheery 'Good mornings' that this good fellowship didn't automatically extend to him.

A son-in-law didn't carry any weight.

The deckhand on the *Island Lady*, a statuesque, blond-ponytailed girl, seemed to particularly resent him; once or twice he had sensed her disapproval, turned suddenly and caught her looking at him; her scowls could have pierced his shoulderblades. He found this terribly unfair when he admired everything about her – her proud Nordic looks, her golden sporty aura, and especially the nonchalant way she tossed the rope – once almost ten metres – so that it looped around the wharf bollard, then secured it to the boat with a nifty figure-of-eight hitch. Her total, one hundred percent unavailability (she, mysteriously, detested the sight of him; he was married and in love with his wife) made her provocatively attractive.

She was insolently beautiful as she strode the deck collecting fares, ignoring crass male glances and leaping spring-heeled between decks. He respected the coordination she showed in all tides, weathers and waves. At low tide she had to throw the rope upwards from the deck; at high tide, downwards. The arrogant way she only half looked at the bollard at the crucial moment reminded him of a matador seemingly ignoring the bull. She'd literally learned the ropes; hours of practice must have gone into that apparently casual toss. Plenty of male deckhands occasionally missed the bollard with the rope, and the ferry had to keep impatiently toing and froing, the water roiling around the jetty pylons, until the embarrassed fellow got it right. But it was second nature to the Nordic girl. He'd never seen her miss.

His secret admiration made her apparently instinctive dislike of him especially hurtful. What had he done? Did she and the
others resent him personally, or were these sneers and glowers
just examples of the great divide that Kate had joked about back in
their Sydney days – a quaint piece of small-community behaviour
that he'd laughed about at the time and immediately forgotten?

The usual scowl from the golden ferryhand on the journey
home, yet more eye-rolling and sighing from Dawn Thirsk when
he pointed out the weevils in a just-purchased packet of rice (in
their financial position rice was a staple diet; why did he suddenly
feel like some prissy urban gastronome?), and, exasperated, he
asked Kate to explain things once and for all. Okay, what did they
all have against him?

She was defensive. 'How would I know? Maybe the beard.
The left-wing student look. And the leather bag of books. I suppose you read books on the ferry?'

Four hours spent travelling every day: of course he read on
the ferry. He took a deep breath. He was quite proud of the beard.
It had come together surprisingly well. At last it made him look
old enough to be a father.

'What sort of anthropologist would I be without a beard?'

She shook her head annoyingly. 'Beard plus book-reading
in public equals university wanker.'

He snorted with outrage. 'I've out-suffered all those lazy,

beachcombing bastards.' He took several more deep breaths. 'Okay, I'll start reading *TV Week* on the ferry. In the meantime you can tell them I'm a poor orphan boy from the bush who ate weevils in his porridge every morning of his childhood and I'll be buggered if I'm going to eat them now.'

'Don't take it personally. It's the locals-versus-touros thing.'

Locals were those whose families went back at least three generations on the island; touros were tourists – anyone with the misfortune to come from somewhere else.

'What about real tourists, the holidaymakers? Where do they fit in?'

She shrugged. 'They just come and go on the ferry, rent their cottages, buy their beer and bait and icecreams, hire their boats, spend money. They're easily ignored.'

'But they'd be on the touros' side?'

She looked at him and slowly shook her head. 'The touros don't have a side. There's only one side.'

This was hilarious, a real case for study. It was thesis material. But tough luck, he was living here now and they'd have to get used to him. 'I've invaded their territory and bred with you,' he said, patting her bottom. 'Widened the gene pool. *Homo sapiens* has come to *Homo erectus* whether they like it or not.'

She ducked from his hand. 'Is that so? Marrying-in isn't enough to bridge the gap.' She appeared to rather relish the fact. Marrying-in was seen as a typical underhand touro trick to ingratiate oneself with the true and unique Lion Islanders.

'Now you tell me,' he said. 'By the way, what are you?'

'I'm a local, but under sufferance for marrying a touro.'

'So,' he said. 'Let's take this to its logical conclusion.' Far from acting responsibly by marrying his pregnant girlfriend, he'd pulled off the sneakiest possible scheme: getting a Prowse pregnant so he could marry into the famous beachshack-rental family. And, to make matters worse, without a big, celebratory island booze-up. A good example of the depths to which a touro would sink. 'There's just one question – why would I want to suck up to a mob of beach-wormers?'

'See, that's the typical superior touro attitude that sticks in our gullets.' She might have been joking. She certainly hadn't talked like this back in town, back at university, back at her flat, in her bedroom with the heroic-worker posters and the mirror ball. But she looked far too smug for his liking.

'Well, I'm proud to be a touro,' he said. He might have been joking, too; it sounded inane enough. At the last minute he'd stopped himself from adding, 'And not an in-bred islander.'

She tapped her temple as if demonstrating age-old island wisdom, or mocking someone doing so. 'We can read you people like a book,' she said.

This was during their early days on the island.

At the outset the neighbours certainly stressed his otherness. On their first night the three teenage boys next door in Monterey – notorious throughout the island as the Cottage Crew, breakers and enterers of holiday cottages – marked their boundary with prawn shells, dog shit, cigarette butts and beer cans over the fence. He collected the garbage and threw it back; they swore indignantly ('The fucking cheek of the cunt!') but held their fire. Then, having observed for a month his early-morning dash out the door and down the cottage stairs to the ferry wharf, the brothers one night strung nylon fishing line across the top step.

When he tripped and somersaulted down the stairs next morning he was fortunately only shaken and bruised. But he was forced to change his torn clothes and so missed the ferry and his bus connection to town. He was angrily ripping the fishing line from the verandah railings *(What if it had been Kate who tripped while carrying baby Grace!)* when he noticed his racing bike missing from the verandah. Next door in Monterey there was no one home; at least no one answered his knocking.

All day he simmered and fumed. That evening, disembarking from the ferry after a useless, truncated day at the university and some murderous looks from the Nordic ferrywoman, he spotted the eldest Cottage Crew member casually riding the racing bike outside the store. The youngest brother was perched on the handlebars. They were circling a couple of girls, round and round in the sunset, cackling and flirting.

Striding towards them, the blood pounding in his ears, he wondered whether he had a late concussion from the fall. His peripheral vision was gone; as if he were looking through a telescope, he saw only the boys, his bike and the black mist swirling around them. He didn't mention the tripwire; he wouldn't give them the satisfaction. Anyway, it was all he could do to talk. 'I'll have my bike back.' His strangulated voice certainly sounded like a stranger's.

The younger boy slid guiltily off the handlebars. But there were girls present and the older boy responded accordingly. 'You mean *my* fucking bike,' he croaked. His eyes and mouth were too sly for his years and he thrust out a foxy chin sprinkled with whiskers.

He could have choked the boy on the spot. 'So you're a liar as well as a thief,' he said and grabbed the handlebars. Jetty fishermen turned to look at the tug o'war. He tugged harder and the boy's legs became tangled in the bike and he fell to the ground. The curses and clatter, plus the obscenities from the other boy and one of the girls, brought a small crowd of curious onlookers, including their red-haired mother.

As the woman dashed her cigarette to the ground in a whirl of instant fury, an odd sense of déjà vu swept over him. Their clash seemed preordained; nothing about it surprised him, not even the realisation that her outrage went much deeper and further back than the confrontation over the bike. It was ageless.

She'd have him in court, she shrieked, for assaulting her son. 'Who do you think you are?'

'The owner of this bike, for one thing.'

'Oh, yeah? Who do you think you are?' she repeated.

One of the fishermen grunted, 'You tell him, Yvonne!' She did. It flooded out. She knew the script by heart. She declared that everyone knew her son (the bicycle thief!) was a decent, hard-working kid who was a great help to her in her single state and that she'd given him this bike for Christmas. Cost a pretty penny. You could ask anyone.

'Anyone', in the form of Frank Thirsk, exited his store holding a cricket bat. 'He bothering you, Yvonne?' he muttered, advancing chivalrously towards the fracas. Emboldened by his support team, the boy had assumed a sort of karate stance and was dancing about, chopping the air with his hands and screeching, 'C'mon, poofter, I'll take ya!'

The age difference was, what, about five years? But how could he hit or even grapple with a skinny boy? An ugly dream was turning uglier by the second. He'd had this one too many times before, and three orphanages had accustomed him to its theme: pride, saving face, means sticking to an outrageous lie. It doesn't even matter that everyone knows it's a lie.

Part of him just wanted to stretch out on the road and wake up in his bed alongside his girls, the waves breaking outside and the palm fruit rolling on the roof. But a brainwave pierced the fog and he said to the thief, 'If it's your bike, your name must be John Molloy.' He up-ended the bike and pointed out his name stencilled under the frame.

There was surprisingly little satisfaction in this victory. Reluctantly the crowd broke up then, having guessed the truth all along. Frank Thirsk, too, gloomily accepted the point and moped self-consciously back to the store. Only the mother and boys didn't attempt to move. The mother's head was an angry blood-knot in the middle of the street. They hunched together, swearing and spluttering, lighting consolatory cigarettes all round and thrusting middle fingers at the world.

He wheeled the bike home, unwilling to ride it. The neighbours' ego-salving curses followed him inside Mariposa and continued to ring out through the night, interspersed with shouted threats and snatches of shrill laughter and sudden slaps and dog yelps and heated arguments among themselves, all punctuated by the staccato clatter of missiles on the roof.

Even after Reece had a word to them and the Cottage Crew gave less trouble thereafter – their tenancy of Monterey depended on it – the red-haired mother's shriek in the street still rang in his head.

Who do you think you are?

He'd almost laughed. *Don't you think I'd like to know that?*

At night her kisses are much the same as they've always been – at night. It's the daytime kisses of ordinary affection that are no more. At night she still kills and licks her victim over carefully, like a poet's tiger.

But before bed they have the habit of walking, ostensibly for exercise but also to chat and get things off their chests. The walks began as her idea. He's usually keen to talk but increasingly she's less so. They set off from Mariposa, a little self-consciously these days, one of them pushing the stroller containing a sleeping Grace, and when they come to a jetty they walk to the end of it. The stroller's wheels rumble over the planks but the two-year-old enjoys the motion and never wakes.

At the end of the jetty there's a bright boating light crackling with moths and beetles. Usually they pause here and peer avidly down into the depths. In the artificial light they spot blue swimmer crabs, ribbonfish and toadfish, occasionally a stingray, riding the tide. Silently they absorb the green aquarium view, the lights across the river mouth, the rock- and gorse-covered hill behind, the silhouettes of palms, then, depending on the jetty, they take deep breaths of either ocean or estuarine air, turn back to shore and resume their walk.

An average nightly walk might include two kilometres of waterfront and three jetties before they turn for home. A more serious walk in which the nature of their relationship is under stricter review could take in four jetties. In all only five jetties, including the main ferry wharf, fringe the island.

Their last evening walk is a rare five-jetty night. These are the most intense, sometimes argumentative and emotionally harrowing of the walks – a complete circuit of the island. Between jetties number five and one is the darkest stretch of coast. Outside the range of the jetty lights the water shines like sump oil; the incoming black tide is swift and only the sky is reflected in its sheen. Every few seconds a mullet leaps from the slick and plops back – as if something big is out there.

The stroller rumbles over the jetty planks as they speed up their steps. In turns they are animated, angry, tearful, confused and, finally, silent. The night is humid but they still shiver. They reach coastal landmarks and can't remember how they got there. They seem to have been talking for hours; they seem to have just set off. Grace's head lolls and bobs but she sleeps on. The shoreline turns with them as they walk, and anxiously hugs their heels.

In weekend attire Reece seems to have a lower centre of gravity. Of broad girth, with low knees, wide feet and calves like serious fists, he wears his shorts well below his stomach, exposing buttock cleavage that lengthens alarmingly as he dips and bends down to the sand.

However, his manner is solemn, almost awe-inspiring. He's frowning with concentration at his task, and the combination of effort, sun and constant bending gives his face a swollen, hectic glow. Veins and eyes look ready to pop out. He appears to be on the verge of some sort of seizure. When he straightens up he holds between thumb and forefinger a stringy red creature about two feet long and whiskery-legged, like an elongated centipede.

'There we are,' he says, and drops it in a bucket. Reece is beachworming. Beachworms are the best bait for bream, whiting and flathead, in his opinion, and even mulloway find the big greenhead beachworms a real treat.

Reece and he are standing ankle-deep at low tide on the shore of the surf beach facing the Pacific. The son-in-law is wondering why he's there, why he's been summoned by this chunky old fish-lover carrying an old stocking filled with rank meat and oily pilchards in one hand and a pair of worming pliers in the other.

'I need to have a word with you,' Reece said. However, he hasn't had it yet. And he isn't looking at him when he speaks now, only at the lumpy stocking he's wafting gently back and forth in the receding flow.

'Sure.' *What's this about?*

'I could put it this way – I need the cottage back. The market's going gangbusters. I'll probably sell it – can't afford not to. Kate's moving in with us for a bit. You'll probably want to move back to town.'

Move? Water circles his ankles – the sand is swampy and sucks at his suddenly leaden legs.

Reece watches for another worm to pop its head up to check where the smell is coming from. One does – right on cue. As if a beachworm is vitally important in the current state of affairs, they both bend over and stare urgently at the little V-shaped worm mouth in the sand. Anything to postpone the talking – the inevitable tidal onrush. An inch below Molloy lives a whole secret stratum of hungry beachworms – he'd have been content never to know of their existence.

He could also do without the quicksand effect. Shifting his feet, desperate for a wider, clearer view, he stares out to sea. Beyond the breakers a flock of terns plummets like a hail of arrows. From bird to spear in a split second. 'A tern for the worse,' he says as they rise, circle and plummet again. One of her old jokes. Apparently it's right on the money.

Reece doesn't say anything; he just anchors the bait bag with a stick so the backwash spreads its smell over the wet sandflats. Then he bends over the worm's head with a small piece of old pilchard in his hand. He's coaxing the worm into tasting it. At the same time as its jaws bite the bait he fits the jaws of the worming pliers around its head. But he doesn't move or tighten the pliers. The thin sheet of ocean flows and ebbs over their ankles. Still Reece doesn't move.

Speak, for Christ's sake! The wave's lip leaves behind a tracery of granular flotsam – specks of weed, leaf, jelly, feather, shell, bits of drowned bee and moth. Reece doesn't seem to want to rush this stage. *Jesus, Reece!* Eventually he closes the pliers around the head and flicks the beachworm out of the sand. Another two-footer.

'Thought I'd missed that bugger,' his father-in-law mutters. 'They've got lightning-fast reflexes. They're very suspicious. When they sense danger they disappear in a flash.'

'What did you say about moving?' His voice is jumpy but he's trying to keep it light. He's shuffling from one foot to the other, back and forth, all those beachworms under him, thousands of optimistic carnivorous mouths rising to the surface. The sand clutches his heels again. 'You kicking us out?'

Still Reece doesn't look up. 'Obviously everyone's given it a good try,' he says. Again he waves his meat stocking over the wet sand. His shorts are so low now that half his broad backside is bared to the elements. Paddling around on his knotty rhino feet. 'I don't mind you. You're not a deadshit or anything. But apparently you're not doing it for her. Not making her chimes ring.'

'*What?*'

'It's not your fault necessarily. Jesus, I'm trying to let you down gently.' He bends, grunts, grips, flicks up another beachworm, runs his sandy fingers down its length to remove its slime, drops it in the bucket.

'Did she say something to you? What's going on?'

When Reece finally looks up, his face is purple and his breath sounds thick and phlegmy. 'Listen, mate.' Pausing for his blood and thoughts to settle. 'C'est la fucking vie. The swinging seventies.

Do your own thing. Whatever turns you on. Frankly, I'm old-fashioned. I don't want to think about that side of it.'

Sure. Old-fashioned Reece tootling up to all the single mothers with an aquacar full of fish.

'But she's always been contrary, Catherine. Her mother's putting a sort of romantic slant on it. She says all she's done is gone back to her first inamorata.' He rolls the word around in his mouth, tastes it gingerly like a risky oyster. '*In-am-or-ata,* that's the word Beryl prefers to use.'

The ferry scene is like a film, and he's both audience and actor. On this cloudy marine set he anticipates something dramatic happening. He's prepared for melodrama. Like an edgy movie-goer, he doesn't want to miss anything.

But he's a protagonist as well, certainly the film's most tor-tured performer, and he's keeping a desperate eye on the smaller tableau of himself, a young woman and a tiny girl standing beside two suitcases tied with yellow twine on the end of the Lion Island main jetty. He and the woman are too wrung out to speak, but the toddler is gesturing across the empty water and chanting matter-of-factly, 'Fairy-fairy-fairy.'

On this late-May afternoon low clouds pressing down on the estuary amplify the ferry's throb and rumble. He feels the *Island*

Lady before he hears or sees it. The water eddies suspensefully around the jetty pylons. Toadfish scatter in anticipation and fishermen shift their lines. Then the ferry appears around the bend and surges towards them, all relentless engines and power, bisecting the outgoing tide. Grey whirlpools twirl away like colliding catherine wheels. In the ferry's wharfbound confidence – in its plan to bear his wife and daughter away – it seems triumphant enough already but it blasts its horn anyway.

On deck, holding her rope at the ready, well before it's necessary, stands the Nordic deckhand, ponytail uncharacteristically loosened, long hair flicking and swaying in the breeze. So athletically golden and high-breasted and long-legged in her uniform white T-shirt and shorts, all that blond hair swishing about, she could be a model in a shampoo commercial. Despite the lack of sun her face is flushed. She's even smiling for once in his general direction. He's almost tempted to wave.

'Judy!' cries little Grace. 'There's Judy!' The ferry goddess doesn't look like a Judy. With her hair swinging in that shining sweep she might be an Astrid or a Nadia or a Frieda. She could have been the boat's figurehead.

However, she's indeed a Judy – Judy Renfrew, non-Scandinavian, a Rocky Point girl and the ferry skipper's daughter. She's Kate's old high-school friend and – he's been definitely the last to learn – both her first and most recent lover.

She's Judy the outdoor girl who didn't join the exodus to the

city and university and Vietnam moratorium demonstrations
and politics. Judy the small-town sportswoman who stayed put.
Judy who tried boys first but found the local larrikin surfers and
junior footballers selfish and wanting. Judy who'd stolen all his
hours of sleep this week, who this afternoon is about to steal his
wife in front of the whole island.

In his youthful male certitude he'd never imagined a woman
cuckolding him. To tell the truth, he'd scarcely thought of a man
doing so. Considering the available selection of varicosed old
beachwormers and leathery fishermen, not here on the island
anyway. But what did he know about women? Less than Reece,
the divorcées' favourite aquamotorist and seafood donor. Until
this week he'd still counted love in the accretion of individual acts; how many times a week they did it – how many times
a *day*.

How could he have known that Kate was accruing numbers,
too? All those ferry trips from Lion Island to Rocky Point, back and
forth across the estuary, once, twice, and lately three times every
weekday. Two years of Kate and Judy rekindling their relationship in
the balmy sea breezes. While he was in town pinning his future and
his postgraduate hopes on the original Grace, she and today's Grace
were publicly plying the estuary in the *Island Lady*. No wonder
he was the island's object of scorn. Or that mother and daughter
were both as brown as old Hawkesbury oystermen. They were on
deck all day, learning the ropes.

Any detachment has vanished now – forget the observer role. It chills him watching Judy loop the rope precisely over the wharf bollard. As the ferry berths, the jetty shudders and he still feels its trembling through his legs as Judy lets down the gang-plank, as Kate motions Grace towards it, as Judy jumps nimbly to the jetty and grabs the second suitcase.

He's still trembling. This is the nightmare moment of his redundancy. They're leaving him. He aches to cling to his daugh-ter until some denouement occurs – even if he has to cause it. (The dramatic abduction? The leap together off the deep end?) But he merely hugs her again and passes her quickly to her mother. As a father is expected to do.

His girls are now on board, standing on the deck. The women's eyes speak for them. Judy seems suddenly self-conscious as she darts forward to retract the gangplank. Now water separates him from his daughter. They're going – it's over – he's been left once more. He could be a child again. The estuary could be an ocean. But, no, the ferry is still tethered to the shore. Judy hasn't yet removed the rope from the bollard on the wharf.

How small Grace's face seems, the dark hair blowing around it. She waves back at him, smiling. To her it's just another of their regular ferry trips. He's the only one finding this too much to bear – the suspense, the urgency of the engines, the ferry straining to be away and gone. However, Judy is brushing her hair from her face and trying to tie it back. She's exasperated with her hair and with herself – it was silly to wear it loose for the occasion – and glancing knowingly at Kate as she picks up the rope.

She's taking much longer than usual. The ferry begins to move off; the captain doesn't realise his vessel is still connected to the land. The rope isn't unfastened yet from the bollard. A little flustered now, Judy darts forward to unhitch it. No matador arrogance – her feet seem uncoordinated – and the rope rapidly tautens, and tangles around a leg. And right here, time and motion accelerate into mayhem.

Tension has a sound. Fibres can scream. It takes only two or three seconds for the ferry's power to tighten the rope enough to sever her leg, much less time than the duration of a scream. A second, higher, scream is time enough for the leg – propelled so forcefully, with a sort of cartoon velocity that defies physics – to shoot over the rail and disappear. As people rush along the deck towards Judy, the rope stretches further, and snaps, and the two ends lash and flay people both on board and on the jetty.

With so much screaming no one observer can possibly take in the aftermath. The skipper leaving the wheelhouse in a panic. After all, it's his daughter who's the deckhand, *his* little girl. And the ferry, unfettered now, running onto the sandbank that he's successfully skirted twelve times a day for nineteen years.

On the jetty, half stunned from the rope blow across his brow – it felt more like a metal rod! – all Molloy can do is shout their names. *Grace. Kate.* He can't see their heads above the deck rail, but that might be the blood in his eyes. The ferry, the means of transport to the mainland, wallows like a squealing sow stuck in mud. This is a quandary, he thinks dully. When will the screams stop? That's another problem. All he can think to do now is call his daughter's name again and again across the water.

Water has never been his forte. First a London orphan boy, then an Australian farm boy, he's never been a swimmer. A sort of anxious, head-jutting breaststroke is his limit. Nevertheless he finds himself in the water. He must have leapt off the jetty into the estuary. It's much colder than he imagined and its weedy taste makes bile rise in his throat.

The sandbank is perhaps three hundred metres offshore. It's shaped like a crescent and across it squats the *Island Lady,* its screws slowly churning the mud. A horn is sounding, a bell as well, and the screams have turned into yells. He paddles onward in a dream. He swallows water, coughs it up, then, before he realises it – before he's even considered sharks – he's in shallow water, his feet touch sand and he's standing by the hull looking up and calling Grace's name.

No one answers him. Bleeding people peer blankly down at him, beyond him, out across the estuary.

The bell still rings somewhere, perhaps in his head. The horn sounds intermittently. How has a particular nightmare turned into something totally different? And certainly not better. His brain struggles back to the moment of their leaving him. His head throbs. How did their little cameo turn into this catastrophe? How unfair that his sadness has been stolen.

There is movement suddenly above, and urgent voices. 'There!' a voice shouts. A passenger lets down the gangplank and they pass Judy down strapped to a stretcher. She's bound and wrapped in blankets, barely conscious. Her ashen father follows. 'Darling, darling,' he moans. 'You'll be all right.'

An improbable vehicle is approaching the ferry: the Skoda *Amphibie* on its busybody afternoon assignations. Reece Prowse ploughs out of the estuary, his windscreen wipers still flicking, and drives right up onto the sandbank. Gently Reece and her father lift Judy from the stretcher and place her in the vehicle. The skipper kisses his daughter and climbs slowly, with immense difficulty, back up the gangplank to observe his captain's responsibilities (for he has no number two, no deckhand, to help now), to wait for the high tide.

And then Kate and Grace, too, appear down the gangplank. Kate's forehead is bleeding from a similar whip slash to his. Grace, short enough to escape the flaying rope, is unharmed. Perhaps ten seconds pass. Then it's on this sandbank, an island outlying an island, three hundred metres from shore, that Kate makes her choice.

Without a word, she gives him custody of Grace's life, passes her over, and climbs into her father's aquacar and holds Judy's hand.

He's not going to risk the icy swim again with Grace. So father and daughter sit on the damp sand and wait for something to happen. The shipwrecked ferry looms above them, but he cannot face it and turns away. He considers the future life and present thoughts of the ferry skipper – and of others, too. He thinks of choices, spur-of-the-moment decisions that change lives, and hugs his daughter. Possibly in shock, he weeps without knowing it.

The tide is slowly turning, the sandbank is gradually shrinking under them. It's almost winter and he shivers in his wet clothes. But boats will come. They will get off this island, and the other one as well. This is their starting point together.

NINE

THE LIVING NIGHT

A wave of ghost crabs ebbed from the van's path and then flowed back over its tracks once it had passed. She drove the twelve-seater along the hard tidal sands under the full moon. The lack of cloud and the bright night sky made perfect conditions for turtle watching. She drove up the beach, stopped by the edge of the dunes and switched off the headlights.

The party of twelve stood around murmuring solemnly and casting shadows. The sky amazed them. A woman exclaimed at a shooting star. They were in awe of constellations and geography, impressed by the blazing night and the encircling silence. The tourists were pleased with themselves just being in this yawning nightscape, especially knowing that where they presently stood would soon be deep ocean.

It was almost eleven o'clock but the moon on the white

sand, the absence of any interfering artificial light – nothing along the silent breadth of land or sea or in the air – gave the night a stark clarity. Stars fizzed like fireworks. The sky was bright enough to read by. Grace could make out individual ghost crabs now resurfacing and regrouping, as well as their whorling sand patterns, as ordered and ornamental as Maori facial tattoos.

Several turtle species chose to lay their eggs on this slope of coast. Green turtles, loggerheads, olive ridleys, leatherbacks, hawksbills, flatbacks. The beach was sheltered and gently shelving, with few outcrops and obstacles to hamper the females' laboured passage up from the sea.

'Okay,' she called out. 'We're looking for semicircular marks in the sand.'

Almost immediately they saw tracks – the intuitive dragging scrape of the flippers. The imperative haul of the body. She handed out torches. 'Use these if you need to. I'd prefer not to use the headlights. We don't want to make the old girl's big night even more uncomfortable.'

She delivered her safety and environmental lecture as the party followed the trail towards the dunes: Try not to disturb the turtle. Don't wander off by yourself. Leave the beach as you find it. No litter, please. No cigarette butts. No souvenirs, if you don't mind. Leave the shells and rocks on the beach. The cliffs above us are three or four hundred million years old and very fragile – please don't try to climb them.

The green turtle sprawled and gasped beside a pile of sandy, pulpy-looking eggs. Its straining face was eaten by the light of the torches. The front flippers, as automatic as a wind-up toy's, constantly flicked sand on the eggs. When the people came nearer, the turtle heaved a phlegmy sigh, as if something important had suddenly registered, and closed its eyes. It gave another shudder-ing sigh and two final eggs dribbled in quick succession onto the sand. Mechanically the flippers flicked sand on them.

The onlookers stood reverently by. In its dazed convalescent state, the turtle ignored them and their doting cameras. Neither its pained expression nor the rhythmic flippers seemed to indicate sufficient resistance to the large sand goanna that emerged then from the cliffs and snatched the last egg, still mucoid and drip-ping, from under it.

'*Oh!*' the shocked people shouted, as one. '*No!*'

A moment later the turtle merely rolled a pessimistic watery eye as a second goanna ambled up with karmic confidence from the other side of the group, darted in and grabbed one of the earlier, dry and sandy eggs.

'*My God! No!*' everyone cried.

'Do something!' A thin, dark-haired woman was clutching at Grace's arms, shaking her. Tears ran down the woman's face. She had an unfortunate undershot jaw and it trembled with fury and despair.

Grace stood there, the sand gripping her feet like cement. She could feel its coldness coming through her soles. It was like watching a film where something unhappy occurred. A bad, unwanted thing. If you could rerun the film, wouldn't you prevent the old and whiskery assistant vulcanologist from falling into the crater of molten lava? Wouldn't you allow the Irish mother of nine to survive TB and hug her weeping children? (If someone had to die, make the drunken layabout father go instead?) No, the informed moviegoer sighed and got over it. The protagonists were intact. The larger drama had to play out.

'It's very sad but that's nature for you,' she said. 'Don't feel bad. What could we do?' Meanwhile the woman was right in her face, all flying spittle and projectile tears. Grace took several steps back. 'We can't interfere,' she announced to the group.

'We can't just stand here and let that happen to her babies!' the thin woman cried.

All torches were now trained on the goannas. They had carried the eggs in their mouths towards the base of the cliff and they stood both facing and ignoring their agitated audience, more at ease in their backlit territory of prehistoric boulders and leached tree branches that gestured like corpse fingers. They were substantial reptiles, more than a metre long, but they still had to throw their heads back and then stretch and extend their jaws in three or four jerky stages in order to encompass their meals. They gulped several times, their gullets swelling to allow passage, and swallowed the eggs whole.

'Dreadful!' said a yellow-haired matronly woman. She put

away her camera and shut the camera case with a snap, as if it would punish them to be so defiantly unphotographed. 'It's like a horror film.'

'Nature does makes allowances,' Grace said calmly. 'That's why the turtle lays so many eggs. There are still quite a lot left.'

'Those lizards are awake-up to that,' commented a burly middle-aged man with a modified Zapata moustache. He wore cargo pants and Nikes and a baseball cap, the daytime clothes of someone thirty years younger. The front of his T-shirt said, 'Hey! Appearances Can Be Deceptive'. The back said, 'I Told You So'.

'Of course they are, Warren,' said the yellow-haired woman. 'Look at their sneaky eyes.'

'Listen, this is the wilderness,' Grace told them. 'As I always tell my groups, you're seeing the real thing, not a TV show. The sand goannas aren't evil, they're just doing what they're supposed to do to survive.'

The woman with the underbite picked up a rock and threw it at the nearest goanna. Her aim was off. The creature shuffled a few steps to one side but it didn't retreat.

'Don't do that!' Grace warned. 'You mustn't do that!'

The woman's contorted face, her skin, eyes, every atom of her, suddenly seemed to resent the life she'd been dealt. 'I'm not letting them get away with it,' she muttered. 'I've been in that situation. They're never satisfied.' Her bottom teeth showed in a determined mandibular grimace: little nippy urgent teeth. 'They'll just keep going and going until there's none left.' She threw another rock, a sharp chunk of cliff-face. It struck one of the goannas on the neck. It hissed and showed its tongue.

Startled, the other goanna darted in the turtle's direction, then thought better of it and stopped in mid-dash, confused and swinging its head, its tongue tasting the air.

'Quick!' snapped the man with the moustache. He flung a rock at the second goanna. The thud was audible. The reptile staggered a few steps, then turned and hissed at its attacker. They faced each other. The man strode up to it and pounded a heavy flat rock on its head.

Grace grabbed the man's wrist. 'Stop it!' she screamed. 'Right now!'

He threw up his arms in mock surrender. 'All over, Red Rover,' he said.

The thin woman was still pelting stones, shells, driftwood, anything she could lift, at the first goanna. It was half buried and hissing fitfully but still not attempting to flee. It merely lashed its bleeding neck about as if savouring the strange fury in the air, and painstakingly extracted one foot at a time from the rubble.

'You're just prolonging the agony,' someone protested.

The yellow-haired woman said decisively, 'Yes, you're right,' and the moustached man said, 'Give us a hand, darl,' and the couple stepped forward.

The crowd parted obediently for them and they brushed

past the hectic thin woman, picked up a weighty rock each, and crushed the goanna's head and spine.

She left them there, their torch beams playing uncertainly over the scene, and walked away. She was too angry to speak. One antagonistic word and she would have struck someone. She was breaking the cardinal company rule for its rangers: never leave your tour party (an imperative of their insurance cover), but she left the nature lovers standing in the sand with the dead goannas and the turtle eggs and stomped away into the night.

The full moon looked trite now, a nursery rhyme in questionable taste. The sea sounded meaningless. Midges scribbled in the torchlit air so she turned off the light. Let them worry where she was – she jiggled the van keys in her pocket – and worry how they would get home.

The old feeling of lost control and ineffectual fury flooded back, as sure as the tide. She wanted them to suffer. More than that. She wanted them to be frightened. She wanted them to be mosquito-bitten and caught by the tide and forced to scramble up the ancient, crumbly, goanna-infested cliffs. She wanted them bruised, scratched and bitten by venomous prehistory. Yes, she wanted snakes. Black-headed pythons and king browns and death adders. She wanted them attempting to walk the hundred kilometres back to town in tomorrow's heat without sun hats, water or sunscreen. She wanted them stalked by dingoes and whirling birds of prey.

All that newfound confidence and outdoor prowess suddenly stood for nothing. In ten minutes – one lone incident – she'd lost most of the self-esteem she'd regained. She should have realised that nothing ever lasted and nothing ever went away.

In the moonlight came a heavy wheezing, then a rhythmic thump, becoming louder and more insistent. The rasp of a throat being cleared. Then a grunt, and another. Who was this after her now?

She swung around and shone her torch into the living night, into an instantaneous cloud of gnats and moths and tiny skimming night-swallows. The beam picked up the lurching hump, then the pained, elderly face. Agonised as usual. In deference she turned off the torch and the turtle wheezed past her like an aged nun and dragged its silhouette back to the ocean.

Of course she didn't leave the turtle watchers stranded. After half an hour cooling off she returned; another silent hour's drive back to town and she deposited the party at the company's office. Were they abashed as they faced again the Eco-Adventures sign on the shopfront (RESPONSIBLE TRIPS TO THE WILDERNESS)? Not that she noticed. Anyway, no individual hotel and motel dropoffs for them, she decided. Let them walk through town. She wasn't going out of her way to make them comfortable; she was still disgusted with them. If they dared take up the matter of the abruptly curtailed nocturnal tour with management, with Garth Stroller himself, then let them. She intended to get in first.

She had paperwork to do. She foresaw Department of the Environment repercussions. Best to write a report on the goanna incident while it was fresh in her mind, while she was still furious. Down the street the waterfront pubs roared competitively into the bay: karaoke night versus an Irish band. She let herself in, locked the door behind her as usual and sat down at the front desk.

The sense of being watched made her look up. The face at the window was sunburned, or perhaps it was just a flush of drunkenness or high spirits. It remained expressionless, however, as unselfconscious as a child's, staring at her for what seemed like minutes. Taking her in, absorbing the look of her, soaking her up. A hot wire seemed to instantly connect her throat to her breast, to her stomach, all of them pierced and burning as it tightened. Somehow, irrelevantly, her brain noted that beyond the glass and down the road by the mudflats the karaoke enthusiasts were singing 'Summer Nights' from *Grease*. Loading up the amps and bellowing joyously into the mangroves.

Meanwhile the face at the window seemed strangely

disembodied, as big as the hackneyed moon over the sea yet still somehow unclear. It mouthed something but she couldn't hear it. It might have been an angry drunken shout or a conspiratorial whisper. Then it was gone.

Adrenaline made her limbs skittish and itchy and sleep difficult. When she finally fell asleep she dreamed she was following a trail of bare footprints in the sand. Clear, crisp prints in damp white sand. Each foot had six toes, with two identical small toes nestled together. For a long while and with increasing urgency she followed these unique tracks over the dunes without getting any nearer to the person who had made them.

In the dream she happened to glance behind her, and saw the six-toed footprints were following her. They stopped right behind her own. She kept turning around sharply, but there was no one in sight.

The mysterious atmosphere segued into an air of crisis. Suddenly the footprints reached the banks of a muddy river and she knew a bad thing had happened. A member of her tour party, a young woman, had been taken by a crocodile while mudcrabbing during the Mangrove Crab Adventure. Brett Stroller and she had to retrieve the woman's body. Because of the danger presented by the crocodile, they couldn't dive down to get her.

It was understood that they had to harpoon the woman to lift her from the river bottom.

The nightmare woke her. Attempting to calm herself, she lay there trying to analyse all the horror and fear out of the dream – squeezing it dry and rendering it harmless with bits of remembered Jung and pop dream psychology and animal symbolism and scraps of Aboriginal legends.

The crocodile. The mythical creature with no voice, symbolising the silence in the Beginning of Time. Sacred to Osiris and embodying the power of so-and-so and what's-her-name and someone else she'd forgotten. In parts of Arnhem Land a revered creature. In Kimberley reality – Clifford snorting just metres below her window – an indiscriminate, opportunistic feeder, taking every prey from water beetle to water buffalo. And humans.

However, the nightmare wouldn't dissipate and she fell quickly back into it. Brett and she were standing on a tin dinghy looking down into the ooze of the river – at the dim shape of the young woman's body. The woman's head gave off a dull green glow like a luminous clock face.

'*You* have to throw the harpoon,' Brett insisted. 'You got her into this.'

LOVE OBJECT

For the first time in more than a year she found the snake-feeding an ordeal. Doing the rounds of the snake enclosures with her plastic container of white mice – humanely annihilated in the Norge freezer – she had an unnerving out-of-body moment. She saw herself from afar: the latex gloves, the container of recently thawed mice (actually an Ikea salad crisper), the abrupt body movements and haunted expression of someone barely holding it together. Wincing while death adders struck at furry little corpses. Why was this tense woman feeding mice to snakes for a living? The vision of herself almost made her weep.

Barely remembering to lock its trapdoor again, she left a king brown imperceptibly ingesting a mouse and took her crisper of remaining mice over to the Hard Croc. It wasn't yet open for business but she begged a cup of tea from Ursula, the Hard

Croc's manager, and sat on the café verandah staring out over the gardens.

The bushes and lawns glistened like wet plastic. Kangaroos shortly began bustling from the vegetation, stretching and scratching and assembling on the dewy lawn, ready to harass the day's first customers for their packets of feed pellets. The kangaroos seemed testy, as if they had all got out on the wrong side of the bed. They gave the impression they were looking at their watches and frowning impatiently at the delay.

She badly needed a Xanax but her supply had run out long ago. She'd woken at the nightmare's most vivid stage – the girl's luminescent body, the harpooning – so now the dream was embedded, not only impossible to shake off but hovering, waiting to return tonight the moment her head hit the pillow.

The goanna aggravation also throbbed in her memory. Then there was last night's face at the window. Of course the face had been pinker, older, fuller; she mustn't let herself imagine it was the Icelander. She had to deny him her fear. Someone merely sitting in the movies, a drunk peering through the shopfront window – it was crazy at this distance and after all this time to succumb to his madness again. How *dare* he have this influence on her? He couldn't possibly be here in person; now it was the *idea* of him she had to keep at bay.

So why was she running through it all again, masochistically dredging up all that erotomaniac stuff she'd pored over back in

Forbes Street? Case profiles. Warnings for the stalker's 'love object'. But she couldn't help it. What was Madonna's modus operandi? How had Jodie Foster handled John Hinckley Jr's obsession with her? Madonna and Jodie seemed to be getting on with life pretty successfully. Was there anything she'd missed, a clue somewhere to help her get back her equilibrium and forget him for ever?

The Icelander was the type of stalker who became fixated on someone through the media – yes, she understood that. He'd built up a delusional fantasy of a unique relationship with her, probably extremely sexual and reflected in the mad way he communicated with her – okay, got it. But her photo and writing hadn't appeared in the magazine for three years. She'd disappeared. Without any stimulation, wouldn't his obsession have eventually just faded away?

But what all delusional stalkers had in common, she recalled from her internet forays, was some false belief that kept them tied to their victims. Back in Sydney the Icelander had believed he was destined to be with her. If he only pursued her hard and long enough she'd come to love him as he loved her.

Wasn't what made erotomaniacs dangerous their tendency to *objectify* their victims? To see them not as human beings but as objects they had to possess and control? It was when their love was persistently denied by the love object, when the love object abandoned them, that these lunatics could get nasty.

Well, this particular love object had escaped his net.

She sipped her tea and felt a little calmer. The heat began to beat down and she imagined she could see all the night's moisture evaporating off the lawns and bushes. The jungle sheen was rising and fading as she watched. A musty mice whiff wafted up from the salad crisper and she tightened the lid and moved it out of the sun. Below her, the kangaroos still scratched themselves impatiently. Two bad-tempered males began sparring, backed off, then shaped up again. Heads leaning back out of striking range, they scrabbled and punched at each other like small boys in a schoolyard.

After last night she had no stomach for an Adventure Tour. For once she was grateful to be rostered for park duties. On this morning's first circuit of the Nature Walk were several family groups – southerners, easterners, foreigners – all pressing hopefully forward as usual, on the lookout for something more dangerous. Only one couple, an elderly woman and her middle-aged daughter, seemed indifferent to the possibility of excitement. The women's features, physiques and complexions were almost identical, only age and its effects providing any difference. Mother and daughter were lagging well behind, barely glancing at the wildlife and vegetation.

Their slow progress along the Nature Walk – the daughter supporting her mother's elbow as they talked – was fragmenting the tour party. The others wanted to walk faster. So did Grace. She was keen for this day to move on.

'Let it go,' the younger woman was insisting in a low voice. 'You can't do anything about it so just let it go.'

'I can't let it go,' said the mother.

'You have to let it go. You're seventy-nine, what's the point? My advice is to let it go.'

'I can't.'

'You have to. Simple as that.'

'Yes, well.'

'I'm right. Let it go. It's happened, been and gone, done with. What can you do? Nothing. You know that. Let it go.'

'I know that. I know it's the *sensible* thing.'

'Then let it go.'

'I can't let it go.'

Yes, you can, thought Grace. You're holding us up.

There was a rustling in the bushes and the agile wallaby darted out on cue. Grace moved back through the group to the two women and started to go through her spiel. Maybe they'd take the hint and get a move on.

'Ladies, let me tell you about this speedy little fellow, the agile wallaby.'

In the brusque manner of the wallaby, someone bounded through the bushes just then, elbowed his way through the tourists and brushed roughly past the mother and daughter. The flushed and angular young man blocked Grace's path, droplets of sweat and saliva flying around his head like an aura.

For a moment the shock locked her brain and shunted memory and recognition aside. He stood before her on the Nature Walk, sweating profusely, his face waxy and glistening, his body shaking with emotion. She could smell his nerves; his chemical body odour hung in the humidity. As she screamed he lurched forward and reached out for her with both hands: a slow-motion sleepwalker, a horror-film zombie.

His hands were on her shoulders, around her throat. 'Oh, harlot,' he said.

There was no doubt about it this time.

At her scream, Verge Action, on the ride-on mower behind the shrubbery, jumped off the machine, burst through the bushes and grabbed the man, then locked him within his own huge tattooed forearms while he tried to work out what was happening.

The Icelander was projecting furious tears, crying, 'Satan's concubine!' and, 'Traitor!' as he struggled in his grip. 'Shut your fucking gob,' advised Verge Action and, still bemused, squeezed the man's ribs until he ceased yelling.

Someone hurried off to get Security. In the big gardener's grip the Icelander withdrew into himself, mumbling and shaking his head. 'The whore finds Our Lord. It's all in Luke. The sinful woman cured. Is it too much to ask?' he pleaded.

'Jesus, what's *your* story, mate?' said Verge Action, squeezing his ribs again for good measure.

Then her legs gave out suddenly, the morning skipped a few beats, and she found herself sitting on the path, little chips of blood-wood embedded in her thighs. A bird shrieked nearby. The old woman and her daughter were pressing her head between her knees and hovering over her, offering water and dabbing her forehead and neck with tissues. The rest of the tour group had shuffled into small muttering clumps and were keeping a decent distance, their expressions registering distaste at what looked like an unpalatable domestic scene.

Somehow diminished in size and fury in Verge Action's grasp, the Icelander swivelled his head in Grace's direction. But he made no further attempt to struggle. 'Galilee?' he murmured plaintively to the sharp sky. ' It's all in Luke? The woman redeemed? Galilee?' he repeated to the bushes.

The pathetic rising note in his words. Perhaps Verge Action was fooled by this passive questioning tone and relaxed his grip, because the Icelander abruptly squirmed out of his shirt and twisted free from his captor. Bare-chested, he sprinted down the bloodwood path towards the crocodile enclosures.

Shaking his head, muttering oaths – what was happening to his sedate morning of lawn trimming? – Verge Action lumbered after him. The Icelander reached the saltwater-crocodile pens, skirted two groups of park visitors, and darted behind another.

Alerted by the shouts, D'Angrusa the security man came out of the Hard Croc then, carrying a takeaway coffee. He dropped the coffee, put his hand on his holster, saw the crowds and thought better of it, and attempted unsuccessfully to cut him off.

The Icelander was side-stepping and feinting like a footballer, dodging in loose figure-eights around the pens and through the tourists. It was easy to pick out the flashes of white skin through the foliage. Among suntanned tourists, that damp bare torso shone with an alien pallor. In any case, the crowd's urgent shouts soon had him pinpointed. He'd clambered up the cement wall of Clifford's pen and stood balanced over the lime-green pool, swaying among the drooping mango leaves, defying logic and bemoaning her failings.

Arms out like a tightrope walker, he strode along the wall until he was over dry land, Clifford's sunning area – its sandy surface whorled by countless sweeps of his tail – and jumped into the pen.

It seemed no time had passed. Everything repeated itself. The emphatic filmic way that day turned into night. The sun exaggeratedly sinking over Indonesia. The strident birds carousing in the palms. The hawks and bats spiralling over the trees. The rustle of emerging night creatures in the bushes. And the Icelander's existence overwhelming it all.

The same cast and props, too, settled on Clara's verandah: the old ladies grumbling stolidly beside the bougainvillea, the Beefeater and tonic bottles, the packets of Dunhills. And Grace sitting rigid in her deckchair, in the same state she'd been in when she first arrived. Worse. She could still feel his hands on her neck.

It was when the hubbub had finally died, while she was dazedly packing her bags in the rangers' cottage, that Angela, the girl at the Crocodile Gardens entrance counter, her eyes still sparkling with the morning's drama, had given her the envelope. This was long after Garth and Brett Stroller had entered Clifford's enclosure improbably armed with long sticks – really not much more than broomsticks or rake handles. With a tap on the nose here, a prod there, they kept Clifford at bay while Armed and Dangerous threw a net over the pale creature sitting crosslegged in the sand. As if he were the killer reptile.

The police had taken the Icelander away of course, but how much leeway would that give her? she wondered. A couple of days, a week, before he was out on the street again? She would hardly press charges and go through all that again. What was the point? The most basic psychiatric report would get him off.

So her troubles had begun again. He was after her wherever she went, for ever. And his timing could not have been worse. Complaints had already come in about her 'callous attitude' to the turtle-egg incident. Garth Stroller had no patience for incidents.

'What's going on? We can't have this crazy stuff happening.

Something eats your suicidal boyfriend, envenoms him, takes just the slightest nibble out of him – my insurance can't handle it.'

'This came for you a few days ago,' Angela had said, not even trying to contain her smirk. She was almost dancing in the doorway. 'I wasn't sure whether you'd want it.'

The envelope was addressed to her by name and, in bigger capital letters, by another epithet: ABORTIONIST WHORE. She snatched it and shut the door in Angela's face. She needed to open the envelope to discover how he'd found her. She had to know. Her hands were shaking; she barely had the strength to rip it open.

Inside was a page cut from a colour travel supplement in the *Sunday Telegraph* headed 'Discover the Kimberley'. The main article, 'Impossibly Luxurious', lauded a new exclusive resort at Impossible Bay that prided itself on its 'barefoot luxury'. But it was the feature below it, 'New Smile on an Old Croc', about the facelift at Crocodile Gardens, that was furiously circled in black ink.

Her face stared out from a photograph whose colour register was surprisingly sharp. There were several gradations of brownness between the khaki of her shorts, the tan of her legs and the liver-coloured woodchips of the path. Framed by fronds of jungle green, she stood on the Ecosystem Nature Walk smiling vivaciously beside a grinning older man. He was silver-haired and tanned and wearing a loud hibiscus-print shirt. He had a proprietorial arm around her shoulders. At their feet, as if it were this roguish couple's droll pet, squatted the ubiquitous agile wallaby.

Scrawled diagonally across the picture in more mad black capitals were two words: YOU DARE!

The car swung into Clara's driveway and drove up to the verandah, squashing fallen guavas under its tyres. As a precaution Sister Joseph had switched vehicles – it was a Mazda station wagon this time.

She and a younger nun got out and spoke quietly to Clara. Clara nodded and they opened the Mazda's rear door. The boy sat up, stretched, and climbed out. He seemed taller and neater looking but his hairstyle hadn't changed. This time he nodded hello to Grace and said her name.

Marion picked up the drinks tray and in a solemn procession everyone moved inside. The air was suddenly redolent with guavas.

TEN

SEWING INSTRUCTIONS

When she was little she would complain to her father, 'The people you work with are *too dead*!'

But she'd become used to them: the brick room in the Randwick backyard was always full of skeletons – some whole ones on display and some skulls rampant on shelves, others neatly stacked away in hermetically sealed cabinets.

He had casts of all the famous fossil skulls, sitting beside skulls of gorillas, orang-utans and chimps, for contrast. As a small girl she couldn't see much difference. He told her that was the point. The room was a former stable from Randwick's more prosperous and genteel nineteenth-century days. He'd had it temperature-controlled and he kept his wine there, too.

The body outside was *too dead*. How dead? For her father's sake, very, she hoped. Eighty thousand plus. From the cabin window she could see the edge of the tarpaulin covering it. The skeleton inspection had finished. According to the motel manager, her father had left yesterday. So had the workmen repairing the cyclone damage. She and the boy were the motel's only guests – if you could call them guests.

The habit of running to her father was hard to break. This time she'd missed him by a matter of hours. She would have phoned ahead but the nuns were worried about security, and there was no mobile-phone reception out here. She'd not been thinking straight. Now she felt even more rattled – stupidly ill-prepared as well as isolated. All she'd thought of was to borrow Clara's car and then fall back on her father; to hand over responsibility while she regrouped.

They must have passed each other on the Salt End Road when she and the boy stopped at the Clayfire roadhouse for a snack. Chips, hamburger, milkshake – teenage-boy food. All that eating recently had filled him out but he was still always hungry.

The window of the boy's cabin looked out on the indigo sky of late afternoon, a small disused landing strip of red pindan sand and weeds, a galvanised-iron hangar, and a tattered windsock drooping down like a leech on a stick. The motel's main building, perhaps a hundred metres away, wasn't visible from here. In the heat nothing stirred and the only sound was the gagging correspondence of distant crows.

She pulled the curtain across the window against the glare. Somehow the flimsy nylon barrier seemed to offer a small degree of security. There was a ceiling fan and she switched it on. It made a great clatter but its draught barely reached the boy on the bed.

There was just one hard-looking formica chair. When she sat instead on the edge of the bed she almost slid off – the bedspread was made of some synthetic tangerine material, slippery to the touch and whorled in looping patterns intended to defy stains. It smelled of cigarettes and stale beer sweat. She pictured legions of exhausted men collapsed on its clammy surface. Although the floor was bare linoleum tiles, the sour smell of wet carpet also lingered mysteriously in the room.

'Just a couple of days,' she said, far more cheerfully than she felt, 'and then we'll head back.' She would have given in to despair if he hadn't been there.

The boy stared dully at the ceiling. His face was more tired than wary. He looked older. She knew he hadn't wanted to leave the Little Company of the Holy Charity. But at least he talked a bit these days; she couldn't have stood his silence as well.

She'd thought she'd better keep him company for a while. Anyway, there was nothing else to do, nowhere to go. How could she have forgotten a book, magazines, board games, something to pass the time? She hadn't thought it out, being on the run again. What was the matter with her? In the meantime there wasn't a TV, or a swimming pool, no normal motel trappings – not even anywhere proper to sit in this sweaty room.

To avoid slipping off the bed she inched a little further from the edge. There was a question she'd wanted to ask him.

'How do you sew up your lips?'

For a moment he didn't answer. Then he put on a serious face. There was a touch of the martyr in his expression.

'You get a needle and thread from the women and some ice from the kitchen freezer. You press the ice on your lips so you can't feel the needle so much.' He touched his mouth. 'And you tighten your lips and push the needle through the thick part of the top lip, in and out.'

She interrupted him. 'Just like girls piercing their ears.' Touching her own pierced lobe. *We have something in common.*

'Ears feel less pain.' Making stitching motions with his hands, he continued, 'Some people just push the needle through the under-skin of the lip, the part with less feeling. But I put it through the full thickness.'

'It must hurt.'

'The thread hurts more than the needle. Pulling the cotton through the flesh makes your whole body shiver.'

Her hand went involuntarily to her mouth. 'Ouch.'

He frowned at her like a parent. 'Shall I finish telling you this?'

She nodded. 'Yes.'

'You push the needle through the bottom lip, and pull the cotton through, then cross over to the other side of your mouth, the top lip, and do the same again.'

She pictured this painful arrangement, the cat's cradle of the lips. 'How do you eat?'

He looked scornful. 'You're on a hunger strike. You're protesting against being locked away in the desert for two years.' Then he softened slightly. 'I found it hard to speak. But laughing hurts most.'

She felt stupid. 'But who's laughing, right?'

He looked at her uncomprehendingly. He didn't understand flippancy. He was just a foreign boy. His lips trembled self-consciously for a second – *all this talking about them* – but then he set them tight.

'When your mouth becomes inflamed and swollen it's difficult and painful to remove the thread.'

Something thumped, scraped and flapped on the tin roof, as if a heavy bird had swooped down on some smaller prey and then taken off again.

'Were you punished for sewing your lips?'

He nodded. The shadows from the blades of the ceiling fan swept across his face. The rhythm of shadows made him any age or race. It was impossible to sit on this slippery bed at such an uncomfortable angle. She moved further inwards and leaned on an elbow. Neither of them spoke.

'I'm being hunted, too,' she said eventually.

'To lock you up or to be killed?'

'I don't know. Just to possess me, I think. Maybe to punish me. He thinks I'm evil.'

His eyes looked surprisingly old.

'He never gives up,' she said, and was annoyed by her sudden needy sob.

He reached for her hand. The shock of skin contact made her gasp. It seemed a long while since someone had touched her sympathetically. She was too exhausted and wrung out to be in control of this novel sensation. Her reaction was almost involuntary.

Like an actress behaving in an inevitable manner, she leaned – slid – across the tangerine bedspread that stunk of hot workmen. This was just an ordinary boy gripping her hand, she thought. She was just an ordinary girl. And if you half closed your eyes it was a dream.

She lightly touched the scars on his lips before she kissed them.

When she came out of the bathroom it was dark. She was grateful for that. He was still lying on the bed. He hadn't switched on the light; maybe he too found the darkness easier. She felt the beginnings of panic, however she couldn't just leave. Give it fifteen minutes. The chair looked even more prim and uncomfortable than before, but under no circumstances could she return to the bed.

She broke out in a sweat of embarrassment and guilt. *Was she genuinely crazy?* Her face felt flushed; thank God for the dark. She sat down self-consciously. In the dark the bedspread seemed to give off a crude synthetic glow.

He was awake. Immediately she rushed to fill the gap of silence – the unbelievable chasm – with businesslike questions. Teacherly words that redefined the age difference.

'What were you boys screaming as you clambered over the fence of the detention camp?' *Yes, boys!*

'Visa! Visa!'

'Oh, on TV your mouths looked like you were shouting, Freedom!'

'No, *visa.*' Because all of a sudden they *were* free, he told her. When it finally happened, the abruptness of the escape had come as a surprise. No one had expected all the guards to hide inside from the cyclone, especially while the protestors were still at the fence.

He seemed grateful to be talking. The guards were not from these parts, he said. They were more scared of the wind than the refugees were. 'No one wanted to be standing in the observation tower when it blew down.'

It had taken their liberators only a few minutes to flatten the weakened fence. They'd brought three trucks but their planning was half baked. Maybe fifty refugees had busted out. There were a dozen activists in the liberation party. But only three vans for about sixty people.

'Only twelve of us could squeeze into our truck. The same

number in the others.' The rest were left behind in the desert, running after the trucks, crying and throwing stones in the wind. The trucks drove off in different directions – north, south and inland. Their driver said, 'No names, man. You can call me Sandman.'

Their truck headed inland, with the rain and cyclone winds behind it, driving into the night. There was no other traffic. They were expecting police roadblocks but saw no one. For food, Sandman had brought a bag of oranges and a bucket of Kentucky Fried Chicken. 'The chicken was very old by then.' Then the truck hit a kangaroo and it flew up in the air and landed on top of them in the back of the truck. 'Everyone yelled. It was wet and still kicking. My friend Fayed was knocked unconscious by the body and the rest of us were covered in blood and scratched by the claws.'

Despite their yelling, Sandman kept driving, and at last the kangaroo stopped kicking and twitching and they lifted it up – it was as heavy as a man – and threw it out. Then Sandman hit a bull – a white bull standing out there in the road all by itself – and this time it didn't fly so high in the air. But it pushed in the radiator and the windscreen and cut Sandman's head, and he drove off the road and bogged the truck. They all had to get out in the mud and push it back on the road. Then Sandman heard on the radio that the other trucks had struck roadblocks and those boys had been told to run off into the scrub.

By now it was light. 'Our radiator was overheating and quickly using up our bottles of drinking water.' Sandman said he wasn't driving into the desert without a windscreen and with a radiator wrecked by animals, so he turned back towards the coast. He said, 'Keep your fingers crossed.'

The further they drove, the more everything was damaged by the cyclone. Fallen powerlines jumped and sparked on the road. Ducks were swimming on the highway. In the new roadside lakes they filled up bottles for the radiator. 'Suddenly we could hear frogs everywhere.' The next afternoon the trees and bushes became thicker and Sandman dropped them off by a muddy creek.

Sandman gave them some oranges and told them to sit tight under a tree and wait for him to return with a different truck. If he wasn't back in two days they should follow the creek to the coast.

'He didn't return, so I did so.'

'What about the other boys?'

'Fayed and his friends were scared of more wild animals dropping on them. They sat by the road to wait for the police. I ran away from the highway.'

'What did you eat?'

'Some blue eggs that tasted of fish and some bitter berries. I drank from the creek.'

'Then I found you in the mud.'

'No. I found you.'

No more teetering moments, she thought. Sentences shouldn't hang in the air gathering freight. A silence could be wrongly construed as intimate, romantic – anything. *Christ*. There must be other things to talk about.

'This used to be ocean here,' she enthused, teacherly again. She told him about how the Kimberley desert used to be an underwater reef, and how her father had found a perfectly preserved fossilised fish nearby.

He didn't seem to be listening.

'A friend of mine has this fish on her mantelpiece. Louise. Imagine that – hundreds of millions of years before the dinosaurs, there were schools of prehistoric fish swimming right where we are now.'

'I would rather hear about crocodiles.'

'"The crocodile kills hungry – it also kills not hungry." That's an Aboriginal saying.'

'It will attack you whether it's hungry or not?'

'If it's in the mood. If it's hungry, of course. If it's not hungry it might kill you anyway and store you in its larder for later. Or kill you just because it feels like it, because you're in its territory. Maybe it's nesting. There's a famous one that attacks outboard motors – tries to chew them up. It thinks their noise is the courtship bellowing of another male.'

'What else?'

'They like to kill each other, too. The big ones like to eat

the smaller ones; the females like to kill the other females –
they're very intolerant animals.'

The silence lay there waiting; it was both a presence and a
common language. It was like a witness to them. No more teetering moments, she thought again. He stirred on the bed, just a
grey shape, but she could make out his wide eyes. The bedclothes
rustled as he moved position. She looked away and he cleared
his throat before speaking.

'Who is hunting you? The secret police? An old lover?'

Was he trying to sound sophisticated? 'A crazy man, sick
in the head. He imagines I love him and that he loves me. It's a
well-known mental sickness.'

'To love you?'

She laughed. 'No, imagining that you're having a big love
affair when you're not. Erotomania, it's called.'

He was quiet for a time. Then he said quietly, 'If he comes
after you again I will kill him.'

'I'm sure that won't be necessary.' She got up from the chair
and opened the cabin door. 'I'm going for a walk and then I'm
off to bed.' She needed fresh air and moonlight, and especially solitude, in which to castigate herself – to really scald and lash.

As she shut the door behind her, he was sitting up and calling
out. 'I know how to kill him! Many ways!'

She almost fell into the skeleton pit. She'd forgotten about
it already. She shuddered. Too much life happening among the

living. Too much chasing and hiding and insanity. She still couldn't believe this evening had happened, or believe it of herself. How could she? There was probably a special Mud Room category for people like her!

For a moment she stood still and slowly inhaled the sweet dusty smell of the scrub. The familiar sentimental smell of this country brought her to her senses. It had been an aberration, quite nonsensical, and she would put it behind her. It hadn't happened.

She stepped briskly around the tarpaulin and police-scene tape and headed towards the lights of the motel. What she needed was a drink and adult conversation. Striding out along the gravel path she felt a trickle down her thigh.

Kelly was behind the bar. The room was otherwise empty when Grace walked in. A couple of desultory pictures hung on the walls: an archaeological dig with kneeling bearded men fiddling with little mounds of sand, like children playing on a beach, and a photograph of the West Coast Eagles football team. Over the bar was a framed caricature of the proprietor ringed by signatures and flippant farewells. One of the clearer messages said, 'You can run but you can't hide! Good luck from Arson.'

'I was waiting for you to come in,' Kelly said. She served her, then switched on the CD player and came out from behind the bar. 'You might want to step outside a moment,' she suggested.

Grace took her glass out onto the verandah; Kelly followed her with the wine bottle and poured a drink for herself. Insects beat past their faces in their race to the verandah light, then thrashed noisily against it.

'Bloody bugs,' Kelly said, and turned off the light.

Silhouettes loomed sharper as Grace's eyes adjusted. Soon she was aware of several degrees of darkness. In the bar Billy Joel was warming up with 'Piano Man'. She looked back towards the cabins. The boy's light remained off. She desperately hoped he was asleep.

As the dark's intensity lessened she thought of all the creatures emerging out there. Scores of nocturnal animals coming to life in the trees, the rocks, the bushes. Under the earth. All the secret marsupial byplay that went on – the scratching, sniffing and tunnelling, the hunting and gorging. Lots of dying. In this climate the nights were far busier and more bloodthirsty than the days. Every morning showed evidence of tiny murders. The scuffle marks, the pile of chest feathers, the ball of blood-stained fluff.

Kelly held up a cautioning finger. She was waiting for Billy Joel's chords and na-na-nas to cover what she had to say. 'I have to tell you this. Of course Evan's suspicions might be quite wrong – the boy might be your Muslim nephew or something.' Obviously she didn't believe this for a second. 'Evan has his beliefs, I guess. His own reasons. Maybe to curry favour. Anyway, he's reported the boy.'

Grace gazed out into the gradations of blackness as Kelly's words sank in. Competing against 'Piano Man', the bush returned a polite hum and chatter.

She drained her glass. She couldn't speak – swallowing so quickly had made her eyes water and bile rise in her throat.

'The thing is,' Kelly went on, 'I've been thinking about this problem for some time – the way I'd handle it if it came to the crunch.' She refilled their glasses. 'I'm thirty next year and I've made a few mistakes so far. This issue is of great importance to me. To do my bit.' She cleared her throat, embarrassed, but then made a sweeping gesture anyway, as if to embrace the surrounding gravel and sand, the hidden insects and reptiles, all those harsh scratchy plants halfway between weed and tree.

'Did you know that this was almost the Promised Land? We came *this* close.'

Grace spoke finally. 'When will they be here?'

'Apparently the authorities want to do it properly and not just rely on the State guys. You know how competitive they are. They want Feds from headquarters. Tomorrow afternoon.'

Returning to her cabin, shining her way with a borrowed torch, Grace saw the path was lined with tiny marsupial mice. They were as recklessly unafraid as cartoon mice and she had to be careful not to tread on them. In the torchlight their eyes glistened like drops of Indian ink.

ROAD MOVIE

Byron and another local elder, his Uncle Walter, arrived in Byron's van marked 'Kularta Tours', and got out rubbing life into their faces. Walter was a bony dignified man in his seventies dressed in the western shirt, worn-down boots and dusty jeans of an old stockman. A cataract had turned his left eye opaque.

The dawn was in its first flush. The sand was still damp and its crust retained traces of the night's small dramas. Without comment they recognised bilby, snake, scorpion, owl. Byron shivered in his Eminem T-shirt. This was early for him and both men had been up several hours already.

There was no sign of life from the motel. Evan Strachan and Kelly Burnish weren't up yet. Anyway, Byron had indicated that their absence would be appreciated. This was a significant occasion. In front of Strachan, Kelly had firmly agreed. It was certainly fine by Strachan. He'd handled this by the book; now he just wanted to wipe his hands of the skeleton and fill in the bloody hole.

Byron brought out a hessian pallet and set it down by the tarpaulin. Then he lifted off the cover and climbed gingerly down the lower side of the collapsed dune, trying to minimise the sliding sand. Working carefully, hands nervous, trying not to look at it too closely or disrespectfully, he lifted out the skull first and passed it up to his uncle.

Walter leaned over the hole and received the skull in cupped hands. His sigh seemed to empty him and almost fold him in two.

Byron worked his way down the body, bone by bone, fragment by fragment, passing each one up in turn. He tried not to rush it. Take it easy, he thought. He's been here a long time already. The ribs were difficult and the fingers and toes were not complete. Sometimes a small piece of bone crumbled into dust and he felt inept and ham-fisted; other times the bone was indistinguishable from the sand and ochre under and around it.

As best he could, Uncle Walter reassembled everything in proper order on the pallet, allowing the man to recline in his familiar position on his side. As he laid down each bone he muttered an incantation of suitable length and seriousness and tears of emotion ran down the lines of his face.

By the time they had finished the sun was up and crows were calling. A wedge-tailed eagle flew low over the cabins and frowned at them. Byron climbed out of the hole and stood by his uncle.

The men looked at the skeleton with their heads half averted, and at the indentation it had left behind. Then Uncle Walter said things softly in his language. As they loaded the pallet into the van they trod carefully around the hole so the memory of the old man would remain stencilled in the earth.

It was just a small tarpaulin-covered bump resting on a straw bed in the back of the Kularta Tours van. Grace and the boy avoided looking back at it. She understood there were important boundaries of race and gender to observe but she didn't want to raise the matter. Once when the van hit a deep rut in the track she imagined she heard a dull rattle of complaint coming from the back.

She and the boy were sitting up front beside Byron. They'd driven Clara's car to Uncle Walter's house, a tin shack surrounded by stringy dogs, goats and rusted car bodies off the Salt End Road, and left it there with him. This was the getaway plan arranged with Kelly Burnish. By the time they were twenty or so kilometres north, on one of Byron's back roads, she'd become used to the skeleton's presence. But she wondered why Byron hadn't left it with Uncle Walter. And why he was helping them.

With Uncle Walter gone, Byron's sombre mood gradually lightened. He giggled at the aptness of Kularta Tours helping their escape. The legendary Kularta, he told them, was an Aboriginal hero from the 1890s – a charismatic fugitive with supposedly magical powers, chiefly the ability to freeze police and black trackers. Kularta meant hunting-spear. When they tried to arrest him for spearing people and cattle he'd immobilise them.

'They'd ambush him, then he'd hypnotise 'em and escape with his women and kids,' Byron said. 'He was a sort of guru. Good-looking bastard with dozens of women. Mad for them.' He drummed his fingers on the wheel in amusement. 'This fella could survive anywhere, no problem. They chased him into bad country, just gravel and sand, with no food there – no worries, Kularta lived on lizards, ants, cats.'

'Cats? Pussycats?'

'Pussycats gone feral. I don't mind cat myself. My kids won't eat it, though. Prefer their KFC.'

'I've seen feral cats around the town. But in the middle of the desert?'

'Cats are everywhere, lady. Big buggers, big as leopards, some of 'em. Some only a generation or two from grandma's tabby, others maybe descended from Dutch sailors' pets five hundred years ago. The tabbies predominate. Their colouring's best for camouflage.'

She was suddenly aware of the boy's leg against hers on the seat. He was staring expressionlessly ahead. He hadn't spoken since they left the motel. She moved away and inquired with fake brightness, 'What does it taste like, pussycat?'

'Not like chicken,' Byron laughed. 'Like rabbit or possum.'

There wasn't much room on the seat. The van's springs were shot. On Byron's zigzagging tracks they bounced around and the boy's thigh touched hers again. She pressed her knees together in a definite gesture.

The boy muttered sullenly, 'I could never eat a cat.'

'No one's making you, mate,' said Byron. 'Maybe I inherited the taste for them. Kularta was my great-great-grandfather.' He laughed again, which set him coughing, and the savage second face swung towards them as he spat phlegm out the window into the spinifex. 'Mind you, I've got the biggest mob of cousins.'

'What happened to him?' she asked.

'His magic powers didn't work while he was asleep. One night when his belly was full of cat the police crept up on him and shot him.'

The boy reminded her then that they'd left the motel before having breakfast.

'How can you think of food?' she said over-cheerily. In her shame she sounded inane to herself. She was cramping with the effort of preventing their legs from touching. On this bumpy road it was impossible. All her weight was forced onto one increasingly numb buttock. Her lower back ached.

So this was what it was like on the far side of a road movie, she thought. On real back roads. Not like a Ry Cooder album at all. Unbearably hot and stuffy. Uncomfortable on several levels. Where was the breathtaking desert scenery? The guitar backing? Where were the dusty filling stations and the diners with the squeaky swinging doors and laconic waitresses and enigmatic cowboy customers drinking coffee and eating pie? Not in this country.

She imagined she could hear the skeleton rattling impatiently behind them but it might have been Byron's old drink cans and food wrappers rolling around the floor of the van. It was getting hotter, and with his circuitous route she had only the vaguest idea where they were. They passed no traffic. Then the boy's leg was pressed against hers again.

Eagles scouted the van and hung low over the track like crows, watching for roadkill.

Veering on and off the highway, they drove north until they neared the coast, although neither the sea nor horizon was discernible. A dusty mist drifted from the earth into the sky. One side of the road was dust; the other, mudflats. The van ploughed through a coffee-coloured haze that only lifted thousands of metres above them. The windows were closed against the dust and the cabin was oppressively hot. Byron coughed and chain-smoked, steering with his knees while he rolled new cigarettes, and they were too drugged by fatigue and smoke to speak.

For once there were no natural borders. From the van it was

impossible to see where the dust ended and the mudflats began. Or where the mudflats ended and the sea began. The whole country was blurred and undefined – khaki tidal mud receding into khaki sky and khaki land, and a flat ocean like a sheet of plywood.

The boy was still complaining of hunger. When they reached the first roadhouse an hour later, Byron stopped.

'We need petrol anyway.'

'Better make it quick,' she said.

She looked up and down the road. There was no traffic in either direction. Would the authorities be after them yet? Would they expect them to flee north, east, or to the more populated south? She had no idea. What about helicopters? In chase movies they always brought in the choppers. With a jolt she remembered the motel's old airstrip. How visible would a black, red and yellow van be from the air? Suddenly she felt panicky and nauseous – the old familiar feeling. They'd stick out like a beetle on a sheet.

She had to remind herself that they wouldn't be looking for the Kularta Tours van – or would they? This was becoming like one of her regular chase dreams. She was relentlessly chased, night after night. By whom was not always clear. Of course in waking life she knew.

Eventually they came to a town. From the road its one hotel, ringed by dense palm trees and bougainvillea, looked like a tropical resort. Perhaps that was the original intention. Up close, however, it was a fortress. Signs at the entrance said YOU

ARE UNDER VIDEO SURVEILLANCE and GUARD DOGS PATROLLING
ALL HOURS.

She was wary. If she and the boy were suspected of fleeing
north, wouldn't they be expected to call in here? Wouldn't the
hotel be checked out? Wouldn't the local police be tipped off?
What a memorable travelling party they must look, too – a black
man with two faces, a Middle Eastern-looking boy, a strung-out
white woman. She almost laughed. This merry band turning up
in the State's most garish and recognisable vehicle.

'I need a Coke,' the boy said. 'And the toilet.'

'All right, all right.'

A flock of yellow-throated miners burst from the surrounding
palms, crying their *people-people* warning.

A jukebox was playing Neil Diamond as they entered the bar.
A couple of whiskery locals and three travelling-salesmen types in
short-sleeved shirts were drinking beer. Two black girls played pool
outside on the patio. A heavy metal security grille enclosed the bar
itself, its steel rods spaced just wide enough for a schooner glass
to be passed between them. A sign over the bar said NO CHEQUES,
NO CREDIT CARDS, NO SHIT WHATSOEVER. From somewhere nearby
came a deep muffled bark – the sound of a big dog kept in an
enclosed space.

The pink-faced barman reluctantly left the company of the
other drinkers, approached them languidly and received their drink
orders in moody silence. Disapproval came off him in waves. 'The

kitchen's closed,' he announced defiantly. 'If you were wanting food.'

'We're fine, mate,' said Byron's smarter face. 'But thanks anyway.'

The bar's atmosphere of deep mistrust was surpassed, however, by the lounge's celebration of doom. It was hard to relax over drinks in a room commemorating chaos and disaster. Blown-up photographs around the walls featured famous local air crashes and the aftermath of the town's worst cyclones. But obvious pride of place went to a selection of framed photographs of this very hotel on fire – ablaze on three separately dated occasions, in May '71, August '79 and July '91 – with flames shooting from the windows.

'I'd say they're overdue for another one,' Byron said.

In all of these scenes of havoc there were townspeople meandering about in the rubble or ashes or twisted metal. The same people seemed to have turned up at each disaster. To Grace, none of them appeared upset or curious, or particularly interested in setting to and cleaning up the destruction in question. They looked stolid and impassive.

But it was the old sepia pictures of the town's two tourist attractions, the former leprosarium and the native prison, that caught her attention. Ragged Aboriginal lepers were arranged in descending physical condition around a stern-faced nun. Gaunt black men in loincloths, fierce cicatrices striping their bony chests, squatting in linked leg irons between two boab trees.

The awfulness of the photographs, especially seeing them with Byron standing there beside her, made Grace squirm with discomfort. The warriors' deadly glares at the camera could have been directed at her. She couldn't wait to finish her drink and leave. But the pictures held no surprises for him. Of course he'd seen them and many others like them before.

'I know this doesn't feel like the right place,' he said calmly. He sipped his beer. 'But with prehistory you never know.'

'What place?'

'Where the old fella landed. But I'd better make sure.'

They drove down to the sea, to a long jetty where muddy waves snapped against the pylons. Signs warned NO FISHING, NO SWIMMING, BEWARE OF CROCODILES. The crocodile warning added LAST FATALITY FEB. 13; the date part of the sign was easily revisable. The emergency lifebuoy was missing from its stanchion. It was high tide; the jetty planks barely cleared the waves. Along the railing a dozen gulls stood in smooth Indian file, feathers flattened back, beaks into the wind. Byron opened the front and back doors of the van to allow the gusts from Asia to blow through.

Over the skeleton, she thought.

Like the seagulls, he stood facing in the direction of Timor, with foam like chocolate-milkshake froth flecking his T-shirt. A small turtle bobbing haphazardly on the surface seemed to divert him for a moment but after a while he turned away from the sea, saying, 'Nup, this wasn't the place.'

They all stretched their legs, hardly speaking to each other. The boy looked tired and cross. Back at the hotel of doom he'd readjusted his hair to its *Titanic* specifications and now the wind had wrecked it.

Then Byron closed the van's back door and they set off again into the dusk. Away from the sea the wind dropped and the evening air felt suddenly sticky and sultry, full of shrieks, laughter, metallic bangs and clangs and the smell of burning.

'We'll be okay,' Byron said. 'They know this old bus.'

They passed windowless storefronts fortified like bunkers against the tempests of nature and man. The portcullises had been lowered for the night ahead. Gangs of ghostly children were already flitting in and out of the smoke, bouncing bricks off security doors, stoning the sparse traffic and overturning garbage bins. Strings of grass fires burned in their wake.

Through the night Byron and she took turns to drive and – fitfully – to rest. Next afternoon they climbed over a jagged range of rust-coloured hills that fell sharply to the sea. They had run out of road – there was nowhere else to go.

Below them shimmered a silver-roofed town set among palms and tall eucalypts. Suburbs of modern tropical-climate houses stretched around a wide turquoise estuary. Sprinklers whirred on lawns resembling bowling greens. Heat mirages flickered across the tin roofs and white lattice. Most houses had a boat on a trailer out the front. Swimming pools the colour and shape of opals shone in the backyards.

They descended slowly, over-braking down the hill, suddenly loath to arrive. The boy sat up and checked his reflection in the rear mirror. Unfamiliar raucous parrots, skimming and diving recklessly across the van's path like dolphins in a ship's bow wave, accompanied them down the hill into the town.

There was an airport, ringed by smoking sugarcane fields, and a six-seater plane scheduled to leave for Darwin the following morning. She booked two seats. The young Timorese booking clerk said, 'Darwin? Cool!' and didn't ask for ID so she extended the bookings to Sydney.

Cars passed the airport towing boat trailers or with fishing rods on their roofs. Byron turned the van and followed the traffic to a river crossing several kilometres from the ocean mouth. Where the banks flattened there was a boat ramp and sheltering paperbark trees and a grassy municipal park running down to the river. A sign by the water's edge carried the usual ferocious toothy illustration and the words DON'T FEED THE CROCODILES! BOAT FISHING ONLY! NO WADING! NO SWIMMING! WATCH YOUR CHILDREN AND DOGS! Another sign nearby said IN MEMORIAM GREG PUDDSEY 30/8/98. Three white men stood thigh-deep in the river casting for barramundi.

The boy reluctantly followed the others out of the van. These crocodiles weren't in cages. He stood well back from the water, unable to take his eyes off the river and keeping a picnic table between him and the bank.

'Don't worry, mate,' Byron said. His gaze followed the bends of the river towards the estuary and then the sea. 'Well-known fact. Crocs only kill bad people.'

He didn't look convinced. The adolescent hair, his tense face, made her feel sad, guilty, sympathetic. Tender. All these emotions swept over her in turn. And shame again.

Ever since they left the Salt End Inn she'd been trying to regularise and justify that afternoon by recalling films featuring this sort of *incident* (not affair!). Even one Hollywood example would ease her mind, help to mainstream the *incident* on the orange bedspread. *Summer of '42* was the only one she could remember (the rest were European, unfortunately). But the attractive older woman in that film (about her age) was sympathetically regarded because she was a sad war widow. Oh, and *Harold and Maude* – but that escaped through zany wit and extreme cultishness: the boy was twenty and the woman about eighty.

Again she foresaw Justin in the Mud Room lecturing censorship applicants about her.

'Only if you transgress the rules, man,' Byron went on. 'Make a stupid mistake, have sex with a girl from the wrong skin group –'

'It's all right,' she interrupted. She'd never felt older. Not maternal, exactly – more like an aunt. An aunt by marriage. 'It's safe. I promise.' He was just an ordinary boy. She came close to patting his silly-looking hair.

Byron was animated now. 'This makes sense,' he enthused. A horizontal strip of Timor Sea stretched taut and gleaming in the distance, like a fluorescent hair ribbon. 'I feel it in my skin. What's the word? Osmosis, eh? I reckon this is where he would've landed. He wouldn't have gone any further east than this. He brought his bamboo raft right in here.' His arm swept over the boat ramp to the gas barbecues and picnic tables and public toilets and the tourist bus parking area and the children's playground and skateboard park beyond. 'And camped here on his first night.'

The boy was still too nervous to stay out in the park, so they got back in the van and sat with the doors open. This time Byron gently lifted the tarpaulin as well and let the sea breeze waft directly over the old man. Grace and the boy remained respectfully facing the front while Byron sat in the back in a deep reverie for perhaps half an hour.

Then he carefully covered the bones again and joined the others in the front. He said, 'The old man says yes.' The river was rising; its surface was dappled with a slick sheen like alcohol. 'I hope some brother does this for me in a hundred thousand years,' Byron said. 'I think I'd appreciate it.'

For another hour or so the three of them sat there together, watching with waning interest to see if a foolhardy fisherman would be taken by a crocodile. Mosquitoes came out from the paperbark trees. An egret stalked and dipped among the sunset's reflections. In the red and gold angled beams the shallows looked viscous, like blood and honey. The boy began sighing with impatience and hunger. At dusk Byron drove them to a motel and said goodbye.

She leaned forward and kissed his original face. 'I feel privileged,' she said.

'You are,' he said. 'It took great discussion. But we respect your dad. It came down to that.'

The Timor View Motel. The name was inaccurate by three blocks and about a thousand kilometres. Except for a thin strip of moonlit sea between the roof gutters and satellite dishes there was no view. It didn't matter. She was so tired she could have collapsed anywhere. They ate early in the motel restaurant and went to their rooms.

Two of her senses woke her – hearing and smell – the faint squeak and whoosh of the door, a soft rustling, then a sweet intrusive aroma.

She jumped up and turned on the bedside lamp. The intruder stood before her in his Crocodile Gardens underpants. He blinked like a possum in the light.

Moths and several flying beetles had raced him inside and

were battering themselves against the bed lamp. From a nearby room an American male voice abruptly proclaimed the CNN news. It startled the boy. A little shakily he declared, 'I've come to protect you.'

As if he weren't entirely sure of this, or of himself, he looked questioningly at her. Going by his scent, he'd liberally doused himself in the motel toiletries. His hair flopped in Leonardo mode. He was shivering.

'Thank you,' she said. So much for adjoining rooms. She had to clear her throat to stop her voice shaking. Every nerve in her body was twitching. Adrenaline – fright, fight and flight. 'I appreciate the thought. Now go back to bed, please.' She turned off the light so he could depart with a scrap of dignity. Also so she could apologise. 'Listen,' she murmured in the dark, 'I'm not heartless. I'm in a mess and I'm sorry for everything.'

It confused things, she thought, as the door closed behind him. The beseeching eyes and recalling the feel of his skin.

ELEVEN

THE SACRED IBIS

He gave Salt End Woman up to Byron O'Malley. That was the deal – a Grace for a Grace. And for the boy as well.

Getting her through airport security, the X-ray machine, was a story in itself. She was too important and frail (her skull alone reconstructed from those two hundred and twenty-one shards of bone) to entrust to baggage handlers. So he took Grace from the preservation safe, packed her up in a royal-blue leather case and took her across the country business class.

Back to Western Australia. On the plane Molloy found himself sitting among a group of five boisterous investment consultants returning from a Sydney conference. It was a Friday evening; their drinking had obviously begun at lunch, rallied again in the club lounge. Now, on the long flight home across the continent, it had become a fully-fledged party.

They all looked to be in their thirties, the sort who liked to be taken equally seriously in nightclubs and boardrooms. The group had its designated roles: comedian, easygoing fall guy and mock-grumpy group leader. Plus two lesser lights who fed the comedian his lines. Every few minutes the funnyman repeated an inside joke born back at their conference, the sidekicks laughed appreciatively, the scapegoat grinned self-consciously, the dour chap weighed in with a cryptic clincher. Everyone roared together. And then they did the routine again.

The clincher line was 'Bring on the snorkeller!' and they found new heights of hilarity in each retelling. Like boys mucking up on the school bus, they were in overdrive, unable to tell any more if they were laughing at their joke or at their own hilarious selves. Meanwhile the drinks kept going down and the butt of the humour, a thickset young man they called Kezza (the snorkeller?), grinned and blushed his way across the country.

Inevitably, they sought to include neighbouring passengers in the fun. The comedian had a brainwave. In a stage whisper he suddenly addressed the cabin. 'Which one of you is the armed guard?'

Business class went quiet. Even his colleagues were momentarily nonplussed at his gall. 'Who said that?' the joker went on, in a different, stern voice. He was a snub-nosed, close-cropped blond fellow, the flush risen in his cheeks and scalp. If nothing else, he *looked* like a stand-up comedian. 'Come on, own up or it's Guantanamo Bay for you.'

'It's always the one who doesn't look like a guard,' said the dour one. 'Probably this bloke here.' He was indicating Molloy, the only male not in a business suit. He didn't look up from his newspaper. A small story on page five. A comprehensive new study by a multidisciplinary team of experts from eight universities, led by Professor Henric Fischer of the University of New South Wales, had corrected previous estimates of the age of Salt End Woman. Their consensus was that she was younger than originally believed – approximately 40 000 years old.

One of the comedian's sidekicks, a balding younger man, leant across the aisle. 'Is that so? Are you the guard? Don't worry. I won't let on.' He winked and put a finger to his lips. 'Sshh!'

Molloy looked up wearily and saw in the young man's face, within his pinstripes, behind the loosened tie, the timid freckled boy he'd been. Eager for peer approval. His eyes were glazed and the acetate from the day's alcohol was on his skin and breath. 'You going to save us from the Muslim fanatics?'

The flight attendant was instantly there, lips tight. 'Do you gents want to be arrested? Those jokes are out of bounds!' You could see her brain working. (*Trouble? No, just Friday-night businessmen. Keep them happy.*) She rolled her eyes and topped up their drinks. 'Had a successful trip, have we?'

'Have we what!' the comedian said. He was off again. 'Kezza, are we snorkelling on this issue or are we deep-diving?'

And it was while the others were reliving some business

battle, braying back and forth in this aggressive alien language (*Aren't we just repackaging the same old Big Mac? Where are the synergies? Is he a warrior or a window-dresser? We'll have to trouser the guy. Bend him over the bonnet. What's the temperature check? How are we going to consummate that? He's a steamrolling guy. No, he's soft-cocking it. We're going to have to take him out . . .*), that the young balding drunk boldly reached across, said, 'You love that bag, don't you? What've you got in there?' and opened the royal-blue bag on the seat beside him.

Molloy was telling his daughter the story. Everything but the news of Fischer's study. He told himself he'd wait for the published research in *Nature* before he accepted that particular blow. Anyway, it seemed like he'd been waiting for it for ever. They were sitting by a pond at the Randwick end of Centennial Park. Sacred ibises pecked around them, a dozen or so birds waiting for their sandwich scraps. In her urban cool-weather clothes – jacket, jeans and jumper – she looked out of kilter, he thought. This morning had obviously unsettled her. Airport farewells did that.

'Ten minutes of chaos,' he said. 'From the moment he saw the skull.'

She pictured the scene. The nut-brown, patched-together skull, the drunken reaction, the flight attendant in a flap, then the real guard appearing, the passenger hubbub, the laboured explanations, the incomprehension, the grim apologies. Later, on the ground, the questions all over again.

'They thought I was some sort of diversion. Causing an incident so something could happen elsewhere on the plane. Skeleton Brings Down Aircraft – make a good headline, eh?'

'Bizarre. Tell me about the handover ceremony.'

She wanted him to keep talking, to take her mind off things.

The formal return of the remains. When he thought about it, it was strange they hadn't asked him to give her back long before now. 'We trusted you to care for her,' Byron had said. (He'd been her discoverer, after all.) 'But now we want her back.' That was it. An arrangement, a deal, he supposed, rather than a forced gift. So they didn't feel beholden.

Back to the spot where he'd found her. Lake Salt End looked just as it had that September morning so many years before. The Great Sandy Desert. The wide basin of red dunes. Stark blue sky blazing down. The air humming. Ants. Bushflies. Crows flopping around the scrub. Animal tracks from the night before. But no Fischer snoring in the tent this time.

It was a smoking ceremony and ritual cleansing. No press or TV of course. They didn't like photographs of human remains being published. More than two hundred desert people present at the ceremony. Rattletrap overheated cars and trucks from all over the north and northwest. The young staying in the background, quiet for once. Solemn old people in their best clothes in the front rows. He was the only white person.

He faced the old people and slowly opened the royal-blue case and lifted out her cranium in his hands. The little pieces of painstakingly reassembled teacup. The head he'd discovered when he was twenty-one. His life's *Eureka!* moment.

He stepped forward and passed the skull to an elder, Byron's Uncle Walter. The old man held it reverently for a moment and then he carefully passed it to another old fellow. And so on. And it was the most amazing thing. Old people previously terrified of touching ancient bones did so with tears streaming down their faces. And he began crying, too. The symbolism was overwhelming. The people believed that the First Woman had risen to the surface to contact them. They thought she'd come to the surface for a purpose – to bring white and black together.

His daughter said fair enough. Excellent. Was that all? *That couldn't be all. The boy, the motel, the van . . .*

Then Byron brought out the male skeleton the cyclone had uncovered at the motel – Salt End Man – and repeated the procedure. And that rounded off the ceremony. Now they possessed the king and the queen. It didn't matter that thousands of years might have separated this woman and man in real life. They were like royalty, or matching religious relics. It was a funeral and a baptism and a coronation all in one, very solemn, but also a celebration. Everything had great dignity. The people placed their palms on the skull of Salt End Man and sort of blessed him, and their faces reacted like they'd been blessed back.

Beatific – he'd always wondered what that looked like, a beatific expression, a beatific smile. Now he knew.

Now what would happen to them? she asked. The remains?

He shrugged. Realistically, maybe nothing. It was up to the people. Science had bowed out. All science could do was stand on the sidelines and wait. At least the descendants knew that the remains of the first modern humans were enormously important to human knowledge.

Anyway, the skeletons were now in Aboriginal custody. Kept in a safe at the ranger's station at Salt End. There were two keys to the safe; Byron O'Malley had one and he had the other. They'd allowed him that. That carried the weight of their trust in him. In a way, that was the point.

History awaited and the people waited on history. The same old two-way relationship. In the meantime they didn't see any rush. They had been around for a long while. These were the world's most patient people.

The boy had looked different when they saw him off on the plane to New Zealand. In the past three months, while the network moved him between safe houses in New South Wales, his lip scars had faded. The *Titanic* haircut had gone. Shorter hair changed his whole appearance. He looked older, more Western. Less *foreign*. Less *just off the boat*.

'How long is the flight to New Zealand?' she asked her father.

'Only a couple of hours. He'd be in Auckland already.'

'He'll have a good life there,' she said. 'In a more sympathetic place. Not running for once.'

'Yes, he will.' He was distracted by a sacred ibis that had strolled up behind him and neatly snipped up a sandwich. He shooed it away but it flapped only a few lazy steps. Several other ibises sauntered by, bobbing those strange thin hooked beaks.

'The number of ibises around here lately!' he said. He sounded put out. 'They used to be migratory birds, flew here every year to Centennial Park and waded about in the ponds and then flew back to Egypt or wherever they used to be sacred – back to the Nile. They don't go home any more. They can hardly be bothered wading – they prefer asphalt. They're worse scavengers than pigeons or seagulls. You see them in Kings Cross eating pizza crusts.'

'Just vagabonds at heart.'

'No, no, something's upset the species' equilibrium. They're sort of footloose and restive.'

'Like the birds in *The Birds*?'

'Almost.'

'Maybe we should put them in detention camps.'

'Without further ado.'

He was still looking askance at an island in the middle of the pond where the birds had taken up residence. They were noisy tenants. As the island's lone, guano-painted tree pitched and rolled with squabbling ibises he was shaking his head in bafflement.

He's disturbed about the sacred ibis problem? After her time away the whole city seemed rattled and out of whack. It was easy to take things personally: the unfamiliar road rage; the orange juice she'd bought this morning tasting of onions; the fake pools of vomit on the footpath – some advertising genius's idea of a cool urban promotional campaign. Everyone and everything seemed to be getting at her. Even her father was becoming self-centred and eccentric. More easily exasperated. Sacred ibises? For the first time she noticed he was getting older.

And on top of everything, the old tension was back. She was back to square one. The suspense. The waiting. The looking over her shoulder. The Icelander.

'I looked them up in a book of Egyptian symbols. The ibis represents the transforming power of the moon, the trickster.'

'Really?'

'It also represents the source of inspiration.'

'What's so inspiring about ibises? Heads like umbrella handles.'

He frowned at her. 'They don't inspire you?'

'Not much.'

He laughed. 'Me either.'

'Sorry I'm not very good company,' she said. How would she tell him, of all people, that she was pregnant? The *why*. The *how*.

Now was not the time, when she already felt so agitated, and with him still glaring at random ibises. It was hard to imagine when the right time would be. She thought to herself, Just don't get him started on gene flow.

'Don't laugh at this,' she said. 'Sometimes over the years when things were going wrong for us I've wondered whether Salt End Woman did have a malign side. What with her having been ritually destroyed and maybe being a witch or something.'

'Then wouldn't the bad luck have gone to the people who destroyed her? Rather than the person who brought her to the surface?'

'Maybe it did that as well. When you think about it, their luck hasn't been fabulous in the last two hundred years.'

'Anyway.' He squeezed her shoulder like he used to when she was a little girl. 'Now I've handed her back our luck will definitely improve.'

'I've got some news,' she said.

SCENARIO

She was back. Amazing how things went your way if you were patient. If you just watched and waited. He'd had three sightings that he ran through his mind. Getting out of her father's car. Checking the letterbox with a frown on her face. Hanging washing on the clothesline. He'd acted quickly on the last one; he had a pair of her panties in his pocket right now.

His plans had changed. Since throwing away the tablets he felt more confident. He had no more use for medication. He wanted to stay on the ball and be his intrinsic self. Original Carl. Already he felt more shrewd and intuitive. The den of crocodiles had been a reality check – to finally realise the lengths she and her friends would go to keep him from her.

No, worse word than friends – *cohorts. Cohorts of Satan.*

Well, he'd tested the faith. Courageously battled the cohorts and the wild animals. Thrown himself into the jaws of death – the literal jaws of the monster, the Biblical Beast! And survived, thank God and the Archangel Michael. They'd come down on his side, no doubt about it.

What a relief to be Original Carl again and have that certainty back. Not confused any more, not bewildered and exhausted by her running from him. No longer having to argue her case with the holy voices – the incessant voices damning her whoring and aborting. He didn't have to block his ears against their furious broadcasts. What a din! And what a relief to just give in to them and quieten them down.

He'd been too chivalrous. Generosity itself. But all that pressure was in the past. It was time to think of unresolved matters. The cohorts. The worm of betrayal still gnawed at his brain. He had a face to link with that particular treachery – that grinning devil in the flowery shirt. Would any young man stand for that – the whole country laughing at his humiliation by a grey-haired old lecher? Not in any movie he'd ever seen. He couldn't think of a single one. The flowery-shirt man was next.

He'd had the right scenario in his mind for a long while now. Ran it over in his mind every night as well. It was all to do with him boldly entering her bedroom. A brazenly feminine room in the scenario, all seductive pillows and fripperies and soft pink lighting. A room like the bordello in *Moulin Rouge*.

So he appears by the bed. She's struck speechless at the

impressive sight of him. But rather than angry, his expression is surprisingly suave and mellow. *So here you are at last. The naked bride in her bed. Declaring a self-evident truth to the world.* He sighs and shakes his head at the memory of the many mischiefs inflicted on him. *An explanation would be interesting, in the circumstances. Do feel free.*

Well, this confounds her. The sheet is all atwist around her bare limbs. She can't seem to manage to cover herself. Playing the virgin or just trying to seduce him again? She's whiny and girly. *I wasn't myself. I'm weak. I couldn't help it. You're my true soulmate!*

He's so cool and sardonic. *How shall I address you? Grace Brand? Mrs Carl Brand? The adulterer? The whore? Or my wife?* All stated drily with a raised eyebrow. Something's different about him. His hair's long and combed straight back, the goatee beard. He looks powerful, even gladiatorial. But more Russell Crowe than Brad Pitt. He strips off his clothes.

My God! / One flesh under God, remember? / Yes, Carl! / So Grace, things are different now! / Oh, yes!

That's when he'd do it – when she desperately wanted him he would withhold himself. Withhold his body from her, then do what he had to do.

The scenario made him shiver slightly although the evening was humid and he could feel his shirt sticking to his back. He'd watched long enough from the street and also from the back lane. The Randwick house was dark. The car wasn't there. They were out.

He moved briskly down the side of the house, away from the street. A jasmine creeper snagged on his shoulder bag as he brushed past, its scent intensifying as he struggled to pull free. The fragrance further provoked him and he tugged the creeper viciously. It riled him with its sexual suggestions.

He picked up the key from where he'd seen her father put it – under the terracotta pot by the back door – and let himself into the brick room at the rear of the backyard.

Two human skeletons, an adult and a child, greeted him inside. Heart and head booming, he reeled back at this devastating message. A gorilla skull glared at him. Pelvises stood shamelessly side by side. There were eye sockets and toothy grins from all continents and ages. A lamp shone at the back of the room. Along two walls ranged racks of wines – some dusty, others, those nearer the lamp, lit by a rosy glow. On top of the wine racks yet more skulls grinned down at him.

On a shelf an Ape Man's head stared down. Nonchalantly propped beside it was an empty wineglass. He could see fingerprints on the glass and a dark scum settled on the bottom. He knew the prints were hers. What depravity occurred in here? First the wild animal den, now this museum of horrors.

There was a permanent silence in the room. All those leering teeth made it seem even quieter than normal silence. Wasn't there a phrase? *Perfect silence? Dead silence? Silent as the grave?* He strode rapidly around the room, running through his scenario again to calm himself. Just bones. Heads. But all this paraphernalia was distracting. A baboon's skull baring its fangs. Prehistoric eye sockets looking into his soul. By the wine racks, the dense masculine smell of red wine that had always nauseated him. Like an old drunk's body odour. He'd underestimated her. *Dark Lady of the Cinema* didn't begin to describe her.

When she was young, Grace had christened the room the Skull Cave, after the Phantom's headquarters in the comic strips. *Four hundred years ago on a remote Bengali beach a man swore on the skull of his father's murderer . . .* John Molloy kept about three hundred complete or part skeletons in there – old and young, most races, both sexes. There were *Homo sapiens* and *Homo erectus* skulls, a cast of Peking Man, a Neanderthal head fleshed out, every kind of ape.

The skulls got progressively smaller, from gorillas and chimps and orang-utans to gibbons and down to squirrel monkeys. He had a few little marsupial skulls too, that he'd picked up in the bush and desert, just for fun. They looked like eggs with teeth.

At the back of the room he kept the treasured Australian *Homo sapiens* bones in plastic bags and marked cardboard boxes, all locked and sealed in airtight lockers. Also at the rear, illuminated by the light he kept on at night – a goose-neck lamp with a burgundy-coloured shade – stood another, bigger metal cabinet. This was a high, heavy safe of the sort made not only to secure unique and valuable contents but also to protect perishable property from Sydney's notorious humidity.

The cabinet was labelled simply GRACE, the name printed on a sheet of art paper in a child's elaborate, keen-to-please hand. The paper had the look of a class project. Below the name was a neat faded drawing of a brown-faced girl ringed by a pattern of boomerangs, koalas and kangaroos, symbols of Aboriginality imagined and drawn many years before by her seven-year-old namesake.

The cabinet was closed but not locked. His hands shook in anticipation but when he turned the handle it opened easily enough. It was empty now.

He stood before the cabinet, rocking slightly, trying to think this through. GRACE. Her personal space. Specifically hers. The aptness of the discovery and especially the breach of intimacy made his skin tingle. He remembered the panties in his pocket then and touched them lightly. Blood pounded in his head and for a moment he was short of breath. Perhaps a minute passed, then he became calmer, without fear.

Original Carl again. He could adjust the scenario. How clear-cut this had become all of a sudden. He undressed hurriedly, took the knife out of his shoulder bag and, with a little difficulty – the overflowing manila folders took up some room – jammed his clothes into the bag.

He discovered the cabinet door was actually three separate metal doors, with three hermetic seals that folded neatly into each other. He spread them all open. Then he climbed inside the cabinet with the knife and bag. He could wait. For years he'd been patient. This was her chamber; it was inevitable she would come to it. It was somehow programmed.

He squatted down, bare buttocks and shoulderblades pressed against the cold metal back of the cabinet. Then he tugged the doors together into one door again, and drew this single heavier door steadily towards him until all he could see outside were two bands of red light – one horizontal, the other vertical – on the linoleum floor.

He dragged the door a little closer and the two bands of light became splinters and joined together into one thin red L. Now he noticed the old-coin smell of the cabinet's interior and also a musty and leathery odour, like old first editions in a second-hand bookshop.

From the point of view of someone entering the room the

cabinet would still appear suspiciously open, he thought, and he pulled the door closer still. Now it was completely dark except for a red right-angle as fine as a pencil line. The musty smell, more pungent now, had overwhelmed the metal smell. In order to listen out for her and to be able to breathe, Original Carl held the door open with the point of his knife.

In the end he certainly hadn't raved on about the importance of gene flow or the future of *Homo sapiens*. His gaze swung sharply from the island of sacred ibises to his daughter. All he said, as a wave of great fatigue swept over him, was, '*Christ!*'

Waterbirds thronged. A passing brown dog sniffed at a discarded shoe, then urinated on it. Small bobbing horse-riders, attempting the rising trot, juddered around the track.

'Are you okay?' he asked.

She shrugged. The brown dog moved on, sniffing the air. A homeless man painstakingly rustling up dinner under the pines from a motley collection of cans, bottles, cartons and plastic bags was forced to stop his preparations to shoo the dog away.

'Have you made a decision?' he asked then. A radio station's traffic-watching helicopter clattered overhead and he had to repeat the question.

'Not yet.'

She was hardly a teenager; he didn't press her about decisions, or the male involved, or anything else.

Back home again, he seemed to her to be pottering more ineffectually than usual, turning on the TV, then despairing of the news (dominated as it was by disasters and terrorism), turning it off again. Making tea, suggesting toast, biscuits, fruit, as attentively as someone's grandma. But staying in her vicinity, she realised. He was making himself available, offering support. She was touched by that. She also couldn't bear the idea of him dithering around like this all evening.

She said there was a film she wanted to see. He was willing enough. But afterwards neither of them was in the mood for discussing it over the usual coffee. They drove home in silence.

As they reached the house she told him the story.

'I need a drink,' he said as he parked the car.

'I'll get a bottle,' she offered, and without waiting for him to open the front door, set off around the side of the house.

In the dark the side path seemed strangely unfamiliar, the space between the house and the fence narrower and more overgrown than she remembered from childhood. More tunnel than path. Her face collided with a coil of jasmine tendrils; the creeper was trailing loose, as if pulled from the fence. Why wasn't the Skull Cave key under the terracotta pot as usual? Although the door was closed, it wasn't locked when she tried it.

In itself this wasn't enough to raise any suspicions. Her

father could have forgotten to lock it. It was only when she stepped inside, past the first two skeletons, the East African man and girl – the welcoming committee, as he called them – that another small irregularity made her freeze. In the draught from the door something fluttered on the floor. A magazine clipping – an old Grace Molloy film review.

A faint but sickly whiff of aftershave hung in the room. She almost keeled over. Sheltering behind a benchtop of skulls, leaning on it for support, she tried to get her voice working. The sound that emerged was the protesting shout produced during a nightmare – a strained croak.

'Come out! Come out now!' she managed eventually.

Nothing moved. The patch of light pooled like spilled wine on the linoleum. Her eyes scoured the Skull Cave, familiar since childhood. It had never seemed quite the chamber of horrors her schoolfriends used to giggle and shriek about, but now the old bones threw ghoulish shadows.

'I know you're there!' she called. But he didn't come into sight. Not yet. Not yet. And not yet.

There was nothing handy or suitable as a defensive weapon. Only skulls and pelvises and, miles away across the room, perhaps a disengaged femur or a bottle from the wine rack.

She moved out from behind the bench anyway. She was drawn
to walk forward. Running back to the house, to her father, was not
a consideration. This couldn't go on – the intimidation, the terror
tactics. She refused to live a film where she was expected to be the
victim again and again. Maybe she had once expected it of herself,
but no longer.

Fuck you! Had she just shouted this or heard it in her head?
It didn't matter. *Fuck you, you fucking madman!*

Whatever happened, this had to end now.

There was nowhere for him to hide except the big cabinet – the
preservation safe. As she approached it her skin and muscles seemed
to be fluttering like tissue paper. From eyelids to buttocks, all her
nerves reacting at once. And suddenly she was standing in the pool
of wine-coloured light in front of that drawing she'd done years
ago. Seeing the name.

Imagine her not as ancient bones but as a girl, her father
had said. Because that's what she was. Only twenty, twenty-one.
Living, breathing, loving. A young human like you. With the
body of a ballerina. Gracile limbs, hence Grace.

At first she presumed the cabinet was shut. Only when she
reached for the handle did she see the point of the knife, the
silver tip, protruding between the edge of the door and the door
frame. She jumped forward and shouldered the door with all
her weight, trying first to engage the handle, then to lock it. The
knife prevented this. Sobbing with frustration, she pushed, and

pushed again, trying unsuccessfully to break the blade. In exasperation she pulled the door sharply towards her and the knife slipped sideways and fell to the floor.

Inside, a naked man squatted, long limbs all bunched together, his face resting on his knees. One arm protectively clutched a bulging cloth bag. She stood there panting, peering in at him. He didn't raise his head. Something told her to quickly pick up the knife, so she did so. The man still didn't move. He was so jammed in there with his bag that he seemed wedged into position. She couldn't tell if he was breathing or not. If he was dead, alive, foxing.

Holding the knife before her, she leaned into the cabinet, held her breath and touched a bare foot. This was the Hollywood moment where they sprang up and grabbed you. Her blood throbbed in her ears. She felt his instep, an ankle, neither warm nor cold. There was no breathing or pulse that she could ascertain, but with her own pulse battering in her ears and throbbing even in her fingertips it was hard to tell.

Did she find a pulse in the ankle? She couldn't be sure. There was a smoky reek in the cabinet, a toxic exhalation that caught her throat and lungs as she quickly withdrew. The Icelander with his worldly possessions sat hunched and still.

She tossed in the knife, stood back for a moment and then stepped quickly forward and closed each of the three sealed doors in turn. Locked them. Tight as a drum, strong as a vault, time-proof.

THE ISLAND

They had never been back, and in any case she wouldn't remember events that long ago. He remembered them all too well. Young married life under Mariposa's tin roof. The feral neighbours. The ghost dog. The gleaming delight of the green-capsicum morning. The last five-jetty night. The ferry.

However, it seemed important to show her the island. There was no bitterness left but maybe she'd get an inkling of her early, other life. He'd never elaborated on the *him* and *her*. The *why*. Shouldn't this gap be filled before she entered her new stage? You couldn't live with gaps in your own story.

'I want to show you where you lived as a baby. Where we all lived when your mother and I were young.' He didn't say, Before you leave me too. Or, Before you become merely one of us.

She went along for the outing, to please him. It was hard to be nostalgic for something you didn't recall, but she reasoned it was a day outdoors, a ferry ride in the sunshine – why not? It was pleasant to get out of the city. These days sentimental good humour struck her in sudden waves.

The island had changed, of course. Mariposa and Monterey were long gone, replaced by architect-designed holiday homes. Expensive yachts and motor cruisers lolled on their moorings in the bay. The general store had acquired an espresso machine and advertised focaccia and sushi and the *Financial Review*. Outside at shady tables men in boat shoes sipped small coffees. Women with bobbed hair power-walked along the shore clutching bottles of spring water. Pelicans still dozed on the pylons, however; children continued to fish off the end of the ferry wharf. Through the cabbage-tree palms and spotted gums the offshore breeze still gusted and the summer sun pressed down.

They took their takeaway coffees to a seat by the wharf and sat watching the tide receding in evenly scalloped stages along the shore. A migratory heron stalked the shallows. The yachts' and cruisers' dinghies rested obliquely in the silt. In the middle of the estuary the sandbank was rising, as enticing as a desert island in the enveloping Pacific.

He was waiting for her to speak. Instead she stood up and slipped out of her dress. She'd worn her black swimsuit underneath. The new defined profile took him aback – her doorknob of a navel, the defiant larger bulge stretching the material so thin that it faded to a pale brown transparency across her stomach.

'Coming?' she asked.

'Not this time.'

Her dive was still surprisingly neat. It was quite a distance, he remembered. The breeze drove small choppy waves against her body. As she swam out across the ferry channel towards the sandbank, he watched her every stroke, lived every breath.

Acknowledgements

This novel was completed with the help of a resident fellowship at Varuna, the Writers' House, granted by the Eleanor Dark Foundation.

It owes much to the generous assistance and patience of Dr Alan Thorne of the Australian National University. For her helpful guidance I'm similarly grateful to Rachel Bin Salleh of Magabala Books in Broome.

I'd also like to thank Candida Baker, Michael Bisits, John Drewe, Alan Gill, Bruce Haigh, Sandra Hall, Sandra Symons, and my daughters Amy and Laura. Special thanks to Anne Devenish in Kununurra and the Western Australian State Literature Centre.

For their enthusiastic editorial support, I'm grateful to Julie Gibbs, Meredith Rose, Robert Sessions, Fiona Inglis, Simon Prosser, Lesley Bryce and Juliette Mitchell.

I gained valuable insights from these non-fiction works: *Orphans of the Empire*, by Alan Gill; *Asylum: Voices Behind the Razor Wire*, by Heather Tyler; *Archaeology: Theories, Methods and Practice*, by Colin Renfrew and Paul Bahn; *The Story of Fossils: In Search of Vanished Worlds*, by Yvette Gayrard-Valy; *The*

Miracle of Man, by Harold Wheeler; *Monster of God: The Man-Eating Predator in the Jungles of History and the Mind*, by David Quammen (as well as Tim Flannery's review of this in *The New York Review of Books*); *Australian Crocodiles: A Natural History*, by Grahame Webb and Charlie Manolis; and *The Skeleton Manual: A Handbook for the Identification of Aboriginal Skeletal Remains*, by Alan Thorne and Anne Ross.

The line about the poet's tiger on page 319 is an admiring reference to 'Tiger-Psalm', by Ted Hughes (*New Selected Poems 1957–1994*).

It's important that my imaginary characters not be confused with real people or their opinions, occupations, accomplishments, locations or tribulations. Fanciful conjectures regarding *Homo sapiens*, as well as any errors of science or chronology, are mine alone.

Incidentally, a place called Lion Island does exist on the New South Wales coastline, but it's an uninhabitable rocky outcrop at the mouth of Broken Bay.

Also by Adam Nevill

Apartment 16

The Ritual